Ca

Freya North holds a Masters Degree in History of Art from the Courtauld Institute. Her first novel, *Sally*, was published to great acclaim in 1996. She has since written *Chloë*, *Polly* and *Cat*, all bestsellers, and her most recent novel, *Fen*. She lives in London.

Acclaim for Freya North:

'Passion, envy, love and sex, topped with lashings of laughs. Freya North has done it again, only better'
Daily Express

'Freya North is on a roll . . . stamped with foxy, feelgood flair' ***She***

'A funny romantic romp . . . and a very happy ending' ***Cosmopolitan***

'Very racy indeed . . . Jilly Cooper on wheels'
Woman's Own

'Funny, heart-warming and full of charm' ***Hello!***

'Just the thing for a Sunday evening in a hot bath with a glass of chilled Chardonnay'
Waterstone's Book Quarterly

Also by Freya North

Sally
Chloë
Polly
Fen

To find out more about the novels of Freya North,
visit her website at www.freyanorth.co.uk

Cat

Freya North

ARROW

Published by Arrow Books in 2002

1 3 5 7 9 10 8 6 4 2

Copyright © Freya North 1999

Freya North has asserted her right under the Copyright,
Designs and Patents Act 1988 to be identified as the
author of this work

First published in the United Kingdom in 1999
by William Heinemann

Arrow Books
The Random House Group Limited
20 Vauxhall Bridge Road, London SW1V 2SA

Random House Australia (Pty) Limited
20 Alfred Street, Milsons Point, Sydney
New South Wales 2061, Australia

Random House New Zealand Limited
18 Poland Road, Glenfield
Auckland 10, New Zealand

Random House (Pty) Limited
Endulini, 5a Jubilee Road, Parktown 2193, South Africa

The Random House Group Limited Reg. No. 954009

www.randomhouse.co.uk

A CIP catalogue record for this book
is available from the British Library

Papers used by Random House are natural, recyclable products
made from wood grown in sustainable forests. The manufacturing
processes conform to the environmental regulations
of the country of origin

ISBN 0 09 944677 4

Printed and bound in Great Britain by
Cox & Wyman Ltd, Reading, Berkshire

For Jeanette – with love,
gratitude and a wink

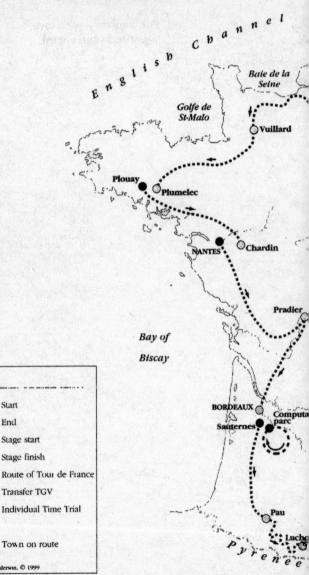

Cat McCabe's Tour de France

English Channel

Baie de la Seine

Golfe de St-Malo

Vuillard

Plouay
Plumelec

NANTES
Chardin

Pradier

Bay of Biscay

BORDEAUX
Computa parc
Sauternes

Pau

Luchon

Pyrenees

Key

◐	Start
◉	End
●	Stage start
◯	Stage finish
......	Route of Tour de France
....	Transfer TGV
╌╌╌	Individual Time Trial
Chardin	Town on route

Map by James Anderson, © 1999

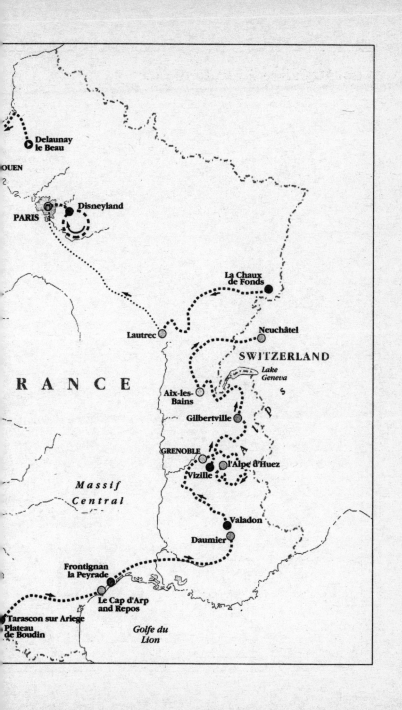

CAT McCABE AND THE
TOUR DE FRANCE

'*I* know that your mother ran off with a cowboy from Denver,' Django McCabe reasoned with his niece, 'but you chasing through France after a bunch of boys on bikes – well, isn't that taking the family tradition to new extremes?'

Cat McCabe, sunbathing, eyes closed, in her uncle's Derbyshire garden, smiled.

It feels funny smiling with closed eyes; like you can't really do both.

So she opened her eyes, stretched leisurely, sat up cross-legged, and picked blades of grass from her body, fingering the satisfying striations they had left on her skin.

'Lashings of lycra!' her elder sister Fen offered from her position under the pear tree.

'Oily limbs a-plenty,' connived her eldest sister Pip, suddenly cartwheeling into view.

Cat tried to look indignant but then grinned. 'The Tour de France is the world's most gruelling sporting event,' she said defensively, hands on hips, to her audience. 'It demands that its participants cycle 4,000 k in three weeks. At full speed. Up and over mountains most normal folk ski down. Day after day after day.'

'And?' said Django, rubbing his knees, bemoaning that the sun wasn't doing for his arthritis what it did last year.

'And?' said Fen, an art historian who was much more turned on by bronze or marble renditions of Adonis than their pedal-turning doppelgangers her sister seemed so to admire.

'And?' said Pip courteously, more interested in perfecting her flikflaks across the lawn for her new act.

Cat McCabe regarded them sternly.

'A Tour de France cyclist can have a lung capacity of around eight litres, a heart that can beat almost 200 times a minute at full pelt and then rest at a rate at which most people ought to be dead. They can climb five mountains in a row, descending them at up to 100 k per hour.'

'Wow,' said Fen with sisterly sarcasm, 'I bet they're really interesting people.'

'Greg LeMond,' countered Cat, 'won the Tour de France in 1989 by eight seconds on the final day.'

'Bully for him,' Pip laughed, doing a handstand and wanting to practise her routine right the way through.

'And that was two years after coming back from the brink of death when he was accidentally shot by his brother-in-law in a hunting accident.'

Now you're impressed!

Fen nodded and looked impressed.

Pip executed a single-handed cartwheel and said, 'Mister LeMond, I salute you.'

Django said, 'Bet the bugger's American.'

Cat confirmed that indeed he was.

'In what other sport would you have participants called Eros? Or Bo? Or teams called BigMat or OilMe or Chicky World?'

'Topless darts?' Pip proposed.

'They can also pee whilst freewheeling,' Cat slipped in before anyone could change the subject.

'In their shorts?' Pip asked, quite flabbergasted.

'Nope,' Cat replied in a most matter-of-fact way. 'They just whip it out, twist their pelvis, and pee as they go.'

'So,' said Django, 'you're off to France to experience a great sporting spectacle performed by superhuman athletes with great bike skills but no sense of urinary decorum?'

'Partly,' said Cat with dignity, 'and because hopefully there'll be a job at the end of it.'

Fen raised her eyebrow.

Pip regarded her youngest sister sternly.

Well aware that her sisters continued to stare at her, Cat looked out over Darley Dale and wished she had her mountain bike with her.

'Oh, all right!' she snapped whilst laughing and covering her face, 'I'm not just pursuing the peloton because there's a job at the end of it if my freelance work is good enough.'

I wish I had my bike. I could just ride and ride and be on my own.

'You are pursuing the peloton—' started Fen.

'Because there's a—' continued Pip.

'Hope of adventure?' Cat tried contemplatively, still covering her face.

'Lashings of lycra,' Fen shrugged as if resting her case.

'Silky smooth shaven thighs,' Pip said in utter agreement. 'Big ones.'

'Over the sea and far away,' Django mused. Everyone mused.

Cat nodded. 'It's time to move on,' she said thoughtfully. Everyone agreed. No one had to say anything more.

'I am Catriona McCabe,' Cat muses to herself, sitting under a cedar in the grounds of Chatsworth House, not two miles from where her uncle lives and from where she was brought up when her mother ran off with a cowboy from Denver, 'and I'm twenty-eight years old.'

And?

And I'm going to the Tour de France, with full press

accreditation, to report on the race for the Guardian *newspaper.*

And?

If my reportage wins favour, I might land the job of Features Editor for the magazine Maillot.

Jersey?

Maillot.

And?

I'll be sorted. And happy.

OK. But all things on two wheels aside, what else?

I'm twenty-eight.

We know.

I live in London. In Camden. In a tiny, rented one-bedroom flat with gay neighbours, a tapas bar opposite, and my two sisters near by.

We met them.

Fenella is a year older than me, Philippa two. Fen's an art historian. Pip's a clown. We're close but different.

Certainly. And you're into journalism?

Actually, I'm into cycling. The journalism part just enables me to indulge my passion.

Isn't a passion for pedal sport rather unusual for a British female? Wouldn't it be more common for you to be into three-day eventing? Or tennis? Or soccer, even?

Cycling is my thing. It is the most beautiful, hypnotic sport to watch. The riders are consummate athletes; so brave, so focused, so committed. My heart is in my mouth as they ride and I watch.

But how and why?

Because I.

That's a fine sentence, Cat.

Because I was . . . with . . . a man who kindled my interest. He left. The interest didn't.

When did he leave?

Three months ago.

A time trial indeed.

Indeed.

4

So France will be good.

France is my dream. France can mark a new me. France can help me heal. Can't it?

I'm sure.

Cat was helping Django prepare supper. Though the McCabe girls visited their uncle monthly, it was rare for them all to be there at the same time. June was turning into July but with his three girls with him, Christmas had come early for Django.

'I'm going to do a Spread,' Django announced. For three girls whose mother had run off with a cowboy from Denver and who were brought up by a man called Django in the wilds of Derbyshire, the Spread was nothing to raise eyebrows at. For normal folk of a conventional upbringing and traditional meal times using regular foodstuffs, a Spread by Django McCabe would cause eyebrows to leave the forehead altogether.

Django McCabe is sixty-seven and, in his jeans with big buckled belts, faded Liberty shirts and trademark neckerchiefs, he looks like he should be an artist, or a jazz musician. In fact, during his lifetime, he's dabbled in both. Twenty-five years ago, in Montmartre, he combined the two rather successfully and sparked a certain trend for neckerchiefs. But then his sister-in-law ran away with a cowboy from Denver and he had to forsake Parisian prestige for the sake of his bereft brother and three small daughters and an old draughty house in Derbyshire. The two men and the three girls lived harmoniously until their father died of a heart attack when Pip was ten years old.

The house is still draughty but Django's warmth, and his insistence on multilayered clothing and his obsession with hot thick soup at every meal during the winter months, ensured that the McCabe girls' childhoods were warm and healthy. They have also developed palates that are robust and tolerant. Soup at every meal throughout the winter months is one thing; that the varieties should include Chicken and Apple, Celery and Baked Beans, and Tuna

Chunks with Pea and Stilton, is quite another. Luckily, it is June and there is no call for soup today.

Pip is having a rest in the back bedroom following further exertion on the lawn. Fen is sitting quietly on the window seat in the room whose name changes according to time of day and current season. On winter mornings and evenings, it is the Snug. On spring afternoons it is the Library. On weekday evenings, if the television is on, it is the Family Room. On weekday evenings if the television is off, it's the Drawing-room. On summer afternoons, it is the Quiet Room. In mornings, it is the Morning Room. When the girls were young and naughty, it was Downstairs. Fen is in the Quiet Room which, after supper, will no doubt be the Drawing-room. Cat is in the kitchen, peeling, scrubbing, grating and chopping and being as diplomatic as possible in dissuading Django from adding Tabasco to the trout, or to the mashed potato, or to the mint and cranberry sauce.

'It's best in Bloody Mary,' Cat informs him. So Django finds vodka but no tomato juice and just mixes the Tabasco in anyway.

'Cheers!' he says, knocking his drink back.

'Cheers!' Cat responds with a hearty sip only to fight back choking and tears.

'I think I'd better name this drink, Bloody Hell, Mary,' Django wheezes, but takes another glug regardless.

Cat nods and wonders if chopped apricots will really add much of consequence – good or bad – to the trout.

They'll counteract the olives, I suppose.

'So, Cat, you'll be a good girl? You'll be careful in France? I know all about Alain Delon and Roger Vadim.'

'I don't,' Cat laughs.

'You watch yourself,' Django cautions, absent-mindedly pointing a knife at her and then apologizing profusely.

'I'll be fine,' Cat assures him, 'I'm in the press corps. There'll be 900 journalists. The Tour is a movable town, a veritable community. I'm in it for the ride, for the duration.'

I'll be safe.

'You look after yourself,' Django repeats, thinking a dash of stout might be welcomed by the mashed potato.

'That's precisely what I'm doing,' Cat says pensively.

The Spread ready, the four McCabes assemble. They stand by their places and look from one to the other in silence. Django gives the nod and they sit. And eat. He's all for picking and dipping and having a taste of this, a soupçon of that. So arms stretch amiably and serving spoons chink and dollop. There's much too much food but whatever's left will be blended together tomorrow, liquidized the next day and then frozen, to reappear as soup in some not-too-distant colder time.

In the Drawing-room, over coffee and some dusty but undamaged After Eights which Pip discovered in her bedside table, Django looked to his three nieces. Fen looked wistful as ever, her blonde hair scrunched into a wispy pony-tail which made her look young and vulnerable and like she should be living at home. Django noticed that she was visibly thinner than when he saw her at Easter and knew that this could be attributed to one of two things.

'Love or money, Fen?' he asked.

She jolted and looked at each of her palms as if assessing the merits of telling him one thing or another.

'Both,' she said, folding her hands in her lap.

'Has he too much or too little?' Django enquired.

'It depends,' said Fen.

Django looked puzzled. Cat couldn't resist. 'One is loaded and the other is broke.'

'Good God, girl!' Django exclaimed in honest horror, much to Cat and Pip's delight. '*Two* of them?'

'Who is it to be?' Cat asked Fen. 'Have you decided yet? The old or the young?'

'Who's the one?' Pip pushed. 'The rich or the poor? Did you toss for it or did they have a duel?'

'Neither,' Fen wailed. 'Both.' She looked out of the window, unable to decipher the night from the moor, or the merits of one love from the other. Django, Cat and Pip gazed at her for a moment.

'Pip,' Django said sternly, 'love or money?'

'I can live most comfortably without either,' said Pip, secretly wishing she had just a little of each.

'Well, a pink afro wig, copious amounts of face paint and an alter ego called Martha the Clown can't help,' Django reasoned.

'I.e., get a proper job,' Pip groaned to Fen whilst ignoring Django. Django turned to Cat who was staring out of the window and way into the night. Her green-grey eyes glinting with the effort of uninvited memories, her sand-blonde hair suddenly framing her face and dripping down over drooping shoulders, her lips parted as if preparing for words she'd never said and wished she had. She looked distant. And sad.

'She's in France already,' Fen whispered to Django, secretly worried that Cat should not be going on her own.

'Best place for her,' Pip colluded, secretly pleased that Cat was guaranteed time alone and away.

'Cat?' Django called softly. Cat blinked, yawned and smiled, hoping it would deflect attention from the obvious effort of pulling on a brave face at that time of night.

'Mario Cipollini's thighs have a circumference of 80 centimetres,' she told them.

I could hear them, my sisters. And they're right – I am in France, sort of. And I wonder if I shouldn't go. I mean, if I stay, maybe He will pop round some time over the next three weeks. Say he wants to change his mind but I'm not here? Might he come back? And say sorry?

As if.

No no.

That's over. Move on, Cat.

But he might.

No, I don't think he will.

How can he love me and then not? And in the same day too?

8

'I love you,' he said in a rare phone call from work that morning. 'I'm leaving,' he said, as so often he did, later that night. 'So go then,' I said, thinking if I stood up to him it would give him the reality check he needed. 'Go then,' I said, presuming he'd stand stock still in horror, sweep me off my feet and cry, 'Never never never.'

Instead?

He went. He ran.

Three months since.

And I cannot bring him back. Yet I left the door metaphorically wide open, hoping he'd come back and bang on it, proclaiming, 'I want to be here with you. Always. What can I do, sweet love?'

So now I think I regret what I did. But they all tell me not to.

The door's still ajar. Soon I'm going to have to shut it. For my safety and my sanity. Let go.

I don't want to. Won't letting go be just that – letting go?

Giving up? Admitting failure? Admitting that it is really, truly over?

And if I let go, am I not saying that I relinquish my hope? Because who am I, Cat McCabe, without my hope?

France. Le Tour de France. La Grande Boucle. *A dream I've had for five years. He was a dream I had for five years – at least this is one I can make come true, all the way to the Paris finale. I will follow the Tour de France, become a part of this fantastic travelling family. From start to finish. All the way, over the flat lands, over the Pyrenees and Alps, through the vineyards and home to the Champs-Elysées. Me and my heroes. Fabian Ducasse. Vasily Jawlensky. Luca Jones.*

You can keep your Brad Pitts and Tom Cruises. You can even keep your George Clooneys. If you want a hero, choose anyone from the Système Vipère or Zucca MV teams. Brad and Tom couldn't do a fraction of the twenty-one hairpin bends on L'Alpe D'Huez. Mr Clooney wouldn't dare descend a mountain with the grace and speed of a peregrine falcon in full plummet.

Bollocks! What on earth has got into me? I mean, I know I

have to move on now – but fantasizing about professional cyclists is not only unrealistic, it's daft and it could be detrimental. Exactly. I'm a professional journalist about to infiltrate a male-dominated world. Not a groupie. Even if I was a groupie, why would they look at me? Put me next to a podium girl with their lips and their legs and their kisses and mini skirts, and I rest my case.

Exactly.

Anyway, the riders are mostly in bed by nine.

And I read something somewhere that hours in the saddle means impotence in the sack.

Only one way to verify that, I suppose.

Cat McCabe!

I meant, talking to the riders' wives and girlfriends.

When Cat arrived home from Derbyshire, her neighbours had left a note inviting her upstairs for a snack and a chat. Eric and Jim (whose fifth anniversary that weekend Cat had missed for Django's Spread) saw Cat's emotional and physical welfare as their responsibility. They were positively parental though they were, in fact, but a year or two older than her. When she had food poisoning, they brought her tonic water and the bucket. When her flat was broken in to, they insisted she slept on their sofabed. When He left, they brought her ice-cream and comfort. They were almost as excited by France and the notion that an adventure and a change of scenery would work wonders for Cat, as they were by the thought of one hundred and eighty-nine amply muscled men in lycra shorts.

'We have a present for you,' Eric said. 'We wanted to give it to you before you leave on Wednesday – by the way, if it doesn't start till Saturday, why are you going so early?'

'Because I have to organize my accreditation and then during Thursday and Friday there are press conferences, team by team,' Cat explained, 'and stuff.'

'Are you excited?' Jim asked, because he was. 'Aren't you nervous?'

10

'I'm very both,' said Cat. 'If that's a sentence.'

'You're vulnerable,' Jim warned her. 'Don't expect too much from France. I know it's a goal that's kept you going, but don't expect too much.'

'And don't go on the rebound,' Eric added, wagging his finger. 'I mean, those riders are considered gods, rock stars, over there, aren't they?'

'I think what he's trying to say,' said Jim, 'is that if you're to go on the rebound – which we sincerely hope you will – a professional cyclist might not be the most suitable participant.'

'I mean,' said Eric, 'just imagine the effect of a night of non-stop debauchery – the poor sod will be too knackered to turn the pedals the next day.'

They all imagined it quietly for a moment and then burst out laughing.

'Which somewhat makes a mockery of our gift,' Eric then continued. 'Here. It's your survival kit.'

They handed Cat a shoebox. She lifted the lid, twitched her brow and then laughed as she fingered through the contents.

'Condoms?' she exclaimed, while Jim shrugged and Eric looked out the window.

'Bic razors?' she asked, counting four.

'We weren't sure if they use Immac on their legs,' said Jim.

'And there's nothing quite like being shaved by someone you fancy,' Eric furthered.

'And there's a lot of leg on some of those boys,' Jim reasoned.

'So am I to suppose that this bumper-sized bottle of baby oil is for after shave and not for me?' Cat asked to meek smiles apiece from the two men.

'Why *do* they shave their legs?' Eric asked.

'To show off their tans and muscles,' Jim cooed.

'Aerodynamics?' Eric pressed.

'Or just a tradition that I, for one, sincerely hope will continue,' Jim said breathlessly.

'Road rash,' said Cat, most matter-of-fact.

'Eh?' said Eric.

'If they crash or fall,' Cat explained, 'it's easier to clean cuts and grazes on smooth skin.'

Jim looked most disappointed with this information. Cat returned her attention to the shoebox. 'Vaseline?'

'We read somewhere that it gives them a, um, more *comfortable* ride,' Jim said ingenuously.

'Not that we're suggesting you offer to apply it,' Eric rushed. Cat raised her eyebrows and held up a wildly patterned bandanna.

'They all wear them,' Eric said, 'we saw them on the TV last year.'

'Extra strong mints,' Cat said, taking the packet to her nose.

'For any, er, passing horses,' Eric said.

'I'm frightened of horses,' Cat said.

'You can befriend them with the mints,' Jim said.

'And that's why you've included them?' Cat pressed with a wry smile. 'Not because I'm going to a country where you have meals with your garlic?' They smiled back at her. Wryly.

Plasters. Antiseptic. A hundred-franc note. A packet of energy bars.

'We'll follow your progress in the *Guardian*,' Eric said.

'It'll be good,' Jim assured her with a squeeze, 'you'll be fine.'

I wonder who'll end up in the yellow jersey? Cat ponders, sitting up in bed with current copies of *Marie Claire* and *Procycling* to hand. *It'll either be Fabian Ducasse or Vasily Jawlensky and I love them both equally but for different reasons. Fabian is stunning in looks and riding, his arrogance is compelling. He exudes testosterone – hopefully in doses that are natural and not administered. Vasily is fantastically handsome too but he really is inscrutable – an enigma. Who do I want to see in the* maillot jaune? *I don't know. May the best man win.*

And the polka dot jersey for King of the Mountains? I'd put my money on Vasily's team-mate, the personable and rather gorgeous Massimo Lipari; the media's dream and a million housewives' darling. I'd like him to make it his hat trick though he'll have to watch out for his Système Vipère rival, the diminutive but charismatic Carlos Jesu Velasquez.

And the green jersey? For points? Can Stefano Sassetta take it back from Jesper Lomers this year?

Then there's the American team, Megapac – Tour virgins, just like me. Maybe I'll try for some exclusives. I'd love to meet Luca Jones – he seems to typify the international camaraderie of the peloton, living in Italy, riding for Great Britain and racing for an American pro team. He's meant to be something of a character – but when you're that pleasing on the eye, it would be a disappointment not to be.

God, I wish I could speak Spanish or Italian. My French is crap. I should have studied harder for Mamzelle at school instead of – how did she phrase it? 'Day-dreaming won't get you a job, O levels will.'

But actually, I've day-dreamt about following the Tour de France for years. And now it's my job to do it.

JULES LE GRAND AND
TEAM SYSTÈME VIPÈRE

*S*warthy, handsome, smelling of Calvin Klein scent and looking very much like someone who might well advertise their wares if he weren't a professional cyclist, Fabian Ducasse strolled through his luxurious Brittany apartment and put a George Michael CD into his Système Vipère mega micro hi-fi station.

'If I rode for the Casino team, ha! I would have only a discount in the sponsor's supermarket chain!' he laughed out loud. 'Or a new vacuum cleaner if I was with Team Polti. If I was with Riso Scotti, I could have all the rice I could eat – so, Système Vipère suits me.' He turned up the volume, reclined his six-foot and twenty-nine-year-old frame on to a leather sofa and listened to George Michael singing about Faith.

Faith. That's what I got to have. Got to win the race or no more super hi-fi for Fabian. Must win. Must conquer. Must blast away any challenge. The maillot jaune *must be mine.*

'Hey, but if I ride for O.N.C.E. or Banesto, I could open accounts with the banks themselves and they could invest all my money and make it even bigger!' He slipped his hand down his tracksuit trousers and grabbed his cock.

14

'Jawlensky? What can Zucca MV give him but building materials? He has a house, so what can he do with more bricks? You can't listen to a brick. A brick doesn't look cool in the lounge.'

With his hand coaxing and rewarding his erection, Fabian walked over to the window and gazed down on the women sipping coffee in the terrace cafés below.

'In four days, the Tour starts. I must win it this year. I should not have let it go last year. I do not like it that this year I am to be categorized "The Pretender". In four days, my future starts again.'

Jawlensky? He took yellow last year only because I wasn't at 100 per cent after that bug. This year is pay back. No one has the maillot jaune *but Fabian.*

One of the women looked up from her *café au lait*. She was blonde and beautiful and he'd seen her before.

'Four days until the Tour. *Bien.* I need coffee. Caffeine is good. And it tastes better when sipped alongside a beautiful woman.'

He made a phone call. 'Hélène? You can get away? Coffee?' His girlfriend of three weeks reminded him that she was at work, in the next town, so he would have to be content that she was having to be content with coffee from the vending machine. Fabian shrugged as he hung up. He went down in to the square and had coffee and an ego-massage by the blonde woman whose name he asked but forgot immediately. He felt incredibly horny. But he forgot that too because he wanted to do 80 kilometres on his bike. Fast.

'Fabian?' Jules Le Grand, Système Vipère's *directeur sportif*, phones his team leader from his mobile phone whilst walking across town from appointment to appointment. A suave man of forty-seven, with an impressive shock of well-styled grey hair, a pair of fabulously expensive gold-rimmed spectacles, a discerning penchant for meticulously designed suits and an almost uncontrollable fondness for exquisite calf-skin loafers, Jules Le Grand would almost look more at home in the offices of a Parisian couturier than amongst the chain grease, muscle embrocation and general blood and sweat that accompanies his job on a daily basis.

Cyclisme is my life, my passion – but why compromise on style? It is not necessary. Only lazy. Laziness is anathema, the enemy, in all to do with cycling, in all to do with life. In that order – compris?

With a phenomenal amount to organize, check and double-check in the rapidly diminishing days, hours, prior to the Tour, the mobile phone, in Jules's mind, is as great an invention of the modern age as the carbon-fibre bicycle frame.

'Fabian?' Jules checks his watch and allows himself the rare luxury of making the call at a standstill.

With a white towel, shorter than necessary (but that was the point entirely) wrapped around his waist, Fabian crooks the phone under his neck whilst trying to figure out the lesser of two evils – to drip on his cream rug or on his fine wood floor. He is going to have to do one or the other because he couldn't possibly tell his *directeur* that now isn't a convenient time.

The Tour de France is not just about cycling your way to Paris, but to the next season also. It's where contracts are confirmed. I must behave on and off my bike, before and during the race.

'Jules,' Fabian says warmly, '*ça va*? I have just done a good ride. I have pasta boiling.'

Shit! I made it sound like he is inconveniencing me.

'I wanted to talk to you before team dinner tonight,' Jules continues. 'About next year. About you and Système Vipère. How is your stereo?'

As head of this company, negotiation is my forte. Or one of my many. As directeur sportif, *it is my business to know what makes my riders click.*

Fabian hops lightly from rug to floorboard, grins at his stereo and grimaces at the two damp indentations of his feet that appear to be indelibly imprinted on his luxurious rug.

'My stereo is great – I hardly ever have it off. Listen.' Fabian holds the telephone receiver out into the centre of the room, presuming his *directeur* can hear Prince. Jules can't but he holds his receiver patiently, checking the battery level and signal strength, until Fabian decides to return to his. 'Did you hear?' Fabian asks. 'Système Vipère is my life – on the bike and off. At all times, I am a Viper Boy.'

That's good – yeah! Jules will like that – a strong commitment that is far more than just a job for me.

'If you like,' Jules says, 'you can have a new stereo. That is, if you stay with us next year.'

The stereo was tempting enough, but Fabian knows it is worthless without a salary to echo, in his mind anyway, his value for the team.

I'll stay silent.

'Plus, of course,' Jules furthers with elaborate sincerity, Fabian's unsophisticated business strategy making him smile, 'a substantial increase in salary. How would it feel to be the highest paid rider in the peloton?'

How does it feel? Fabian pondered moments later, staring at the replaced handset, glowering at his footprints on wood, glaring at the marks still defiant on the rug. *It feels fucking great. I feel like fucking. See, it has made me hard.*

But the Tour de France starts in four days. Shouldn't you save your energy? Celibacy is team policy. Jules is fairly firm on where he stands on sex.

Fairly firm – ha! From where I stand, I am downright hard. I know my body. In bed. On a bike. No problem.

'Fabian, Fabian,' Jules cooed triumphantly, checking his messages and finding four were left during the call to his key rider. Before responding to any of them, he phoned the team's sponsors.

'*Bien*,' Jules told them, 'no problem with Fabian – unless Zucca MV try to sabotage him with a hundred blow jobs.'

'And Jesper Lomers?' they demanded to know. 'Has he signed?'

'Jesper will not be a problem,' Jules assured them.

It's his bloody wife who will cause trouble, Jules hissed to himself as he listened to yet another message left during his call. *All wives are bloody – I've had three, I should know. Maybe Jesper would function better with a mistress – I certainly do.*

I can focus all my attention on the team, Jules mused, *and yet have a woman, at my behest, focus all her attention on me. Perfect!*

His phone rang. It was one of the team mechanics. Jules listened, said, 'Spinergy wheels of course – *imbécile*,' and hung up. The phone rang again. It was the French sports newspaper *L'Equipe*. 'Système Vipère are supreme at the moment,' Jules quoted with bravado, 'Ducasse, Lomers and Velasquez – they will be beautiful to watch. On paper, it is the toughest Tour for a long time, but the Vipers' strength will be like venom to all other riders. You can quote me.' He hung up.

Jules tried Jesper Lomers. No reply.

But no reply is good – it means he is training. And no reply is better than Anya answering the phone. Irritating female – she sees Système Vipère as the 'other woman'. Would Jesper be happy if he was not racing? Would he be a good husband then? She thinks it is she who makes him happy, fulfilled, loved. I know it is Système Vipère. Luckily, I don't think Jesper gives the theory much thought at all. I'll try him again. No reply. Good. Later.

The phone rang again. It was a young rider. 'If you have diarrhoea,' Jules said patiently, 'what must you eat? That's right, hard-boiled eggs, rice and live yoghurt. How much water did you take? That's not enough. We'll put you on electrolytes tonight.' He hung up and laughed.

Directeur sportif? *Call me* père des coureurs – *am I a trainer, a manager or papa?*

'That is why I am strict, a bastard,' Jules muttered,

temporarily changing his pace to a stroll. 'I can shout at a rider in the morning, yell at him from the car during a race, yet by the evening, when he has finished, he is desperate for my embrace. I have to be a father figure to my racers for it is essential that they trust me and crave my approval through their excellence. Why else would they ride? Fabian only for money? Jesper only for his wife's love? Get real.'

Jules marched purposefully across the *place* to the restaurant he had granted the accolade of hosting that year's pre-Tour team dinner. In the town of Eustace St Pierre, it was an honour that all restaurants strove for each year. The proprietors wanted to pamper Jules with complimentary drinks, some fish soup, *tarte tatin*. Jules refused. He was there to check on the menu and arrange the seating plan. Busy. Too busy to eat or socialize, no time for pleasantries at all really.

The Tour de France is on Jules's mind 365 days a year. And because of this, his popularity never suffers. The Tour defines a Frenchman's calendar – for Jules Le Grand to be so unwaveringly committed to it sets him up as a hero amongst his countrymen. The Tour de France preoccupies Jules throughout the season, even when it is still months away. Paris–Nice, Tirreno–Adriatico, Catalan Week, Criterium International, Liège–Bastogne–Liège, the Dauphiné Libéré. Though each race, revered enough in its own right, is given focused dedication, Jules thinks of them all as but preparation for the great one. The Tour de France is always on the tip of his tongue, behind the sparkle in his eye, ever simmering in his mind. The Tour commands his every thought, awake or asleep. Strategy becomes all-consuming.

Directeur sportif? *I am a brilliant tactician.*

Tonight's strategy was for no strategy to be discussed and yet the very purpose of the evening was utterly strategic – team bonding and last mouthfuls of haute cuisine before all vestiges of normal life were relinquished to the clutch and drive of the Tour, to pasta at every single meal, to conversation, dream, thought, breath, devoted exclusively to the race.

More than father to the riders, more than director of a small company whose location changes on almost a daily basis, more than diplomat, or supreme strategist – ultimately I am an army general. The Tour de France is not just about teams of riders going to war against each other; frequently the most severe battle for a rider is an individual one with his own self-belief. I must try Jesper again. That is why I must get to Jesper.

'Hey!' Fabian drawls when he arrives at the restaurant and sits himself down, 'it's our Super Sprinter, the Blond Bomb, the Rotterdam Rocket – you're looking good!'

The compliment, laced with sarcasm, is directed at Jesper Lomers. The Dutchman regards Fabian with a smile and a shake of his head to conceal any hint of embarrassment. Fabian lifts a lock of Jesper's hair. It is very blond, like straw, but soft, a little spiky here, charmingly floppy there.

'That crazy magazine,' Fabian remarks, referring to a recent adulatory article in Italian *Vogue* in which he and Jesper were featured, 'they'll be mourning when your hair is shorn within an inch of your scalp for the Tour. What was it that they wrote about your legs?'

Jesper waves his hand dismissively and busies himself tearing open a bread roll, buttering it well, yet not eating it.

This is good, Jules thinks, *humour, laughter, the team is reacting well.*

He answers on Jesper's behalf. 'The article said – team, listen up – *Jesper Lomers has the most beautiful thighs in the peloton.*'

The team fell about laughing.

Jesper shrugs. 'They're the tools of my trade, guys, the tools of my trade. I'm a good rider – not a sex symbol.'

'Where's the problem in being both,' Fabian comments, knowing his own blend is consummate.

'Anya would beg to differ, I'm sure,' chips in a team member.

'Anya wants to go back to Holland,' Jesper says to everyone but looking steadily at Jules.

'And we want the green jersey,' Jules responds, holding the eye contact whilst aware and pleased that the restaurant saw fit to serve him first, 'and we want you, Jesper, to win it for us again this year.' He regards his rider, one of the most consistent he has ever known. 'The *maillot vert* is yours. You can take it again, your riding warrants it.' Jules knows he can keep Fabian – a little flattery, a lot of money. Jesper he is not so sure about and it unnerves him.

I've never known a rider who can win so spectacularly but with such good grace. Nor have I known a rider so keen to kiss his wife whenever she's at the start or the finish. Increasingly, though, she's been at neither. It unnerves Jesper, I know. She wants to go home. And that unnerves me. Jesper must stay. She has plans. But so do I.

'That's why no wives,' Jules, musing to himself over the three he'd regrettably suffered, proclaims. Luckily, Jesper is preoccupied dunking his bread into the soup like a tea bag and appears not to have heard, let alone taken offence. A couple of the other riders, however, shoot blade-sharp looks at their *directeur*. When they are sure he isn't looking.

'I ride better if I sleep better and I sleep well when I share with my wife,' says one under his breath.

'*Vraiment*,' agrees the other. 'I need a bed-mate on the Tour, not a room-mate. No offence.'

'None taken,' his team-mate confirms. 'So, are we rooming again, this Tour?'

'I would think so,' the other shrugs. 'I've requested it.'

'So have I.'

'You nervous?' his team-mate asks, despite knowing it is a question that will never be answered directly.

'You?'

Clever but fairly standard answer.

'No Weakness,' the rider proclaims as if it is some mantra.

'*Précisément!*' The team-mates, soon to be room-mates in lieu of their female bed- and soul-mates, chink glasses and drink the red wine as if it is nectar.

'Jules, where's Carlos?'

'A Spaniard riding for a French team is a coup enough,' Fabian interjects, touching his nose as if it is out of joint. 'Can we really expect him to turn up any earlier than the last minute, for something as trivial as a team meal?'

Before Jules can answer on Carlos's behalf, the waiters arrive with miniature portions of sorbet which everyone samples but, being tomato and basil sorbet (of which, undoubtedly, Django McCabe would have been proud), no one much likes.

Jules raises his glass of Burgundy. 'Here's to the jerseys. And they are most definitely plural. The yellow. The green. The polka dot. Fabian. Jesper. Carlos. Here's to Système Vipère. *Salut.*'

'*Vive le Tour,*' says Fabian, gulping wine and then tucking into duck.

'*Vive le Tour,*' says Jesper, thinking of Anya, wishing she were here and apprehensive about a certain coldness that will greet him at home that night.

Carlos Jesu Velasquez had no compunction at being absent from the team dinner in France.

'I am to spend over three weeks in your country so that night I will dine with my wife,' he had said to Jules previously by telephone.

He must feel special, Jules had reasoned to himself, *so I will make it seem a gesture of my respect that he needn't be present for the dinner. Realistically, he would not add much in the way of scintillating conversation to the evening. In truth, it is not important to the team or the Tour whether he eats escargots with us or paella with his family.*

Carlos Jesu Velasquez is nicknamed the Pocket Rocket, like the energy bars of that name which the riders carry with them, on account of his small stature but enormous potency.

Carlos Jesu is also known as the Cicada for he speaks little. He speaks no other language than Spanish but even amongst the Spanish riders he is frugal with communication. He uses his tongue and his lips to address the peloton, hissing or clicking at riders to move away, to work with him, to get out of his line. Carlos is also known as the Little Lion, for when the little climber wins at a mountain finish he lets out a guttural roar utterly inconsistent with his diminutive size and quiet mien. His wife, Marie-Christina, however, calls him Jesu with a throatily pronounced 'h'. His three children call him Papa.

This evening, he walked his three children across the street to his mother-in-law's. He then went back to his house, closed the door and made love to Marie-Christina. Then he sang to her. Tomorrow, he will travel to Eustace St Pierre.

'Away on business,' he whispers soothingly to his wife, 'but home again soon.'

* * *

If I were to meet the inimitable Fabian Ducasse, what exactly would I say? Cat wondered, on her way in to the *Guardian* office to discuss their requirements and other practicalities.

He's famed as a womanizer, so should I concede that he might be more willing to talk, to grant me an audience, if I wore a skirt? I'd have to think of a slant – not just 'Are you going to win the Tour de France, Monsieur Ducasse?' Perhaps I could ask him about sport and adulation – would he do it if he didn't get it? I want to tap in to that arrogance to see if it's a front or genuine. Not that I care which – it has the desired effect on me for one.

Is there time to learn a little Spanish? Mind you, just a grunt from Carlos Jesu Velasquez would suffice. And how about Jesper? Is there anything that comes close to hearing English spoken with a Dutch accent?

I can't believe I'm soon to be there. In France. With them. What'll I say?

RACHEL McEWEN AND
TEAM ZUCCA MV

'Jesus!' cried Massimo Lipari, grasping his left leg and stroking his hamstring tenderly. 'Holy Mother Mary – you are in one fuck of a bad mood.'

Rachel McEwen looked down on the rider's prostrate nakedness, his nether regions covered only by a towel, nappy-style; his lanky, lithe frame the colour of mocha ice-cream, which enabled him to skip up mountains like a gazelle, his huge brown eyes regarding her dolefully, full lips puckered into a somewhat theatrical pout. She looked at her hands, bit her lip and apologized.

'I'm sorry, Mass,' she said, using her hands more gently and reminding herself that his thighs were flesh and not meat, 'I have a lot on my mind.'

Shit, poor Vasily – I must have pummelled him to hell and back half an hour ago. And yet I never heard even a wince – just a 'thank you, Rachel, thank you'. Vasily Jawlensky, the committed and consummate sportsman for whom, no doubt, 'pain is gain', a man frugal with words but abundant in his triumphs. And now Massimo, Italy's heartthrob, the team's key personality, one who loves to make drama out of the ordinary, let alone a crisis. Was I rough? Did I hurt you? Sorry.

Rachel shook her hands as if they were wet and, despite fingers glistening with massage oil, scrunched her wavy hair into a haphazard pile on top of her head. She returned her hands to the rider's inner thigh and then moved her fingers as if she was playing the piano.

'You know,' said Massimo, 'when they said we were to have a female *soigneur* – well, I almost went on strike, I could have left the team, to and fro.'

Rachel laughed. 'You mean *there and then*, Mass. I thought you'd have been delighted, being the Casanova that you are.'

Massimo grimaced as Rachel worked at a particularly tight knot near his knee, as if she was making pastry. 'Well, girl, if they had said we were going to have a, how do you say, female doll?'

'Mascot?' Rachel suggested.

'*Si!* Mascot – that would have been different. But I never thought the words female and *soigneur* could really be – how do you say? Married?'

'What you mean, you nasty man,' Rachel retorted with no malice, 'is that you didn't think a female *soigneur* would be any good.'

'*Si*,' said Massimo, his eyes still closed, 'paint and pasta.'

'Chalk and cheese,' Rachel corrected. 'You thought that she'd be too weak to give a good massage.'

'*Si*,' Massimo smiled, looking at the ceiling of Rachel's office at the team's Cambiago headquarters while she continued to untie his muscles and unravel his ligaments.

'That she'd worry more about her fingernails than your welfare?'

'*Si!*' Massimo laughed, remembering how Rachel had stayed up with him during the Giro, the prestigious Tour of Italy, last month, so that he could repeat over and over his anxieties for the next day's Stage.

'And that she might shrink all your gear in the wash?'

'Ha!' said Massimo, suddenly realizing he didn't even

know what happened to his dirty gear once he had stripped after a race.

'Moaning about boyfriends the whole time?'

'That too,' Massimo agreed, having no idea if Rachel even had a boyfriend, current or past.

'So,' said Rachel, lifting Massimo's leg over her shoulder, pushing against it for the stretch whilst doing something extraordinary to a point just below the buttock, 'all in all, I suppose I've completely let you down then? Utterly destroyed your preconceptions of a female *soigneur*?'

'Rachel,' said Massimo, turning to lie on his front and inadvertently presenting her with a sizeable portion of hairy bottom from behind the slipped towel, 'you are my *soigneur*. You are the best *soigneur* for Massimo. I don't think of you as a girl at all.'

Well, I suppose that was the definitive compliment, Rachel muses as she washes her hands of oil and changes the towel on the massage table in preparation for the next rider. *But odd too. Out of all the* soigneurs *on the Tour – three or four for each of the twenty-one teams – I'll be one of only two females. And though it's nice that Emma and I, in this hugely male-dominated world, are not hassled, it's a bit bizarre that everyone completely denies us our gender. It's like, in life there are men, women and* soigneurs. *I mean, I know I'm a woman, but it is a fact of negligible interest to the cycling fraternity.*

'It doesn't bother me,' she says out loud, allowing herself a fleeting glance in the mirror and thinking her hair really does need a cut. 'This is my job. It's appallingly paid but I love it.'

Rachel McEwen is twenty-seven years old and looks far too slight to be hoiking the heavy limbs of exhausted men and dispelling the lactic acid in their tense, brutalized muscles. But that is what she does and she does it very well.

'But what the fuck is a *signor*?' her best friends had enquired when she told them she was leaving Edinburgh for Italy to be one two years ago.

'*Soigneur*,' she stressed. 'It means "one who looks after" – the riders' needs are my responsibility.'

This was greeted, much to her consternation, by a rapid chorus of wink-wink, nudge-nudging.

'I'll be doing their laundry, for Christ's sake!' she retorted, twisting her hair around and around in frustration before pinning it to her head precariously. 'And preparing their race food each day. And going on ahead to the hotels to check out the rooms and the menus. And giving massage and minor medical assistance. And counselling – many riders look on their *soigneur* as their confidante.'

'Back track, back track,' they had implored, 'to the "massage" bit.'

'Yes?' Rachel had replied ingenuously. 'It'll be good to put it to some practical use after two years of training.'

'They'll devour you,' one friend said. 'You're such a wee lass and all that friction against the chamois lining of their shorts must make 'em horny bastards.'

'Numb, more like,' Rachel had said, 'and anyway, I can't be doing with love at my age.'

I haven't the time, Rachel reasons, remembering that conversation well and realizing with horror that she hasn't been back to Scotland for almost a year. She prepares the table for Stefano Sassetta's arrival and skims through the sheaves of lists for the Tour that she started compiling during the Giro.

Shit! Frangipane.

Is that an expletive?

No, I really do mean the cake. It is a fantastic energy burst for the boys and it keeps moist and fresh for ages. I'm in cahoots with a local baker – he has broken an age-old family custom to make the cake square just for Zucca MV, because it's much more practical to cut and divide.

So, a *soigneur* is a masseuse and a patisserie expert?

And a rally driver too – watch me bomb along the Stage route to the feed station or the arrivée *where often I have to rescue my riders from the media scrum.*

It is my job to be the first person my rider sees on finishing a Stage.

'Shit,' says Rachel, running fingers still rather oily through her long-suffering locks, 'I must check on disposable flannels. Stefano is due in ten minutes and I'm a little concerned about that shoulder of his.'

Stefano Sassetta, who should have been on Rachel's massage table ten minutes ago, was parading around his apartment in his Zucca MV team strip.

'God, this blue and yellow suits me,' he commented to his current girlfriend. 'If I had taken up Team Mapei's offer, I wouldn't look half as good. It was reason enough to stay with Zucca MV.'

While Stefano gazed at his opulent if vulgar kitchen extension, a gift from the team's sponsors and designed by Stefano himself, his girlfriend could barely keep her eyes from the semicircle of stitching around the reinforced groin area. It was like a magnificent sunburst and she was hot for what was behind it.

'You want to work up an appetite, baby?' she said coyly, fingering the spaghetti straps of her negligible sundress. Everything about the man was big – his baritone voice, his legendary thighs, his hands, his nose; they all complemented the biggest treat of all, currently concealed but far from hidden behind his shorts.

'I just did a good ride,' Stefano countered as if his appetite were indeed her exclusive concern.

For Zucca MV's Stefano Sassetta, Système Vipère's Jesper Lomers was his nemesis. Jesper was undoubtedly a better rider technically; Stefano knew it and loathed the Dutchman for it; loathed, too, the way Jesper was always so courteous and affable towards him. Jesper might be the better rider but the crowds loved Stefano's flamboyance. However, though the fans might adore Stefano, the peloton had more respect for Jesper.

Whereas Jesper regarded his physique merely as a by-product of his career, at this point in the season Stefano was increasingly obsessed with his own beauty. Specifically, his thighs. Measurements, dimensions and cross-comparisons with last year, and with the thighs in the peloton in general, had become a fixation. Stefano was almost more pre-occupied with having his thighs praised over Jesper's than he was with taking the green jersey off him. He thus presented his body to his girlfriend as if it were a statue. You can look but you cannot touch. He has told her to expect no sex until September.

Consequently, it is also around this time of year that a change of girlfriend is imminent. They leave him. It's an occupational hazard. He would never ask them to stay. For Stefano, riding slowly is boring. It's nice to have a change of strip.

'Did you read that thing?' Stefano asks Rachel who is trying to loosen his right shoulder.

'God, you're tight,' Rachel murmurs.

'Hey,' Stefano jests, 'that's my line.' Rachel does not react. 'Did you?' he repeats, his contrived nonchalance failing to mask his unease.

'Did I what?' Rachel asks, feeling something give high in his neck, and glancing at the flicker of subconscious relief across Stefano's face.

'Read that thing?'

'What thing?'

Stefano, you're such a dick. It's the bloody Jesper issue, isn't it?

'That thing. About Lomers. In *Vogue*.'

'Stef,' Rachel chides in a very grave way, 'would you give up? The *look* of a thigh is utterly superficial. It's what they can do that's the issue.'

She rubs his hard for emphasis.

He looks like a sulky schoolboy. And he won't race well. OK, Stef, for the millionth time, I'll say it again.

'Don't your women go wild for both the look and the feel

29

of you?' Rachel asks in a totally fresh way, despite it being an enquiry Stefano likes to hear on a weekly basis at least. Nevertheless, Stefano squints at Rachel as if she has just posed a really taxing question.

'Who does the crowd love?' she presses kindly and with convincing ingenuousness.

Stefano pulls a face as if assessing every member of the peloton. 'Stefano Sassetta,' he declares, as if it was a most considered answer.

'How many Stages did Lomers win in the Giro?' Rachel asks. Stefano holds up one finger.

'And how many did you win?' she furthers. He holds up three fingers and then starts laughing.

That's better, thinks Rachel, laughing at him and not with him.

'And how many are you going to win in the Tour?' she pushes, taking his foot in her hand to work on.

'It is not the Stages of the Tour,' Stefano says, his eyes dark and glinting, 'but the colour of the jersey. You know, I think green on your back completely alters the impression of the thigh. If they see me in green, they'll think of my physique as supreme within the peloton. I want it to be written that *Stefano Sassetta, this year's winner of the green jersey, has the thighs of a Greek god.*'

'Och, you're so full of crap, Sassetta,' laughs Rachel, for whom it is impossible to look on Stefano's thighs as anything other than pistons for which she is caretaker. 'What was that saying you taught me?'

'More shit than in the backside of a donkey.'

'Aye, that's you,' Rachel laughs again. 'Now turn over. I need to do your glutes. By the way, how are your haemorrhoids? I think that new cream is probably better – yes?'

'*Oh la la, chica chica la la. Le Tour, oh yeah, le Tour. Yeah. Yeah. Le Tour. La!*'

Massimo Lipari, pleasantly rejuvenated from his session

with Rachel, is singing in his apartment, gyrating his way from bathroom to bedroom, giving a good shimmy by the cupboard door and then delving around his quite extensive wardrobe. Never mind the imminence of the Tour de France, it is the team supper itself tonight that requires greatest application from Massimo. He repeats his song and sings it fortissimo.

If I were not a professional cyclist, I would be a pop star. He regards his handsome reflection and gives himself a wink. His cheekbones are as sharp as his eye reflexes when he's descending mountains at 100 kilometres an hour. His smile is as dazzling as the way he can dance up the ascents of the most unforgiving climbs. He sings his pop song again. The tune is the one he recorded as the official song of the Giro D'Italia last year which made it into the top ten.

It was almost as thrilling as finishing third overall in the race itself. Almost – but not quite. Cycling defines me. A cyclist could, conceivably, become a celebrity. But a pop star could not decide to become a pro racer.

Off his bike, Massimo lives as a star and loves it. He's on adverts on television and billboards, he's been in the hit parade, his face is on a particular brand of chocolate-hazelnut spread and his local bar is bedecked with Massimo memorabilia. And yet astride his bike, he is utterly focused, racing brilliantly and seemingly independent of crowd adulation. The transformation to superstar occurs the moment he crosses the finish line. He always wipes his mouth and zips up; there are thousands of cameras, press and TV, fans staring everywhere – he believes it his duty to delight them both in and out of racing conditions. He wants to take the King of the Mountains jersey this year, to make his hat trick.

He goes to the vast gilt mirror above the flamboyant paved fireplace that his sponsors built for him. He gazes at himself and nods.

'I am *Donna* magazine's "Sexiest Man on Two Wheels",' he remarks. 'Nice! But if I can take the polka dot jersey for a third time – well! National hero comes home to party time!'

Looking like a healthy composite of mafioso, pop star and Milanese advertising executive, Massimo Lipari leaves his apartment for the team dinner. He could drive. He could take a cab. He could have taken up Rachel's offer to taxi him there as she is doing for other members of the team. But Massimo decides to walk. He likes to hear the calls of '*Ciao*, Massimo!' He likes to feel people looking, he likes to sense the recognition, he likes to imagine what they say to each other when he has passed by. He is a local hero, all the Zucca MV boys are, living in close proximity just north of Verona and in the shadow of the foothills of the Dolomites.

With his hair gelled and tweaked, his goatee beard clipped to perfection, his jet-black eyes hidden from view behind Oakley sunglasses despite it being dusk, Massimo Lipari cuts a dashing figure, slicing into the fantasies of the women he passes on his way to the restaurant with much the same force as when he slices through the pack on a mountain climb.

Rachel is wearing a skirt, not that anyone has noticed and not that she's noticed that it's gone unnoticed. It is pale blue linen, straight, and to the mid-calf. She has teamed it with a white linen shirt and white lace-up pumps. It suits her. Her hair is down but scooped away at the sides. She is wearing perfume but no make-up, her fresh complexion giving a radiance to her already pretty features.

It's the last bloody time for over three weeks that I'll be able to wear light colours and not smell of embrocation. The Tour de France, and the perils of being a soigneur, mean dark plain clothes are not just practical but a necessity. Anyway, I still haven't had the chance to do my own laundry. Poor Paolo has had a very bad stomach which he is playing down because this will be his first Tour and he doesn't want to miss it. However, his shorts have really taken the brunt. Terrible mess. It's taken me most of the afternoon. Poor boy.

Rachel, you're a saint.

Bollocks. I'm a soigneur. It's my job.

She looks around the table at the team and realizes she is on tenterhooks on their behalf.

Look at you all, seemingly so relaxed. My God, when I think what's in store for you.

And for you, Rachel. It's your first Tour de France.

Me? Oh, I'll be fine. The Tour, the Giro, the Vuelta – surely just the scenery is different. But the boys have the Col du Galibier, the Madeleine, L'Alpe D'Huez – not to mention the fucking Pyrenees beforehand. Shit, I must remember cashmere socks.

'I must remember cashmere socks,' Rachel all but shouts. The table falls silent, pieces of pizza halt half-way to mouths; spaghetti unravels itself from motionless forks.

'Huh?' says Massimo shooting glances to his team-mates.

'In case it becomes cold, in case you develop sore throats. If Benylin is a banned substance, a cashmere sock worn round the neck at night surely is not.'

'Rachel,' said Stefano very seriously, stretching his arm across the table and laying his hand on her wrist for emphasis, 'we finished work for the day. Shut the fuck up, relax, eat. Please.'

The team cheered and raised their glasses in support. Rachel twitched her lip and then raised her glass too.

'Here's to you lot,' she said with immense feeling. 'Have a good race.'

*   *   *

Rachel knows that she is to be one of only two female *soigneurs* on the Tour de France and the thought doesn't worry her in the least. Cat has no idea that, in the *salle de presse* of 1,000 journalists, she will be one of only twelve women.

If I were to meet Vasily Jawlensky, Cat muses, coming

33

home from the *Guardian* office, *what on earth would I say to him? Ought I to bow? Curtsey? In his presence, surely major genuflection is highly appropriate. I wish I could speak bloody Russian.*

I can't wait to meet Massimo Lipari, he always kisses everyone three times, regardless of their sex or relationship to him. Remember how last year, Phil Liggett from Channel 4 was given the Lipari smackers live on TV after Massimo won at L'Alpe D'Huez? Liggett looked lovestruck and told the viewers he'd never wash his face again. I'd like some Massimo kisses. But how would I go about getting them? What exactly would I ask him?

I'd love to set Stefano Sassetta off against the inimitable Mario Cipollini. They're both the most extravagant, over-the-top personalities in the peloton. Stefano tall, dark and handsome; Cipo with blond highlights, a pony-tail and a great line in outrageous one-liners. There's Stefano banging on about the aesthetic excellence of his thighs, and there's Cipo saying if he wasn't a cyclist he'd like to be a porn star. Italian stallions, both.

But.

I suppose it's not so much what I'd say to them, but whether or not they'd talk to me.

Oh.

BEN YORK AND TEAM MEGAPAC

*B*en York, born thirty years ago in Hampshire, studied medicine at Guy's Hospital, London. It was perfectly reasonable for his mother, his father, his friends and his then-girlfriend Amelia, to assume he'd take the position offered to him by Guy's, further his career, become as brilliant as everyone had always anticipated, marry Amelia (as she anticipated), afford a very lovely place in Notting Hill and take up golf.

Ben York, however, hates golf.

Ben turned down the job at Guy's, let down Amelia, appalled her parents and stunned his parents when he announced he was going to downtown Chicago to live and work.

'Chi*cago*, Ben?' his father had protested. 'When you have so much going for you here, why move to America of all places? What about the lovely Amelia? And Guy's? Have you really thought this through?'

I've thought of little else. Upsetting women is what I seem to do effortlessly if wholly unintentionally. This isn't about the Ben you all want me to be, but about the one I know I am. I'm not a Guy's man, and I can't be Amelia's man because, lovely as indeed she is, she isn't Ben's woman.

'But sweetie,' Amelia sobbed, 'what about our life in London? Notting Hill, for heaven's sake. Marriage and babies? And a brilliant career at Guy's? How could you do this to me?'

I'm not doing this 'to' you, I'm doing this for us – because of me. I don't want a place with you in Notting Hill – I don't even like Notting Hill. Marriage and babies? Maybe one day. With you? No. We're young. You're staggeringly beautiful. You'll be OK.

That was five years ago. Amelia married Charlie three years ago and has just given birth to baby James. The nursery at their place in Notting Hill is exquisite. She's idyllically happy. Ben spent three years in Chicago, another in Denver and was then head-hunted by Team US Megapac who made it worth his while to embark on a new and unusual career based in Boulder, Colorado.

And I bloody love it. Not so much the US specifically, but the job itself. This is medicine, the fact that I am needed to oversee the health of these riders, that I must observe how their bodies work, how they need to heal and what I can do to help them win and what I must do to keep them healthy too. Many of my riders have wives, girlfriends – and it is for them that I keep their men safe.

And you, Ben?

I love watching a body function – and pro cycling often means that the body is at its absolute peak but also its ultimate limit. I have to keep those bodies continually at the summit of the climb – I cannot let them hurtle downhill. It's my job.

Interesting, but I was referring to the 'wives and girlfriends' bit. Do you only live for your job? Who is Ben when he isn't assessing tendons or administering balancing doses of B12 and electrolytes?

I don't understand the question. This is my life.

It's your job.

Exactly.

Exactly. Who are you when you're off duty?

What the fuck does that mean?

I said 'off duty', not off your guard. Ben York, you're a doctor, but you're also thirty, brawny, caring (and don't just say that's your job) and something of a catch yourself. It is an undisputed fact that doctors are fantasy men for many women. Especially one with an English accent out in America. That you should also be aesthetically charming on the eye – by that I mean six foot, fit and handsome – well, you're the cake, the icing and the cherry on top that most women would want to consume in its entirety.

Most women are too calorie conscious.

Oh, very droll. Come on, Ben, post-Amelia details?

In the States they call it dating. If dating goes well, one proceeds to going steady.

How's the dating going?

Fine.

That sounds final.

I date. But then I steady up.

Why?

As I say to my riders when they ask, sex is very good for mind and body.

And love nourishes the soul.

And can be utterly exhausting. These chaps need to be focused to race.

I wasn't referring to your riders.

Ben York isn't the only one in Team Megapac whose accent gains him much attention. Luca Jones was born to an Italian mother and English father and his resultant Anglo-Italianisms are inimitable and do strange things to women. He lives partly in Italy, partly in America. Currently, he is in Colorado, at the team headquarters. They leave for France tomorrow. As is Luca's wont, he met a pretty girl in a bar last night, stayed up far too late, went way too far and is now not only tired but also late for a physical with Ben.

'I'm later than late, bugger damn.'

Luca hurries himself into a tracksuit, winces at the bags

under his eyes, slaps his cheeks to shift the pallid evidence of the previous night's over-exertion, and darts out of the apartment to cycle the short distance to Ben's surgery.

'Have you seen it?' Ben laughed, holding aloft the beautifully bound press information booklet the Megapac PR department had produced for the Tour. 'It's a fucking novel! A cheesy, toe-curling, piss-takable collectors' item.' He took Luca's blood pressure, unwrapped the band from the rider's arm and then took a sample of blood from the crook of his elbow with no more ado.

Luca flipped through the booklet. 'The media are going to love this,' he said. 'Have you seen the pamphlet Zucca MV produce? I thought the team looked ridiculous posing amongst the brick and cement of the sponsor's factory. But at least their riders are wearing their kit and have their bikes. This bloody photographer took hours. They put make-up on me, goddamn!'

Ben took the booklet from him and found Luca's page. The photograph flattered a face that needed no flattering. Underneath it was Luca's 'mission statement'. Under that, his biographical and career details. Ben skimmed through it and laughed.

I love riding a bike – the thrill of racing, the dream and possibility of winning. Being part of a team is like being part of a family. Racing for Megapac has been, well, MEGA! For our sponsors and our supporters, thank you – I'll race hard for you.

Luca Jones

'Did you write that all by yourself?' Ben asked jovially, fond of Luca, six years his junior, looking on him as a kid brother.

Luca punched him lightly. 'Some woman phoned me and we talked about bikes for an hour. Somehow, she got it all into four sentences. I was so impressed – and she had a very nice voice – that I asked her out for a drink.'

'Unbelievable,' Ben shook his head.

'As old as my Mama!' Luca rued. He took the pamphlet from Ben. '*Ben York, a brilliant young British doctor,*' Luca read very theatrically, '*whose wisdom we admire, whose care we are so grateful for, whose advice we trust, whose friendship we cherish.*' Luca regarded Ben, clicked his heels and saluted the doctor. 'Hail, Mighty Medicine Man, my Lord, my Keeper, Great and Godly Giver of Vitamin B12 and Creatine.'

'You know they've printed over 3,000,' Ben informed him, taking the pamphlet from Luca to fan himself.

Luca nodded. 'And have you seen the baseball caps and T-shirts? The journalists are getting them too.'

'Not to mention the cereal bars,' Ben elaborated. 'You know they're emblazoned with the logo and the words "as depended on by our brave team"?'

Luca's jaw dropped. 'I never bloody ate one in my life!'

Ben manipulated Luca's ankles. 'If you riders don't impress the media, this treatise and accompanying branded freebies certainly will.'

'We're a friggin' *wildcard* team,' Luca exclaimed. 'It was only confirmed we'd be racing the Tour a month ago.'

'Megapac are a wildcard team only because they're not ranked in the UCI top sixteen,' Ben said, almost sternly. 'It has nothing to do with the quality of the riders – merely that you're a relatively new team and therefore have amassed no track record.'

'Yeah, yeah,' Luca said, leaning forward so Ben could listen to his chest.

'Don't rush your career,' Ben mused. 'If you went to Mercatone Uno or Saeco, you'd be a much smaller fish. You can really shine at Megapac – you already have. A Stage win in your first Giro – bloody marvellous. Now, let me listen to your heart,' Ben said, stethoscope at the ready.

'My heart,' Luca proclaimed, with his right hand clasped at it for emphasis, 'belongs to Megapac. God Bless America.'

Ben and he laughed heartily and then fell silent while Luca's impressive organ was analysed.

'Good,' said Ben, 'you're really in good nick. Just take care, young man. Recuperation is the key to success.'

Luca sat up on the side of the examination table and took a couple of deep breaths. 'Drink tonight?'

'You can have *a* beer,' Ben cautions, 'and no women. Or vice versa.'

'Yeah,' Luca laughed, 'something like that.' He sprang down from the bench, slipped into his tracksuit, gave Ben a high five and arranged to meet him later.

Ben smiled as he prepared for the next rider.

For me, Luca personifies the point of the Tour de France – the international flavour and colour that epitomizes the peloton. He's going to hit his peak during the Tour and do great things for the team. It's going to be his first Tour de France, coming only a month after his first Giro where he won a Stage in fine style. He'll go far. With my help. Ambition is in his soul but his body is in my hands. That's the kick for me.

Ben is sharing beer and banter with Hunter and Travis, the two American stars of Megapac. Hunter Dean and Travis Stanton are as focused and earnest as Luca is cavalier and spirited. Both are all-American boys: Hollywood handsome, open demeanour, and awesomely fit, for whom Commitment is their creed, Dedication their dogma and very much with capital letters. They're ambassadors – representing Megapac and the United States in general, cycling in particular, their families, their colleges, their home towns specifically. They love their bikes and their moms and dads and kid siblings, their buddies in the teams and their fiancées with dreamy daft names to whom they dedicate race wins, Stage wins, tough days or good rides.

'Cycling is lucky to have been chosen by you,' Ben says, eating peanuts, 'because I suspect you could have turned to any sport you wished and excelled.'

They know more about vitamin supplements than I do. They love sports massage; they love citing their VO_2 Max *and how many kilometres they ride a year. They love knowing what their ideal body fat percentage is and they love training hard and eating the right things to ensure that they maintain it. They love quoting their power output in terms of watts, and mantras which they chant and believe in. They believe in themselves. Belief is both the ultimate and minimum requirement for any cyclist who wishes to survive the Tour de France, let alone do well.*

'As I said in my mission statement,' says Hunter, touching a peanut and then forsaking it, '*When I was a kid, I had a dream and my dream was to represent a great national team, to represent my country.* I'm living my dream, man, living my dream.' He sighs and nods gravely at Ben. 'My statement continued: *They say that racing takes it out of you, but by racing, I believe I'm giving something back. I ride because I love it but I race for all of you.* That's me, Ben, that's how it is for me.'

Ben sips his beer thoughtfully.

I don't know whether to kiss the bloke or piss myself laughing.

'Your mission statement,' Ben says instead, 'did you write it? Were you interviewed?'

'*Interviewed*? Was I fuck,' says Hunter. 'Sure I wrote it.'

'And you, Travis?' Ben asks.

'It's a mission statement,' Travis exclaims, as if Ben is mentally deficient, 'of course you write it yourself. Or it ain't yours. What would that make the mission? Fucking bogus.'

'Do, er, you know yours off by heart?' Ben enquires, grateful that Luca is out of earshot or keeping his straight face would be a physical impossibility and mental torture.

Travis balks, as if Ben has asked a most ridiculous question. 'It starts off: *They say you never forget how to ride a bike and I guess that's true. Racing professionally enables me to make my living out of a pastime that is a pleasure for so many people.*' He pauses and shrugs. 'And it goes on, you know?'

Ben is saved a rendition of the entire statement by a rumpus at the other end of the bar. It is Luca, surrounding himself with an impressive, hungry female entourage. 'What is it about Luca?' Hunter shakes his head. 'Huh, Ben?'

'A blend of sound and vision,' Ben shrugs, raising a bottle of beer on catching Luca's eye.

'Huh?'

'The aural senses send nerve impulses to woman's carnal core,' Ben expostulates, knowing it's bullshit but that Hunter would never think so. 'At least, that's my theory.'

'Huh?' Hunter repeats, wondering whether it is a finer point of medicine, Ben's grammar or the effect of the rare beer that is making comprehension a little difficult.

'Ears, right?' Travis clarifies.

'The *accent*,' Ben specifies. 'Luca's curious blend of Italian and Carnaby Street peppered with Americanisms causes an involuntary chemical reaction in womenfolk.'

Hunter laughs and chinks bottles with Ben and Travis. 'Way to go, Luca!'

'*You can kissa my ass 'cos I'm not going up that fuckin' 'ill,*' Ben imitates Luca perfectly.

'Fucking A1!' Hunter proclaims, chinking bottles again and taking a good swig.

'Plus,' Ben continues in all seriousness, 'it comes out of the mouth of a perfectly formed, aesthetically pleasing twenty-four-year-old.'

They observe the younger rider, in his element, flirting for England, or Italy, or America. Wherever. Perfect white teeth surrounded by pillowy lips, set into a boyish face atop a beautifully athletic physique.

'Look at those women,' Ben remarks objectively, motioning to the throng with his beer bottle, 'they are utterly bewildered. They are caught in an extreme dilemma.'

'They are?' Travis probes, inquisitiveness keeping him in the bar though he's glanced at his watch and thinks that, at half past nine and after half a bottle of beer, he really should be leaving so he can get eight hours' sleep. 'What's the problem?'

'Well,' says Ben contemplatively, 'they don't know what

they want more – to mother him or fuck him.'

'Je-sus!' Hunter exclaims. 'He's a fucking *bike* rider.'

'Exactly,' says Ben, 'they can't decide whether they'd rather run their fingers through those soft, Botticelli curls or grab hold of his buttocks and drive their nails right in.'

'Go, Luca!' Travis jockeys, ordering another beer and thinking what the hell.

'Son of a bitch,' Hunter agrees with admiration.

Luca extricates himself from the tangle of women and saunters over to his team-mates and doctor. 'You guys, you talking about me, hey? What you saying?'

Bottles chink.

'You're a chick magnet,' Hunter congratulates him so solemnly that it should be impossible to take seriously.

'Cheers!' Luca responds ingenuously. 'Here's to France and the *belle femmes*.'

'Coming hot on the heels of the Giro and all those *belle signorine*,' counters Ben.

'Ah, the Giro,' Luca says wistfully, as if it were something he'd done as a young man. 'All those pretty babes in denim shorts and bikini tops, waving and calling your name from the roadside, coming to you at the *village départs* wanting an autograph—'

'And being rewarded with your double kiss,' Travis adds.

'Gawping, in hot-flushed awe, as your legs were rubbed,' Ben remembers.

'All our legs are rubbed at the finish,' Luca remonstrates.

'Yes,' Ben says, 'but the rest don't spread their limbs quite so wide while maintaining unflinching eye-contact and suggestive smiles with young ladies.'

'I'm a young man, man,' Luca shrugs, 'and strong. I'm a bloke. The crowds, the passion, the girls – *vive le Tour*.'

'OK guys,' says Hunter, suddenly horny from the beer, the conversation, the freedom of the evening and the realization that he won't see his fiancée again for nearly a month, 'I'm out of here.'

'Me too,' says Travis. 'All set?'

Ben nods approvingly and raises his eyebrows at Luca. 'You should do the same.' Luca looks petulantly over to the posse of pussy whose eyes have not once left him. He regards Ben and then nods.

'I'm going to have a great Tour, hey doc?' Ben places a supportive hand on his shoulder in response. 'I'm going to make the sponsors proud and they'll sign me for next year – with a raise, perhaps elevate my status in the team.'

Ben steers him through the bar and out into the night. The mountains lumber and slumber in dark mauve velvet masses against a sky smattered with an inordinate array of stars.

'And my Mama and Dad – make 'em proud too,' Luca continues. They stroll to their bikes. 'Podium girls,' Luca says, swinging his leg and freewheeling away. Ben catches him and they pedal slowly back to the apartments, the lethargic pace caused as much by their intent conversation as from a little alcohol.

'Podium girls?' Ben repeats.

'Yeah! I want to be flanked, Ben – flanked, kissed and zipped into that yellow jersey – just for a day. I'd die happy.'

'You can't die,' Ben reasons, 'or you won't be able to bask in glory, sign more autographs, dish out more kisses and increase your female fan base.'

'I want to have fun,' Luca says, 'you know? On the Tour. On my bike and off. It's the fuckin' Tour de France, man – it's my dream. I'm going to be living it. My goal is to finish in the top thirty in Paris. My dream is a Stage win. My ambition is recognition for my skill, to be recognized by the spectators, the media, my sponsors. Yeah, and the girls!'

They pedal thoughtfully, virtually tasting the imminence of the Tour, the hopes that might be realized or could be dashed.

'You know,' Luca says imploringly to Ben as they arrive outside the doctor's apartment, 'I don't mind the hills, I like the flat, I enjoy Time Trials.'

Ben pats him on the back and bids him a good night's sleep, stressing the word sleep with a slyly raised eyebrow.

'You'll have a great Tour,' Ben says, 'and it won't end there.'

Luca grins and spins away.

I want to have fun. I am twenty-four years old and I want the world to know who I am. Luca Jones and the Tour de France – awesome.

Ben closes his apartment door and regards his suitcase, packed and waiting.

'Let's have a good race, boys,' he says, wandering over to the window and rolling down the blind. He sits on the sofa and looks at his fingers. 'I would rather they ride well enough and safe enough that I end up twiddling my thumbs instead of using healing hands.'

I know what the team are doing with their hands right now, Ben muses as he slips naked between his sheets. *Hunter and Travis are running them all over their fiancées' bodies, with courtesy and their partners' sexual gratification leading the route. Luca, no doubt, now has a minimum of two pairs of tits to choose from and grope. I'll put money on him having cycled back to the bar. No amount of sport – indoor or outdoor – alters his testosterone levels.*

He switches off the light and wonders whether he's too tired to masturbate or tired enough not to have to.

Shit, when was the last time for me? And not by me? That girl in Paris with the gecko tattoo?

What was her name, Ben?

Annabel? Annie? It was three months ago. I can't remember. Well, I can add another month now – I would say that there's not going to be time for anything on the Tour de France unless it's cycling-related.

* * *

Cat's mind is meandering while she deliberates over the pros and cons of a rucksack versus a suitcase for three weeks in France.

It's not so much an 'if I meet Hunter or Travis' as 'when' – because I know that they're happy to talk to any journalist who expresses an interest in their ride. So, when I meet Travis and Hunter, what shall I ask them? Dare I tap into their feminine sides and ask about the importance of their girlfriends to their performance? Would that be acceptable? Maybe I could find the girlfriends and ask for their stories – that would be a great idea. I could branch out, perhaps pitch an article to a women's magazine.

Cat decides on the rucksack and proceeds to lay out the contents of her entire wardrobe on her bed, sectioning the clothing into don't-take, might-take and must-take.

Mistake? Is He thinking of me preparing? Is He impressed? Untouched? Is He ever coming back? Please let France enable me to let go, to move on. Please let the physical distance mean that I won't have to think of Him as much as I do now, when we still share the same city and my home houses His ghost.

Alongside shorts, cotton T-shirts and cotton short skirts, Cat chooses a couple of frocks but then wonders if she is being a little too hopeful. She knows there are dinners hosted by the teams, and parties on the Sunday evening of the Champs-Elysées finale. She should be ambitious.

What the hell, they don't take up much space and they won't crumple.

Yes, but you'll need a suitable pair of shoes – trainers and pumps are certainly practical, but somewhat spoil the line of a nice little slip dress. And remember, the Alps and Pyrenees are prone to suddenly clouding over and becoming very wet and cold. You'll need a fleece or two, and something highly waterproof. You'd better pack your Timberland boots.

I hope Luca has a good Tour – he's a great rider and so colourful. The Brits are as sceptical of him taking our nationality as they are about Greg Rusedski, but I think Luca could be a useful sidekick to Chris Boardman as a publicist for the sport in my country. Chris is the consummate champ

– he is to cycling what Gary Lineker was to soccer. So Luca, with his trendy haircut and his haphazard speech and flamboyant losses and crashes and triumphs, could play a different role entirely. He'd be as useful to the profile of cycling in Britain, especially awareness amongst women, as the Hollioake brothers are to cricket. I want my girlfriends to say to me, 'Cat, when's the Vuelta? Will Luca be racing? He's such a spunk – that photo Marie Claire *published of him alongside your article – well!'*

You and me, Luca my boy, we can do something good for cycling – and, of course, for ourselves.

Cat props the packed rucksack upright on her bed and shuffles herself within its straps. She meanders around her flat and kids herself that the pack on her back is really rather comfortable and not nearly as heavy as, well, as it is.

It's loaded – and yes, all symbolism absolutely intended.

My God, France tomorrow. I hate ferries. I can't believe I'm almost there, that I'm going, period, that I will indeed be there. Cat McCabe and the Tour de France. Please let it last for ever.

SETTING THE WHEELS IN MOTION

Wednesday. The English Channel. 10 a.m.

How strange. On the ferry's deck, Cat McCabe, who has fantasized about following the Tour for years, who has recently acknowledged that a change of country – if only for three weeks – would be a sensible and constructive option, has found that she is wishing she'd stayed put, that she could be back at home. She is very nervous, convinced she's bitten off more than she can chew and fears she might choke. Oughtn't she just to watch the Tour on Channel 4, in privacy at home as she always has? She could be on her settee, with a nice cup of tea, proclaiming aloud that the presenters, Phil Liggett and Paul Sherwen, should have their own TV series. Or run for Parliament. Or come over to her flat for coffee and a chat.

Maybe it would just be better if I had no interest in cycling at all.

Cat experiences lurches of homesickness when the white cliffs start to shrink. Wafts of the panicky emotion gust through her more strongly than the buffets of sea air which, she kids herself, are the sole cause for her smarting eyes. Having enjoyed umpteen imaginary conversations with real or fictitious characters in the months leading up to this day of departure, Cat suddenly realizes she has no idea where she'll find the confidence to approach such people in the flesh.

I haven't the balls. Quite literally. They'll take the piss, surely. Me – British and female – amongst all of them.

Furthermore, she's had her hair cut yesterday and, though merely a variation on her common theme of shoulder length plus fringe, she doesn't like it and feels self-conscious. The blasts from the sea breeze seem alternately to blow and suck her hair into configurations she cannot see but is convinced are queer and most certainly unattractive. She gazes at the white cliffs for as long as she knows she can really see them, trying very hard to ignore the fact that she now feels seasick as well as homesick, attempting to focus instead on France France Tour de Bloody France and all it is going to do for her sanity, her career and her future.

When does the English Channel become La Manche? Soon? Already?

Only a good few moments after Dover has unarguably disappeared can Cat finally turn her attention from inward and England, forward to France and, for the time being, her immediate surroundings. She turns her back on all she is leaving and faces the direction of travel, France, forwards, ever onwards. She glances around the deck, simultaneously keen for someone to recognize her yet desperate that no one will.

It's strange. I suppose I presumed the entire ferry would be peopled by those going to the Tour – that we'd all be recognizable as a club of sorts and, of course, that there would be this wonderful familial feeling amongst everyone. And yet now I'm here, I have no idea who is who. Most of the passengers look like standard holidaymakers. But what specifically distinguishes cycling followers? I don't even see any of the stalwart, anoraked, club cycling crowd that spend their Sundays traipsing the Trough of Bowland or struggling in Snowdonia. I mean, there's a small group over there in tracksuit bottoms who look young and sporty – but they're just as likely to have hired a villa in Brittany.

Though Cat half wants to be recognized – as a cycling aficionado of the non-anorak genus if not as the sports journalist she is hoping to become – the other half of her is quite content to be invisible. She ventures inside the ferry and queues for rubber sandwiches and plastic coffee, trying not to scan the tables too obviously for that elusive quiet spot, a hiding place. She spies one that might suffice and heads for it, looking at no one and trying to look nonchalant herself despite her bulky rucksack and wobbling tray.

'The Prologue will definitely be Boardman.'

The sentence causes Cat to slow up instinctively.

Brilliant! I think it'll be Boardman too!

'I'd say Jawlensky,' comments another voice.

No, I think your colleague and I have it with Boardman. And it's Yav-lensky.

'*Yav*,' says the first voice.

'Hey?'

'*Yavlensky*.'

See!

'I hardly think my pronunciation will make much difference to the outcome. Jawlensky is going to take the Prologue from Boardman, thus ending his reign.'

'Bollocks.'

Yeah – bollocks!

Cat aborts her journey for a place squeezed in at a table neighbouring that of the two men discussing the Prologue Time Trial, which forms the inauguration of the Tour de France. She eavesdropped as subtly as she could, listening without looking.

'Did you go to the Giro?' the man *au fait* with Russian pronunciation asks the other.

'Nah. Actually, I haven't covered a race since the Tour of Britain.'

But I was there! Cat starts to herself with pleasure superseded by dread. *Oh God, who are you though? I did the whole of the Tour of Britain for* Cycling Weekly – *up and down the UK for seven days. Did I meet you? Have you* already seen me today and decided not to say hullo? Or seen me, perhaps, but not recognized me at all because you didn't notice me on the Prutour?

She regards her sandwich as if staring at food might nourish her nerve.

Do I dare turn around? Nonchalantly or with intent? Brazenly or with contrived innocence?

She scrunches her hands into fists, digging her nails reprimandingly into her palms.

Come on Cat, get a grip.

She grips herself hard.

Right, I'll turn around, pretend I'm looking for a – for a clock – then I'll shift my gaze and say, 'Oh hi! Weren't you on the Tour of Britain?' Or maybe just regard him like I know I know him but can't figure out where from, and then snap my fingers and say, 'Tour of Britain?' Or maybe—

'Shall we go on deck?'

No! Wait! I haven't turned round yet.

'Yeah, sure – another beer?'

'Yeah – start as we mean to carry on.'

'You're telling me! Come on, let's split.'

Wait – I'm going to turn around right now and say, 'Hi, I'm Cat McCabe, I'm reporting for the Guardian *– I think I met you at the Tour of Britain.' See – now!*

But it is too late. The backs of two men are all Cat sees and she cannot deduce whether or not she has met one of them.

Tomorrow. I'll find them tomorrow and I'll introduce myself then. And if they ask when and how I arrived, I'll feign surprise that 'No way! I was on that ferry too!'

Oh God.

Me, myself and I for over three weeks in France.

Wednesday. Hôtel Splendide, Delaunay Le Beau. 2.30 p.m.
Rachel McEwen banged her clenched fist down on the concierge's counter. Her treacle-coloured hair was loose and rather wild and her eyes were ablaze with fury and indignation.

'*Mademoiselle?*' said the clerk, with a superciliously raised eyebrow that made Rachel clench and reclench her fist as if she was about to aim a blow.

'Look,' Rachel said in a cold, courteous voice that served to accentuate her outrage more descriptively than any physical attack, 'it is not *my* room I want changing, but room 46. I am *not* having one of my riders sleeping on a camp bed in a cramped room with crap curtains.'

'Wait,' said the clerk witheringly, dropping the one eyebrow and then twitching the other, along with a slight smirk, as he disappeared. He returned with his smirk and also a smartly dressed woman.

'Good afternoon,' said Rachel. 'I was trying to explain to your colleague that I find it unacceptable that there is only one decent bed in room 46. I have two riders sharing and I will not have either one sleeping on a camp bed.'

'Miss?' the manageress, as she transpired to be, enquired.

'Mc–Ewen,' said Rachel briskly, breaking her name as she only ever did when she was deadly serious and very annoyed. 'I am *soigneur* for Zucca MV.'

'Zucca!' the lady marvelled quietly, flushing slightly. 'Miss McEwen, I am terribly sorry. I will of course rectify this problem immediately.' She rustled through an index file, tapped officiously at a computer and gabbled at the clerk who scurried off, the smirk wiped from his face. She raised an eyebrow in a much more impressive way than her male junior. 'Room 46 – Massimo Lipari? Ah, and Gianni Fugallo – a good *domestique*.'

Rachel smiled.

Here's the link. Here's the bond. A passion shared is a problem solved.

'I shall put them in room 40 – I don't know how this could have happened and I apologize.'

'Thank you,' Rachel said, the relief in her voice softening her tone, her hair no longer seeming wild but, rather, merely unkempt through stress and a devotion to priorities in which concerns for coiffure were too petty to feature.

'Miss McEwen,' the manager cleared her voice, 'if it is possible, an autograph? From Massimo? For me – Claudia?'

'*Bien sûr*,' Rachel nodded.

Funny how I know just enough idioms in French, Spanish, Italian – even Portuguese and Flemish – to get by! If we ever raced in Latvia, no doubt I'd learn the lingo for 'no problem', or 'cheers', or 'put your hands away I'm not interested in sleeping with you'.

Rachel marched back to the lifts, back to room 46 and told a dejected-looking Gianni not to worry. Then she made two trips to room 40, transferring the riders' bags and belongings while they sat on the one good bed, resting their legs and feeling the minutes ebb away and the Tour loom ever nearer.

Wednesday. Hôtel Splendide, Delaunay Le Beau. 5.30 p.m.
'Yes?' said the manageress to, remarkably, another British girl.

'MissMcCabe,' Cat strung in a rushed whisper, looking around the foyer, her heart still racing from the excitement of spying the cars of three different teams in the hotel car park, emblazoned with logos and crowned with the bike racks.

Cofidis! Banesto! Zucca MV!

'Ah, Miss McCabe, your room is on the fifth floor. Number 50.'

When Cat arrived at the lifts she grinned, for there, as in all races, regardless of prestige, a list of the teams and their rooms was pinned unceremoniously.

Jesus – what a perfect, God-given sandwich I have become!

Temporarily flabbergasted, Cat scanned the list over and again, pinching herself that what she saw was correct.

It says so! Massimo Lipari and Gianni Fugallo directly below, Jose Maria Jimenez directly above. If Jimenez and Lipari want to vie for pin-up of the peloton, they can always meet half-way at room 50 and let me be the judge!

The fact that room 50 turned out to be rather small, with

the teak veneer fittings and meagre chewing-gum-grey towels typical of a sub-2-star hotel, was of no consequence to Cat.

I'm here in France surrounded by the boys!

Wednesday. Hôtel Splendide, Delaunay Le Beau. 11.29 p.m.
Stefano Sassetta is delighted. Thanks to Rachel, his *soigneur*, he does not have to share a room. He had a great training ride this morning and is confident he will attain peak form during this first week, be invincible in the sprints and start hoovering up bonuses for the points in the green jersey competition. His thighs feel good and, after Rachel's incomparable massage and Stefano's lengthy scrutiny in the bathroom mirror, they look sublime to him. Stefano has been zapping through the television channels. His French is poor so he continues to flick the remote control, stopping awhile at MTV, enjoying a few minutes of boxing on Eurosport before it becomes tractor racing or dominoes, or some commensurately poor excuse for a sport. On he zaps. He is tired. He should sleep. But he is too psyched. If his manager came in and suggested a night ride, he'd be on his bike in a flash. He feels powerful and proud. And now he is delighted, for, two channels on from Eurosport, a porn movie is in its throes. Now he'll be able to sleep. Masturbation is a great idea. Masturbation is better than sex – no energy wasted, as an ejaculation uses only sixty calories. No energy thrown away on pleasuring anyone but himself.

Thursday. Delaunay Le Beau. 10 a.m.
In the timescale of the Tour de France, Thursday is the dawn of two days of medicals for the riders, accreditation for the journalists and press conferences for both.

The previous evening, though Cat had tried valiantly to stay awake and recline demurely on her bed reading, neither Jose Maria Jimenez or Massimo Lipari had come to see her. She had woken in the early hours, dejected and still clothed.

As if they would have come to my bloody room.

Feeling a little foolish, she had crawled under the bed-covers, still clothed, for a few more hours of exhausted sleep.

Now, showered, changed twice, breakfasted and disappointed that there were no riders in sight, Cat left the hotel; the whirlwind of butterflies in her stomach at odds with the balmy climate outside. The trees, lampposts and road signs in the town of Delaunay Le Beau, which was hosting the Prologue and housing the Tour entourage, were bedecked with arrows pointing the colour-coded way for anyone who had anything to do with the Tour de France. For Cat, to follow the green *presse* arrows was like being led on a treasure hunt.

Somewhat circuitously (the prerogative of the town's *chambre de commerce*), the route took her past picturesque squares, the main shopping area, the university and the hospital – anyone who was anything to do with the Tour de France was to be subliminally persuaded that Delaunay Le Beau was a pretty town with excellent facilities. For Delaunay Le Beau, paying to play host, the Tour meant Tourism. Eventually, she arrived at the *Permanence*, an ironic title for the eternally temporary headquarters of the Société du Tour de France. In Delaunay Le Beau, it was housed in the grandiose town hall.

Cat McCabe had no idea what to expect – from Thursday, from the *Permanence*, from anything at all. For Ben York, however, an anxious female chewing her lip while her eyes darted as if on a pinball course was certainly not what he expected to see when he escorted his Megapac riders to the *Permanence* for their physical assessments. His groin gave an appreciative stir and his lips a flit of a smile at the sight of her. He felt almost privileged, as if spying the first swallow of summer before anyone else.

Here comes Cat, trying to saunter down the sweeping staircase of the town hall, hoping her grip on the banister seems nonchalant. She has been queuing for her accreditation in a vast room throbbing with strangers. Now she is wearing her green pass and she displays it with pride; it hangs from her neck and is as precious to her as pearls. It is the reason for her heightened state of excitement and the resulting lack of composure. It is her access to the real Tour de France; this year she has backstage privileges. Last year, and the years before, the cyclists were one step removed behind her TV screen.

I'm a journaliste. *See? It says so: Cat McCabe,* Journaliste, Le Guardian. *That's me. That's what I do and who I am.*

Ah, but Cat, how many journalists hover half-way down a staircase, fixated by the middle distance and gripping the banister with both hands?

I hate stairs. Please emphasize the 'eeste' – journaliste *sounds far more delicious, much more prestigious than the English pronunciation.*

All right, Cat McCabe, *journaliste*, walk on down the stairs and do your thing.

See her taking the stairs slowly, trying to absorb everything that is going on around her without looking quite the goggle-eyed devotee that she in fact feels?

I hate stares. Someone down there is looking at me. Keep walking. Oh Jesus! It's Luca Jones! I'm going to have to stop again. That's the medical check. Shit shit – what should I do? What am I allowed to do? What do journalists-istes do? Dictaphone? Yes, of course I have it with me. Ditto notepad. I have everything a journalist on the Tour de France could possibly need. But what I have most in abundance is nerves.

Establish eye contact with Luca, Cat. Why don't you give him a smile? You needn't say anything, but a smile today might mean recognition tomorrow, perhaps another smile the following day and huge familiarity thereafter.

I know. I know. I'm metaphorically kicking myself already for being so stupidly shy. But I have over three weeks. I won't go home till Luca and I are on first-name terms.

We'll hold you to that.

Don't. Oh! It's Hunter Dean! Dark, handsome and utterly Hollywood.

Hunter appears from his medical and beams at the loitering media consisting of six or seven tall men. Hunter really is the personification of his mission statement. Tipping his sunglasses up on to his head, courteously, he permits the clutch of journalists to surround him and systematically attends to all questions and answers them well, with considered replies and great charm.

Fuck fuck!

Cat is in a quandary. She has reached the bottom of the staircase and is so overcome by her proximity to her heroes that she feels much more like running from the building and hyperventilating somewhere in private, than in doing her job extracting soundbites.

What should I do?

They won't bite.

Shall I just breeze up to the group and stick my dictaphone under Hunter's mouth?

She ventures over and does just that. It's the kind of thing a journalist does, Cat deduces from the bouquet of hand-held recording equipment already thrust at Hunter's lips. She stares unflinchingly at the Megapac logo on the breast of Hunter's tracksuit top. Hunter speaks, his voice pulls Cat's gaze to his face while her dictaphone scrounges for soundbites with the best and rest of them.

Hunter's lips. God, he has a beautiful neck.

Six male journalists stare at Cat who is incapable of controlling a creeping blush.

Oh shit, I didn't just say that out loud, did I?

Cat nods earnestly at whatever it is that Hunter is saying. She praises gods of all creeds for the invention of the dictaphone because whatever he is saying, that the current thrill of it all prevents her from hearing, she can listen to later anyway. She focuses hard on the bridge of Hunter's nose, to discipline her desperate-to-flit gaze.

'Initially, Megapac may be an unknown quantity in terms of the Tour de France,' Hunter is expounding, 'but we'll be the team on the tip of y'all's tongues by the end – that I can assure you. You can quote me on that. We're the best thing to happen in American cycle sport since Greg LeMond and Lance Armstrong.'

'*Bonne chance!*' Cat surprises herself by responding unchecked, anticipating that Hunter might very well start to sing the Star Spangled Banner or quote the Constitution.

'Hey, yeah, right!' Hunter responds.

With a wink! Did you see that? A wink! I've died and gone to heaven. Does a wink come out on a dictaphone?

'Cute,' Luca nudges Ben, out of Cat's earshot. Ben gives Luca an exasperated look that prevents him having to agree and thereby present himself as a contender. Fortuitously, Luca is called through for his medical and Ben can regard the lone female with a certain private pleasure while Luca creates a diversion. He sees her redden as she focuses on Luca.

Bastard boy racer, he frowns to himself, *but why on earth wouldn't she blush? There'd be something wrong with her if she didn't. And, anyway, it's proof to me that she's a healthy, sexual person. And that's good.*

A couple of journalists call greetings to which Luca replies with the victory sign before disappearing into the open arms of the Tour's medical team.

I should have called out something, Cat reprimands herself. *Wouldn't my voice have stood out, made him stop and perhaps notice me?*

Cat looks a little forlornly at the space on the bench Luca has left. Her gaze shifts to the right and clocks a nice pair of Timberland boots, good legs clad in black jeans, a white shirt. Her eyes travel automatically upwards, over a strong neck, ditto chin, to a pair of just parted lips. She finally alights on very dark brown eyes which won't let her go. She notes a handsome face enhanced by a wry smile, crowned by dark hair cut flatteringly close to the head and quite strikingly flecked through with grey. Momentarily, Cat wonders who he might be. But she knows he's not a rider so her interest wanes.

Anyway, I have to go. I have to find the salle de presse. *I'm working. It's my job.*

Ben watches her leave, rather gratified by the fact that he'll see her again over the next three weeks.

Thursday. *Salle de presse.* **1 p.m.**
Starving hungry, Cat's appetite disappeared on entering the press room. Dread instead filled her stomach until fear was a hard lump in her throat and panic was a terrible taste to the tongue. She felt immediately that she had been transported back to Durham University, that she had just entered a vast exam hall and was ten minutes away from the start of her finals. The comparison was apposite but, as in an anxiety dream, disconcertingly twisted too. Noise. Too much of it. You can't sit the test of your life amidst such a din. There again, you wouldn't really sit your finals in northern France, in an ice rink requisitioned by the Société du Tour de France.

What had happened to the ice was initially of little relevance for Cat. Rather, she was transfixed by line upon line of connected trestle tables on which, at regular intervals, an army of laptops were positioned, gaping like hungry mouths eager to gobble down the information in any language as long as the topic was cycling. At the front and to either side, a brigade of industrial-sized televisions was mounted on tall stands, surrounding the journalists and perusing the scene like phantasmagorical invigilators.

If I'm not at Durham University, then I'm in a George Orwell novel or a Terry Gilliam film. Am I really at the Tour de France? It's all so vast – anonymous, even. What on earth am I meant to do now? Where should I sit? This is my workplace for the next three days, how am I ever going to be able to concentrate?

Cat felt much sicker and far less steady on her feet than she had for any exam, or even on the ferry. But she made it to a space on a run of trestle conveniently close and which, to her relief, had an expanse of at least three metres between where she set up and the next journalist.

I'm in Babel. Did no one say hullo in Babel? Isn't my pass enough – do I need a password too?

After a quick, furtive scout around, Cat plugged in her laptop, positioned her mobile phone near by and fanned out a selection of the booklets she had been given at accreditation.

See, now my workspace looks no different from any of those around me. I'm one of them, now. So, now someone should say hullo. I'm going to busy myself. I'd like to scrutinize this one: 'Les hôtels, les equipes' – see if any of my other hotels during the Tour might house teams too. Better not – that's something I can look forward to doing later tonight when I'm in my room pathetically deluded that Jimenez or Lipari might come and find me.

I'll start by flipping through this booklet – 'Les régions, la culture'. Fuck, it's all in French. I'll just skim the pages as if I'm speed reading – oh God, but if I do, they might presume I'm fluent and come up jabbering away at me. PR packs from the teams. That's better. I'll start with Zucca MV.

She was staring at photos of the team when her mobile phone rang, causing her to jump and fumble with the handset.

'Hullo?' she whispered, her hand guarding her brow, her eyes cast unflinchingly down towards the keys on her laptop.

'*Bonjour!*' boomed Django so loudly that Cat glanced around her expecting to find the entire press corps listening in, knowing it wasn't work, that she was but a pseudo *journaliste*. However, her presence, let alone that of Django's voice, was obviously still undetected. Now she was relieved.

'Hullo,' she said, 'Django.'

'How are you?' he asked, slurring his words in his excitement. 'Where are you? What's happening? Keeping a decorous distance from all that lycra, I do hope?'

Though she'd hate herself for it later, Django's enthusiasm irritated Cat.

I'm working. This isn't a holiday. Take me seriously.

Ah, but don't deny it is a pleasure for which you yourself cannot believe you are being paid.

I bet nobody else's uncles are phoning them.

Well then, you should pity them.

'I'm fine,' Cat said quietly, 'but busy – press conferences, deadlines – and then some.'

Haven't actually been to a press conference. My first deadline is tomorrow.

'And the people?' The pride in Django's voice caused Cat's eyes to smart. 'Are they nice? Have you made friends? And the riders, girl – have you met and married?'

'Oh,' Cat sighed, swiping the air most nonchalantly, unaware that it was a gesture wasted on Django, 'loads – great. Everything.'

'Well, I'll phone again,' Django said gently, sensing her unease. 'Just had to make sure that you're really there – now that I hear you, I can continue with my jam-making. I'm trying damson and ouzo. I thought an aniseed taste and an alcoholic kick might be an interesting addition to an otherwise relatively mundane preserve. There'll be a jar, or pot, probably plural, awaiting your return.'

Django's culinary idiosyncrasies suddenly touched Cat. She closed her eyes and listened. It was like a voice not heard for a long while and yet its immediate familiarity was so comforting it was painful.

'Thanks, Django,' Cat said, smiling sadly, 'but I have to go. Bye.' She switched off, stared hard at the phone and forced herself to switch off. Back she was, in the formidable ice rink.

Too many people were smoking too many cigarettes. A man with a handlebar moustache was smoking a cigar. A large one.

He looks like an extra from a spaghetti western. What do I look like? A journaliste? I don't think I'm noticeable at all. Do I want to be? And I haven't done any work, I haven't even switched my laptop on.

And there's the Système Vipère press conference in ten minutes.

Good, I can get out of here.

Thursday. Team Système Vipère press conference. 1.30 p.m.
Cat just sits and stares. Her physical proximity to Fabian Ducasse is causing her to hold her breath. It is as if she fears that if she doesn't, unless she keeps utterly still, he'll disappear and all of this will have been some tormenting apparition. And what a shame that would be, with Fabian currently smouldering at the press corps, his mouth in its permanent pout, his eyes dark, his focus hypnotic. He is taller, broader, than Cat had previously assumed from television appearances. His skin is tanned, his hair now very short and emphatically presenting his stunning bone structure. His cool reserve, the aloof tilt of his head draw all present to his every move, his every word, at the expense of his equally hallowed team-mates sitting alongside. The conference is conducted in French and fast and, to Cat, the very timbre impresses her far more than the specific words she can pick out and string, if not into a sentence, into the gist of one. The room is charged. Or is it? Is it Fabian Ducasse's doing? Or is it just Cat?

On the platform at one end of the conference room, Jules Le Grand has flanked himself with Fabian Ducasse, Jesper Lomers, Carlos Jesu Velasquez and the youngest member of the team, Oskar Munch, whose first Tour de France this is. Oskar appears as awestruck as Cat – if they caught sight of each other they could exchange empathetic gazes. This, though, is unlikely to happen in a room of at least two hundred people.

For Oskar, I'd like to write a piece about domestiques, the unsung heroes who work away selflessly for the greater glory of their leader, their team.

Carlos is about to speak.

Fuck, all in bloody Spanish! Mind you, he's a man of few words and his grunts are unilaterally understandable. He's

62

probably just been asked if he feels in any way compromised riding for a French team. That shrug-mutter I take to mean 'Amigo, I am doing my job – a fine company wishes to employ me, to pay for my skill – where's the conflict or compromise?' Ah Oskar, someone's asked you your ambition for the Tour.

'Paris!' Oskar announces as if to an idiot.

Shall I ask him about preparation? How well he knows the route? How much is a technical, theoretical study of alpine gradients and Pyrenean cross-winds, how much is physical familiarity with specific climbs? Oh, and mental attitude – will his spirit ensure entry into Paris even if twenty-one arduous days have broken his body?

Yes, Cat. Go for it.

Me? No. Maybe tomorrow.

This is Oskar's press conference today.

In twenty-one teams, there are approximately six domestiques in each. I'll have my pick.

You're contradicting yourself – you just said how much you respect *domestiques* as riders in their own right. I think you should go for Oskar.

This is my first press conference. Give me a break.

The *Guardian* newspaper is giving you your break, remember.

Thursday. *Salle de presse.* 2.30 p.m.
There's a lot of bad typing in the press corps and a quite startling array of awful footwear, thought Cat on returning to the press room and making it back to her seat without anyone acknowledging her presence, which, in truth but to her surprise, caused her a little consternation. All around her, mobile phones were bickering to outdo each other with terrible jingles in place of regular ringing tones.

Cat opened a new file in her laptop and plugged an earpiece into her dictaphone, swooning slightly and smiling broadly at Hunter's American tones. The blank screen was far too intimidating so, etching an expression of utter concentration over her face, Cat looked up and around her, as if deep in thought rather than analysing the particulars surrounding and distracting her.

I mean – look at him, very thin and pale, wearing too short shorts, no socks and shiny black brogues. And that one looks like something out of a Brothers Grimm fairy-tale in those suede pixie boots. And with toes like that, that man there should certainly refrain from putting them on public display.

Cat placed her fingers rather primly on the keys, then took them off again. What to write, what to write? What on earth was everyone else writing?

I don't want to start – not that I know where to. I'm surrounded by two-digit keyboard bashing and inefficient finger knitting – how can they manage entire articles using the index finger of their left hand and the third finger of their right? There again, I can touch-type – and fast – but I can't write a bloody word.

Cat was subsumed by an illogical fear that, as soon as she started typing, there'd be silence and all eyes would be on her, assessing how fast *she* types, *how* she types, what she *writes*, even what *shoes* she wears. She stared at her screen then glanced around her, momentarily bolstered by the fact that though everyone's screens were on view, it was impossible to discern what they'd written, never mind in what language. Her fingers hovered and then alighted softly on the keys. She cocked her head, as if Hunter had said something of supreme interest, and allowed her fingers to skitter randomly over the keyboard.

akdjoii sdiuej fdiknvoiq=- jdoaign kdjlau SODIJA L.upoadj lkduflakdkruoqemma d OKLAKEUR .kdug; ae#q,dkafp9cekjr9 diuarslkqjwlfre0 dpsofiqawe.wer fdfpiaduf lksadurmq pe9981ek cagl9igdam.s .. diew r l;sie. 932 ..xouawpoe w.e;

She looked away from the screen and was momentarily

staggered, soon relieved, as she realized her hot flush and racing heart were pointless. No one met her gaze, no one laughed at her work, everyone was utterly preoccupied with all things other than Cat McCabe, *journaliste*. Cat allowed herself a smile, looked at her screen and thought, *well – it could be Finnish*, deleted the lot and started to transcribe Hunter's soundbites. Her typing speed matched the pace of his voice perfectly.

Now I'm going to sketch out a piece for the Guardian *focusing on the non-European element of the Tour de France – mention Luca Jones and whether winning a Stage in the Giro D'Italia can translate to winning one at the Tour de France.*

'Hullo.'

I might do an 'introducing Megapac' – use my Hunter quotes, bring the riders of this wildcard team to the public's notice.

'Bonjour?'

In fact, it would be interesting to do a piece as an exposé of the cliques in the peloton according to nationality or language.

'Buenos dias?'

There's often inter-team friction, or factions, due to language – how does that change within the peloton at large?

'Buon giorno? Guten Morgen? Hola!'

Cat looked up with a jolt.

'Bonjour,' she mumbled, wondering if she'd been talking her ideas out loud. She glanced at the man and was able to assess immediately that he appeared, physically at least, non-intimidating and relatively normal. For a start, he was wearing khaki shorts of decent dimensions and had a pen rather than a cigarette between his fingers.

The man flicked over a page of his notebook, squinted and then spoke.

'Cat-riona McCabe?' he asked. '*Guardian*?'

And he's British.

'Yes,' Cat beamed, standing up and shaking his hand.

'I'm Josh Piper,' he said, extending his hand.

'Oh – *Josh*-ua!' Cat proclaimed, with a familiarity and joviality that made her cringe because they far exceeded the mere expression of recognition and relief she'd actually intended. 'You're English *and* you're Joshua.' She shook his hand anew.

'Er, yes,' he said, regarding her quizzically, 'but please – it's Josh and I'm relieved you're Catriona McCabe – I've been standing here for ten hours saying hello in every language I know and some I probably don't. You were miles away – where were you? Half-way up L'Alpe D'Huez already?'

Cat gave a guilty grin. 'Not quite, but I was preoccupied. I'm sorry.' To emphasize the point, she sat down again and stared concertedly at her screen.

Noticing that she still had her earpiece in place and that the dictaphone appeared still to be whirring and that her fingers were over the keys, Josh put his hands up in surrender.

'You're going to share the driving with us – right?' His hands were now on his hips, as if it aided him in assessing her potential behind the wheel.

'Yup, absolutely, thanks so much,' Cat rushed.

'This is your first Tour,' he told her.

Am I that transparent?

Cat shrugged and nodded, trying to wipe the daft grin from her face.

But this is *my first Tour – I'm here at the Tour de France – automatic smile drug.*

'It's my seventh,' Josh continued. 'I read your Tour of Britain report for *Cycling Weekly* – I thought it was quite good.'

'Thank you,' Cat smiled, closing her eyes temporarily, revelling in such praise from a seasoned and respected journalist.

'Good,' Josh said. 'How's Taverner doing at the *Guardian*?'

'My boss?' Cat smiled on. 'He's fine – stressed out, as ever, but fine. Still racing a fair bit, winning not a lot but forever exhibiting his war wounds!'

'I bet he was pissed off having to delegate this job out – it would have been his thirteenth tour.'

God, I have so far to go. So much to catch up on. Shoes to fill. A spectre to cast off. An impression to make.

'Well,' Josh continued, 'nice to meet you. I'll see you around.'

'Thanks,' said Cat, watching Josh blend with the press corps and suddenly kicking herself for not asking for his mobile number, or where they should meet on Sunday for Stage 1, or what she should do with her bags and what sort of car it was she was to help drive.

Why didn't he invite me to sit by him? Or suggest coffee or sandwiches? Or ask where I'm staying?

Because you're at work, not at a dinner party. Anyway, he was friendly and he did come to find you. Now write. Work.

I don't know where to start. I'm still starving. Anyway, it's the Saeco-Cannondale press conference in twenty minutes and I want to get a seat near the front so I can concentrate on Mario Cipollini.

Ten minutes later, as Cat was on her way out of the main ice rink to the press conference room, she came across Josh Piper headed in the same direction. It transpired they were staying at the same hotel.

'Cipo, Cipo,' Cat whispered as they took their seats and waited for the team. She turned to Josh and regarded him earnestly. 'Mario Cipollini,' she said, eyes asparkle. The sentence was complete, the profundity of its meaning and the depth of associated emotion were encapsulated in those two words.

'I fucking love Cipo,' said Josh, 'I love him.'

'So do I,' Cat breathed, 'I love Cipollini too.'

Josh shook her hand. 'Can I call you Cat? We should meet for dinner this evening,' said Josh, 'there's a few of us at the hotel.'

'That would be lovely,' said Cat earnestly, 'and of course you can. Can I have your mobile number?'

Josh tipped his head. 'Won't it be easier if I just call your room from my room?'

'Oh yes,' said Cat, biting her lip and hoping that a grin might, in some way, counteract her inanity. Josh looked ahead and nudged her. She grinned at him again.

I have a friend!

She nudged him back. He turned to her, swiftly regarding her with a flicker of a frown, tipping his head towards the platform at the front, giving her a sharp nudge. Cat followed his gaze.

'Cipo!' Cat proclaimed involuntarily, her voice hoarse and regrettably loud. The two rows in front of her turned and stared. Mario Cipollini, however, nodded at her. Josh nudged her. She could feel him smile. Cat swelled.

Friday. *Salle de presse*. 10 a.m.

The press room wasn't quite so unnerving, did not seem nearly as cavernous or quite so cacophonous the next morning, nor did the press corps seem as intimidating. Not least because there were now two faces known to her. Nevertheless, Cat set up her work space, settled herself down, opening a file and typing a few lines, before she scanned the mêlée and finally recognized the backs of Josh and also Alex Fletcher a few rows in front of her. She grinned at their shoulder blades, felt settled and keen to work.

I do hope Jimenez and Lipari weren't twiddling their thumbs and at a loose end last night – because I was otherwise occupied. Josh did indeed call my room and we went out for a meal, with Alex Fletcher who is also travelling with us. Alex is very tall but his stature seems disproportionate to his demeanour – he's like an excitable schoolboy – deplorable expletives every other word and a quite staggering lack of respect for his expense account. I had heard he can be brusque, that he requires an ego massage. But I like him, he's amusing – it might even be fun with the three of us in the car.

'Morning, Cat,' said Alex, right on cue and towering above her, 'fucking shit night's sleep last night.'

Cat wasn't quite sure how to respond, because she had slept very well, so she gave what she hoped was a sympathetic tip of her head. Alex loped off. Cat rèturned her attention to her still ominously blank screen.

I have to write my piece – Taverner wants 800 words on the Tour de France in general for Saturday's issue as a prelude to the daily reports on each Stage.

'Coming for coffee?' said Josh. 'Then the Zucca MV press conference?'

'Sure,' said Cat, quickly exiting her empty file as if it was full of secret scoops; grabbing her notepad and dictaphone, checking her back pocket for francs. 'Bugger,' she said, looking aghast, 'I've come with no money.'

'Money?' Josh laughed. 'You won't need it – did you not eat during the day yesterday?' Cat shook her head. 'Well, Cat, Christmas comes early for the *salle de presse* – follow me.'

Josh took her out of the main ice rink and through to a much smaller hall where three sides of the room were lined with tables heaving under what appeared to Cat to be a veritable banquet.

'No one loses weight on the Tour de France,' said Josh, assessing Cat openly and deciding, in her case, that was a good thing.

'Apart from the riders,' said Cat.

'Huh?' said Josh, looking at his watch and then taking some baguette and brie.

'The riders,' Cat repeated, sitting down beside Josh and Alex, '*they* lose weight – they can lose around 4 pounds of muscle alone when the body starts to use it for energy.'

The baguette Josh was about to eat stopped midway to his mouth. Alex had a mouthful of coffee but put the gulp on hold.

'How many calories a day do the riders consume?' Josh asked, as if merely interested though Cat could tell she was being tested.

'Between six and eight thousand,' she shrugged, '60 per cent from complex carbs, 20 per cent from protein and 20 per cent from fat.'

'Liquid?' Alex demanded, having swallowed his.

'Well, on a long Stage, and if it's hot,' Cat recited, 'they need about 12 pints – but you see, the body can only absorb around 800 millilitres an hour, so fluid is always going to be a major concern. That's why the drinks must be cold and hypertonic – they need to be absorbed quickly and to work efficiently.'

'Also—' Alex started but Cat hadn't finished.

'All riders fear thirst,' she said gravely, taking a contemplative sip of Orangina, 'because if you're thirsty, it's basically too late.'

'Who rode the most Tours?' Josh enquired, as if he had temporarily forgotten.

'Joop Zoetemelk,' Cat reminded him kindly, 'sixteen in all.' She regarded Alex, who was obviously musing over some taxing question. She saved him the trouble. 'Maurice Garin,' she said, 'won the first Tour in 1903. Of course, the free wheel wasn't invented until practically thirty years later,' she added as an aside.

'How many hairpin bends on L'Alpe D'Huez?' Alex asked.

'Twenty-one,' replied Cat.

'Fastest time trial?' Josh pumped, raising an eyebrow at Alex over Cat's split-second silence.

'I reckon that would be Greg LeMond in 1989 – I think he averaged a fraction under 55 kph.'

'Name the infamous Uzbekistan rider who won the green jersey and was—'

Cat interrupted Josh: 'and was thrown off the 1997 Tour for testing positive?'

'Him,' Josh confirmed.

'In fact,' Alex mused, '*spell* him!'

Cat laughed. 'I've named my two goldfish after him. Phonetically speaking, "jam-ollideen abdoo-jap-arov" have to be the most delicious words to roll off the tongue. Ever.'

'Want a coffee?' Alex asked, a certain reluctant admiration on his face. She nodded. He went off and brought back just the one, just for Cat. Josh took another chunk of baguette, laid two slithers of brie within it and proffered it to Cat. She accepted graciously.

Respect!

Friday. Zucca MV press conference. 12 p.m.

'Come on, guys, or you'll be late. Massimo – where's Stefano? And where's Vasily?' Rachel McEwen was irritated; swinging the keys to the Fiat loaned to Zucca by the Tour de France, around and around her index finger. She had so much to do. Retrieving errant riders was not on her list.

Vasily Jawlensky, last year's winner of the Tour de France, walked in a leisurely way across the car park. Rachel could never be cross with Vasily as he never intended to upset anyone.

'Vasily,' she said in a theatrical whimper, 'where have you been?'

'Viz my bike,' Vasily replied as if Rachel really should have known the answer. Rachel smiled, nodded and laid a hand on his shoulder. She should have known. The majority of riders finish a race or a Stage, dismount and have no idea, or interest, in what happens to their bicycles. Most riders have little technical knowledge of their machines. But not Vasily. His first love, no doubt his dying love, is the bicycle.

Frequently, after his massage, he will venture to the car park of the hotel, to the team truck, and see to the wash-down and check-over of his bicycle himself. It helps him relax. He loves the company of the team mechanics. He is relaxed among them. When he looks back at the newspaper cuttings, the photos and film of his brilliant career, he does not look at himself, at the grimace of pain or the expression of elation he might be wearing, he does not look at the colour of the jersey on his back, or which rider is in front of him or, more likely, behind him. Unlike his team-mate Stefano

Sassetta, Vasily would never consider analysing the dimensions of his thighs, the condition of his physique, the aesthetic merits of his categorically handsome face. Vasily Jawlensky's attention in such instances is purely for the bike that is carrying him. He is the jockey, they are his transport to success.

To women, Cat most certainly amongst them, Vasily Jawlensky is a most gallant, enigmatic knight in shimmering lycra. For Vasily Jawlensky, his cycles are his magnificent steeds, his high-modulus carbon fibre and titanium chargers. He salutes them.

'Just Stefano now,' said Rachel, looking at her watch and then at Massimo and Vasily, who looked a little sheepish for having upset his *soigneur* whom he respected and liked. She unlocked the car and ushered the two riders in to the back.

'You two,' she said sternly, as if to a pair of dogs, 'stay!' They watched her sprint back into the hotel and, a few minutes later, pelt out again. She ran around to the side of the hotel where the team trucks were parked, disappearing from view just as Stefano appeared from the front of the hotel. He sauntered over to the team car and slipped into the front seat.

'*Ciao*,' he nodded to his team-mates.

'*Buon giorno*,' Massimo said.

'How are you?' said Vasily with great thought. The two riders communicated warmly but sparely in pigeon English.

Rachel reappeared, her hair loose and all over the place. She saw the laden car and walked briskly to it, settling herself in to the driver's seat, studiously ignoring Stefano.

'*Ciao*, Rachel,' Stefano beamed, 'where the fuck you been, hey?' Rachel knew this scenario well. Accordingly, she switched on the ignition calmly and drove away. However, the frequent screech of brakes, the taking of liberties as she took corners, coupled with her loaded silence and wild hair told Stefano all he needed to know. He sat quietly and listened to Vasily and Massimo read all the signs they passed.

'Bou-lang-er-ie.'

'Mon-o-prix.'

'Lin-ger-ie.'

Stefano tittered.

Rachel escorted her precious load to the conference room, swinging the car keys around her fingers. She smiled at Vasily. She smiled at Massimo. She even smiled at Stefano. When he took her hand to kiss, she stared at him very coldly, kept her hand to herself and marched away.

'Where *were* you?' Vasily asked Stefano as they took the stage in the conference room.

'In the bar,' Stefano shrugged, 'coffee. With a nice girl.'

'What are Vasily Jawlensky and Stefano Sassetta saying? Can you lipread?' Cat urges Josh, who sits beside her. He shakes his head forlornly. 'Can Alex?' Cat implores, looking past Josh to the other journalist.

'Only if the language is foul enough,' Josh whispers, 'or the topic suitably scandalous.'

Alex leans across them and giggles. 'What a cunt!' he exclaims; the fact that, being so tall has indeed brought his face about in line with Cat's nether regions is momentarily alarming for the young *journaliste* who has known him for less than twenty-four hours. But Alex talks quickly and Cat, to her relief, discovers his foul fulmination is in fact peculiar praise for Stefano Sassetta. 'He just said to Vasily that he was in a bar all night surrounded by women.' Chinese whispers on this year's Tour de France have begun.

Alex can speak Russian, Italian and French; his German is good, he can get by in Spanish and understands Portuguese. Zucca MV have no French riders and though they are predominantly an Italian team, the presence of their leader Vasily Jawlensky, last year's yellow jersey, ensures that English is their chosen language when in any country other than Italy. Alex, however, giving Josh a nudge which, from its severity, is passed through his body and on to Cat, decides that familiarity will win him friends. And friends in the peloton will be an enviable commodity. So, in Russian, he asks Vasily probing questions about whether his new Pinarello bike for the Prologue Time Trial will reward him with the yellow jersey; then, in Italian, he asks Stefano Sassetta directly about his rivalry with Jesper Lomers.

Cat has been building up her nerve to ask Massimo's opinions on the climbs of this year's Tour but Alex's bravado, his confident language-hopping, intimidates her and the confidence and acceptance she sensed from her facts-and-figures discourse over coffee evaporates. She is not consoled by the fact that Josh has just called Alex a show-off wanker, which, perversely, he has taken as a compliment. She wants to return to the *salle de presse* and make an inroad into her first article. Deadline is five hours away. She ought to start.

Stay put, Cat, the rest of the room is. Megapac are about to come in for their press conference.

Friday. Megapac press conference. 12.45 p.m.

Alex leans across Josh to Cat and racks his body into a brief silent laugh. Cat wonders which term for the female genitalia can possibly come out of his mouth next, most having done so already this morning. Alex surprises her.

'Hey, Cat,' he whispers, while the Megapac boys, a vision in burgundy and forest-green lycra, take their seats and tap their microphones and Josh regards Alex's body sprawled again over his knees with exasperation, 'what would you bid for Luca Jones?' Alex winks suggestively. Cat regards him full on, glances at Luca and then back to Alex.

'Why,' she says with a very straight face, 'everything I own and my soul to boot.' This delights Alex. Cat and Josh share a flicker of a raised eyebrow and all three look at Luca, sandwiched between Hunter and Travis as if it is team strategy that some of their upright morals might just rub off on the young Lothario. Neither Josh nor Alex seem particularly interested in Megapac's presence in the Tour de France but for Cat, there is a certain resonance for they, like her, are new to the show. On show. On trial. In France with dreams in their hearts and hope in their legs. Accordingly, fresh-faced earnestness replaces the showmanship exhibited by players in more established teams. Cat salutes Megapac.

The sight and sound of Hunter Dean, twice in twenty-four hours, lulls her into a false sense of familiarity and friendship.

He gave me a wink, remember.

Of course. Keep grinning and gazing at him as you are, you may even be awarded another.

Alex and Josh are comparing mobile phones like errant schoolboys might electronic pocket games during morning assembly. Somebody has asked the *directeur sportif* about sponsorship and the *directeur* is coming to the close of an informative but monotone soliloquy. For Cat, her surroundings have suddenly become dark, the sounds around her muffled. She feels detached and yet focused. She clears her throat, swallows once, carefully sets her pad and dictaphone to one side and then stands up.

'Hunter?'

God, that was my voice. What the fuck was my question?

Cat's voice seems to her too loud, too detached even to be her own. Its very femaleness has created a hush around her. Alex's and Josh's jaws have dropped.

'Hi there,' says Hunter, tipping his head and granting Cat his undivided attention. The other members of Megapac, racers and managers alike, are regarding her too. She daren't look. She stares fixedly at Hunter.

Oh Jesus, Hunter Dean has just said hullo to me.

So, say hullo back.

'Hullo. Um,' Cat coughs a little, 'what's the strategy and is it personal or team?'

Hunter licks his lips and Cat, to her horror, realizes she has inadvertently licked hers in reply. 'Huh?' he responds.

'Are you – singular – after a Stage win for yourself,' Cat enunciates, involuntarily loudly, terrified she might fart or lose her voice with nerves, 'or are you – plural – pursuing a complete team finish in Paris? Which is the greater glory?'

That sounded good! Very professional. Very salle de presse. *Cat McCabe* – journaliste.

'Man,' Hunter responds in his North Carolina drawl, 'who says we can't have both? The team's strong – hey, y'all? I'm real strong. Mental confidence and physical strength feed each other, you know?'

Cat nods earnestly, hoping Josh has all this in shorthand or on tape. Luca leans forward to the mike, nods at Cat and then bestows upon her a dazzling smile that she is too stunned to reply likewise to.

'You know,' Luca says, keeping eye contact direct, 'I would say each and every Megapac guy has a Stage win in his legs plus – *plus* – the desire for us to arrive together in Paris in his heart. We're a team – you know?'

Now Hunter is nodding alongside Luca and Cat wonders if the three of them shouldn't just quit the room and go and have a coffee somewhere. Which is pretty much what Luca is thinking, observing the pretty girl all serious and attentive – although he would of course drop Hunter from the equation.

'The Tour de France,' says Hunter, 'is about team effort, team spirit, personal triumph plus – *plus* – pain. We'll all be suffering, but hey, you're not given a dream without the power to realize it!'

'We are nine great riders racing under the Megapac flag,' Luca proclaims in his gorgeous accent which today he sees fit to infuse with a twang of American. 'You watch us go.'

'I will!' Cat enthuses. 'Thank you.'

'You're welcome,' says Hunter, who's never been thanked in a press conference before.

'It's a pleasure,' Luca smiles, thinking that a one-on-one interview with this girl would be a dictionary definition of pleasure.

'You're well in there,' Alex growls under his breath, most impressed as Cat takes her seat, stares at her lap and wonders just how red her cheeks are. A healthy blush? Or downright crimson?

'Good call,' Josh says, reading through his notes and congratulating Cat genuinely, the facial colouring of his now-esteemed colleague being of little consequence to him.

I'm a bona fide journaliste, Cat thinks, trying not to let an ecstatic smile expose her as an adoring fan foremost.

'I got propositioned by a total babe,' Luca told Ben an hour later.

'Oh Jesus!' Ben exclaimed, dipping litmus paper into urine samples. 'Are the groupies out in force already?'

'Actually,' Luca explained, 'this one is a very welcome addition to the press *corps* – cor blimey!' he added, tittering at his pun.

'And she propositioned you?' Ben laughed. 'In the middle of a fucking press conference? Now, what did she say, I wonder? "Luca, Luca, after Stage 3, can we shag if you're not too tired?" Something along those lines?'

Luca looked quite hurt. 'Fuck you,' seemed the most appropriate response, 'she questioned me, man.'

'And what did she ask?' Ben asked with a wry smile giving a lively sparkle to his eyes. 'Did she enquire as to the dimensions of your cog? How long you can keep going for?'

Luca did indeed hear the word as 'cock' and gave Ben a larky look which, predictably, said 'fuck you'.

'Well,' he rued, 'she actually asked about Personal Glory and Survival to Paris and shit – but she was a babe, let me tell you.'

'I do believe you already have,' said Ben. 'Please ensure that for you, Personal Glory on the Tour de France is about racing your brilliant best. Keep your head down and direct all your energy – physical and mental – to *la Grande Boucle*.'

'The big, beautiful, killer loop,' Luca sighed, the route of this year's Tour clearly mapped out in his mind's eye. 'Sure, Pop. Work first, then play – hey? That's what I'm paid for.'

Ben cuffed Luca's head and sent him on his way.

Friday. Team presentation. Hôtel de Ville, Delaunay Le Beau. 7 p.m.

Cat finished her piece. She polished the words and tweaked the punctuation until her brain felt frazzled. But the true headache befell her when she tried to e-mail it to the *Guardian*. In the phone room, the expletives in various languages from fellow journalists suffering similar telecom trauma were mildly comforting. She swore with the best of them for half an hour before technology kicked in and swiped her work away from her in a matter of seconds.

'It's the team presentation,' she said to Josh and Alex, who were still in the throes of adjective selection.

'It's just the entire peloton in their gear but minus their bikes, poncing across the stage,' Alex dismissed. Cat could think of nothing she'd like to see more.

'It's more for the VIPs and local dignitaries,' Josh added, 'like in horse-racing when the nags are paraded around before the off.'

'Well,' Cat said breezily, 'this is my first Tour and I feel I ought to experience everything that's going. So, *à demain, mes enfants.*' She left the *salle de presse* and made her way to the town hall. It was humid, the still air hanging thick with the sense of anticipation felt by all connected with the race.

As thrilled as Cat was that she had made friends already, now, at the town hall, sneaking a seat near the front, she was most pleased that she was by herself. She wanted to soak up, savour and smile her way through the team presentation without being laughed at by Alex or, worse, perhaps to be judged and discredited by Josh.

I want to see my boys, standing before me, complete as teams, their bodies unharmed as yet by the traumas of the Tour. I want to keep the image – it's important. Tomorrow changes everything.

Cat had come into close quarters with lycra-clad bike racers many times but it was bizarre, unsettling almost, to see the élite peloton so very out of context, paraded before her, for her, strutting their stuff without a bike in sight.

I almost don't know where to look – because wherever I try to look, my eyes seem drawn back to the bulges. They'd give male ballet dancers a run for their money.

It was like a fashion show. Deutsche Telekom team, looking pretty impressive in pink, left the stage and Cofidis filed on, the riders' chests and backs emblazoned with a vibrant golden sun symbol. Système Vipère looked stunning in their predominantly black lycra, a viper picked out in emerald and scarlet curling itself round each rider's body and left thigh. Despite it being almost eight o'clock, Fabian Ducasse was wearing his Rudy Project sunglasses but Cat was perfectly happy that he should for he looked utterly stunning.

'What do you miss?' Cat understood the compère to be asking Fabian. Fabian replied with an expressive Gallic shrug-cum-pout and said wine and women. 'What does Paris mean to you?' the compère furthered. Fabian looked at him as if he was dense. 'Wine and women, of course.'

And the yellow jersey, perhaps, thought Cat, *not that Vasily will let it go easily, Oh, why can't you both have it?*

Zucca MV, in their blue and yellow strip, striped into rather dazzling and possibly tactical optically psychedelic swirls, sauntered on to the stage next and stood, legs apart, hands behind their backs. Though there was no music, Massimo Lipari was tapping his toe, nodding his head and grabbing his bottom lip with his teeth as if he were in a night-club and on the verge of dancing his heart out. Cat smiled. Stefano Sassetta smirked arrogantly, his torso erect, his thighs slightly further apart than those of his team-mates and, Cat noticed, tensed to show off their impressive musculature. Her eyes were on an involuntary bagatelle course; if they moved upwards from Stefano's thighs, they hit his crotch from where they rebounded back to his thighs before being sent north again.

There's padding and there's padding – and I estimate that only a fraction of what Stefano has down there is padding. Blimey!

Zucca's six *domestiques*, staring earnestly into the middle distance, same height, same build, same haircut, now the same peroxide blond, looked utterly interchangeable and Cat cussed herself for confusing Gianni with Pietro or Paolo and Marco and Mario or Franscesco.

They're the cogs that keep Zucca's wheels turning. If these boys weren't domestiques, they'd most probably be working in their fathers' restaurants. Not as head chefs or maître d's, but as waiters, scurrying back and forth, keeping everybody happy. And they would indeed be happy – working for others is what they do. And they do it brilliantly and with pleasure. Their sense of family is strong. A family is a team. A team is a family. Put any obstacle in front of a line of soldier ants and they will not look for a way around it, they will climb up and over it and so it is with the Zucca MV domestiques. Their selflessness is legendary within the peloton. I'd like to write a piece about them.

Cat was making a mental note to phone the publishers of *Maillot* on Monday morning to propose such an article, when Megapac replaced Zucca MV on stage, the nine riders fresh-faced grinning virgins in comparison to the suave comportment of the Italian team who had a long-standing relationship with the Tour de France. She had to physically stop herself from leaping to her feet and waving at Hunter and Luca whom she now thought of as personal friends.

We meet again. You all look so lovely. Please take care. Have a good race. See you tomorrow. Adieu.

Catriona McCabe. *Journaliste.*

Cat McCabe is exhausted. She is back at the hotel, in her room, praying that neither Alex nor Josh will call for her. In fact, tonight she wouldn't even open the door to Stefano Sassetta or Jose Maria Jimenez, no matter how insistently they knocked. The team presentation has been a reality check; she is truly here, on the eve of the Tour de France. She really is a journalist and a *journaliste*. She's written her piece which Taverner rather liked, allowing her to keep the extra forty-four words which exceeded his word limit, and it will be published tomorrow morning.

Will He read it, I wonder?

He? Taverner? He has already – he liked it.

No – Him.

Why are you thinking about *him*, Cat? Aren't your three weeks in France meant to be putting that all-important distance, in time and space, between you and all that?

I'm just wondering. I still miss Him, all right?

Who, Cat, or what? Do you miss the status of what *he* was – a long-term boyfriend – or do you miss the person *he* is? If it's the former, that's understandable; if it's the latter, it's unacceptable.

I know. It's just the world seems a very spacious place without Him.

And your world was an unhappy one *with* him. Let him go. Let go. Here you are – just look where you are. You're going to be fine.

Am I?

See her sitting up in bed. She is wearing a Tour de France T-shirt and a Team Saeco-Cannondale baseball cap. All the journalists are bribed with branded clothing and yet none are wearing them in public. Cat is disappointed. How can so many seem blasé when she herself is brimming with excitement? Cat has noted how it appears to be cool to wear branded items from previous Tours, but no one wears the current gifts as if somehow that would be too obsequious. Next year, though, no doubt they'll be an enviable commodity and worn with pride and panache.

Cat, anyway, is wearing hers in bed, scanning *L'Equipe* and pleased that she can understand most of what she reads. She hauls her laptop from chair to bed and reads through her article. She pulls the neck of the T-shirt up and over her nose, inhaling deeply and knowing that, whenever she smells this T-shirt again, it will say to her 'Tour de France, eve of the Prologue, Hôtel Splendide, Delaunay Le Beau.

Room 50. Jimenez above, Lipari below. Alex Fletcher and Josh Piper in the bar. I was there.' Cat pulls her cap down over her brow and reads.

COPY FOR P. TAVERNER @ GUARDIAN SPORTS DESK FROM CATRIONA McCABE IN DELAUNAY LE BEAU

The Tour de France is the most prestigious bike race in the world. It is also the most extravagantly staged event, not just in cycling but in sport in general.

La Grande Boucle does indeed trace a vast if misshapen 3,800 km loop across France. An entourage of 3,500 people, the Garde Républicaine motorcycle squad, 13,000 gendarmes, 1,500 vehicles and a fleet of helicopters escort the peloton whilst 15 million roadside spectators salute its progress as it snakes its way through France with speed, skill and tenacity in a gloriously garish rainbow splash of lycra.

The Tour de France is the race that every young European boy fantasizes about riding just as soon as the stabilizers are removed from his first bicycle. It is the race that is the inspiration for an amateur to turn professional, that every professional road-race cyclist desires to ride. It is the pursuit of a holy grail: to wear the yellow jersey, to win a Stage, to ride in a breakaway, or just to finish last in Paris albeit having lost three and a half hours to the yellow jersey over the three weeks.

Hell on two wheels, the Tour de France breaks bodies and spirits as much as it does records. It is also a beautiful and frequently moving event to watch, to witness. It is an adventure, a pilgrimage, a piece of history, of theatre, a soap opera unfolding against a stunning backdrop of France. For riders and spectators and organizers alike, it is a journey.

The Tour de France is a national institution raced by a multinational peloton, accompanied by an international entourage and broadcast to the world. It defines the calendar in France in much the same way as Bastille Day or Christmas. Similarly in Spain. And Italy. Belgium. Switzerland. Just not in Britain.

Ask any child anywhere European and hilly for their great idols and they will always name a cyclist. Ask any European sports star to name a hero, they will always hail a cyclist. Ask anyone, in fact, about their country's key national figures, and they will invariably list a cyclist among them.

Why? Cyclists are heroes because of the bicycle itself; the ultimate working-class vehicle. Many cyclists come from modest beginnings and then achieve something great with their lives. Anyone can ride a bike. Anyone who rides a bike knows the effort it takes and will at some time experience pain – if it's hot, cold, wet, hilly. The knowledge of that pain and that it is but a whisper of the pain and suffering which will be confronted and vanquished by a Tour de France rider, is why the peloton is considered to be made up of superhumans. They cross the Pyrenees and then head straight on to the Alps. Triumph over adversity. Man against mountain. May the play begin. Let the battle commence. May the best man win. Vive le Tour.

<ENDS>

PROLOGUE TIME TRIAL
Delaunay Le Beau, Saturday 3 July

*Z*ucca MV's Vasily Jawlensky, last year's yellow jersey and riding now with Number 1 on his back, had been awake, steeling himself for the day ahead, for hours before Cat arrived at the *salle de presse* as soon as it opened. He had reviewed the Prologue Time Trial course again and again before retiring last night; had ridden it in his sleep and awoke with his legs twitching. Lying awake, yearning for dawn, he pelted the course in his mind's eye, waiting for it to be light enough, for the roads to be closed to traffic, so that he could be on his bike analysing the route and his form for real. Resting his long limbs on top of the bedcovers, his hands clasped behind his head, he contemplated the day ahead. He knew well how all eyes would be on him and yet his sole focus would be on the tarmac unfurling ahead of his front wheel. Vasily is one of the sport's great heroes. However, unlike Massimo or Stefano, the fair, blue-eyed Russian projects no secondary image as pop star or superhunk. Nobody really knows Vasily. His fame comes solely from the genius of his riding. Everybody wants to know him because he is such an enigma. A courteous yet non-committal character. Statuesque. As silent as a sculpture. As beautiful as one too. It's a challenge that journalists and groupies, even his team-mates, relish; to get blood from a stone. That scar slicing his cheek – how did he come by it? No one has been able to find out. Did the sculptor's chisel slip? Is it the only scar he carries? Are there any inside? His heart is huge, twice the size of a normal man of his build. It can pump at almost 200 bpm. It rests at an awesomely relaxed pace. Is that all it does? Is that all he commands it to do? Does it carry anything other than oxygenated blood? Memories? Hurt? Passion? Who knows? Who can find out?

As Cat begins planning her article, Vasily's Zucca MV *equipeur* Stefano Sassetta is yawning leisurely, deciding to rise in a short while and ride the course once or twice. He shaved last night and is somewhat appalled that razor rash on his right leg sullies the sculptural beauty of his famous thighs. Massimo Lipari is singing in the shower. Their *soigneur* Rachel has already mixed the energy drinks, thrown out a box of energy bars a day off their sell-by date and prepared the *panini* – scooping out the centres of sweet rolls and packing in honey and jam.

The Megapac guys are breakfasting as a team, squashed around a long table, interrupting mouthfuls of pasta with the occasional 'yo!' and high five. Luca is positively hyper, Hunter is focused, Travis contemplative.

At the Système Vipère hotel, Jules Le Grand is having to recharge his mobile phone already. Jesper Lomers has phoned home but found no answer. Anya must be on her way to Delaunay Le Beau. He hopes. Fabian Ducasse is staring at himself in the bathroom mirror, giving himself a pep talk concluding with a quiet, prolonged chant proclaiming himself invincible. His brow is dark, his excessively fit heart is thumping its extraordinary resting pace of 30 bpm. To Fabian, it is like a portentous, growing drum roll. In the depth of his soul and absolutely out of earshot of the *salle de presse*, he ranks Chris Boardman's chances more than his own but he knows that public consensus fancies his adversary Vasily Jawlensky over Boardman. What can he do about it? He does not want the man who wore yellow in Paris last year to begin the race in yellow again tomorrow, but what can he do about it?

Fabian joins the rest of Système Vipère, along with many other teams, to ride the Prologue course, to learn the corners, the cobbles, the drag in the middle off by heart. He is focused and tense and his team know to give him a wide berth. He has sworn at the *domestiques* and he has snapped at his *soigneur*. He has said not a word to Jules Le Grand, even ignoring his *directeur*'s morning salutation.

Tour personnel are checking the barriers, hanging banners and liaising via walkie-talkies. They hardly notice the riders warming up. Spectators have already started to mill about, gazing almost in disbelief as riders zip by. The circus has come to town. This year's Tour de France will soon be under way.

Jules Le Grand's mobile phone lives again. He is wearing new shoes today, exquisite Hermes loafers. He has opened a new bottle of aftershave even though he has a bottle three-quarters full.

'Everything starts again. Today is the first day of this year's Tour de France and our lives begin anew. There is no continuation with last year's race. No link. We start afresh. Jawlensky taking yellow last year is now history, I see it as a gauntlet he threw to us last year. We accept. We take it. Jawlensky can only defend what he took last year. It is us who attack. We are the aggressors. We are ready to duel. He should be afraid. *En garde.*'

Jules regrets the fact that it is only to himself, to his reflection in the team car's rear-view mirror, that he has just spoken.

'*L'Equipe* would have loved that. Never mind, I can regurgitate it at will for the *salle de presse* and I shall be sure to do so later on.'

The Prologue Time Trial, the inauguration, the thrilling fly-past, of this year's Tour de France will take each of the 189 riders in turn 7.3 km around the pretty town of Delaunay Le Beau, hosting the race for the first time (check with Alex or Josh how much tourist blurb is the norm). Today's distance, from the total of over 3,500 km, might seem insignificant but with no great time gaps achievable, a rider's placing today can have a psychological bearing on himself and his competitors. Prologues are won and lost in fractions of seconds so the riders must race on the rivet. They are set to race at an average of 51 kph to complete the challenge in around 8½ minutes (check with Josh), confronting a couple of taxing corners (two or three – check), dealing with a drag quite soon after the start, a stretch of cobbles half-way and then a 400 m straight run to the end. Whether Vasily Jawlensky wins today or not, the pressure will be firmly on his back regardless of the colour of jersey he will wear tomorrow for Le Grand Départ.

'I really can't do any more,' Cat decides, after reading her paragraph, 'not until it's all over.' She lays her hand on her diaphragm. She is brimming with adrenalin. *How on earth must the boys feel?*

Her Tour de France is about to start, her sense of anticipation is as much for her own race as for the riders for whom she feels so much.

None of us can do more just now – it's a waiting game. First rider on the course in just under four hours' time. Vasily goes last at 18.33. How on earth can they be feeling?

'Coming to the *village*?' says Josh.

'Sure,' says Cat.

Josh had to contend with Cat stopping still every now and then to focus on riders warming up along the circuit.

'You've got three weeks of them,' he said, over his shoulder as Cat focused on Bobby Julich until he was round a corner and out of sight, 'you'll be sick of the sight by the end of it.' He laughed, knowing that she wouldn't, nor would he, or any of the entourage of the Tour de France. 'In truth, Cat,' he said surreptitiously, 'we're a bunch of frauds. First and foremost, we're fans. This isn't a job, it's pleasure for which we're paid.'

'Jalabert!' Cat, giving immediate flesh to Josh's theory, gasped and clapped as the legendary French cyclist zipped past them. '*Allez*, JaJa!'

If Cat had been surprised by the lavish buffet provided for her and the other journalists at the ice rink, the *village* had her positively gobsmacked. The large courtyard at the Hôtel de Ville, through which she had walked last night to the team presentation, was now plotted and pieced by a vast array of marquees, canopies and awnings, each commandeered by a sponsor and bedecked with an array of refreshments, brochures and promotional merchandise. The air was perfumed with the smell of coffee, of meat, of wine and cheese. There was an entire suckling pig gracing a table on which cold cuts from surely a whole herd of suckling pigs were laid artistically amidst a tapestry of fruit. Further on, an enormous omelette pan was being put to great use by three moustachioed chefs. Tables heaved under huge cartwheels of soft cheese amidst forests of baguette, counters groaned under the weight of local wines and liqueurs and all the Coca-Cola in the world seemed to be available right there. Everywhere Cat looked, people were eating and drinking.

They could be at a wedding, a ball, as much as the Tour de France. Do they actually realize where they are? I do. I couldn't possibly eat – my stomach's full of butterflies. God knows how the riders can eat – and yet they must.

Despite the opulence, variety and availability of all the hospitality, Cat took only a small nutty roll and a plastic cup of orange juice as she circumnavigated the *village*. She grinned at Channel 4's Phil Liggett who had no idea who she was and she found the courage to say to his co-presenter Paul Sherwen, who also had no idea who she was, 'I'm Cat McCabe – this is my first Tour.' She glimpsed Josh with his notepad tucked under his arm so that he could hold a laden paper plate and plastic wine glass. She glanced at the roll from which she'd taken a few small nibbles and deposited it in a bin. Even the juice tasted too sharp to be pleasant and was no longer cool so she threw that away soon after. She was too excited to eat, too nervous to drink but too worried about missing a thing to phone home and recount her surroundings with glee. She checked her watch. Three hours to go.

Come on, come on – start!

Outside the hallowed area of the *village*, into which admittance was strictly by pass only and controlled by scrupulous sentries, the public was gathering along the Prologue route. The crowds were massive, holding flags that they'd wave frantically every now and then if any Tour vehicle should pass. Cat felt enormously privileged, being able to walk inside the snaking barriers, on the very surface that each of the 189 riders would soon be pedalling for position. Just then, she did not feel like a *journaliste* at all, merely an ardent admirer blessed with a pass and she felt extremely lucky. She would walk around for a while, soak up the atmosphere whilst noting specific details of the course. If she could infuse her article with her experience of the former, the details of the latter would surely interest her readers all the more.

'I want to do eight thirty,' Luca says to Ben. The doctor nods, just as he had for Travis, who wants to do eight thirty-two, and just as he did for Hunter, who wants to do eight twenty-seven.

'You coming to watch?' Luca asks. Ben hadn't intended to but as both Hunter, Travis and two other members of the team had asked the same question, he has changed his mind.

'Of course I'll be there,' he says to Luca, 'just don't make me scrape bits of you off the tarmac. Have a good ride. Go for your eight thirty but remember there's tomorrow and tomorrow and tomorrow.'

'*Creeps in this petty pace from day to day*,' Luca says wistfully.

'Fuck me!' Ben exclaims, looking at Luca in genuine amazement. '*You*? Shakespeare?'

'Fuck you,' says Luca, frowning, 'and I'll tell you something for free, I'm not going at a creeping, petty pace. I'm going to ride for all I'm worth, race my heart out.'

Over an hour before the start, the colourful conga line of the 220 novelty vehicles in the publicity caravan was delighting the crowds, already six deep, with their flamboyance and freebies. The riders were arriving in their team buses and campers, parking *en masse* in the Place Victor Hugo. Bikes were held stationary on blocks and the riders were warming up, their fans gawping just inches away from their noses. Some riders stared fixedly at the frame of their machines, or their knuckles, or the ground, as they pedalled; others gazed, glazed, directly ahead, directly at some stranger without seeing them at all.

Cat caught sight of Alex chatting to a girl at the Zucca MV bus and walked over to see if chance might provide her with Massimo Lipari or Stefano Sassetta. Or even Vasily Jawlensky.

For a soundbite. OK, then, just for a glimpse!

She smiled quickly at Alex and the woman.

'Cat, this is Rachel – the *soigneur* nine out of ten riders said they'd like to, er, *have*.'

This typical remark from Alex enabled Cat and Rachel immediately to share a look that shot heavenward and was followed by a conspiratorial smile apiece.

'Cat McCabe,' said Cat, holding out her hand.

'Press?' Rachel asked. Cat nodded. 'First Tour?' Rachel enquired. Cat nodded again, matching the girl's smile with one of her own. 'Me too,' said Rachel. 'Welcome.'

'Thanks,' said Cat. 'It's great to be here.'

She seems my type – I could have a good natter with her, but I'd better be a bit more journalisty.

'How's the team?' Cat asked nonchalantly. Rachel looked over her shoulder to the closed door and blacked-out windows of the camper.

'Tense,' she said.

'I'll bet,' Cat colluded. Massimo Lipari appeared and Cat had to ensure she did not break into a wild grin though a small smile crept out unannounced anyway.

'Hey, Massimo,' said Alex. The rider tipped his head in recognition, asking Alex, in Italian, how he was and Alex, in Italian, rabbiting away until he had achieved an obvious goal of making the rider chuckle. Rachel was gladly telling Cat about how she came by her job – she'd never had a journalist express interest in her career, she'd never actually talked directly to a female journalist – when Massimo tapped Rachel on the shoulder, stood for a moment before tapping her again, staring intently at Cat all the while.

'Rachel, I need the jacket, yes, for here?' he proffered his left elbow displaying a glistening and pretty grave graze acquired from a careless fall whilst training yesterday.

'*Jacket*?' Rachel asked, shooting a glance at Cat. 'You mean the gauze tube? Excuse me,' she said to Cat with an apologetic shrug, 'it's been nice talking. Pop by again some time, hey?'

'Brilliant,' Cat enthused. Massimo stared at her again. It was only when Rachel had turned from her and led the cyclist into the secret interior of the van that it struck Cat that Massimo had actually stared at her quite accusatorially.

And why shouldn't he? I was hogging his soigneur. *How awful of me.*

Alex had disappeared. Josh was nowhere to be seen. Cat turned and decided that to walk around with purpose even if she hadn't a clue what to do next, was a sensible option. Everywhere she looked, she now saw the faces and bodies of the men she had previously known only second-hand, behind the glass of a television, or two-dimensionally in print. Now they were surrounding her, life size, in the flesh, *en masse*. It was so overwhelming, she found herself unable to establish eye contact with any of them. In turning away from the awesome Mario Cipollini whom she could see from the corner of her eye, hands on hips and a vision in a red lycra skinsuit, she found herself by the Megapac vehicles. By concentrating on not catching sight of her best friends of yesterday – Hunter or Travis or Luca (whose eyes were in any case shut as he pedalled the course in his mind whilst his bike remained stationary on the blocks), her eyes went instead to someone else. Or were they pulled there? Or were they caught?

It's that guy. The one who sat by Luca at the medical. Oh blimey, what a smile. Hey! I didn't say that I could smile back.

The man stepped towards her and fingered her pass. 'Hullo, Catriona McCabe,' he said, '*journaliste*, the *Guardian*.'

'I'm, er,' she cleared her throat, 'Cat.'

'Are you now?' he said. 'I'm *er* doctor.' Cat regarded him. He gave her an open smile.

'I'm Ben. York. Hullo.'

Cat nodded rather enthusiastically because she had no idea what to say. She then smiled fleetingly but not directly at Ben York, sweeping it instead quickly and non-commitally over the riders, the Megapac vehicles, and Dr York's shoes before nodding, biting her lip and moving away, rifling through the pages of her pad whilst chastizing herself silently.

He's English. That's nice.

It was gone three o'clock and she thanked God that it was. Cat made her way slowly to a vantage point near the starting ramp and gazed at Travis Stanton as he and his bike were held steady or, Cat felt, perhaps embraced, by a blue-blazered official. She watched another official count the rider down, she observed the rider's face, the focus, the deep inhalation and exaggerated exhalation. The official's fingers had finished the count and he sliced the air with his hand. Off. Go. The rider swept down and away towards a lonely, strenuous eight and a half minutes. Cat found that she was holding her breath and had her fingers crossed.

'My legs. My heart. My mind. My soul.'

Hunter Dean chants the familiar phrase to himself as he pedals slowly through the mêlée around the team cars and on towards the starting ramp.

'My legs. My heart. My mind. My soul.'

He spits. He is wearing his burgundy and green skinsuit and space-warrior style helmet.

'I am aerodynamic. My legs. My heart. My mind. My soul.'

He spits again. He does not notice the crowds, nor does he hear them banging on the barriers, cheering. He does not listen to the fading, megaphone drone from a team car out on the course yelling '*Allez! Allez! Allez!*' at the rider it is following. Hunter notices in a glance that his own team car is ready and he sees his name, printed on a board positioned above the front bumper. *Dean.*

'Hunter Fucking Dean. Strong legs. Strong heart. Strong mind. Strong soul.'

He sweeps his bike through two controlled circles and ignores a fellow competitor leaving the ramp.

'I am fit for this. I am prepared. I am built for this Time Trial. Legs to pump. Heart to pump. Mind steady. Soul ready.'

He takes his position, aware there is a man's arm under his saddle, which presses lightly against his back.

'Backbone – strength. Legs – stamina. Heart – power. Mind – focus. Soul – commitment. I am good. I am ready.'

The official is counting him down.

'Open, lungs – fill. In. Out. Ready.'

Away. *Allez.*

'Corner. On. On. Go go go. Corner. Done. Propel me, legs. Drive me, back. Cobbles. Take them. Take them. On. On.'

Hunter is riding well. He is surrounded by noise, but that of the ecstatic crowd is but a sub layer deep in the recesses of his awareness. What he hears is his breathing. As he sweeps the wide arc which takes him to the finishing straight, he does not listen to the growing clangour of the spectators thumping the barriers, he hears instead the pounding of his heart banging in his chest and in his mouth and in his stomach, flat out.

'Legs. Legs. Legs. Eight twenty-seven. Eight twenty-seven. Come on, you fucker, go.'

Hunter is out of the saddle, stamping down hard, making a great sprint of his final metres. His head is down as he thrusts forward for the line, then it is up and over his shoulder immediately, to clock the time.

Eight minutes, twenty-seven point six eight seconds.

'Point six eight. Shit.'

Django McCabe took three plain chocolate digestive biscuits and carefully swiped a lick of Marmite over the chocolate sides. He steeped three tea-bags in a small teapot, added three spoonfuls of sugar to the inch of milk in the china cup, selected a non-matching but china saucer and put everything on a tray. He went into the Quiet Room and turned it into the Family Room merely by way of flicking on the television set. He selected Channel 4, muted the volume on the closing scenes of *Brookside* and made to telephone both his nieces, sipping tea but saving the biscuits until later.

'Fen, darling, Django here – are you switched on? The bike race is starting in five minutes or so.'

'God, I almost forgot,' said Fen, untying and then rebunching her pony-tail two or three times, the telephone receiver tucked under her chin. 'Does Pip know?'

'Isn't she with you?' Django enquired, a little perturbed. For some reason, Fen actually looked around her flat before replying.

'No, she isn't – should she be?'

'Well, you two live in the same town, I thought perhaps you'd be sharing the experience together.'

'Django,' Fen laughed, 'London's a sprawling metropolis. I don't think the bike race is an experience I, or Pip, have been waiting with bated breath for.'

'I didn't really mean that,' said Django, 'not those shiny boys and bikes themselves, I meant your sister. I meant Cat. This is her experience – I think we should take an interest.'

Fen felt humbled. Suddenly, she wished Pip was here. 'You're right,' she said quietly, 'maybe we might catch Cat on screen. She's there, after all, in the thick of it. So we should switch on and tune in.'

'And share,' mused Django, quite relieved he was on his own and could have his biscuits to himself.

'Don't worry about phoning Pip, I'll do that right now,' Fen said. 'You warm the TV up,' she told her uncle, using a phrase Cat had frequently employed in childhood.

('Cat? Where have you disappeared to? Pip's clearing the table. Fen's washing up and there's a tea towel with your name on it.'

'Oh. Sorry. I was just warming the TV up.')

'Hey, Pip, it's me.'

'Hi, Fen. Get off the phone. The Tour de France is about to start.'

Half an later, the phone lines of Django, Fen and Pip were jammed engaged as each tried to contact the other. Ten minutes on, Pip arrived at Fen's flat and they called Django together.

'Wasn't that exciting!' Django boomed, wishing they could see the two uneaten biscuits as proof.

'It was,' Fen agreed, 'I had no idea!' Pip, bobbing up and down on the spot, took the phone from her.

'That famous bloke won!' she exclaimed breathlessly. 'I remember Cat talking about him.' She handed the telephone back to Fen and executed a handstand against the wall in celebration.

*

'Josh,' Cat asked, 'might you cast your expert eye over my piece?' Though she was confident about the quality of her copy, her request had a twofold function. She was rather proud of her first race report and felt it warranted immediate approval before she wired it to London. Also, she still wanted to consolidate her new colleague's respect for her journalistic abilities and her cycle sport knowledge. Josh was flattered, more so when Alex looked up from his laptop, regarded Cat with a 'Why not me?' glance and bestowed on Josh a glare that said 'Wanker!' a little enviously.

'I like it that you've explained the gap of 53 seconds between first and last rider being in contrast to the hours that will develop as the race progresses,' Josh defined and read on, sometimes to himself, sometimes out loud.

During a day in which the sun shone unabated and lively crowds chanted indiscriminately, Britain's Chris Boardman, riding for the French team Crédit Agricole, equalled the great French rider Bernard Hinault's five Prologue triumphs. He turned a heavy gear throughout, his extraordinary aerodynamic position complementing his futuristic Time Trial bike whose handlebars he designed himself.

'Good for Chris,' Cat mused, recalling the rider's consummate Time Trial. 'Might we raise a glass to him tonight?'

Aren't I being brave, organizing après-*race activities!*

Alex, however, laughed. 'If we manage to leave the *salle de presse* before last orders.'

Cat shrugged as if to say 'Whatever', whereas actually she was shaking off the sudden embarrassment she felt. She read her article over Josh's shoulder. He could feel her breath on the side of his neck. It felt nice. He didn't comment.

'So,' Cat said, 'Fabian stormed to second place today, 0.19 of a second faster than Vasily.'

'Yes,' clarified Josh, 'but Jawlensky still has the incentive of racing with Number 1 on his back.'

'But Fabian is tasting blood,' Cat commented.

'Well, it'll be Boardman wearing the first *maillot jaune* of this year's Tour when the race starts in earnest tomorrow,' Josh said.

'It will be interesting to see who makes the first assault on the jersey,' Cat pondered, 'Vasily or Fabian.'

'I like the way you've commented on how Ducasse showed greater bravura but Jawlensky looked consistently more comfortable,' Josh remarked.

Alex, who had left the *salle*, returned with cans of Coke for everyone. He read Cat's work over Josh's other shoulder. 'I don't know whether you should be using solely their Christian names, girl,' he commented.

But they're my boys! Cat protested to herself, with no intention of changing a word.

'Good closing paragraph,' Josh said.

Tomorrow, the Tour de France will be under way with a week of flat road racing Stages providing the spectators and sponsors alike with the flamboyance and daredevilry of the sprinters.

'Good comment on strategy,' Alex furthered, 'to explain that those aiming for overall victory will be keeping quiet in the centre of the bunch, maintaining a safe distance from the unavoidable mayhem of sprint finishes.'

'She calls it "*the broiling hurl*",' said Josh approvingly.

'Come on,' Cat tried again, 'let's finish up and toast Mr Boardman.'

'Maybe,' Josh said, to her satisfaction.

'Could do,' Alex said. Cat allowed herself an inward smile.

STAGE 1
Delaunay Le Beau–Rouen. 195 kilometres

*W*hen Luca Jones tripped on the stairs of the start podium to sign in, he did not see it as an omen for his ride but as cultivation of his popularity. He recovered his composure, signed the vast chart and beamed and waved at the crowd as his name was blasted out by the PA system.

'Stage 1 of the fucking Tour de France,' he marvelled to Travis as if he might not have realized, while, astride their bikes, they waited for the ceremonial off.

'Watch yourself,' Travis laughed.

'Everyone's watching!' Luca responded. He felt absolutely ready for the day's racing and was looking forward to enjoying himself. 'It's fairly flat today,' he had reasoned to his *soigneur* who was slapping his legs warm earlier, 'I'm just going to hang out with the bunch, turn and tune my legs. I'm going to clock the crowds, even the landscape – perhaps there'll be some gorgeous scenery along the way, softly undulating and bikini-clad – you know?'

Luckily for the riders around Luca, the weather was dry, bright but too cold for bikinis. Crashes were a foregone conclusion without the added jeopardy of roadside distractions on Luca Jones. The peloton rode in unison for a while, teams happily dispersing to chat in native tongues to fellow riders.

'You're a tart, Luca,' Stuart O'Grady teased when Luca came back to the English contingent, having ridden leisurely with an Italian posse for a few miles.

'Yeah, but my tan, man,' Luca reposted, 'better than you, Stu.' After tapping on for a few miles more, the bunch stepped up the pace and began to race. For over two hours, the only view Luca examined was the colourful contours of the mass of torsos around him. He was well prepared therefore when a Banesto rider took down four others just far enough ahead and to the left to avoid the pile up. *Lucky Luca*, he said to himself. He worked his way to the front forty for a while, rode alongside Vasily Jawlensky who gave him a nod of recognition, which served as fuel injection to the legs. *Lucky Luca*, he said to himself, *Vasily fucking Jawlensky*.

Then what happened? To be suddenly staring at the still mass of blue sky after concentrating for so long on the multicoloured movement of the peloton was momentarily disconcerting and dazzling. It was not Lucky Luca who found himself all but sitting directly on top of JaJa. The famous Frenchman Laurent Jalabert had Fucking Luca Jones sprawled over the top of him.

'*Merde*!' Jalabert swore as he and Luca extricated themselves amicably enough from one another.

'Wank,' said Luca, seeing blood on his shin and wondering where his bike was.

'*Ça va*?' someone asked.

'*Oui*,' Luca muttered, 'wank.'

There's my bike. There goes Jalabert. Skill. How come I'm bleeding? Do I hurt? I don't think so.

Riders were picking their way cautiously around Luca and a few other floored men. Luca was aware of the thrum of the TV helicopter overhead, of the whirr of press cameras near by, of the yellow-clad Mavic neutral service personnel swarming around like helpful worker bees. After so long in the saddle, to stand upright felt a little odd. To the French family previously enjoying their annual institution of picnic and peloton, the stooped Luca looked injured enough even before they saw his ripped shorts. It was time to do their bit; what an honour, what a conversation piece. Luca was bent over with hands on knees, collecting himself and his Oakleys, when someone put an arm around his shoulders.

'*Monsieur?*'

Fuck, look at my shorts. Where is the blood on my leg coming from?

'*Monsieur – ici.*'

Luca was gazing at the sky again.

I'm lying on a picnic table. I'm being photographed.

He sat up. On the road, riders were remounting. He looked to his right and stared blankly at he photographer. He looked to his left and a small child stared at him whilst sucking hard on a straw in an empty bottle of Coke. He looked down and regarded a pile of picnic victuals hastily dumped on a chair. He looked at his left thigh and observed slivers of baguette crust speckling his skin with shards of gravel.

'*Ça va?*' a photographer said perfunctorily, looking around for another photo opportunity.

Luca shrugged, got to his feet, set his bike upright, spun a wheel and grinned through 180 degrees. 'Yeah – I'm fine.' He saluted the family who nodded humbly. Off he went, shorts in shreds, left hip stinging, reputation intact, popularity increased.

'It's not your blood,' said his *soigneur*, sponging Luca down at the team car when he arrived an hour or so later.

'Huh?'

'Not yours,' the *soigneur* said, almost accusatorily.

'Jeez, must be Jalabert's,' Luca muttered as if he ought to return it.

'Great butt,' Hunter laughed, raising his eyebrows at Luca's flank on view through his tattered shorts.

'You want to change?' his *soigneur* asked.

Luca nodded initially but then said, 'Nah.' Narrowing his eyes, he correctly deduced that the three girls hovering would prefer him this way.

'From Denmark,' said one, holding out her T-shirt for an autograph and exchanging three kisses.

'Me too,' said the other, proffering a felt tip and her forearm for signing and her lips for direct osculation.

'And me,' the third said, offering Luca her autograph book and a respectful if solemn handshake.

I feel better already. Bye bye girls, come again. Oh look, there's that girl from the press conference. Come and ask me how I am. Don't just mouth 'You OK?' Come nearer. I don't bite – unless you like. How about I give a shrug and look blue? Yes!

'Hullo,' the girl from the press conference said, 'are you hurt?'

Luca responded with his heroic shrug.

'What happened?' she asked, pen poised, eyes concerned.

'One minute I'm sitting on the bike,' Luca drawled, staring at her steadily, 'next I'm sitting on Jalabert. Hey, but we both live to ride another day!'

'Hullo, Catriona *journaliste* McCabe,' said Luca's doctor, suddenly at his side.

'Oh, hi,' said the girl with a swift but sweet smile. Luca's doctor looked hard at her, Luca gazed at her almost imploringly. 'Just checking the wounded soldier is all right,' she said.

'Er, that's my job,' his doctor teased.

'Yes, of course,' the *journaliste* said ingenuously. She tipped her head and regarded the rider. 'Glad you're OK – good luck tomorrow.'

'Thank you, Catriona,' Luca Jones replied, rolling his 'r's and disjoining her name with strange emphases.

'Cat,' the *journaliste* all but cautioned. Rider and doctor regarded her. 'I'd better go,' she said, brandishing her notepad. 'Bye – see you.' She walked away briskly, scribbling in her pad all the while.

'Close your mouth,' Ben said to Luca, who didn't know his doctor had only just shut his. 'Do you hurt?'

COPY FOR P. TAVERNER @ GUARDIAN SPORTS DESK FROM CATRIONA McCABE IN ROUEN

For the first time in the history of the Tour de France, the yellow jersey and the first five places in Stage One went to English-speaking riders. Chris Boardman, losing only 2 seconds off his lead, keeps the golden fleece of his Prologue win. Stefano Sassetta of Zucca MV was relegated to the bottom of this first group for a flamboyant swerve dangerously close to his sworn rival, Système Vipère's Jesper Lomers. Whether plain careless or downright malicious, Sassetta was not given the benefit of the doubt. In the city of Rouen, Sassetta should think himself lucky – Joan of Arc was burnt at the stake here in 1431.

Nice opening paragraph, Cat. But you're reading it to yourself today. Wouldn't Alex rather like your next sentence – '*As Samson lost his strength when his hair was cut, so it appears the sprinters lose their memories once their legs are shorn*'? Oh, Alex is sitting nowhere near you. Nor is Josh. You have a pungent Belgian journalist on one side and a hirsute Spaniard on the other. The *salle de presse* seems a little like the peloton itself as you describe it in your next paragraph, somewhat fresh and disorganized at this early stage. Where's your Luca quote? Have you woven it in?

As in all wars, the innocent are frequently victims. Laurent Jalabert (O.N.C.E.), an elder statesman of the Tour peloton, and Luca Jones (Megapac), a virgin soldier, were amongst the casualties brought down when wheels touched ahead of them at the last sprint point. Jalabert recovered to finish with the main bunch, his fingers bloodied and his brow dark. Jones, whose major injury was dramatically ripped shorts, took time out prostrate on a spectator's picnic table, much to the delight of the public. 'One minute I'm sitting on the bike,' he recalled, 'the next I'm sitting on Jalabert.'

Good work, Cat.

The green jersey, worn by the rider with the most points accumulated en route and for finishing in the top 25, is on the broad shoulders of Mario Cipollini. The true contenders for overall victory were hardly seen today. Just as the villages along the route cluster around their omnipotent churches, so Vasily Jawlensky and Fabian Ducasse were flanked at all times by at least 3 devoted team-mates. Wisely, they kept well away from the broiling at the very front yet still finished with the same times as that group.

    And so began the week-long campaign by the audacious pure sprinters to retain the top positions. Soon enough, the Pyrenees will rip the peloton apart.

<ENDS>

Right, Cat, it's gone nine in the evening and you're only just leaving the *salle de presse*. Alone. You've positively slunk out, hoping no one's noticed. Why? Didn't you bond further with your colleagues last night whilst toasting Boardman's superb win? He's in yellow again today – isn't that *carte blanche* for a celebratory evening tonight?

There are no plans for tonight. The only toast last night, literally, was the tough bread roll I ate by myself in my room. That's my phone.

'Hullo?'
  'Cat?'
  'Hey, Fen.'
  'Cat?' she said. 'You OK?'
  'Tired.'
  'Where are you? George Hincapie is gorgeous! Did I pronounce that right?'
  'Spot on.'

Cat listened to her sister enthuse about the day's Stage. She closed her eyes, wishing she was in Fen's house, settling in for an evening of wine and wittering.

'Pip and I watched it together at her flat this time. We spoke to Django during the adverts and then had a major three-way analysis when the programme ended. I love that nice smiley man from Channel 4 – Leggings.'

'Liggett,' said Cat with a little laugh.

'Do you know him?'

'No.'

'Have you met him yet?'

'Almost.'

'What did you *do* today? I'm fascinated. I mean, we're only granted half an hour's summary of the whole day – how does it pan out for you?'

'Oh –' Cat said breezily, swiping the air nonchalantly with her hand, a gesture of course lost on her sister.

'Cat?' Fen asked again. 'You OK?'

'It's odd,' Cat defined softly, 'I'm finding it difficult. I'm fighting homesickness already. I was hopeful of a family atmosphere here. I think that was naïve. We didn't even have a drink to celebrate Boardman's win.'

'It's very early days,' Fen said sensibly, 'riders and everyone else finding their feet, surely. Anyway, I'm concerned that drink, or lack of, is the prime reason for your melancholy.'

Cat sighed. 'Don't be daft,' she chastized her sister, 'today I was sent flying in the finish-line scrum.'

'God!' Fen sympathised.

'I was pushed and shoved, trodden on and ignored,' Cat elaborated. 'I don't stand a chance. Now, I feel on the verge of floundering, of becoming lost amongst it all.'

'Is it every man for himself, then?' Fen asked.

Cat nodded and then said, 'Yes.'

'Who's the gorgeous one who stopped off for a picnic?' Fen probed.

Cat grinned and felt a softening of her tangled brow. 'Luca

Jones,' she said, 'and he gave me a super quote.'

'There you go!' Fen encouraged.

'I know, I know,' Cat conceded, 'but I just feel a little, I don't know – out on a limb. It's only just started, I'm here for a long time – and yet this was supposed to be my fantasy incarnate and a world in which I'd find all the answers.'

'You've only just arrived,' Fen pointed out. 'I bet you anything tomorrow will be fabulous.'

'Fen, I feel too small and female.'

'Bollocks, Cat,' Fen said strongly. 'Yes, you're an anomaly out there – small and female – so you *must* be a breath of fresh air. I'd use it if I were you.'

Cat observed Josh and Alex turning the corner a hundred yards away.

'Fen, I have to go. This must be costing you a fortune.'

'Phone bill? You're far more precious, stupid!' said Fen, thinking herself to sound like a mother – a proper one, not one that had run off with a cowboy from Denver.

'I'll call you tomorrow,' said Cat.

'Promise?'

'Yes.'

Cat walked off briskly. Her ears, however, were peeled. She was listening for a half-hoped-for 'Wait up, Cat,' from Josh or Alex. And yet half of her hoped they had not seen her, that she could go and sit by herself in her hotel room and ruminate on her day.

Rachel McEwen's room at Zucca MV's Rouen hotel was cramped enough as it was, without the addition of three strapping riders and the veritable grocery shop Rachel set up each day. Her portable massage bench held *domestique* Pietro Calcaterra. He'd swerved to miss the knot of Luca Jones and Laurent Jalabert but had careered into Fernando Escartin instead. Now his knee was hurting. Massimo Lipari sat at the small table, softly humming his Giro pop song, helping himself to a huge bowl of cereal and arranging a diced banana artistically over the top. Gianni Fugallo, the team's *super domestique*, lay on Rachel's bed reading her *Cosmopolitan* magazine whilst listening to a Walkman.

Suddenly, Massimo exclaimed, 'StefanoStefanoStefano!' through a mouthful of cereal. 'Big trouble,' he declared, 'very big trouble for Stefano.'

Though the riders discussed their errant team-mate's aggressive swerve animatedly, Rachel did not comment. The *directeur* had already forewarned her that Stefano would be coming for his massage after a strict pep talk; consequently, the rider would be either deeply despondent or darkly defensive. It would be Rachel's job to massage his psyche into fit shape for the next day's Stage.

When she had finished Pietro, she asked Massimo if he had had enough to eat and pinged back the earphones on Gianni's Walkman to ask him if he needed anything. Massimo had eaten sufficient but took another banana, slipping it down his tracksuit bottoms so it poked out like an erection. The first time Rachel had seen this, she hadn't known where to look. The second time, she hadn't known how to react. The third time, she'd laughed heartily. Now (and Massimo was in to double figures) she just ignored him. As did the other riders. Massimo still found himself thoroughly amusing. Gianni asked Rachel if he could borrow the *Cosmopolitan*.

'What's mine is yours, Gianni,' Rachel said magnanimously, 'you know that.'

Massimo grabbed the magazine, flipped through it with much exaggerated ogling, fingered his goatee lasciviously, performed some lewd pelvic thrusting until the banana slipped down his tracksuit and poked out at the side of his leg like some gruesomely broken bone.

With the three riders gone, the room seemed temporarily vast until Stefano entered without knocking and filled it entirely with the thunder that was swept about him like a cloak. In fact, it was a voluminous, somewhat incongruous peach towelling robe but his blazing eyes and the muscles in his cheeks twitching furiously deflected attention from it.

'Never do I be speaked to as that!' he spat, his command of English suffering in the clasp of his indignation.

'Never have I been spoken to like that,' Rachel placated, smoothing a fresh towel on the massage bench. Stefano stripped and stood before Rachel in his naked glory though she had ceased to see it long ago. She handed him a towel, which he slipped between his legs nappy-style once he'd climbed aboard the table.

'Lomers!' Stefano growled like an expletive directed at the vigour of Rachel's massage. Rachel took her hands away from his body, wiped them and put them on her hips.

'Stefano,' she said, 'shut up. It's Lomers who should be spitting your name.'

'It was my line,' Stefano protested, sitting up and regarding Rachel squarely, 'I rode it correctly. I did not flick him.'

'On the life of your mother?' Rachel challenged him. Predictably, Stefano, ever the dutiful Italian son, fell silent.

'Take risks by all means,' Rachel said, gently pushing the rider's shoulder so he lay back down. She looked down on him, her hands on her hips again, 'but don't ride dangerously. You will either get hurt or disqualified. Then Lomers will wear the green jersey and you will be watching him from the TV in your apartment. And your mother will weep.'

'Still, no one speaks to Stefano Sassetta like that,' Stefano said petulantly, referring back to the *directeur*'s rebuke.

'They will if you deserve it,' Rachel said. She massaged him hard. He stared unflinchingly at the ceiling. 'Beware,' she said as she sent him on his way, down to supper, 'rain is forecast for tomorrow. The roads could be hell.'

Cat sits in her hotel room, ruminating on her day.

Three elements have made her Stage 1 not such a good one. Disappointment. Bewilderment. Trepidation. She had not considered having to confront such emotions, not on the Tour de France. She'd only anticipated tiredness, stress and irritability at some point surely much later in the race.

I need to consider these new three before I'm allowed to go to sleep.

Start with Disappointment.

I did not see one wheel turn of cycling today – not live. We drove directly to Rouen, missing the route altogether. The itinéraire direct was 46 k. We did it in forty-five minutes. The boys did 195 k in just over four and a half hours.

Couldn't you have suggested to Josh that you drove the route ahead of the race?

I did. He frowned and laughed. It was embarrassing.

Number two, Bewilderment?

I miss the ice rink. I miss little Delaunay Le Beau. I knew it well – five days there. The salle de presse in Rouen is this 1950s clump of glass and concrete – civic and austere. Josh and Alex.

That's not a sentence.

Didn't save me a place.

Oh. But on purpose?

I mean – I only nipped to the loo. This hefty German journo pushed by me. He dumped his stuff by Alex.

So they *had* saved a place for you.

But they didn't defend it. They just shrugged. I had to set up in the smaller press room. The only cycling I saw was one step removed, via the press TVs.

Cat, can you hear yourself?

I know. I'm feeble. In the finish-line scrum, I was just plain flimsy.

Is that number three, Trepidation?

Absolutely. An all English-speaking result – not only did I not get a word in or out, I didn't even manage to get close to any of them. I stood on tiptoes near the swarm around Hincapie but learnt my lesson when some Bavarian brute sent me flying. Then I tried for O'Grady, but a wall of men was formed around him, not even a chink to wriggle my arm and dictaphone through. Alex had just left the Jay Sweet mêlée and looked straight through me. Seeing Josh having to barge for a soundbite from Travis Stanton decided me not to even attempt to approach. So then I wandered off and came across the lacerated Luca.

How can you be glum about that?

Because I was pretty shaken and didn't come across as I wished I had. As I'd envisaged I'd be.

Good quote, though.

I suppose.

And a smile from Luca and his doctor.

I suppose. He's strange, that bloke, Ben. I find him a bit unnerving.

Because he's good-looking and direct?

OK, don't answer.

Sleep well.

STAGE 2
Rouen–Vuillard. 260 kilometres

*T*he next morning, the whole of Rouen awoke to the incessant thrumming of rain. Rachel was pleased – Stefano would be forced to be more vigilant. On the whole, the riders from the lowlands didn't mind such weather, but those from southern Europe mostly hated it. For physiques attuned to long hot summers, the cold or the damp could infiltrate their bodies swiftly and disrupt the pursuit of prime form. Stefano Sassetta was only too aware that he was of the latter persuasion but that his arch rival Jesper Lomers was of the former. In kilometres, it was to be the longest Stage of the entire race. If the wind was north-easterly, as it had been, it would be three-quarters behind them and the day would be fast. Breakfasting with the team, Stefano theorized that he would ride carefully, commandeer a posse of *domestiques* throughout and ensure he had at least two lead-out guys for the final sprint. His *directeur* nodded his approval and team orders were given. Rachel, who had snatched a bowl of cornflakes two hours previously, was now hauling the team's luggage from foyer to van.

'Want a hand?' Ben York, standing amongst the Megapac baggage, asked her.

'No, you're all right, Ben,' Rachel replied.

'Only all right?' Ben teased.

'In your dreams,' Rachel responded, knowing full well that she'd never been in Ben's dreams because, for the cycling fraternity at large, her gender went unnoticed.

The rain did not deter the crowds. The city of Rouen, birthplace of the great Jacques Anquetil, the first man to win the Tour five times, appeared to have turned out in its entirety. Cat went to the *village*, to the press stand to shelter and see if yesterday's *Guardian* was there. It was. Taverner hadn't cut a word.

'Good work.'

She turned. Josh, in an extremely colourful cagoule, was reading over her shoulder. 'Alex has wangled a ride in the Vitalicio team car,' he continued, 'so it's just you and me. Shall we drive the route or the *itinéraire direct*?'

Cat beamed. 'Route, please.'

Josh regarded her. 'We might be able to nip in behind a break if we're lucky – we'll have to leave at the first bell, though. See you by the car.'

Cat felt back on track, read great significance in to the fact that the rain had abated, flipped over to a clean page in her pad and left the *village* to be amongst the teams.

'Morning, Dr York,' she said as she passed by, without stopping, without really looking.

'Miss McCabe,' he responded, businesslike in tone but with a glint in his eye which went unnoticed.

'Cat,' she said over her shoulder.

'Ben,' he called after her.

Ahead, Rachel raised her hand at Cat who waved back. Rachel beckoned her over.

'Hey, Rachel,' Cat said warmly.

'I have something for you, Cat,' Rachel replied, 'hold on.' The *soigneur* went to her team car and ferreted around in the glove compartment, retrieved what looked like a small make-up bag and rummaged around the contents. 'This,' she said to Cat, 'is a talisman – and I think it's my duty to pass it on to you.' She proffered a closed fist. Cat held out her hand. A pencil sharpener.

'The lovely Emma O'Reilly – US Postal's *soigneur*, I'll introduce you – gave it to me at my first Vuelta,' Rachel explained, as if that was enough. 'Now I pass it on to you.'

'Thanks,' said Cat, trying to figure out the symbolism.

'It's for your elbows,' Rachel whispered, chuckling conspiringly. 'I saw you yesterday, getting knocked and shoved and more than ignored. Bastards. Make sure your elbows are sharp. At our height, we can give a most efficient jab at *their* waist-height.'

Cat laughed and thanked her sincerely, touched by the gesture.

'Keep it with you at all times,' Rachel said.

'You bet I will,' Cat replied.

'I have two more things for you,' Rachel continued, 'my mobile phone number and also some advice.'

Cat jotted down the *soigneur*'s number. 'We could meet after school,' Rachel suggested wryly.

'Yeah, right,' Cat responded, giving Rachel her number, 'have a quick drink after work.'

'Like normal people,' Rachel said, shaking her head at such absurdity.

'As if!' they said, almost in unison.

'Now for the advice,' Rachel said. 'This is also from the wise mouth of Emma.'

'Shoot,' said Cat, pen poised, feeling bolstered that there was a girls' club.

Rachel regarded Cat, twitched her lips into a sly smile and whispered, 'Never answer your hotel door after midnight.'

Then she winked, turned her hand into a telephone, turned from Cat and gave her attention to Stefano Sassetta who wanted more embrocation on his thighs.

'So,' said Josh, almost as soon as they'd driven out of Rouen, 'who's holding the fort for you?'

At first, Cat thought he said fork and had no idea how to answer him.

'Fork?' she asked, glancing around the Peugeot hire car that seemed the height of luxury after her clapped-out Beetle.

'Fort,' said Josh. 'This rain is bollocks.'

'The forecast says bright and dry later. I don't have a fort,' Cat added, regarding herself in the side mirror, noticing she looked tired already, 'just a small flat.'

'Who's—' Josh began.

'I live by myself,' Cat preempted.

'Who's keeping the home fire burning?' Josh probed, peering through the windscreen wipers swiping at full speed.

'I have gas central heating,' Cat replied primly, now knowing exactly what he was searching for and wanting to deflect further investigation as politely as she could.

'Got a boyfriend, then?' Josh asked her.

'Yes,' Cat proclaimed. 'You?' It was a fair question to put to a man with fine features and closely cropped hair, who marvelled at bike boys.

Josh, however, swerved. 'I'm bloody *married*,' he said defensively. Initially, his information pleased Cat, made her feel safe and relieved. Then it worried her.

Oh shit, is he coming on to me? I'd better ask about his wife. Thank God I lied about having a boyfriend.

'How does your wife feel about you being away so much?'

Why the fuck did I say 'Yes I have a boyfriend'?

'That's cycling,' Josh shrugged.

'Par for the course,' Cat defined, 'riders and writers and mechanics alike, hey? A life on the road. Presence of partners rare, discouraged even.'

'Exactly,' Josh replied. 'How does your bloke feel about you being out here? Surrounded by menfolk away from their womenfolk?'

'He's not bothered,' Cat said quickly, wondering quite what Josh was trying to ascertain, 'he knows that consummate athletes have very low levels of testosterone.'

Josh roared with laughter. '*Should* have! We're in *cycling* – the levels *should* be low but most of the peloton probably have pretty normal levels.'

'Hmm,' Cat acted, holding her finger to her lip in exaggerated contemplation, 'how can that be? Can you imagine! If all that training *depletes* their testosterone level to that of a *normal* man – imagine their levels if they *weren't* pro cyclists. Stallions!'

'Oh my God,' Josh feigned, 'Cat McCabe, is that sarcasm? You wouldn't be suggesting that their testosterone levels are unnaturally enhanced?'

'*Doping*?' Cat gasped theatrically. 'In cycling?'

'Where does medical care end and doping begin?' Josh said with a serious edge. 'Low testosterone can cause osteoporosis.'

'Too true,' Cat replied honestly, 'let's not talk about it.'

'You sound like the UCI,' said Josh accusatorially, referring to an accusation frequently levelled at cycling's international governing body.

'Doping is cheating,' Cat defined, 'but health is another matter altogether. How does the UCI set this arbitrary level? They're saying that if the cyclists take stuff to boost their levels to within a hair's breadth of the set line, it's not doping. But they're taking stuff – period.'

'There's the rub,' Josh said, 'let's not talk about it.'

'More banned substances than any other sport,' Cat continued quietly, looking out of the window at wheatfields winking in the sudden sun after the rain, 'and more dope controls too. Let's not talk about it. Not today.'

'Sure,' Josh said, 'because there'll be many occasions when we will.'

'Is it still rife?' Cat asked.

'Some do, some don't,' Josh said, 'it's difficult to quantify, what with sophisticated masking agents and the fateful turning of blind eyes – which I would rank as being more criminal than substance abuse itself.'

'Let's not talk about it,' Cat said for him.

Don't fall from grace, heroes mine. Don't shatter my

admiration. Or that of that lovely old boy by the roadside over there with his grandson, waving. Don't bring shame on your beautiful sport. Don't harm yourselves. Ride well. Ride from the heart, but use your heads.

They drove on, noting banal agricultural details of the route that would nevertheless add essential colour to their reports.

At least I've deflected attention away from my love life.

'Anyway,' Josh said, 'before diving off on such an unsavoury tangent, I do believe we were talking about testosterone and your bloke.'

'Who?'

'Your boyfriend.'

No he's not. Not any more. I don't have a boyfriend. I've lied and I don't know why and I don't know how to get out of it.

Cat, you should say something. Your silence is too loaded. Josh might read into it; might think he's in with a chance if that's what he's into.

'Does he not mind you being in such a vastly male-dominated world?'

'Oh,' said Cat, noticing with great interest that the blue tone to the land had changed to lime green over the last few miles, 'I can look after myself.'

Get yourself out of it – tell him 'Actually, we just broke up'. Say 'Sorry, Josh, I don't know why I said that because, in truth, my boyfriend left me'.

Yes, but if I do, he'll know I'm available. It will be hassle I don't need and I'll be judged on my sex first, my journalistic skill second.

Luckily for Cat, Josh was suddenly far more interested in the race report coming through on Radio Tour. 'Did you hear that?' he asked, turning up the volume. 'Fabian Ducasse and the Viper boys are still at the front – I don't know why they're putting on pressure today.'

'It's probably like an army parading tanks and weaponry,' said Cat. Josh agreed.

'One six three,' Josh said, quoting riders' numbers off the radio, 'thirty-one, seventy-five.'

Cat checked her list of riders. 'Thirty-one is Cipo,' she said, 'seventy-five – Tom Steels. Hey! 163! Go Travis!' she cheered for the victor of the first hot-spot sprint. With the memory still vivid of Hunter Dean's wink, of her quote from Luca Jones, US Megapac had swiftly become her personal team.

'Stanton's good,' Josh nodded, 'maybe not quite a Stage winner but his riding's already respected.'

'Look at this road,' Cat remarked. It ribboned out before them, seemingly for miles, straight and mostly flat.

'Meaning?' Josh tested.

Why are you still testing me, Josh?

Why not ask him?

No. I'll just answer him. Obviously I still need to earn my wings.

'Well, a road like this hardly encourages anyone to attack – it would be much ado about nothing. The pack would just watch such a rider peg off. He might manage around 45 kph but the bunch could stream after him at 60. Of course, there was that Stage where—'

'Jesus!' Josh whispered, his hand on the volume control. Cat concentrated hard.

'Fuck!' she exclaimed. Josh had been about to say the same.

'Two-thirds of the bunch have gone down,' he murmured.

'Shit!' said Cat and Josh in unison.

Gratitude to God spread through the sixth of the peloton ahead of the crash like a united whisper. Luca Jones, however, thanked Rudyard Kipling. Walt Disney, rather. *The Jungle Book* was still his favourite film (joint first with *The Exorcist*, followed closely by *9½ Weeks*). He especially loved the scene where Kaa hypnotizes Baloo. He had been riding in the middle of the bunch when the magnetic pull of the nine Système Vipère riders leading the race had lured him through the pack. The Viper boys rode in a long sinewy formation, taking turns at the front to confront the headwind before peeling off to take a rest in the slipstream of the eight team-mates. Judging the wind like migratory birds flying long haul, they chevroned themselves across the road when the wind decreed it. It was textbook team riding. To ride in such formation brings a rhythmic security, even a certain vicarious peace. To observe a team working so adeptly is thrilling – for spectator, seasoned hack or fellow racer. And so it was for Luca Jones. With the 'Bear Necessities' song on his mind, his eyes were drawn to the snakes slithering around the lycra torsos of the accomplished team. His *directeur* would want to know what the fuck he was doing, taking chances at the front, especially after his tumble the previous day. Hunter and Travis would have liked him to have looked over his shoulder to locate them. What if they needed him? But Luca was fixated on Système Vipère. For a few miles, he eschewed his Megapac colours and imagined himself to be a Viper Boy, a member of the highest-ranked team in the world. He did not feel a traitor to Megapac but an honoured young citizen of the peloton. The fantasy not only sustained him on the long, arduous Stage, it kept him out of danger too.

'How on earth does one relate the drama of six hours, twenty-four minutes and sixteen seconds in only 500 words?' Cat complained, mainly to herself but loud enough to amuse Alex and touch Josh.

'Practice,' Alex defined.

'Passion,' Josh added.

COPY FOR P. TAVERNER @ GUARDIAN SPORTS DESK FROM CATRIONA McCABE IN VUILLARD

Chris Boardman gladly relinquished his yellow jersey today. On a day when crashes made nightmares of the dreams of a handful of key riders in the Tour de France, Jesper Lomers won the 260 km second Stage from Rouen to Vuillard and took the yellow jersey. 'He's welcome to it,'

Boardman said. 'Sprint mayhem and mass pile-ups? I'd rather make it to Paris in one piece.' With the long straight roads which dominated the Stage discouraging lone attacks, the peloton surged forward together at a high speed, riders occasionally going for a sortie at the front merely to give their fresh legs a stretch and their sponsors a few metres' exposure before slipping back to the pack. A touch of brakes can cost a rider up to twenty places, but to keep off the brakes keeps the pace fast and dangerous. As the peloton journeyed from Rouen through the Eure to Calvados, a consistent north-easterly wind propelled the bunch even faster and Lomers won a clean sprint to take the Stage in 6 hours, 24 minutes and 16 seconds. Consuming two out of the three intermediary sprint bonuses, Cipollini retains the green jersey on points, today resplendent in matching shorts.

For five riders, the Tour de France ended way before the Stage finish in the heart of Basse-Normande. Jalabert and Olano most notable among them, retired gracefully. Pietro Calcaterra, an esteemed domestique for Zucca MV and key lead-out man for Stefano Sassetta, was scraped off the road and helped back to his team car, too devastated to cry. He had landed heavily on a knee already bandaged from his collision with Kelme's Fernando Escartin yesterday. 'Though the pain from his knee must be excruciating, it doesn't even register against the agony he feels at the termination of his race,' said Rachel McEwen, his soigneur.

Lomers's victory is a popular one. Though the crowds love Stefano Sassetta for his flamboyance, it wins him few friends in the peloton. Jesper Lomers, universally respected, may find that his triumph today is redefined by Sassetta as a veritable gauntlet. Demoted yesterday for dangerous riding and held up today by the crashes, Sassetta will be tasting blood tomorrow; primed, charged and desperate for a good ride.

<ENDS>

'Brilliant!' Cat says quietly to herself, stretching her fingers out and glancing around the *salle de presse*, the majority with heads down, cigarettes hanging from lips, fingers scooting in organized chaos across keyboards. 'I'm pretty pleased with that. I had a good day. I hope Rachel likes her soundbite. Oh God, poor Pietro Calcaterra.'

Poor Pietro Calcaterra indeed. But his girlfriend was waiting for him at the team hotel. Her tenderness dressed his injuries far more curatively than the stitches from the Zucca MV doctor; her support settled his psyche much more quickly than his meeting with his *directeur*; her embrace was infinitely more soothing than Rachel's massage.

Poor Jesper Lomers, therefore. On paper, as all the journalists were busy lauding, Jesper won not just the Stage but the yellow jersey too. However, though he has a wife, she is not here. Nor was she at home. She had left no message on his mobile phone. Jesper craved her congratulatory embrace but he had to settle for his *directeur*'s praise, his team's delight, the deluge of attention from the media. Though Jules Le Grand did not particularly like Anya Lomers, banned mere girlfriends of riders from the Tour and actively disapproved of the presence of wives during the race, today he would have welcomed her. The key sprinter of his Système Vipère team should be euphoric, buoyed by his victory and hungry to keep the *maillot jaune* for the team. Instead, Jules observed him at the team supper looking detached.

If I offered him the maillot jaune *in one hand*, Jules contemplated, *his wife in the other, I fear I know which he'd choose. Wives are more disruptive, more harmful to my Viper Boys than the crashes. They can cause my riders more pain, more suffering, than back-to-back mountain Stages.*

'Women!' he hissed with venom under his breath.

Fabian Ducasse heard him. *Women indeed!* he smirked to himself. *I am Ducasse. I am a national hero. I can have any woman I want.*

*

Système Vipère are having supper when Cat gathers her laptop and cables and goes to send her article down the line.

What a day!

She returns to the main hall and searches out Josh.

'Coffee?' she asks.

'Can't,' he says, looking frazzled.

'Alex?' she offers. He's typing so hard he does not answer, so she does not press.

'I'm through,' she says apologetically to Josh who regards her accusatorially as if she can't possibly be a bona fide *journaliste* then.

'Lucky you,' he says, not unkindly.

'I thought I'd phone *Maillot*,' Cat whispers, 'see if they'll take an article. I so want that Feature Editor position, I thought some earnestness now wouldn't go amiss.'

Alex and Josh nod politely but she sees they're too engrossed in their work to be especially interested in her career development so she goes to the hotel to make her call.

'Sutcliffe.'

'Andy? This is Cat – um, McCabe.'

'Hi Cat, how's the Tour?'

'Fine, brilliant – have you seen my daily reports?'

'All two of them?'

'Oh. Um. Well – I've had an idea for an article for *Maillot*, can I run it past you?'

'Are you sucking up to me?'

'No! Well – I'm serious. About the job – I know I don't have it yet, that I have to earn my position, I know I'm out here for the *Guardian*, but I'm thinking ahead, thinking laterally.'

'Shoot.'

'Well,' Cat clears her voice and wonders whether this conversation is as bad an idea as foisting even more work upon herself, 'how about an interview with Rachel McEwen – Megapac's *soigneur*?'

'I know who Rachel McEwen is,' Andy replies in a tone of

voice Cat can't really decipher, 'but I don't think it's fleshy enough.'

'OK, not an interview,' says Cat, not wanting to sound disheartened but not wanting to sound like she's clutching at straws either, 'how about an article on *soigneurs*?'

'I've asked Josh to do something along those lines.'

'*Female soigneurs*?' Cat specifies.

'There are only two.'

'Women in cycling?'

'Why don't we discuss your ideas after the Tour?' Andy suggests. 'See how it goes.' There's not a lot Cat can say to this. She nods at her hotel room walls and says OK as brightly as she can.

I'm not going to give up. Nor am I going to be fobbed off. I'm going to formulate my ideas and bloody bombard Maillot *again. Before the end of the Tour.*

It was nine thirty. Neither Josh nor Alex were in their rooms but, aware that she was sharing the hotel with Megapac, her confidence and determination in fact bolstered by her potential future boss's rejection, Cat left her room and, eschewing the lifts, meandered along the corridors as if that was the way to reception anyway. She was on a quote hunt; not quite brave enough to phone specific riders' rooms, she was hoping to come across them accidentally-on-purpose.

She should have known that Megapac, by this hour, would mostly be asleep. She would not have known that Luca and his room-mate Didier LeDucq were deep in the pages of *Penthouse* and a Dutch magazine that made the former look like the *Beano*, but as all doors were shut, she was saved this unsavoury revelation. She found herself in reception with no real purpose at all. However, a huge rumble from her stomach suddenly gave her one. The humiliation of Ben York's presence was almost enough to make Cat want to march purposefully back to her room but her hunger and his hypnotic eyes kept her exactly where she was.

121

'Jesus,' he said, 'was that thunder?'

Cat swallowed down an embarrassed laugh but this lacked the substance and nutrition that her stomach needed so it groaned again, loudly in protest.

'Yes,' said Cat, surprisingly cool, 'there it goes again.'

'I was going to the bar for a quick drink,' Ben said. 'Do you want to join me?'

'OK,' said Cat, hoping she looked neither keen nor shy, for suddenly she was feeling a very odd combination of both. She was following Ben, just about to make small talk, when her phone rang. She stopped, Ben turned to her. She shrugged and regarded her handset.

Fen. It's bloody Fen. No, not bloody at all. I have to take it.
Take it then.

'Aren't you going to take it?' Ben asked, not moving a discreet distance away, if anything leaning towards her, appearing closer, invasive almost.

'Hullo?' Cat said.

'Hullo!' Fen replied.

'Hey girly!' Pip cried, from another extension. 'We're a bit drunk. We want to know about lycra.'

Oh God, thought Cat, holding the phone tight against her ear in the hope that her sisters' voices were not transmittable to Ben who continued to stand close.

'Please can you explain what on earth is going on?' Fen asked.

'And can you tell us what the jerseys are *actually* for?' Pip interjected. 'And why that gorgeous Dutchman took the yellow one from Chris Boardman today?'

Oh God, thought Cat, *I don't want to explain such rudimentary details. Not here, not now. Not at this time of night.*

Not in front of Dr York?

What's he got to do with it?

What's the time got to do with it? It's hardly late. What you mean is, you'd rather drink with your doctor than speak with your sisters.

122

Bollocks. He's not my doctor. He's physician to US Megapac.

'How exactly do you *win* the Tour de France?' Fen was asking.

'Um,' Cat replied, 'what is it you don't understand?'

Don't turn your back on Ben, it's rude.

Yes, but so is hovering. See? I've now turned my back and he hasn't budged. It's a bit – odd.

So move.

I can't – it's a bit odd.

'What exactly *is* the yellow jersey?' Pip all but whined.

'*Et le maillot vert*,' Fen said extravagantly, 'oh, and that spotted one too.'

I'm not going to look at you, Ben. Stop it. I'm going to stare at your shoes and speak to my sisters.

'At the end of each day, the race leader – the yellow jersey – is the rider who has spent the least amount of time in the saddle so far in the Tour,' Cat said, trying to infuse her voice with a tone that would inform any eavesdroppers that she was having to assist some imbecilic person with no knowledge of the grand sport. She knew Ben was regarding her unwaveringly. For a split second, Cat wondered whether her answer had been wrong.

Go away, Dr York. This is not a good time. You're off-putting.

'And the green?' Pip was asking. '*Vert*?'

'Each day,' Cat explained, 'there are points to be won at hot spot sprints along the route, as well as finishing in the top twenty-five. The green jersey is thus for the most points, for the most consistent daily finisher. It's the second most important accolade. Cipollini took sprint points along the way today, plus finished high – giving him green. Lomers has the fastest time – a further twenty seconds were deducted for him winning the Stage today – hence the yellow.'

Oh. Ben. You're going.

'So he'll wear it tomorrow?' Fen asked. 'He's winning?'

'Who?' said Cat, noticing that Ben was wearing a very nice polo shirt which caught his shoulder blades most becomingly.

'The flying Dutchman?' Fen prompted.

'Yes,' Cat expounded, 'yellow is supreme.'

Is that the bar through there? Should I move in a bit?

'And the dotty?' said Pip, correcting it to 'spotty' to prevent insinuation from either sister.

'Each day, the hills are marked according to their steepness,' Cat explained most informatively. 'Today, as yesterday, there were only fourth-category climbs. Climbing points are awarded to the riders reaching the tops first. Hence our David wearing the King of the Mountains jersey at this stage in the race.'

Maybe I should go back to my room and just order room service.

'Who's "our David"?' Pip asked in a whisper as if, unbeknown to her, he might be related.

'David Millar is a British rider in the French team Cofidis,' Cat elaborated. 'He's not a specialist climber but a very promising *rouleur* – all-rounder. At this stage in the Tour, the hills are not taxing enough to be the exclusive domain of the *grimpeurs*, the specialist climbers, who are wiser to save their energy and steer clear of trouble in anticipation of the main mountain Stages later.'

If I say 'I'd better go now', they'll ask why. If I tell them, they'll make me go to the bar and not my room.

'So it's fifteen minutes of fame for Our David,' said Pip.

'I think he'll have more than that,' Cat said, 'just you watch him in the Time Trials.'

'Not another bloody jersey,' said Fen.

'No,' said Cat, 'no jersey for Time Trials.'

'I think we understand,' said Pip, 'do we?'

'Yes,' said Fen, 'we'll ring Django and tell him. Who should we look for in tomorrow's Stage?'

'I'd better go now,' said Cat.

'Why?' said Pip. 'It's our call – we don't mind.'

'I'd better go to my room,' said Cat, who'd noticed that the bar was filling up.

'Why?' Fen probed.

'Where are you?' Pip asked.

'In the foyer,' Cat said, a little deflated, 'near the bar.'

Both her sisters were silent.

'So?' said Fen.

'Sounds good,' Pip commented.

'Don't you scurry away,' Fen said, 'you're no mouse, Cat.'

'I know that,' Cat remonstrated, 'but it's a tough call, trying to carve a niche in unfamiliar territory – especially in a new world where everyone but me seems so at home, so *au fait* with the routine.'

'But you said they're a friendly bunch,' Fen said.

'He is,' said Cat, quickly changing it to 'They are.'

Back in England, Fen winked at Pip who grinned back.

'Who is *he*?' Pip whispered.

'Just a team doctor,' Cat whispered back.

'Just!' Pip shrieked.

'Just have a drink,' Fen said nonchalantly, glowering at her sister who was doing a jubilant handstand against the wall.

'OK,' said Cat, who quite liked being told what to do.

Cat has switched her phone off. She has taken two deep breaths. It took courage not to go back to her room. It's going to require pluck to walk in to the bar. In she goes. There he is. He's sitting on a small settee in front of a low table. He is sipping from a bottle of beer. Cat doesn't really want to notice that he has lovely forearms.

'Sorry about that,' says Cat, 'my sisters are watching the Tour for the first time.'

'And they are calling on your expertise,' Ben reasons, 'can't say I blame them.' He smiles at her. It is unclear to Cat whether this is a compliment for her knowledge, or a critique on the vagaries of the Tour de France rules.

'Let me get you a beer,' Ben says, going to the bar before

Cat can say she'd prefer a glass of wine. He comes back with a bottle of Kronenbourg 1664. 'Some advice,' Ben says, whether she wants it or not, holding the bottle aloft, 'if you want to impress, you abbreviate it to *Seize*.'

Do I want to impress? Cat wonders.

Of course you do. Sip *Seize* sexily, Cat. Ben does so quite inadvertently.

He does. He keeps his eyes on me while he swigs, they narrow slightly. They open when he licks his top lip.

Ben York is interested in Cat. He asks her many questions. The beer is cool and fizzy and, for Cat, on an empty stomach, pleasantly tongue-freeing. She answers him happily and slips in questions of her own. First about Megapac. Then about Luca. Soon enough about Ben. Momentarily, she is disappointed that it was not a love of cycling that saw him search out such a job, but she is impressed that his reputation as a physician saw Megapac approach him. Anyway, he speaks with enthusiasm and in depth about the sport and he is a kindred spirit for sure. Ben is friendly and attentive and she wonders whether he is flirting with her. She tells herself she must be imagining it, that it must be the beer. Certainly, it's something of a novelty for her. It's refreshing for Cat, having been the brunt of constant criticism and no praise for such a long time.

I'm in France. On the Tour. Away from home. Away for the summer. Away from Him. I'm glad I came. I'm pleased I didn't go back to my room.

'*Croque monsieur, mademoiselle?*' Ben asks, raising an eyebrow which seems to insist his lips part.

'Only if you have one too,' Cat says, really quite coyly. They allow a look between them to linger before Ben grins and Cat grins back. He goes to the bar to order and her eyes follow him before she glances around the room as if to see who has observed. There are quite a few people but none seem remotely aware of or interested in her presence or the chemistry she feels she and Ben surely must have been exuding like a visible glow. He returns.

'Do you like olives?' he asks.

'I love olives,' Cat enthuses.

Ben leans towards her with a dish of olives; black, green, stuffed, glistening with oil, permeated with garlic, enhanced with rosemary.

'Excuse me,' says Cat, her thumb and forefinger hovering before selecting a particularly plump specimen.

'What for?' says Ben.

'No,' says Cat, still chewing, standing up, 'I mean, excuse me but I'm going to the toilet.'

She takes a stone from her mouth and plinks it daintily in the ashtray. Off she goes, trying to walk slowly, trying not to wiggle, or wondering if she does indeed wiggle and whether it's becoming. She sits in the cubicle and regards left hand and right hand like Fen tends to – but she has no dilemma on her hands, she is not searching for advice or answers. She just wants to collect herself, calm down and return to the bar, to Ben's restorative and compelling company. When she washes her hands, she catches sight of herself in the mirror. She gives herself a little shrug, a little smile.

It's OK. This. It's good. I'm having a great evening. I think he really is flirting with me. I'm not sure. It's been a while. Is he?

Go back and see.

Oh. Alex and Josh are sitting by Ben. Eating olives. Drinking *Seize*. Oh.

'Hey, Cat,' Alex says, a little dishevelled in the hair and somewhat wild about the eyes.

'*Finito completo*,' says Josh, who looks utterly exhausted.

'Hullo, guys,' says Cat, taking her seat, glancing at Ben and wondering if that really was a glimmer of a remorseful shrug he's just given her. 'I'm having *croque monsieur*,' she announces as if her fellow press men had been pondering a reason for her presence at the table with Ben and his olives and the strong beer.

'So are we,' says Josh.

They eat. They talk. Cat concentrates only on Josh and Alex, studiously avoiding any eye contact, any direct anything, with Ben, though she so wants to. Ben, however, ensures he speaks to Cat directly; he buys her another beer, he even answers on her behalf.

'No,' he tells Josh, 'the guy at *Maillot* didn't seem very interested in her ideas for an article on female *soigneurs*.'

Josh yawned. 'Shit,' he said, 'I forgot to phone home.'

Cat wonders whether this has been said for her benefit and wonders again whether Josh has designs on her. And she wonders if she has designs on Ben and whether it's presumptuous or OK for her to wonder whether this is reciprocated. And then she thinks what utter nonsense. This is the Tour de France. It's work. Her livelihood. Absolutely no room for anything else.

'Beer?' Alex asks.

Ben yawns. 'I'd better push some zeds,' he says.

'Pardon?' Cat says.

'You know,' Ben explains, with a chuckle at his wit, touching her arm, 'like a cartoon character asleep with "z"s coming out of their mouth.'

Cat finds this funny. So do Alex and Josh. But Cat laughs longer, and more loudly. In fact, she gives Ben's knee a quick push and wonders whether that's OK. It felt OK to do it. More than OK. Was it OK for it to be felt by Ben? Witnessed by the other two?

Can't we stay a while longer?

Alex stands and stretches and blasphemes whilst yawning. Josh rises too and does the same, without the choice epithets. Ben stands up. He doesn't yawn but he clasps the back of his neck drawing Cat's eyes to his elbows before they meet his. Cat is disappointed.

Please stay. I'm enjoying myself. This is what I was hoping for, camaraderie. Colleagues becoming friends. That we'd work hard and earn evenings like this.

Exactly. You're all here working. So there will be tomorrow. Indeed, just under three weeks of tomorrows.

'Night all,' Ben says, heading for the stairs.

'Later!' says Josh, as is his wont.

'See you,' says Alex through a yawn, pressing for the lift.

'Night, Ben,' Cat says, though he has now gone.

'I think you've pulled there,' Alex goads, leaning against the mirror in the lift, regarding Cat quizzically.

'Don't be a wanker,' says Josh, rubbing his eyes, his bristled chin, 'she's got a boyfriend back home.'

STAGE 3
Vuillard–Plumelec. 225 kilometres

I *don't want Josh to fancy me and I don't want Josh to tell Ben*, thought Cat, quite urgently when waking with a start in the early hours. *I don't want Ben to think that I have a boyfriend. Because, of course, I do not. Oh. But that means I actively want Ben to know I'm single. If I fancy Ben, which I do, it must mean that I now feel single. If I'm feeling single, it is the lid on the coffin of my time with* Him. *To fancy another, to want another, to be with another, would symbolize the ultimate sealing nail in that coffin. How do I feel about all that?*

Her meanderings led her to a thick sleep for a couple of hours. She awoke again, still way before dawn.

Fancying Ben might allow me to bury my past relationship, those intrusive memories and my deluded hopes of Him. *That would be wise.*

Cat slept for an hour more and then rose before six thirty.

Bullshit, Cat. Ben has no purpose, nothing to do with Him *back home. The point – and it is indisputable – is that I fancy Ben, full stop. He turns me on. I want him.*

She rummaged around her rucksack and laid out a selection of her clothing in various configurations. Really, it was far too early to start dressing. The riders would not be signing on until 10.30. Cat therefore had four hours to decide what to wear and she tried on a number of alternatives. Soon enough she was sitting despondent on her bed, in a mismatched bra and knickers. She took her mobile phone and dialled.

'Hullo?' Fen was startled. It was an hour earlier in GMT after all. An early phone call was often a harbinger of death, of doom at the very least.

'It's me,' Cat whispered, fearing the walls might be thin enough to entitle her neighbours access to her revelations.

'Jesus, what's up?' Fen asked.

'Up?' Cat replied, concerned at her sister's tone.

'It's so early – are you OK?' Fen persisted.

'Oh shit!' Cat exclaimed, the time difference dawning on her. 'I'm fine. I just wanted to call. To say hullo.'

'I see,' said Fen measuredly.

'Um,' Cat faltered, 'also for some advice.'

'Advice?' Fen asked. 'About—?'

'What to wear today?' Cat said meekly, peeping through the curtains and assessing the flat but dry prelude to dawn.

'What to *wear*?' Fen repeated, looking out the window to a rain-dressed pavement. Fen contemplated her sister's loaded silence and wondered if Cat could sense that, back in Camden, she was grinning. 'What to wear,' Fen repeated, this time as a statement. 'Tell me it's the doctor and not some oily bike boy,' Fen whispered with glee.

'It's the doctor,' said Cat, eyes squeezed shut as if a revelation out loud might ultimately jeopardize the actuality of a currently non-existent situation. 'Do you think that's OK?'

'More than OK,' said Fen, 'it's about time.'

'I thought of my khaki shorts,' said Cat.

'What's his name and age and vital stats?' Fen asked. 'Khaki sounds good.'

'And my little stretchy vest from Gap Kids,' Cat furthered.

'Ben York, probably a few years older than us, tall but not too tall – handsome, oh yes, very.'

'I like your stretchy vest from Gap Kids but what's the weather like? Perhaps add a white shirt, loosely tied not buttoned,' said Fen. 'So where is he from? Does he speak English?'

'I have that great shirt that Pip gave me,' said Cat, taking it from the pile on her bed and holding it to her nose. 'He's British but lives in America.'

'That's no good,' Fen groaned.

'The white shirt?' Cat asked, scouring the pile for an alternative.

'No – the America bit,' said Fen, 'an intense three weeks in France and then what?'

'I hadn't thought that far ahead,' Cat said, 'it's nice just to feel those feelings of, well, lust – anticipation. Have we decided on the white shirt?'

'Yes,' Fen declared. 'Is there chemistry?'

'I think so,' said Cat cautiously, hoping that she had neither misread nor read too much in to what she believed had been a mutual frisson, 'it's been a long time for me. Timberland boots or trainers?'

'Sweet girl,' said Fen, 'I wish you all the luck and lust you'll have time for once your reports have been filed. But be careful – it's the Tour de France, you're not living in real time or a real place. In reality, Cat, you need a *fling*. You deserve fun and frolics. He sounds perfect. Fling Thing. He sounds,' said Fen, 'pretty gorgeous. Timberlands.'

'His name is Ben York,' Cat remonstrated, 'and you're making him sound like a cheap package holiday. Timberlands it is, then.'

'He'll do you the same power of good – a golden tan from the sun equates with the healthy glow of a well-laid woman,' Fen theorized earnestly.

'Fen!' Cat giggled. 'What are you *like*? You loose lady, you – you who can't decide between two – have you chosen yet?'

'No,' Fen said sadly after a long reflection. 'Tell me more about Ben.'

'He has odd eyes,' Cat said with a swoon.

'Odd?' Fen reacted, imagining one brown, one blue, perhaps cross-eyed or else one lazy and staring.

'I mean,' said Cat, '*strange* – they're the colour of Cadbury's Dairy Milk and they hold your gaze.'

'Think about your underwear,' said Fen. 'Not that he should be seeing it quite yet but your deportment is directly accountable to the pants you wear.'

'He has odd hair,' said Cat. 'I'll wear my Calvins.'

'Odd?' Fen asked, imagining a ginger bonce of unruly curls not dissimilar to the wig Pip wore when she became Martha the Clown.

'Short,' said Cat, 'dark but not really – heavily flecked through with light.'

'You mean,' Fen deduced, 'he's going grey prematurely. Well, George Bloody Clooney watch your back! Calvins – definitely.'

'I think he likes me,' Cat said. 'I won't bother with a bra – my Gap Kids vest is supportive enough. And clingy.'

'Go girl!' Fen marvelled. 'Of course he bloody likes you – why on earth wouldn't he? Can I tell Pip?'

'Isn't that tempting Fate?'

'Bollocks, Cat,' Fen laughed, 'have a little confidence.'

'I lost it a while back.'

'No!' Fen said sternly. 'It was stolen from you. You're entitled to its return. Can I tell Pip?'

'OK!' Cat laughed. 'Tell her about his eyes – and that he's a doctor and all.'

'Can I tell Django?'

'Wouldn't that be bad karma?' Cat asked. Fen, who felt more for karma than she did for fate, pondered this quietly. 'Tell you what,' Cat said, 'if Sassetta wins the Stage today, you can tell Django.'

'Better make that the *maillot vert*, Cat,' Fen said very seriously. 'If he scoops up the intermediary sprints and finishes higher than Cipollini, he needn't win the Stage to claim the jersey.'

Cat smiled. Her sister had caught the bug. There was no cure. It was in her blood. She would never be rid of it.

Where's Ben? Dr York – ou es tu? And can I 'tu' you or ought I to 'vous' you? You're not with the Megapac entourage.

Cat was milling about the teams enclosure with hundreds of other journalists, Tour and team personnel.

Oh, there's Mario Cipollini.

'Mario! *Ça va?*'

'*Buon giorno!*' said Cipollini whilst wondering who this girl was who greeted him with such warmth and familiarity. How charming. 'I'm well – today SuperMario to be LionKing again – *compris?*'

'Oh, *compris* very well, Cipo,' said Cat, not giving the abbreviation a second's thought. '*Bonne chance.*'

'*Merci, grazie,*' said the flamboyant Italian before brandishing his best English, 'thank you so very much, *signorina.*'

Cat brazenly waved her hand as if to say heck, Mario, don't mention it. Off she went in search of Dr York, smiling directly at Laurent Dufaux on her way. Jan Svorada, Jose Maria Jimenez, Jacky Durand all raised a hand at a girl they had never met, who was wearing a pair of shorts as flattering as her smile and who gave them salutations of great feeling as she strode past.

Where are you, Dr York? Might you be in the village? I'll go and check. Bugger off, Alex, I'm on a mission. I'm thirsty. Ah, the Maison du Café stand. I'll have an espresso, please. Merci beaucoup. *Good God – Eddie Merckx – good God himself.*

'*Bonjour,* Monsieur Merckx.'

'*Eh? Ah oui – bonjour, mademoiselle.*'

'*Café?*'

'*Pour moi? Merci.*'

Don't mention it. It's on tap. I can get another. Where are you, Ben? I'll circumnavigate once. Well, if that's Luca, his doctor surely must be close to hand.

'Hey, Luca,' Cat beamed, 'how are you? Bloody good ride yesterday.'

'Thanks, babe,' said Luca, delighted to see her but wracking his brains for her name and squinting behind his Oakleys to try and read it from her pass.

'Any thoughts on today?' Cat asked.

Any idea where your doctor is?

'Well, Catriona,' said Luca, most pleased with himself, 'it's a weird finish – you hit Plumelec and then have to do a 12 k circuit before an uphill home stretch. Not really sprinter's domain – but if anyone wants to win it more than Delongue, whose birthday it is, it'll be Sassetta – he's out to kill, man, out to kill. You know what I mean, Catriona?'

'Luca,' Cat reprimanded the rider lightly, 'you really can call me Cat. You take care today.'

And tell your bloody doctor I'm looking for him.

Luca tipped his head. 'Thanks,' he said. Cat's 'Take care' was so much more humane than the perfunctory 'Good luck' from most journalists. 'Come find me at the finish – I'll give you the scoop of the day!'

'That, Luca, would be an honour,' said Cat. 'Promise?'

Make sure your bloody doctor's there.

'Sure,' Luca shrugged. He tipped his Oakleys on to his forehead, flashed excellent teeth, held out his hand and kissed Cat's when she took it.

If I feel this floaty from Luca's kiss to my hand, how am I going to feel when Ben takes my mouth?

With Stefano Sassetta, he of the spectacular thighs, on the war path for a Stage win, or the green jersey, potentially both, Cat and her fellow journalists took the *itinéraire direct* to the *salle de presse* in Plumelec to scrutinize the race from the bank of televisions there. On the way, they pooled notes about the buildings changing in colour from grey to beige, that the small town of Josselin with its stunning river-hugging château and sharp right-hand bend over a narrow bridge was worthy of mention, that rosebay willowherb and other meadow flowers were abundant and that the villages became increasingly bedecked with bunting and Breton flags.

In the *salle de presse*, one of the technicians tested the microphone with a lengthy impression of an orgasm. While most of the 1,000 press men shared a titter, the dozen female *journalistes* bonded immediately by locating each other to share eyebrows raised in exasperation. Having grabbed and then bolted down baguette and pâté from the buffet, Cat sat and allowed the live pictures of the peloton to seduce her, to mesmerize her. Had Ben York appeared, bollock naked with a rose between his teeth, Cat would have given him but a cursory glance and requested that he return later.

The bravery of a breakaway, the beauty of the bunch streaming along to bring them back. I love watching the Tour aerially – a flock of geese, a shoal of fish, a single arrow – the comparisons are poetic. When seen from above, the pack moves as one, surging along harmonious and unified. See them approach that roundabout?

Cat's lips parted as she watched the bunch split and streak around either side of a flower-encrusted roundabout before fusing together again and streaming ahead. Like mercury.

And yet, an aerial view of the Tour, aesthetically moving as it is, is somewhat misleading. Looking down on the peloton from on high, it is easy to forget that this apparently single mass is in fact 189 riders – oh, down to 184 – jockeying for position, shouting and swearing, psyching each other out.

Cat contemplated the fact that this beautiful streak of colour, skating along the tarmac, slicking around corners, enhancing the Breton countryside and the lives of the native spectators, was made up of each man turning his pedals, watching his line, monitoring his pulse, pacing himself, performing his job for his team, his sponsors, making it a day closer to Paris, surviving to ride another day, period.

Twenty-one teams. 184 individuals at present. The peloton of the Tour de France. A river of bright energy when seen from above. Down there, in the bunch, in reality: war.

With over 100 kilometres to go, Megapac's Hunter Dean and Travis Stanton grouped together with three other riders and shot away from the peloton.

'Fuck, it's humid, man,' said Travis.

'Wind's behind,' Hunter replied encouragingly, taking the front. The five-man break kept their heads down and pedalled with conviction.

Back in the bunch, Stefano Sassetta summonsed his team car. 'Who's gone?' he asked his *directeur*. 'What do you want me to do?'

'No one for you to worry about,' his *directeur* answered him, 'let them have the last sprint point. They'll tire soon enough. They're nothing. Some Americanos – let them fly their flag a while.' Sassetta made his way back through the bunch, catching sight of the yellow-clad back of Jesper Lomers. He felt his blood chill and then immediately boil. He pedalled until they were shoulder to shoulder. The Dutchman was looking studiously ahead. Apart from gesture, English was the only language in which these two riders could communicate.

'Enjoy your shirt,' Sassetta hissed, 'you no have it long time. Green suit me only anyway. Bad with your hair colour.'

Jesper regarded Stefano briefly and then returned his concentration directly ahead. Jesper had no intention of reacting. It was not his style. He was a sportsman. For him, manners were integral to his vocation. And his mind was on Anya, who was never at home.

With just over 25 kilometres to go, Travis and another rider dropped back, eased off and returned to the peloton. Hunter and the other two soon hit Plumelec, knowing there were a further 12 kilometres to race. Looking briefly over his shoulder, Hunter knew that the bunch would be on them soon enough but the Stage might, with a miracle, be his. Just. Was it worth riding himself out today? What would be the consequence for his legs tomorrow? There were two Stages later in the race he had earmarked for himself. But the opportunity was here.

'6 k to go – I'm out of here,' he said to himself, summoning up reserves to surge away from the other two. Hunter was riding at 46 kph. With 3 kilometres to go, Hunter's lead was eleven seconds and he was charging along on adrenalin and desire. With just 1 kilometre left, he swept perfectly around the right-hand bend and narrow bridge, stood on his pedals and honked towards the finishing climb.

Then he heard it; it was all he could hear. Not his heart. Not his breathing. Not the yelling crowd. What he could hear he could sense too. He wanted to go forward yet sensed he was being sucked backwards. As his legs and arms felt the drag of the finishing incline, Hunter took a fateful glance over his shoulder. The motion cost him seconds yet he knew the sight he would see was of the deafening, deflating sound that was filling his ears. The peloton of the Tour de France was surging towards him, a swarm in a heat haze with no affection for him, no malice either, but certainly no consideration for the stamina he had exhibited for over 100 kilometres. With dignity intact, Hunter sat up. He was caught. He was back in the bunch. He was anonymous once more.

COPY FOR P. TAVERNER @ GUARDIAN SPORTS DESK FROM CATRIONA McCABE IN PLUMELEC

Mario Cipollini conceded the green jersey to fellow Italian Stefano Sassetta in Stage 3 of the Tour de France. In an uphill finish not conducive to sprints, the powerful Zucca MV rider pumped away from the bunch. As he crossed the line he punched the air, perhaps not so much in ecstasy of the victory as in the sweetness of revenge. He won the Stage; tomorrow he will ride in the green points jersey. Jesper Lomers is in yellow for another day but soon he will relinquish the jersey when the true all-rounders come to the fore. Lomers will no doubt do this with grace and equanimity. He will then focus his efforts on the maillot vert. To claim it will require more than excellent riding – it will demand a certain stoicism to disregard the crowd-pulling arrogance Sassetta displays when flaunting his power in the maillot vert. There will be as much a fight for the green jersey as there will be for the yellow. The Tour de France this year is a duel between Système Vipère and Zucca MV.

Against the verdant verges of cycling's heartland, speckled with rosebay willowherb and throbbing with Breton aficionados, a five-man breakaway led the race in the last 100 km, at one time achieving a 3-minute lead over the pack. A bid for freedom by the US Megapac star Hunter Dean, with 6 km to go and the bunch hot on his heels, was more heart-rending than it was realistic. However, success in the Tour de France can often be achieved with the spirit stronger than the body. If Dean's passion can be maintained, even if the mountains mangle his muscles, he might well shine in one of the final Stages of la grande boucle.

Tomorrow, the 184 riders of the Tour de France will race 248 km from Plouay to Chardin. With wide, flat roads, the winds could well be strong and potentially disruptive. The peloton should devour the tarmac and rebuff the wind with textbook team riding – a pleasure for the spectators to observe but in truth the only way the riders are going to get from A to B as unscathed as possible.

<ENDS>

'Because of the bloody cricket, Taverner gave me only 350 words today,' Cat says petulantly to Josh. 'I chose to slip in the rosebay willowherb, rather than to mention that Millar gave the polka dot jersey to US Postal's Jonathan Vaughters.'

'Alan Titchmarsh will be pleased, but you've probably blown your chance of a ride in the US Postal team car,' Josh said before returning his focus away from horticulture and chit-chat, back to his laptop.

'I'm going out for quotes,' said Cat, leaving.

To try and find Luca. For his promised soundbite. And his doctor. Oh – there's my friend Rachel.

'Hey, Rachel,' said Cat, standing by smiling, watching Rachel wipe down the legs of the team's *super-domestique*, Gianni Fugallo, with a wet flannel.

'Not a good time,' Rachel said, barely looking up. Though momentarily taken aback, Cat quickly reminded herself where she was and why she was there and thus held her hands up in affable surrender, telling Rachel she'd give her a call.

'Cheers,' said Rachel, who was hot and tired, 'that'd be great.'

There's the Megapac lot. Where's Luca? There's Hunter.

'Hullo, Hunter,' says Cat, 'great ride.'

'Hey, thanks,' says Hunter, vaguely recognizing her.

'Yo, Catriono!'

Luca!

'It's Cat,' she says, delighted none the less. 'How are you?'

'I'm good,' he says, looking very tired, his eyes a little bloodshot, their sparkle somewhat dulled, his blond curls slightly lank, 'thanks. Cat.' He approaches her, his hard shoes giving his walk a Chaplinesque gait, and at once she wants to gently put her arms around him, to lead him to a chair, sit him down and put his brave legs up. She notices a fleck of dried spittle on the corner of his mouth, grime on his calves; the paradox of the impressive musculature of his legs against the fragility of his gait which six hours of racing have caused.

He needs his soigneur. *Or his doctor. It always gets me – on his bike, a rider looks so strong. Off it he appears almost vulnerable.*

'Have you a quote for me?' Cat asks.

'Sure,' says Luca, hands on slim hips. 'Where you staying, babe?'

'Plouay,' Cat replies.

'You come round the hotel, to my room, I'll give you soundbites,' Luca says, his accent making her smile more than any ulterior motive detectable.

'That would be great,' Cat enthuses, 'I'll see you later.'

'*Ciao, bambina,*' Luca says.

Cat hovers.

I'd better go. I need the doctor. Where's Ben?

There's Ben. With a woman. She's standing coyly with her back against the truck of that tree. He's standing in front of her, as close to her as he was to Cat yesterday. Not so much invading the woman's space as dominating it. There's a difference – Cat has already experienced it. It's subtle – the former would be undesirable, intrusive. The latter is disconcerting and compelling.

Poor Cat. This is not jealousy but despondency. There's Ben, whom Cat has longed to see all day. But he has not been looking out for her. His attention has been caught by this other woman. Look at them now – Ben has cupped the woman's face in his hands and is looking into her eyes intently. Look at her, all legs that are brown and a face that is perfect. It doesn't matter that she is wearing a minuscule scarlet frou-frou frock, nor that her head is crowned with a ridiculous hat in the shape of a Coke bottle top. The point is, she is a podium girl and she is stunning. Cat is a *journaliste* in a pair of now creased khaki shorts, a vest from a children's department and a white shirt with ink on the cuff and a coffee stain down the front. She is also wearing boots that might very well carry the Timberland seal of authenticity, but objectively they are what her Uncle Django calls 'clodhoppers'.

Oh God. Uncle Django. I told Fen that if Sassetta won, she could tell Django about bloody Ben.

Cat turns her phone off, turns and walks away quickly but not briskly. There is no spring in her step. She takes herself off to an area behind the finish line where officials are busy

141

dismantling the temporary grandstands. She finds a crate and sits down, head in hands.

Shit and double shit. Now everyone at home knows about Ben bloody York – whose attraction for me obviously doesn't exist apart from in my delusions. Josh, whom I like and respect, now knows and defines me by a boyfriend who doesn't exist – which leaves me vulnerable. For Ben York, though, I don't exist.

Cat, you sound adolescent and rather pathetic.

I'm trying to fucking heal, to make my way forward.

Does that take a man? How about Luca then?

Fuck off. He's a rider in the Tour de France. He's super-human. I absolutely wouldn't dare touch him or even encourage him. Think of the consequences.

What about Josh?

I think I'll end up adoring Josh. But for me, there's no possibility there beyond good friendship.

'I'm a *journaliste*,' Cat says softly, repeating it louder. 'I'm here working. I have an idea for an article for *Maillot*. I must phone them.'

Cat returns to the *salle de presse* and phones *Maillot*.

'Hullo, it's Cat McCabe – how about a feature on podium girls?'

'Podium girls?' Andy responds.

'Getting to the substance behind the skirt?' Cat elaborates, a twang of desperation to her voice causing Josh to look up and regard her with a flicker of concern.

'Perhaps,' Andy says. 'OK?'

'OK,' Cat says forlornly, 'podium girls – who the fuck are they?'

'Sure,' says Andy, 'let me think about it.'

STAGE 4
Plouay–Chardin. 248 kilometres

*B*en was concerned about
Didier. Didier LeDucq was an accomplished *domestique*;
professional for four years, he was riding his second Tour de
France in his first season for Megapac.

'What worries me,' Ben said to himself whilst examining
his chin and wondering whether he need shave that
morning, 'is that Didier has been so damn quiet. Over meals
he usually regales the team, all of us, with tales and
anecdotes of his antics on bike and off. Yesterday he was all
but silent. If he's sickening, I wish he'd tell me now.'

*I'd better shave. You never know whom you might come
across.*

Ben was concerned about Hunter Dean. Patting foam
across his bristles, he stared at the vision of Santa Claus in
the mirror. He bared his teeth, observing that they did not
appear unduly yellow next to the shaving foam.

*Hunter is so focused, he feels so much for the team, for the
sponsors and his belief in himself is immense. Good. Great.
But we've only had three days of racing. I can't have him
burn out. He's a potentially brilliant all-rounder. He can
delve into all the disciplines of pro cycling and come up with*

results. But I don't want him riding like a sprinter. Or anywhere near them really. I'll talk to the directeur. Maybe his soigneur too. I'll talk to his girlfriend. Maybe I ought to talk to him. I'll go down to the start today.

Looking out through the curtains, Ben saw clear skies and a breeze that gave the impression that the trees were breathing gently. He dressed in shorts, slipped bare feet into docksiders, wrapped a sweatshirt around his waist and headed out for the *village*.

I'll breakfast there. The company is usually good.

'Hey, Alex.'

'Morning, Josh.'

At a rickety table in the breakfast-room of their hotel, which was really a glorified *pension* without the nice personal touches, the men rubbed bleary eyes and bemoaned the stream of beer which had found its flow down their gullets the previous night.

'Have you seen Cat?' Josh asked, picking up a croissant, scrutinizing it from various angles, before forsaking it in favour of a second cup of black coffee. Alex, who had a mouth full of croissant and lips coated with crumbs, shook his head.

'Nah – not since she left the *salle de presse* yesterday.'

'Talking of the devil,' Josh said, 'morning, Cat.'

'Morning,' said Cat.

'Have some breakfast,' Alex said, offering her a croissant in his fingers and munching on it himself when she refused.

'Coffee?' Josh offered, pouring himself a third cup when she declined.

'I'll see you at the *village*,' Cat said. 'Are we going *avant* or *arrière*?'

'Who's driving?' Josh asked.

'I'm probably still over the limit,' Alex said with a certain pride. Josh looked beseechingly at Cat.

'I don't mind,' Cat said, 'the route is pretty straightforward – shall we follow it?'

'*Avant*!' Alex proclaimed, like an army general.

'Can you load my stuff if I leave it in reception? I'm going to stroll over now,' said Cat, 'we'll meet by the Maison du Café stand at the second bell.'

'Sure,' said Josh.

'Yes, ma'am,' said Alex, saluting and burping simultaneously.

'Is she all right?' Josh asks Alex, glancing at Cat disappearing from view, thinking how this morning she looks somewhat deflated.

'Huh?' Alex responds, turning to scour the space she has left.

'She's all right,' Josh declares.

'Then why are you asking?' Alex retorts.

'I mean,' Josh says, 'I was sceptical initially but actually I rate her – her writing's good and her knowledge is sound.'

'I must admit,' Alex nods, drinking the juice set for Cat, 'I agree. She's one of us – but with great tits. Which is refreshing.'

'God, you're a twat,' Josh laughs.

'Street cred for us in the *salle de presse*,' Alex shrugs. 'I've seen the *L'Equipe* hacks regard us approvingly.'

'We must remember that this is her first Tour,' Josh reasons, 'and that she's a girl.'

Alex winces and tuts theatrically. 'You sexist sod, you!'

Josh is serious. 'Fuck off. She *is* one of us but she is *not* one of us. I mean – she *is* a girl. And she is a novice. We must remember that and we should respect it. But don't you think she seems a bit – I don't know how you'd call the condition – quiet?'

'Maybe,' says Alex, reaching for the remainder of Josh's croissant.

'Hey, Hunter,' said Ben, laying a hand on the rider's shoulder.

'Yo,' Hunter replied. The rider was sitting on the steps of

the Megapac van in a picturesque green, plotted and pieced by birch trees – near the start line. Just one rider from the group of 184 wondering how his day would pan out and how much control he could ultimately exact on the outcome.

'You have a nice mention here,' Ben said, holding up the *Guardian*.

'What is that?' Hunter asked.

'A newspaper?' Ben cajoled before answering honestly, 'It's British. Listen up. *If Dean's passion can be maintained even if the mountains mangle his muscles, he might well shine in one of the final Stages of* la Grande Boucle. She terms your ride yesterday "heart-rending".'

'Who the fuck is "she"?' Hunter asked.

'The journalist – the British one.'

'Oh sure, right,' Hunter nodded, 'Luca's one.'

'Luca's?' Ben asked quizzically.

'Sure,' Hunter shrugged, 'he feels like she's his – saves up his best quotes for her. I was in his room yesterday. He put on aftershave after dinner even though he hadn't shaved. And clean track pants. Said he'd invited her for a soundbite.

'And?' Ben enquired.

'She didn't show,' Hunter said. 'Hey, let me read that.' He scanned the article quickly, then folded the paper angrily and thrust it back at Ben. 'I'm not waiting till after the fucking mountains to go for it.'

'Hunter,' said Ben sternly, 'that's the point – if you go for broke now, you'll bonk – you'll hit the wall – you'll break. This first week is for sprinters, some of whom won't even make it half-way up the first hill – you know that. Be consistent. You're a *rouleur*. You're team captain. Why else would the bunch insist on chasing you down? Your strength is known – you're a rider to be reckoned with. And you've got to get yourself and the boys to Paris. What sort of example are you setting the likes of Luca, Travis even, if you don't?'

Hunter regarded his legs, smooth, hard, glistening, and

glanced across to Ben's which looked unnaturally hirsute in comparison. It made him remember who he was and where he was and his function here, his purpose, his gift, his aim in life. He looked up at Ben and rose. 'Sure thing, Doc. You're right. I'll ride as I should. I'll lead the guys home.'

Hunter Dean, Ben marvelled as he tweaked the peak of the rider's logoed baseball cap, *when you hang up your pedals you can slip straight into Congress. Or Hollywood. You're a star.*

Ben went in search of Didier LeDucq. Luca said he'd seen him heading off towards the toilets. Luca looked at his feet. Then Luca told the doctor he'd heard the French rider throwing up before breakfast. Then he looked down at the doctor's feet. When his doctor ventured off to track down his ailing *equipeur*, Luca winced.

If I felt shit, but I wanted to race, would I want my doctor to know? If I felt shit but I wanted to race, would I tell my team-mates? If I'd thrown up and chosen not to tell my team-mates, would I want them to dob me to the doctor behind my back? Fuck me. I'm a jerk. I'll go find Didier – before Ben. Oh. But not before I have a quick chat with my journaliste.

'*Gatto!*'

Cat turned, wondering who was crying for cake. Luca walked towards her.

'I'm calling you *Gatto*,' he declared, kissing her somewhat startled cheeks once apiece. 'I'm basically bilingual but *Gatto* is Italian for cat.'

'Oh,' Cat nodded, her eyes caught by the tan line on the rider's arm, revealed by his jersey sleeve being a little bunched up. Seeing the glimpse of pale skin created similar maternal affection in her as witnessing the riders tottering in their cycling shoes.

I want to straighten his sleeve for him.

Go on then, no doubt he'd love you to.

Don't be ridiculous.

'I like pussy,' Luca said, regarding her directly. Cat jolted and any feelings of maternal affection were swiftly replaced by consternation. She tipped her head to one side, hoping she was regarding the rider in a suitably stern way.

'Is that a quote for me?' she asked, matter of fact and tongue in cheek.

'I mean,' Luca said ingenuously, frowning for good measure, 'I like "pussy" – but "*gatto*" is better. Italian is a beautiful language. Italian is really my mama tongue. I just speak English also.'

'You could just call me Cat,' the journalist suggested, 'it's simple English.'

'No no no,' the rider said emphatically, 'I want a special name for you.' Luca narrowed his eyes, straightened his shoulders and poked Cat gently in the stomach. 'Last night, how come you didn't want me?'

Cat clasped her hand against her mouth. The gesture was immediate and honest. She had indeed completely forgotten, having wrapped herself in her insecurity blanket just as soon as she'd reached her room. Luca grinned outwardly, felt appeased inwardly and was suddenly keen to find Hunter, to restore the American's belief in Luca's irresistibility.

'I was knackered,' Cat said apologetically whilst reprimanding herself. Unprofessional. Stupid. A wasted opportunity.

'You were shagged,' Luca elaborated very seriously. Again Cat jolted. Luca was a little alarmed. 'It's a good English expression – very, very tired. Right? Poor pussy Cat,' he continued, 'let me give it to you later. I want to.'

'What?' the journalist exclaimed quietly, her eyes skittering all over the rider's face.

'You come and see me – we'll have a good long one,' Luca shrugged, wondering why Cat continued to look less than ecstatic.

'Pardon?'

'We'll go somewhere quiet,' Luca said openly, 'and I'll give it to you there. You staying in Chardin tonight? I don't know where the fuck the team are staying. You find me. You call me. We'll take it from there.'

Cat stood and stared at the rider.

'You want it – don't you?' he asked.

Though she was listening hard, Cat could not hear any lascivious undertone lacing what appeared to be genuine concern.

'Come after dinner,' Luca said, 'I do it better on a full stomach. *Ciao, Gatto.*' He walked away from her, turning his attention to Didier's whereabouts.

Alex walked up to Josh, who was talking to Ben and Didier at the *Coeur de Lion* marquee in the *village*. Didier ambled a few strides away to his bike and cycled off slowly, through the *village* and back to the team van, via an undisclosed visit to the toilets. Josh had got to the rider before Ben had and now the rider had left before Ben had him alone.

'He says he feels strong,' Josh said, looking at his notepad. He looked at Ben. 'He looks like shit.'

'Who are we talking about?' said Alex, now joining them.

'LeDucq,' said Josh.

'He always looks crap,' Alex said, laughing, 'he should get rid of his stupid pony-tail. I'm going over to catch Max.' Ben and Josh watched Alex join a small posse of journalists surrounding the ever popular Max Sciandri. Neither of them could see Cat amongst them. They turned their attention back to each other and the absent LeDucq.

'I'm his doctor,' said Ben, remembering he was talking to a journalist. 'He's fine – if he isn't, I'll know about it. That's my job.'

'It's going to be hot today, I reckon,' said Josh, still thinking LeDucq looked awful. Ben nodded. The men looked at the sky and noted the very few, high clouds that were there.

'It's bizarre, isn't it?' the doctor said. 'Talking about the weather is never idle chit chat here at the Tour.'

Josh laughed and nodded. A bell rang. The VIPs started to gather together, leaving the *village* to be transported along the route to hospitality at the *arrivée*, wined and dined with

149

elaborate packed lunches on the way in cars invariably driven by ex-Tour racers.

'I think we're staying at the same hotel tonight,' Josh said.

'Great,' said Ben, 'maybe we'll have a few beers later.'

'Providing Sassetta behaves,' Josh reasoned. 'Zucca are staying there too.'

'There's your colleague,' Ben said, nodding towards Cat who had just appeared in the *village*, making her way straight to a booth and taking a long drink of juice. 'Is she staying with you?'

'Cat?' Josh replied, glancing in her direction. 'Yeah, she is, all the way. I didn't know her before – shit, I've actually only known her a week. But she's OK, she really is.'

'Yes, she is. Her work's good too,' said Ben, flashing the *Guardian* as emphasis.

'Yup,' said Josh, 'it's great to have her on board.'

'Makes a change,' Ben said, his eyes not having left her.

'Doesn't it just?' Josh agreed. They regarded her as she meandered from one stand to the next. She was wearing a short denim skirt and white pumps, a T-shirt and a Nike baseball cap. She looked preoccupied. Ben fixed his gaze on her face to no avail. Josh raised a hand in a futile wave. A few stands on, she caught sight of the two men. She stood stock still momentarily before turning on her heels, leafing with urgency through her notepad and walking with huge purpose out of the *village*.

Neither Ben nor Josh knew she'd gone directly to hide behind a tree, feeling knotted. Ben presumed she was gleaning gems from Luca. Josh assumed she was just going about her job.

'Catch you later,' said Ben, catching sight of Didier sitting with Travis, both with cups of coffee. Travis sipped his with his little finger extended genteelly; Didier just raised his cup, contemplated its contents and then replaced it. Ben was alarmed. Few riders forsake their legal caffeine entitlement.

'Yes, this evening,' said Josh, suddenly feeling the impact

of the vast amount of restorative breakfast caffeine and thinking he really ought to piss before they set off, 'we'll have a few beers.'

'Hey, Cat,' says Rachel, the boot of the car open to reveal a veritable booty of clothing, bidons, food, and first-aid accoutrements. 'I'm sorry about yesterday.'

'Sorry?' Cat asks. 'For what?'

'I was so stressed out I might have to borrow back the pencil sharpener,' Rachel says, lowering her voice to a conspiratorial whisper. 'Stefano is – well, he drives me mad, let me tell you!'

'Do tell me,' Cat implores.

'Yeah, right,' Rachel laughs, 'but as a mate, as a fellow female – not as a *journaliste*.'

Cat holds her hand to her heart. Rachel beckons her closer until both women are leaning deep into the car. 'When he won the Stage yesterday? He said to me – and excuse my accent – *Where is Lomers? I want give him these flowers – I want say him "Hey Lomers – give these for your wife because she think you no love her because you no fuck her no more".*'

The women regard each other and then laugh in horror but not quite in disbelief.

'What did you say?' Cat gasps.

'I said I would tell Jean-Marie Leblanc,' Rachel says, referring to the revered and omnipotent Director General of the Société du Tour de France.

'What did Stefano say?'

'He gave *me* the fucking flowers and looked pretty sheepish. I massaged him viciously last night,' Rachel declares with certain glee and sparkle, '*viciously.*'

'What a character,' Cat laughs, adding, 'Bloody men!' as an aside.

'Stefano's a prat,' Rachel says, not unfondly. She tells Cat the name of the hotel that Zucca are staying at that night.

'I'm pretty sure that's where we are,' Cat responds, delighted.

'Cool,' says Rachel, 'let's have a beer later.'

'You're on,' says Cat.

'*Ciao*, Cat,' Rachel says, though Cat has gone. She slams the boot of the car, consults the map and heads for the feed zone midway along the route. Then she'll head straight for the finish line, stocked with everything a rider could ask for after racing for 248 kilometres. Everything from antiseptic to a quick leg rub, from fresh socks to a banana, from tracksuits to a warm and welcoming smile.

'You're happy about driving on the wrong side of the road?' Josh asked Cat as she took her seat behind the wheel.

'I'll take it slowly,' she replied.

'No you fucking won't,' Alex cried from the back. 'To the *salle de presse* – and don't spare the horses.' He leant forward, removed her baseball cap and thwacked the roof of the car with it. 'Vamoose!'

Josh and Cat shared a quick glance of exasperation. Cat drove off, cautiously but at a pace that could not be castigated.

'You OK?' Josh tried.

'Fine, thanks,' said Cat from behind sunglasses.

'You're not your usual perky self,' Alex said, replacing her baseball cap sideways on her head so she looked quite the little urchin. 'Tell Uncle Alex what's wrong.'

'Alex, fuck off,' Josh said, shaking his head, catching Alex's glance in the rear-view mirror and giving him a loaded look. Cat removed her sunglasses, righted her cap and looked at both men, assuring them she was fine, just tired.

Bloody boys. Males. The lot of them.

She only swerved twice. First when Alex enquired, innocently enough, after what Luca had had to say that morning – all of which Cat was still trying to remember word for word, the intention in particular. Then she swerved again, with equal severity, when Josh remarked that both Zucca MV and Megapac were staying at their hotel.

'Ben said to meet in the bar for a drink,' Josh said.

'Ben?' Cat said.

Bloody Ben.

'Yeah, you know, the Megapac doc,' Alex said rather slyly, leaning forward between the two front seats and grinning at Cat.

'I was talking to him at the *village*,' Josh said. 'We saw you and tried to call you over but you were on a mission.'

On a mission not to be seen by him. What did he say? Did he mention podium girls? What did you say? Did you mention my fake bloody boyfriend?

'He asked after you,' Josh continued.

'Oh?' said Cat, eyes on the road but mind far from it. 'What about?'

I don't want to know. I do want to know. What did he want to know? That I have a boyfriend? Please say you didn't say so. Because I don't. Oh, but what does it matter – Ben's hardly interested anyway.

'This and that,' said Josh casually, 'where you fit in – he'd read your report of yesterday.'

'Oh,' said Cat.

Mine? He searched it out and read it? What should I read into that? Shut up, idiot girl.

'Anyway – he suggested beers tonight,' Josh continued.

He did? With whom? All of us? Just me? Or minus me?

'I'm having a beer with Rachel,' Cat said, almost as a safeguard.

How on earth am I going to concentrate on the race, let alone write the report, with the distraction the impending evening poses?

COPY FOR P. TAVERNER @ GUARDIAN SPORTS DESK FROM CATRIONA McCABE IN CHARDIN

After just over sixteen hours of racing, with just under seven minutes between the maillot jaune *of the leader and the Lantern Rouge of the 184th rider, the Tour de France left Brittany today for the Vendée with a 248 km road race from Plouay to Chardin. For 96 km, while the landscape masqueraded as Cornwall, a 30 kph north-westerly wind gave the peloton a helping hand, propelling the bunch forward together and providing light relief from a sticky 29 degrees. However, as the riders crossed over the mouth of the Loire via the stunning Pont du Saint Nazaire, no doubt they would have preferred high humidity to the sly cross-winds which slicked about the bridge, disturbing the bunch.*

'I'm stuck,' Cat sighed, observing with envy that both Josh and Alex were not. 'I'm going out for a breather,' she said, disappointed that her colleagues were not just staying put but far too preoccupied to have even heard her.

What is going on with Luca? Cat wondered, walking fast to she didn't know where. *And Ben has suggested a drink to Josh. Is that why my work is slow today? Because I'm disconcerted? Some time with Rachel will be good.*

She found a small café, ordered a *latte* and made a conscious decision to devote no more time to fretting about Luca, Ben, beer and her fabricated boyfriend.

I must head back and wrap up my report.

'The bunch devoured the final 20 k of tarmac in twenty minutes flat,' Cat marvelled out loud.

A very chic lady, sitting at the neighbouring table with a tiny dog on her lap and a Chanel handbag by her feet, looked at Cat. 'That touch of wheels,' she said, clearing her throat as if to lighten her accent to complement her very good grasp of English, 'when the road drops with 500 metres to go!'

Cat smiled and nodded and suddenly her closing paragraph was clear. She asked for the bill but the lady waved her hand and insisted on paying. 'Tomorrow,' she asked Cat, 'what are your thoughts?'

'Keep an eye on Tyler Hamilton,' Cat said.

'*Bonne chance, mademoiselle,*' the lady said.

'*Bonne chance*, Tyler Hamilton!' Cat laughed.

*

Cat slips back into the *salle de presse* unnoticed by Josh and Alex, by anyone really. She doesn't mind. She has work to do. She skims through the first chunk of her article and raps out the concluding paragraph with speed.

A touch of wheels with 500 m to go brought down the section of the peloton containing nearly all the key sprinters. While the speed meisters untangled themselves from each other, their lead-out men hammered ahead unaware. Luckily for Chris Boardman's Crédit Agricole team, Australian Stuart O'Grady was not down under and utilized an excellent if wholly unintended lead-out from Zucca MV's Gianni Fugallo to take the Stage. Fugallo looked simultaneously staggered and quite horrified to see the befreckled Antipode on his wheel instead of his dark duke Stefano Sassetta. Jesper Lomers and Stefano Sassetta hold on to the yellow and green jerseys respectively. The next two Stages will suit them well but the Time Trial on Saturday will suit their team leaders Fabian Ducasse and Vasily Jawlensky better.

<ENDS>

'How bizarre,' Cat says aloud, laying her palms on the trestle table and leaning back in the plastic chair.

'Huh?' mumbles Josh, swigging from one of the three Coke cans lined up in front of him.

'You wha'?' Alex mutters, not looking up from his laptop.

'The Time Trial is on *Saturday*,' Cat proclaims in a tone of disbelief. Her colleagues regard her. 'Today is *Wednesday* – right?' Alex and Josh look at each other. 'How amazing!' Cat declares.

'What the fuck are you *on*?' Alex asks, regarding her two cans of Orangina and a fairly decimated packet of Petit Beurre biscuits.

'I forgot all about *days*,' Cat says, offering the biscuits to the men. 'To me, today is Stage 4, the day after tomorrow is Stage 6. None of this Saturday Sunday Solomon Grundy nonsense.'

'Welcome to the Tour,' Josh says, realizing he would have had no idea what day it was had he been asked.

'What are you going to be like when we hit altitude?' Alex teases affectionately, cramming a whole biscuit in his mouth, rubbing his hands and returning his fingers to the keyboard.

'Is Taverner going to let me get away with "*dark duke Sassetta*"?' Cat wonders. Josh roars with laughter. Alex buries his face in his hands.

Jesper Lomers and Fabian Ducasse walk down their hotel corridor to Jules Le Grand's room to which they have been summoned for a strategy meeting. Apart from riding for the same team and being pretty much the same height, similarities between the two end there. The Dutchman is blond and brawny, the Frenchman dark and lithe; Jesper is courteous and temperate with the team, the peloton, the media, Fabian is indiscriminately temperamental. Jesper exudes a modesty for his successes, for which he is universally admired; Fabian's arrogance when victorious augments his magnetic appeal. Jesper will actively try to put anyone at their ease ('I'm just a guy who can ride a bike,' he shrugged to Alex who interviewed him after his victory at Milan–San Remo), whereas Fabian relishes the fact that his stature and demeanour are famously intimidating ('*En Français*!' he demanded witheringly of Josh who merely wanted to congratulate him on winning the Dauphiné Libéré). Though they have little in common on a personal level, they are good colleagues, respectful of each other's strengths and supportive during and after racing.

'I am keeping the *maillot jaune* warm for you,' comments Jesper, who knows he can never win the Tour de France.

'Green's more your colour,' Fabian laughs, with deference to Jesper's consistency as a rider – the domain of the *maillot vert* contender. Jesper knocks on Jules's door but Fabian opens it and walks straight in.

*

If I venture out of my room, Cat considered, in her small room in a nondescript motorlodge on the ring road of Chardin, *I might come across Luca or Ben*. She unpacked the entire contents of her rucksack, hanging as many garments as she could. *I don't really want to see either as I really don't know what to make of them. If I stay here all night, I'll forfeit my drink with Rachel – which I'd really like to have.*

She ran a bath, squirting in a little shampoo to give the semblance of bubble bath.

Luca bloody Jones. Was that humour or was I missing the point? Or did I have the point perfectly? Mind you, at least he'd like to give me one, which is more than can be said for his doctor.

Her bath was ready. The phone rang. It was Josh, informing her that he and Alex were driving in to town for dinner in half an hour.

'I'm not really hungry,' Cat said, 'I stuffed myself at the press buffet and then all those biscuits.'

'Are you OK?' Josh enquired.

'I'm fine,' Cat said.

That's kind of him.

'Are you sure?' Josh pressed.

'Honestly,' Cat stressed, suddenly wondering if his probing had a motive.

'Women's things?' Josh attempted.

No, he's just being kind.

'Yes,' said Cat smiling, glad that she didn't have him wrong, 'women's things.'

After her bath, swathed in a towel pleasingly luxurious for the rating of the hotel, Cat phoned reception for Rachel's room number. There was no reply from the *soigneur*'s quarters.

She's probably in the team bus, preparing for tomorrow. I'll get dressed and go for a recce.

'Luca Jones!' Ben exclaimed, coming across the rider in the foyer.

'Hey, Doc,' said Luca, 'I'm fucking knackered.'

'Have an early night, then,' Ben said, as if to an imbecile, 'it's almost eight thirty.'

'I'm waiting,' Luca said.

'For what?' Ben asked.

'For my *journaliste*,' Luca said.

'Who?' Ben asked.

'The lovely pussy Cat,' Luca said openly.

'I hope you don't call her that to her face,' Ben exclaimed.

'Yeah,' Luca said, 'I tried but she didn't seem to like it. I went for *Gatto*. She did say she'd rather just be a simple Cat but I won't listen.'

'Why are you waiting?' Ben asked. 'When are you meeting?'

'Yesterday I asked her to come to me if she wanted one. This morning, I told her if she found me tonight, she could have it.'

Ben stared at him. 'You said what?'

'That I'd give her one,' the rider shrugged, 'a long one even. Somewhere quiet, I told her. After supper.'

'You said that?' Ben asked, not able to mask amazement.

'Sure,' Luca shrugged, 'she told me she was shagged last night.' Ben's jaw dropped. 'So,' Luca continued, 'perhaps tonight.'

'And she's on for it?' Ben enquired nonchalantly.

Luca looked at him in amazement. 'She's a fucking *journaliste* – why wouldn't she want an exclusive interview with Luca Fucking Jones? Man!'

Ben bit back laughter, nodded sincerely and then walked away.

I must find her. This is too good to miss. She can't not go to Luca Fucking Jones if he wants to give her a big one somewhere private.

If I take the stairs, Cat theorizes, *I can avoid bumping into anything I'd rather not.*

She takes the stairs, forgetting it is the mode by which Ben chooses to travel upwards. She is humming the jingle played each day at the *village*. She skips down a flight, turns a landing, skips down another and all but collides with Ben on the next landing.

'Miss McCabe,' he says, staring at her measuredly, his hands on her shoulders to steady her but, in reality, making her quiver all the more.

'Oh,' says Cat, not able to look anywhere but right at him, 'Ben.'

'Where are you skipping to, all merry?' he asks, removing just one hand from her shoulder.

'I'm going to find Rachel McEwen,' Cat says, wanting him to take away his other hand but also to leave it put. 'We're going to have a quick drink.'

'A quick one,' Ben plays with a wry half-smile. Cat frowns fleetingly. 'And young Luca?' Ben asks.

'Luca?' Cat responds, regarding Ben warily.

'He tells me he's going to give you one,' Ben informs her, 'this evening.'

Cat bites her lip. 'I know,' she says quietly.

'What exactly did my rider say?' Ben asks sternly, his voice low and doctorly and coursing through the blood in Cat's veins like a tonic.

She drops her gaze to his lips fleetingly then regards him full on. 'Your young rider invited me to come and find him tonight if I wanted it – that he'd take me somewhere quiet and give me a long one.'

'Cat McCabe,' Ben breathes, 'my rider is waiting for you in the foyer. He needs an early night. He needs minimal exertion. I think I'll join you both on this one. Come on.' Ben takes her elbow. 'I promise to be just a silent observer.'

Cat is too stunned to respond, let alone stand her ground or insist on her intended path to Rachel.

'Do you use a gadget?' Ben asks, innocently enough. 'The riders usually prefer them – it makes it so much quicker and smoother.' He looks at Cat. 'Don't you agree?'

Poor girl – I am a sod.

In the foyer, Ben and Cat come across Luca talking to Rachel.

'Hey, Cat,' Rachel says. Luca stares intently at the *journaliste* who is trying to transmit to the *soigneur* desperate pleas for assistance via eye flickers, lip twitching and general woman-to-woman telepathy.

'Luca tells me he's having you to himself for a while,' Rachel says. 'I'll meet you in the bar. How long will you be, Luca?'

'As long as it takes,' Luca replies, looking adoringly at the *journaliste*. 'It's up to my feline friend, hey?'

'He won't last long,' Rachel whispers to Cat. 'God knows why he wants to do it now – he's shagged already.' She winks. 'I'll leave you to it,' she says to Luca and Cat, 'see you in a while.'

Ben is hovering.

'You want to join us?' Luca asks him begrudgingly.

'Cat?' Ben asks her. She does not know where to look, what to do. She turns her head towards the bar. She cannot see Rachel.

'You have that thing?' Luca asks her, 'the machine? The batteries?'

Cat shakes her head and upends empty palms. She is wearing an obviously pocketless tube skirt. She looks down, wondering if her knees are knocking. Certainly they feel that they are.

'Oh,' Luca says, 'why not? It's better for you, no? Personally, I like the machine – I prefer it that way – and it is better for you, no? The results are stronger, in my experience.'

Ben can't bear it any longer. He is about to laugh uncontrollably and Cat looks like she is about to weep. 'Call yourself a *journaliste*?' he goads her gently, giving her shoulder a little shove. 'It's part of the job, isn't it?'

Cat regards him blankly.

Bloody fucking men. I'm in the wrong fucking job.

'Necessary equipment?' Ben furthers, captivated by the sight of her heaving chest.

She's not wearing a bra.

'A dic-ta-phone?' he enunciates clearly.

'Ah!' Luca responds cheerfully, 'that's the sodding word – dictaphone.'

'How are you going to remember Luca giving you a long one if you don't have a dictaphone?' Ben asks her, crossing his arms and raising an eyebrow.

Cat's jaw drops. She looks from one man to the other. Luca with his lovely, boy-beautiful open face; Ben, handsome and magnetizing. She could cry.

I could kiss them both.

But of course, she does not. She gives Luca a gentle shove. Then she gives Ben a sly, sideways glance coupled with a fleeting squeeze to his biceps. Just to steady herself. Just to feel. An exploratory squeeze? A gesture of gratitude? She's not about to tell us, she's far too absorbed by the fact that Ben's hands are lightly at her waist and he has kissed very quickly, just catching the tip of her earlobe with his lips.

'Luca,' she beams, 'you know what? I *do* want my dictaphone – and I want to speak to my boss about the slant of the interview. It's late – it's nine o'clock. Tomorrow is a short but intense Stage for you, the first Time Trial is looming too. I want you to have a good sleep,' she says, looking from Luca to Ben and then moving back to Luca, 'more than I want you to give me your big one in private.'

'You are so much more than a *journaliste*,' Luca praises her, 'you *care*.'

'I care about every pro cyclist,' Cat says honestly, 'you're my heroes.'

Luca loves the compliment. 'A good idea,' he agrees, 'let's do it properly, let's do it after the Time Trial. I'm going to bed. *Buona notte.*'

'Good night,' says Ben.

'Sweet dreams,' Cat says, waving as the rider disappears

into the lift. 'You're a sod,' Cat says to Ben, her eyes fixed straight ahead.

'I couldn't resist,' says Ben, gazing at her neck.

Eyes meet and fuse.

Is it chemistry? Cat wonders, patting a hand unconsciously against the butterflies rampaging around her stomach. Ben's lips part slightly as his gaze burrows further into her.

'Cat,' he says. She purses her lips and then licks them, observing how it releases his eyes from hers to focus on her mouth. 'You're having a drink with Rachel.' It is a statement and not a query.

Cat nods.

'I'm having a drink with Josh and Alex,' Ben says.

Cat nods again. She clears her throat.

'We could join forces,' she suggests.

'We could,' Ben answers, 'but where's the fun in that? I'd rather have you to myself.'

His tone is matter of fact. His eyes have her captive again. 'Another time,' he says. He smiles at her and then heads off into the bar. Cat remains stock still.

Chemistry. Undeniably. I don't need my O Level to tell me so.

But yesterday?

The podium girl?

He held her face and looked into her eyes?

Maybe he's morally inept.

The thing is, my desire is so strong I'd probably sleep with him regardless. What would that make me? And where would that leave me? And what if Josh tells him about my non-existent boyfriend?

It was a relief to be with Rachel. Cat chose to sit with her back to Ben, Alex and Josh, who were at the other side of the bar. The room was crowded and noisy. Rachel was relaxed and she and Cat chatted easily, whiling away the evening, sipping *Seize* and eating garlicky olives. By the time they suggested they really ought to retire, they knew each other well. Well enough to kiss goodnight, to look forward to seeing each other the next day, to hoping that there'd be many more occasions both during the Tour and after when, as friends, they could indulge again in each other's company.

Cat is knackered, shagged, bush-whacked, simply exhausted and desperate to 'push some zeds'. She's made the fateful move of flopping on to her bed fully clothed and is tempted to greet sleep dressed as such. So what if she hasn't cleaned her teeth? So what if she hasn't checked whether her mobile phone needs charging? So what if she hasn't examined tomorrow's route or found where she needs to be and when?

I'm so tired. What a day. Fucking Luca Jones. Bloody Ben York. Lovely Josh. Inimitable Alex. Fantastic Rachel. I'll just have a quick shut-eye. Just for a mo' or two.

No you won't. You'll sit bolt upright at the sound of knocking at your door. You'll check your watch. It's almost midnight. Heed the advice of Emma O'Reilly, the *soigneur's soigneur*, passed down to you by your friend Rachel.

Yes, but it's not midnight for another seven minutes.

Cat pads over to the door. There is no spy hole.

'Hullo?' she asks, through the wood, her hand hovering over the handle.

'It's me,' comes the unmistakable voice of Ben York.

Oh fuck.

Cat bites her lip and regards her left hand on the door knob.

What do I do now?

It's six minutes to midnight. You're wasting time.

Cat opens the door a little and looks up to Ben's face slowly, via his legs, quickly over his crotch, his torso, his gorgeous strong neck, over his chin, hesitating at his lips – parted and dark – and suddenly swiftly upwards, on and into his gaze.

'What do you want?' Cat asks softly.

'What do you want?' Ben echoes. They stare at each other.

'I need to give you something,' he is saying, making to take a step forward as Cat instinctively takes a step back. He has crossed the threshold. It's OK. Midnight is still a few minutes off. He is inside the room. It's OK. The door has not quite closed. 'I need to give you something,' he repeats, 'before it is offered to you by anyone else.' He steps towards her, glances down at her bare feet, up to her knees, lingers over her breasts. With one hand, he gently holds her neck so that his thumb is at the base of her throat, his index finger is behind her ear and the remaining fingers are encircling the back of her neck. Cat can't breathe. He can detect her quickening pulse.

Fuck. It must be midnight.

No, not quite.

Ben dips his face down a little, comes closer, their clothing touches. He takes her wrist with his other hand and puts his lips against hers. They alight softly for just a fraction of a second and seem to heat on impact. Suddenly Ben is kissing Cat so intensely and she finds herself responding likewise. She's grasping his neck. She's grabbing his trousers. She's pulled him against her and has herself been thrust against the wall. They are tonguing each other with abandon. Cat can taste toothpaste. Ben can detect beer, garlic. Who gives a fuck? They taste fantastic to each other. Ben pulls away.

'I wanted to give you that,' he says hoarsely, 'I've been carrying it around with me since I first saw you.' Staring at her, he backs out of the room and does not relinquish eye contact until the door is closed completely.

Cat regards the door. She takes the fingers of one hand to her lips, she places her other hand between her legs. She's throbbing, she's on fire; everywhere. She glances at her watch. It's midnight.

STAGE 5
Nantes–Pradier. 210 kilometres

'*C*at? It's Andy – from *Maillot*. Is this a good time?'

A good time? It couldn't be better. I'm having a fantastic time, here in Nantes, in a particularly opulent village on a glorious morning, awaiting the off for the fifth Stage of this year's Tour de France. It's a shorter Stage today – which is a good job really, as Ben York has just brushed past me, turned and winked, and I can hardly wait for later, that we might track each other down long before midnight.

'I can call back later,' Andy was saying, 'if it isn't.'

'It's fine, Andy,' Cat said. 'How are you? I'm brilliant.'

'You are, are you?' Andy responded. 'Now, podium girls.'

'They're nothing,' said Cat absent-mindedly, grinning as she placed herself far higher on Ben's dais in her mind's eye.

'Sorry?' said Andy.

'What?' said Cat.

'No go, I'm afraid,' Andy said, 'we don't feel there's enough substance – not what the readers of *Maillot* want.'

Cat felt momentarily deflated, but then she heard Luca's name being announced at the signing-on stage.

'How about an exclusive interview with Luca Jones?' she

suggested brightly. 'He's keen. It's all organized.'

'Luca?' said Andy. 'Farrand did one last month – of course, he's fluent in Italian. It's coming out next issue.'

'Oh,' said Cat, 'but mine would be different.'

'How?'

'A mid-Tour analysis?' Cat clutched. 'A woman's per-spective sort of thing?'

'Sorry, Cat,' Andy said, 'just bad timing on that one. Look, your reports are good – I'm sure we'll be able to find you something here at the end of it all.'

Cat went cold. 'You mean the Features Editorship isn't in the bag?'

'We agreed it would be dependent on the quality of your race reports,' said Andy, now sounding disconcertingly officious.

'But you just said they were good,' Cat all but whispered.

'They are,' Andy reassured her, 'they're excellent – even the "dark duke Sassetta" stuff. But the job is dependent on whether or not it exists, you see. Nothing personal.'

'No,' said Cat, quite cross and taking it personally, 'I don't see.'

'We're having something of a reshuffle – the staff, the layout – everything. But don't worry – I'd love to have you in some capacity.'

'OK,' said Cat, appalled that she sounded so grateful and meek.

I'm bloody worth more than that.

'Do you mind if I continue to bombard you with my ideas?' Cat asked, wincing at her tone of near-desperate deference.

Andy laughed. 'I wouldn't expect anything less from you,' he said.

Some hours later, Cat was feeling stressed and distracted in the *salle de presse*, today a large marquee set up in the grand municipal park of Pradier. Josh and Alex had no advice for her – they assured her that her ideas for articles were sound, that no one at *Maillot* was remotely sexist.

'You've chosen to fall in love with a minority sport in Britain,' Josh said, by way of explanation, 'that's all.'

'The audience is limited,' Alex furthered, quite serious for once, 'and there are more than enough freelancers touting ideas.'

'*With* a track record,' Josh elaborated, no offence intended or taken.

'Stephen Farrand lives in Italy and has been involved with the sport for some time – if he interviews Luca Jones, editors know what they'll get. They don't know what they'll get with you,' said Alex.

'Why can't they give me a fucking chance?' Cat declared.

'Because that's mag publishing in Britain,' Alex shrugged. 'Took me fucking ages.'

'Me too,' said Josh. 'Don't worry, I'm sure something will turn up.'

'Jesus Fucking Christ,' Alex shouted whilst around them, journalists fulminated equivalent blasphemies in their own languages. Everyone turned to the TV sets and stared. Riders were piling into each other, a couple were flung right out from the bunch, their bodies still attached to their bikes. Riders were lying all over the road, strewn like litter. They were in the ditches to the side, they were on top of each other. One somersaulted straight over the mêlée and landed smack on top of a flung bike. The *salle de presse* watched in silent horror.

Not only the TV cameras and those of the press were trained on the carnage – an elderly lady stood in the road transfixed, her camera at her eye but her finger hovering above the shutter button. She'd only wanted to take a photo, that's all. She's from San Diego, here on holiday. Just wanted a snap of the bike race, that's all. Didn't mean to be a distraction. Didn't mean to be a menace. Didn't know the speed would be so fast. Didn't mean for the men to fall off their bikes. Are they meant to do that? Is it like American football – part of the entertainment? Sure is exciting, and all.

The TV cameras, simultaneously vulturine yet providing essential service, focused mercilessly on the tangle of limbs and spokes. Gradually, the riders extricated themselves, retrieving their arms and legs from the knot of others, picking themselves up, sorting out their injuries and their bikes; spinning wheels, rubbing muscles, changing tyres. Most were remounted, pedalling off with a helpful running shove from their team mechanics or neutral service men. Two riders remained down. A Système Vipère rider was one of them, the snake encircling his body staring blankly at the TV cameras.

'Ducasse!' the murmur went round the *salle de presse*.

'Fabian!' Cat exclaimed in horror.

Merde. I have to get up. I don't want to eat tarmac. It tastes like shit. I must finish in the first group – as I have every day. I don't want to lose a second before the Time Trial. It will make no difference if I do, but it would piss me off. I want my margin in the Time Trial to set the tone for the rest of the race. That is why I have ridden quietly this week, I have made no noise yet still I am up there, top ten. The day after tomorrow, I will take the lead. My body is so strong now, ready to Time Trial, eager to climb, fit to take me to the podium in Paris. So, Fabian, up you get. Carefully.

'*Ça va?*' the race doctor asks the rider, helping him to his feet. Ducasse looks himself over, straightens himself. *Ça va?* That's a good question. How does he feel? Not broken but, having been hurled on to tarmac at 42 kph, somewhat winded all the same. But broken? Injured? No. At least, not enough not to go on. Jules Le Grand is at Fabian's side, not saying anything, just standing tall in nubuck loafers the colour of Fabian's bronzed legs. The *directeur*'s mind is racing – much faster, much harder than hitherto any of his riders have. And yet, there is nothing he can say or do – only Ducasse's body can dictate what will happen next. It is one of the few things over which the *directeur sportif* of Système Vipère has absolutely no control.

'*Vélo*?' Ducasse says quietly at last, contemplating the somewhat mangled remains of his bike lying some metres away. Freddy Verdonk, who did not fall but has hung back to remain with his leader, pushes his own bike forward. Freddy rides anyway not at his measurements but at those of his leader so that he can be on standby for an occasion like this when it is quicker for Ducasse to change on to his faithful *domestique*'s bike. Verdonk can wait for his mechanic to bring a replacement. Patience and humility, rare in a team leader, being the defining qualities of the *domestique*.

The *salle de presse* watch in hushed anticipation as Fabian Ducasse remounts. The race doctor is now looking him over, somewhat cursorily, as if Ducasse is a car that has been merely pranged. The wadge of gauze taped to the side of Ducasse's knee will last the Stage through. This evening, the wound can be looked at more thoroughly. There is no reason why Ducasse shouldn't carry on. Nothing is broken, not least his spirit. Jules Le Grand places his hand on Ducasse's lower back and runs, pushing the rider for a few metres. Verdonk is given no helping hand; that's OK, he doesn't need it, he *is* the helping hand. Cat and the journalists watch in hushed reverence as Ducasse and Verdonk make their way through the convoy of team cars, past a posse of riders at the back, up and through a string of stragglers hanging like a tail to the back of the main bunch. Système Vipère are back in the race. Ducasse has lost no time at all; moreover he has gained publicity, popularity and respect. People will want to watch for him tomorrow, every day, a force to be reckoned with; they'll be looking out for him, wishing him success. Hero.

The cameras pan back. The other rider is still on the tarmac, sitting up, hunched, head in hands. The woman from San Diego finally presses the shutter on her camera.

'I got Bobby J!' she says delighted to her husband. 'That's cool – I got Bobby J!'

In more ways than one.

Bobby Julich tries to stand. He manages it but he cannot walk. He is out of the race. His Tour stops here, but not his reputation. A battle-broken body leaves his heroism intact. There's next year.

On the other side of the road, the cameras focus momentarily on two figures. One is an old farmer standing very still, clasping his cloth cap to his heart. The other is a young boy standing by his small, basic bike, holding on to the handlebars hard. His mouth is open, his eyes are huge. When I grow up, I will cycle the Tour de France. I will be that brave. I will be a hero.

It was just one more crash in the Tour de France but for Cat, the image of Ducasse fallen and then up and away, of Julich down and then stretchered away, lay resonant in her mind's eye constantly. If the Stage had been as exciting, as traumatic, as exhausting for a mere journalist to experience, how can it have been for the riders? The atmosphere in the *salle de presse* was thick and intense. It was also too hot, and somewhat odoriferous. Too many men with a dwindling awareness of personal hygiene, a slackening interest in the merits of laundry, an increasing appetite for nicotine and, Cat detected, for garlic sausages.

'I need some air,' she told Alex and Josh, 'coming?'

'Bring us a Coke, will you?' Alex asked.

'Just Evian for me,' said Josh, eyeing up the line of empty cans in front of him.

It was still incredibly hot. Inland now, and with very little breeze, the peloton were currently racing in 30 degrees. Having been seated herself for almost three hours, Cat was stiff and sticky. Walking slowly amongst the trees, she chose a sturdy old trunk to lean her hands against, stretching out first her right leg then her left behind her. Then she picked up each foot in turn to hold against her bottom, giving the fronts of her thighs a good stretch. She put her hands on her hips and rolled her head very slowly about her neck. She reached up high above her head with arms extended;

relishing the feeling of release from the pull on her waist. She swooped her arms down in an arc, holding them out horizontally at shoulder height before clasping them behind her back and pulling upwards. She held her pose and breathed deeply, her eyes closed.

'Fantastic tits, Catriona McCabe,' said Ben York desirously, feeling the objects of his adulation gently and swiftly before Cat could open her eyes in amazement. She grabbed her breasts protectively, glanced around aghast for fear of witnesses, and had no idea how to respond.

'Cat,' she corrected, indignantly.

Ben held her face and kissed her lips, flicking his tongue tip over them before standing back and grinning at her broadly.

'Ready to play?' Ben asked. Cat shook her head solemnly. Ben regarded his watch and then raised an eyebrow. 'I'd timetabled you in,' he said, 'my only free slot, young girl.'

'I haven't finished my work yet,' Cat apologized, 'old boy.'

'Fresh air and a banana,' Ben proclaimed, 'brain food — mark my words.'

'*Trust me, I'm a doctor*?' Cat cajoled. Ben acquiesced with a tilt of his head. 'Well, here's the fresh air,' Cat continued, 'and I'll grab a banana from the buffet. Promise.'

'Let's go and sit somewhere,' Ben suggested, his hand lightly at the small of Cat's back, guiding her through the park, down a deserted narrow side-street and to a small *tabac* on the corner with just two tables outside.

'How much caffeine have you had today?' Ben asked. Subconsciously, Cat pulled her bottom lip through her top teeth as she thought. When it sprung out, Ben's mouth was there. He bit her bottom lip and then sucked it quickly. His eyes open, observing that hers were closed. Cat had to sit down.

'Five,' she said at length.

'Five?' Ben asked. 'Out of five? Out of ten — are you grading my osculation?'

'Coffees,' Cat explained, licking her lips to lap up the taste of him.

Your kissing is way off any scale I know.

'You're on the Tour de France,' Ben said gravely, 'you're over the caffeine limit.' He ordered two *citron pressés*. 'Had a good day?' he asked.

'No,' said Cat forlornly, 'poor Fabian, poor Bobby.'

'But *you*,' Ben stressed, 'how's *your* day been, *journaliste* McCabe?'

'Not so good, Ben, not so good.' Cat explained to him the uncertainties at *Maillot* in great detail. 'I'm brimming with ideas and overflowing with passion.' Ben raised his eyebrows in delight. 'Seriously,' Cat implored, punching him gently, jolting his glass and causing a dribble of *citron pressé* to course down his chin. She took her forefinger to it, ran it up to his lips and let him suck it. 'I'd justified following the entire Tour as having supreme purpose: a dream job at the end of it. Now that is uncertain, being here feels like an indulgence. I'm barely covering my costs.'

'Don't go home,' Ben said seriously. Cat's look of utter distaste at the thought brought the doctor instant relief. 'There are so many people here,' he continued, 'something'll come up.'

'Would Luca mind me interviewing him after the Time Trial?' Cat asked. 'Even if I can't guarantee a publication date?'

'Luca,' Ben proclaimed, 'would be delighted. Where are you staying tonight?'

'I don't know,' Cat said. 'Josh knows all that stuff. I just take my rucksack from his car to a different but basically interchangeable room each night.'

'Well, I'm staying at the Ibis. Room 324. Finish your work, feed and bathe and revive yourself and then come to me. I'm going to have another *pressé*,' said Ben.

'I'd better have that banana,' said Cat, feeling a little giddy. She rose and thanked Ben, leaning down to kiss his cheek and then taking her lips to his and giving him a hint of the tongue she intended to use to great effect in room 324 of the Hôtel Ibis later. He gazed after her as she walked away.

She looks quite lovely in shorts. And how I'd love to run my finger tips ever so lightly over the imprint the woven plastic chair has left on the backs of her thighs.

Ben looked at his watch. There was just time to enjoy his *pressé* before he went in search of Didier LeDucq's *soigneur* to discuss the rider's health.

COPY FOR P. TAVERNER @ GUARDIAN SPORTS DESK FROM CATRIONA McCABE IN PRADIER

On a day when it seemed at times too hot for even the sunflowers to keep their heads up, the peloton rolled out of Nantes today at 11 a.m. this morning when it was 25 degrees in the shade, travelling south before scooping inland to Pradier. By lunch-time, when the bunch streamed past the feed station at Doré to pluck the cloth musettes filled with victuals held out by their soigneurs, it was over 30 degrees. It was here, at the 100 km mark, that Tyler Hamilton (US Postal) flew off, as if he had suddenly traded his bicycle for a 900 cc motorbike. The bunch were either too engrossed in the contents of their musettes or too sensible to exert themselves in such heat and so early in the race, Hamilton was thus left alone to establish a lead that at one time was just over 7 minutes. He needed to win by 1 minute 15 seconds to claim the yellow jersey. In the last 30 km, the peloton somewhat begrudgingly began to work to close the gap. Hamilton came in with 2 seconds to spare, the maillot jaune was his. Stefano Sassetta, lying a sulky second, is still triumphant in the green jersey two points ahead of arch rival Jesper Lomers. Jesper, however, lies two placings higher than his Italian adversary in the overall standings.

A horrendous crash at 34 km, just after the first sprint point at Courbet, took Bobby Julich not just out of contention but out of the race altogether. Fabian Ducasse was lucky; his was but a taste, albeit unsavoury, of tarmac. If he is sore tonight, racing to Bordeaux tomorrow will ease his joints and restore him for the Time Trial on Saturday when he will throw down the gauntlet to Zucca's Vasily Jawlensky. Vasily has been as enigmatic as ever; keeping a low profile, riding quietly, steering away from the action, the cameras and Fabian Ducasse. He lies in twelfth place, just 18 seconds behind Fabian.

Tomorrow's Stage will be the last opportunity for the pure sprinters to display their daredevilry and thrust their stuff at the finishing line before the toil of the Time Trial and the misery of the mountains will send some of them home.

<ENDS>

'I need something,' Cat wails, 'can I have a quote?' she asks Alex.

He rifles through his notepad and shrugs, 'Can't help you – I'm having enough trouble making mine fit.'

'You owe me one,' Josh says, moving his chair nearer to her. 'I got Lomers at the media scrum. He said, "*Good for Tyler. Strength is a system of will and fitness – he has the* maillot jaune *because he deserves it.*" I'm using it, but you can too – there were quite a few people around him.'

'Josh,' said Cat whilst typing in the quote at the end of her report, 'I love you.'

Josh looked rather pleased with himself. Alex looked somewhat taken aback and, after a surreptitious flick through his notebook, a little deflated too.

I need something, Fabian Ducasse thought to himself. *I was down on the ground tasting dirt – that's no place for me to be.*

His body was sore and his psyche felt bruised. Sure, his *soigneur* could tend to the former, Jules Le Grand the latter, but Fabian knew his requirements better than anyone. He had to feel on top, in control; that he was a man who could dominate anything he wished. He needed to reassert his strength, his supremacy. He regarded himself in the mirror in his hotel bathroom. He needed a shave. More importantly, he needed to rid himself of the hint of unease he alone could detect in his eyes. Easy. It would take one thing. He pulled a baseball cap on low, donned sunglasses and a non-branded sweatshirt. He regarded his reflection again and nodded. He still needed a shave but he liked what he saw. He phoned one of the Système Vipère mechanics and demanded to be driven across Nantes to an insalubrious area he had discovered on a race some years ago, and had subsequently revisited on a few occasions since.

'Wait around there,' he ordered, watching until the mechanic was out of sight before opening a front door without knocking. Of course it was open. It was a brothel.

Fabian was out less than quarter of an hour later, the swagger in his step reflected in the burning glow of his steady eyes. He licked his lips and than spat in the gutter. He felt much better. Restored. And look! Only 8.45 p.m. He'd be asleep in an hour.

Cat was in her hotel room, doing as Ben had requested. She'd finished her work, wolfed down steak frites with Alex and Josh at a small brasserie just near their hotel, she had just had a shower and was contemplating what to wear and quite when to sneak out to the Hôtel Ibis when her mobile phone rang.

'Darling?'

'Django!'

'Cat, my girl,' Django said, 'you sound quite awful.'

Cat was taken aback. 'I feel,' she told him, 'fine. More than fine.'

'Well,' Django said, 'you sound lousy. How is it all going? It was fantastically exciting today – all those bodies all over the place – and then that Yankee bloke winning.'

Cat smiled: that her passion for cycling should be so contagious was a delight. 'I prophesied that – good old Tyler. It

was a terrific Stage. Tomorrow should be more of the same –
though rain is forecast here. How are Fen and Pip?'

'Hooked!' Django proclaimed. 'We speak just before the
programme starts, catch up briefly during the adverts and
then have a full post-Stage analysis straight after. Are you
eating? You do sound terrible.'

'I'm fine,' Cat pleads, 'I just had steak and chips.'

'I made pizza tonight,' Django says proudly. 'I had some
bread that was going a bit off so I tore it up, added a little oil
and beaten egg and a drop of ketchup, formed it into a base
and baked the bugger.'

'And?' Cat asked, somewhat horrified.

'Fantastic,' Django swooned. 'I added a topping of sar-
dines, chicken liver, a little more ketchup and some Stilton.'

'And?' ventured Cat, clutching her stomach.

'If I say so myself,' Django proclaimed, 'absolutely
delicious. I'll make it for you girls when you're next here
all together,' he continued, 'perhaps garnish it with a few
pickled walnuts.'

'Can't wait,' said Cat sincerely, about the visit more than
the meal.

'Darling girl,' her uncle was saying, bringing her back from
her family in Matlock to the bedroom in the hotel, 'you
really don't sound good.'

'I'm fine,' Cat said, feeling her forehead and poking out her
tongue at the mirror for good measure.

'Well,' said Django, 'I rather think you should go and see
the doctor.'

Cat and Django were quiet. As Cat watched herself break
into a smile, she heard her uncle's triumphant sniggers.

'That is precisely what I'm about to do,' she said.

'Can I tell your sisters?' Django asked.

'If you can name the *maillot jaune*,' Cat demanded.

'Tyler Hamilton,' Django replied, as if she was dim,
'fellow US Postman Jonathan Vaughters is in polka dot and
Stefano Sassetta in green. Must go, I have two phone calls
to make.'

'And I have a doctor's appointment to keep,' Cat said.

Cat needed to be incognito. Though she would have loved to have worn her floaty short bias-cut skirt and clingy little top, she opted for cream jeans and a denim shirt. She remembered Fen's advice and chose underwear that gave her walk a wiggle and her eyes a sparkle. She took the fire escape stairs, ducked out into the night and walked very quickly down a number of streets just to put some distance between her and anyone who might know her. When she found a quiet bar and asked the whereabouts of the Hôtel Ibis, she discovered she had charged off in completely the wrong direction. Her composure remained intact and she enjoyed the walk to Ben's hotel.

In the car park, she noted that the Cofidis team was staying there too and wondered if many journalists would be loitering for news on Bobby Julich. She could see the foyer clearly and that a number of people were milling about. She circumnavigated the building, found a side door, said a quick prayer that the entrance would not be alarmed and gave a pull. She was inside. She scaled the stairs. When she came to what she deduced to be the third floor, she stopped. She pressed herself against the wall, turning her cheeks one at a time against the cool concrete.

My heart is going fifty to the dozen. Am I about to have sex? It's been so long – since I've had sex with a man other than Him, since I've had sex full stop. Shit, I don't have any condoms – I'll be telling Ben 'if it's not On, it's not In'. Oh God, is this a good idea, a bad idea or a crazy idea? Is crazy good or bad? It's ten past nine. Fuck, I'm excited. Deep breaths. Ready. Off I go. Wish me luck. And fun.

Cat is in the third-floor corridor of the Hôtel Ibis in Pradier. The carpet is new and makes the hallway smell vaguely like an aeroplane. She passes doors that are closed though sounds of life can be heard within: showers, television sets, animated conversation, singing. Then she passes doors that are shut but with the Megapac riders' names tacked to them. There is nothing but silence emanating from these rooms. 329. Sweet dreams, Luca. 327. Other side, Cat. 328. How are you feeling, Didier? 326.

Oh God oh God oh God.

The door of room 324 is opening. A woman steps out into the corridor. She is laughing over her shoulder. She is out of the room. She turns back towards the door and waves; smiling, gorgeous. It's the podium girl. The same one. The same fucking gorgeous, leggy, luscious woman. She's laughing. She's been in Ben's room and now she's leaving it, laughing. Not a hair out of place. Lips licked with lipstick, requisite almond eyes enhanced with a lash of mascara. She's wearing a skirt shorter than that of her uniform. No daft hat to detract from her silken tresses. She's been in Ben's room, this vamp has. Number 324 at the Hôtel Ibis in Pradier. What is Cat meant to do? How is she meant to feel?

She feels sick. She turns on her heel and walks away, retracing every step that brought her here.

'**A**re you OK, Cat?' Josh asked, handing her a can of Minute Maid orange juice at the Pradier *village*. 'You look shagged.'

Cat couldn't even be bothered to muse upon the irony to herself. 'I didn't sleep well,' she told Josh.

'Are you homesick?' Josh asked gently.

'Homesick?' Cat retorted, banishing an intrusive image of her sisters from her mind. 'No way. Not at all.'

Go away, Django. Derbyshire, be gone!

'I am,' said Josh, 'I miss my wife and my dog.'

- *Oh Josh, why don't I just tell you that again I feel I shouldn't be here, that I feel a little fragile, that it's exhausting to feel I'm constantly swinging from new confidence back down to plain old inconsequential.*

Cat had no need to tell Josh any of this. He saw a tear smudge across her right eye and decided not to pry in case she broke down right then and there, in the middle of the *village*, twenty minutes before Stage 6 began, twenty yards away from five times Tour winner Bernard Hinault. But he did lay a hand on her arm and give it a conciliatory squeeze which made both of them feel a little better.

'Let's try and get behind a breakaway today,' Josh suggested. 'I'll put money on some loopy Italian fucker going for broke.'

'Look! There's Vasily,' Cat cooed, welcoming the all-encompassing distraction of the tall Russian tottering his bike through the throng of VIPs and media. They watched him ride to the barber's booth where two other racers were having their hair cut.

'Have you met Jawlensky?' Josh asked her. Cat shook her head. 'Come on, I'll introduce you, he's lovely.' Cat looked at Josh and beamed. 'Were you too tired to put your top on the right way round?' Josh continued with a grin. Cat was horrified. Not only was her top inside out, it was back to front too. 'Go and change,' Josh said. 'I assume you want to make an impression on Jawlensky – and the information that you're a small, Dorothy Perkins, wash separately, no tumble dry, kind of girl might detract from your journalistic credentials.'

Cat went hastily to the women's portaloo, smiling to herself that a Banesto rider came out of it with not so much as a shrug of apology, let alone a glimmer of embarrassment. If the men's loos were engaged, why shouldn't a rider have priority for any cubicle currently vacant?

Pro cyclists really do have the most uncouth urinary proclivities, Cat mused to herself as she took off her top, hitting her elbow against the formica partition and crying '*merde!*' *It's a perverse reworking of Pavlov's theory. Prior to the final* départ *bell, riders naturally use the conventional facilities – regardless of the gender ascribed to a cubicle. As soon as the bell has sounded, even if they've just emptied their bladders, the boys piss everywhere and in full view. Maybe* Maillot *would like a wry little piece about that? I'll call them later.*

Cat righted her top, cleared her throat, tucked her hair behind her ears and wondered if the Tour barbers could trim her fringe. She gave herself a supportive smile. She was going to be introduced to Vasily Jawlensky and she was more than ready to meet him.

She was not ready, however, to bump into Ben. But there he was, talking to Emma O'Reilly and Rachel, the two *soigneurs* and the doctor right in Cat's path. It was impossible to pretend she hadn't seen them, especially with Rachel calling to her. Cat waved swiftly and tapped at her watch and her brow to justify what she hoped was a plausible exit. At the entrance to the *village* a few metres later, a hand caught her by the shoulder.

'Cat?'

Ben, of course.

'Oh,' Cat said, not establishing eye contact, 'I can't talk, I'm expected elsewhere.'

'Where *were* you?' Ben asked with a hint of rejection which made Cat want to hit him.

'Where were *you*?' she countered, brandishing her pass at the sentries on watch at the *village* entrance. Ben, of course, had a pass too.

'I was waiting for you,' Ben said, following her through, 'I thought we had a date?'

Cat stopped, turned, and regarded him directly, wishing he wasn't so handsome, nor that she should so crave a kiss right there and then. '*You*,' she declared, 'can have too much of a good thing.' It irritated her that he should stare back and look perplexed.

Don't play with me, Dr York.

'Now excuse me,' she ordered, turning and marching purposefully away.

Too much of a good thing? Ben pondered as he strolled back out of the *village* having high-fived Hunter on the way. *What was she on about? How can I have had that if I've hardly had her at all.*

'Oh well,' he said out loud, nodding to Jules Le Grand as he passed.

Maybe she just got out of the wrong side of bed this morning.

The fact that it wasn't my bed means it was wrong, full stop.

With the first Time Trial tomorrow, tension was high in the peloton today. It was the last chance for the pure sprinters to grab the limelight and also for the opportunists to make a name for themselves by making a break. The serious contenders needed to keep out of danger. Ominous cloud cover hung like a headache throughout the Stage but ultimately, all that rained down was trouble, giving practically every rider on this year's Tour de France a liberal dousing.

'*Hung like a headache,*' Cat repeated out loud.
'I'm hung like a horse,' Alex quipped.
Josh regarded both his colleagues and looked baffled.
'Clouds,' Cat explained.
'Oh,' said Josh.
'Maybe a pony then,' said Alex, 'if I'm honest.'

At 80 km, just after the Category 4 climb of Côtes de Morrisot, Max Sciandri (Le Français des Jeux) surged away with Paolo Gabicci (Zucca MV) and Franz Marc (Telekom) in keen pursuit. Lying in 51st place and 1 minute 52 behind the yellow jersey of Tyler Hamilton, it was not unfeasible for Sciandri to bring to fruition the attack he engineered with Freddy Verdonk during Stage 4, to take the Stage and the yellow jersey. Initially, it seemed a dose of luck might assist when, soon after the three attackers had honked away, a crash in the main bunch floored scores of riders, slowing up those behind and putting the brakes on those in front who needed to ascertain whether their leaders had been involved.

Sciandri's group rode positively, retaining a 4 minute 40 second lead for some distance. Though the Anglo-Italian was deserving of victory today, the peloton was not in a generous mood and had their sights set on capture. The last 10 km was slightly downhill which would have been much to the breakaway's advantage. But with a gentle but lengthy drag before that, the peloton pulled together to swallow back the three riders and the Stage headed towards a classic sprinters' finish on the majestic Quai Louis XVIII.

The average speed today was a swift 41.8 kph, touching almost 60 kph in the closing straight. The sprinters certainly gave the crowds something to remember them by; all the key players were there, all desperate to win. None wanted victory so badly as Stefano Sassetta who'd squandered all of the hot-spot sprints to arch rival Jesper Lomers. Pietr Rodchenko was disqualified for hurling his bidon at Stuart O'Grady for no other reason, it seemed, than that the Australian was riding a clear, clean, straight sprint much faster than him. Sassetta crossed the line first but was later demoted to last in the group and fined for dangerous riding, having crashed shoulders with Mario Cipollini and then impinged on Jesper Lomers's line. Lomers's consolation was taking the green jersey away from Sassetta.

The Tour de France has reached the eve of the first Time Trial. New names will no doubt grace the leaderboard tomorrow and then new terrain beckons as the bunch commence their journey south to the gateway to the Pyrenees.

<ENDS>

Bordeaux. Beautiful, elegant, quintessentially French Bordeaux. Cat was pleased to be back there, a place she had liked but not returned to since visiting as a backpacking student with a summer's railcard and a shoestring budget ten years before. She was surprised to remember sections of the town. If she took a left and then first right just there, she would arrive at that lovely little *boulangerie*. If it was still there. It was. She would treat herself. She would treat herself to half an hour of life outside the entourage of the Tour de France, to food other than the now somewhat monotonous press buffets. She would grant herself a little peace and quiet, a *café au lait*, a slice of *tarte aux pommes*, a glass of Badoit too. She fancied *citron pressé* but it was too Ben York. She wanted just to be a young woman, sitting by herself at one of the shop's impromptu tables. Though verging on sacrilege, she even removed her press pass. She just sat awhile, did Cat McCabe, sat and sipped and munched and looked around her. She didn't think of bike riders and she tried not to think of their support teams, certainly not their medical men. She switched her phone off, put her sunglasses on, hitched up the sleeves of her top and concentrated on nothing but the warmth of the afternoon sun seeping through her arms.

There is only so long that surroundings can be observed before they are known off by heart. There is only so long one can watch a game of *pétanque* and retain concentration. There is only so long one can smile blandly at nothing in particular before the mind wanders. What are you thinking about, Cat, sitting there, gaze flitting from building to tree to Gitanes packet in the gutter?

Him and Him.

Who and which?

Ben.

And?

Him – back home.

In that order?

Yes.

Well, there's a start.

Do I really want either?

Do you?

Do I want both?

Do you?

No.

No? To which?

I don't know. I tried, you know. I tried very very hard to make Him happy, to make Him want to stay, to furnish His life with all He could ever require. I feel I've failed in some way.

We gather that. Move forward – and stop capitalizing the 'H'. Move forward – you're allowed to, because you can rest easy that you did do everything you could for that relationship. You also mourned at base level. You swept nothing under the metaphorical carpet. You reached absolute rock bottom emotionally but therein lie the strongest foundations upon which to build. Nothing hidden. Nothing more you could have done, should have said. You do know that?

Yes. I'm just not good at goodbyes. They make me sad. Amor vincit omnia – *and all of that.*

It is good that you feel that way. It means you are undamaged. Imagine if you felt bitter and twisted – how destructive would that be? How awful would it be if you were now hardened and cynical? He was mean to you, Cat.

He was mean to me.

Ultimately, it had nothing to do with *you*. You do see that?

It had nothing to do with me.

That's right. That's to be your mantra.

It had nothing to do with me. I was dealt a bad card, hey?

Good theory. On to Ben. Another good theory, I think.

I don't.

Have another *café au lait.* No, Cat, have the *citron pressé* that you really want. Add some sugar. Have a sip. Nice?

Lovely.

As nice as in Pradier? Nostalgic? If a day's grace can amount to the past? OK, don't answer, just enjoy.

Ben York.

How do you feel?

If I'm truthful, I feel disappointed. If I'm completely honest, I feel insecure. You see, I don't really know Ben at all, do I? And yet there's something there – physical attraction is uppermost at the moment and it's exhilarating to feel this frisson. But I really quite like him too. If I didn't, if I just wanted a fuck, I'd go get it from him – regardless of podium girls or Josh's opinion of me.

You're trailing off.

I'd like another pressé.

There. Continue?

I didn't have the chemistry wrong, I'm sure of it. I don't know what I want from Ben, or what I can expect, or to what I'm entitled. I'm cross with myself for having revelled in being the centre of his attention – and yet, I was obviously foisting on him an attachment that in reality isn't actually there.

Podium Princess?

Yes. I know exactly what Fen would say to me. I'd be calling him a bastard and my sister would calmly theorize that I'm mad at him because of my own indignance that his interest is not exclusively focused on me. That's a distorted view of myself, isn't it? Ben is Ben – Ben is who he is. But, and here's the rub, my consternation, my dejection – OK, my petulance – doesn't really stem from Ben at all. I wanted him to want me, you see. That he doesn't, or at least not in the capacity I'd ascribed to him, makes me hurt, makes me doubt myself, makes me feel insecure. Oh, the ignominy of it all.

You're rambling there. You mean, outwardly you're doing the 'men – pah! – bastards!' and within you're whimpering for what you perceive as inadequacy, as rejection?

I suppose. Yes.

But the crux is that it hasn't actually dampened your ardour. Ben continues to make you swoon. You'd like to go to bed with him, become tangled, embroiled, involved.

Yes.

So, perversely, you're on your high horse with your nose in the air, primly principled when still you're craving to have sex with him?

Yes.

It's called self-protection, Cat.

I'm in Bordeaux. I'd better go. I need to speak to Taverner. To Andy at Maillot. I need to find Josh and see where we're staying for the next two nights. I'm working. I'm a member of the press corps of the Tour de France. I haven't got time for sex or romance or any of that fluff.

So you're going to ride your high horse all the way back to the *salle de presse*?

Sorry, she's decided not to answer.

Half an hour later and Cat suddenly loved Podium Princess, felt immensely strong and wanted Ben York's blood. As she and Josh left the *salle de presse* they passed by a bench on which sat two podium girls. There was a Crédit Lyonnais girl, dressed of course in the yellow of the bank's sponsored *maillot*, the other was Cat's podium girl, or Ben's, or Coca-Cola's actually. The Crédit Lyonnais girl was talking quietly but in audibly soothing tones to Miss Coca-Cola whose eyes were very red, swollen and watery. Cat felt vindicated.

So all men are bastards.

She felt sudden sympathy for the girl.

He's not worth crying over.

She felt relief.

Thank God it's not me weeping.

'What are you grinning at?' Josh asked Cat as he unlocked the car, threw her the keys and slumped into the passenger seat, rubbing his eyes and flexing his keyboard-weary fingers.

'Oh,' Cat breezed, turning on the engine and giving it a good roar, 'women's things.' Josh nodded sagely, rather keen to pry but far too nice to do so.

Auberge Claudette was a breath of fresh air. Two star, of course, but a welcome change from the recent nondescript hotel chains. Cat loved her bedroom, furnished with an old iron bed once painted white, a Lloyd Loom style chair a little threadbare, a clothes rail behind a swathe of calico and a rickety chest of drawers lined with the same *Toiles de Jouy* wallpaper which decorated the walls in a lovely time-faded hue. The tiny en-suite bathroom had a small but deep sitting tub, an incongruously vast porcelain basin and a very low toilet. Best of all, it had a window and Cat realized how, prior to this, she'd been tolerating neon strips and no natural light. There were long windows in the bedroom with shutters inside and out. Cat leant out of the window and smiled into the first signs of sunset. She wasn't so much on the Tour de France as in a Louis Malle film and, to her delight, she could string out the fantasy for more than just a night. With the next two Stages starting so close to Bordeaux, Auberge Claudette was home for the time being.

What better way to settle than to unpack, to hide her rucksack under the bed and to run the tub and luxuriate. Who had tied the pale lilac ribbon into a bow on one of the bedposts? A previous guest? The *patronne*? Was there any significance? Could Cat please have it? She pulled at it gently and then utilized it to fix her hair into a high pony-tail while she had a bath. With the tips of her hair and the ends of the ribbon tickling the nape of her neck, she closed her eyes and momentarily traded her Louis Malle role for that of bathing belle in a bubble bath advertisement. She giggled, opened her eyes and cleared her mind. She sat a while longer in the warm water, grinning at the walls, humming the soundtrack of *Betty Blue* and planned to forsake the hotel breakfast the next day for a circuitous trip to her *boulangerie* so she could complete her picture by strolling the streets with a baguette tucked under her arm.

It was still very warm, even the breeze that whispered in to the bedroom, so Cat let her body air dry. She lounged naked on her bed, reading (Rose Tremain and not *La Route, Les Etapes*), running her fingertips along her thigh and now forsaking an imaginary part in a Jean-Jacques Beineix movie for that in a Degas pastel. She felt soothed and contented and was enjoying her own company immensely until a gentle rap at her door disrupted her peace.

Bugger, must be the patronne – I asked for an extra pillow.

'*Un instant, s'il vous plaît,*' she called, grabbing a little floral sundress and slipping it over her nakedness. Barefoot, she crossed the floorboards lightly, the lilac ribbon starting to work its way loose from the hasty pony-tail she had tied.

'I'm coming,' she said, her hand already opening the door.

Ben York pushed into her room, shut the door more strongly than was necessary, scooped Cat against him so tightly that she was momentarily lifted off the floor, and plunged his tongue deep into her mouth (which was so startled that it was conveniently open anyway).

Don't let him kiss you. Don't! Pull away. Don't bloody kiss him back. Don't fling your arms around his neck – take them away! Don't drop your hold to his biceps. Why are you grabbing his shirt? Stop it! Pull back.

'Don't pull back,' Ben murmured, standing still while Cat all but leaped backwards. She was speechless.

Say something!

'Say something,' Ben said, hands on hips and forearms distractingly on display. 'What's with you?'

Say something – what should I say to him?

Ben advanced towards her more quickly than she could retreat. He pushed her on to her bed and fell on top of her, his lips at her neck, his hand at her thigh. *Get the dress up.* His hand at the flesh of her thigh. Cat wriggled away from him though her body begged her to writhe against him.

'Fuck off!' she hissed. Ben looked utterly taken aback but he broke into a broad smile, reclined on her bed and raised an eyebrow at the obviously furious girl who now stood by the window unaware that her dress was enticingly transparent.

She'd know if she chances upon the state of my cock. Ah! She's seen. She knows. But see? She doesn't move.

'Go,' she said, 'please.'

'Why?' he replied, not moving an inch and pulling his infuriating, gorgeous smile over his mouth and into his eyes.

'Because you're a wanker,' Cat protested, clenching her fist when she observed him bite his lip to conceal his amusement.

'Well,' he said with consideration, 'that must make you a cock-teasing bitch.'

'I beg your pardon?' said Cat, now flushed, and quite the picture of consternation which made Ben's cock twitch with delight.

'What's with you, Catriona McCabe?' he asked again.

'You need to ask?' Cat responded.

'I need to ask,' Ben replied, propping himself up on an elbow and anticipating Cat's reply with genuine interest.

'You shouldn't need to,' Cat protested rather primly, 'I'm not joining the queue.'

'The queue?' Ben repeated, really looking quite puzzled.

'Kiss the girls and make 'em cry?' she elaborated, knowing it sounded daft. He considered the accusation but looked just as bewildered after a moment's contemplation.

'Sorry, Cat,' he said, 'you're talking in rhymes, or bullshit, or something. And I've got to have you,' he said, laying his hand over the bulge in his jeans '– and soon.'

Leisurely, he left the bed and came towards her, observing that her hastened breathing presented him with those gorgeous breasts heaving away in earnest. He didn't touch but he looked long and desirously. He cupped her face in his hands and made to kiss her again.

'Fuck off,' Cat implored flimsily.

'Why?' he whispered, hovering his mouth over her forehead so that she could feel his breath trickle over her face like a waft of warm silk.

'Because!' she proclaimed in a whisper.

'Because what?' he murmured back, tracing her eyes, her nose, her chin, with his lips. He laid his lips over hers but did not move them.

Don't kiss him! Don't.

But Ben detected her lips give an almost imperceptible tremble so he encouraged them by parting his just slightly.

'Why not?' he mouthed, barely speaking.

'Because!' Cat tried again. He pulled away and treated himself to the sight of her; momentarily, her eyes still closed, her cheeks flushed, her lips waiting, worried. God, he found her gorgeous.

'Because *what*?' he asked loudly.

'Because *you*,' Cat hissed, 'you asked for me but you hadn't even finished with *her* and if I'd have been earlier or later – well! Well then! Fuck you!'

'Huh?' Ben shook his head.

'Yesterday,' Cat said, stamping her bare foot indignantly, 'I bloody came to your sleazepad and saw her coming out – all right?'

'*Her*?' Ben queried.

'You know who!' Cat growled. 'She was coming out of your room!'

'Yesterday?'

'Don't play naïve!' Cat shouted. 'And today I saw her crying!'

'Who?' Ben implored.

'Jesus! How many were there traipsing in and out of your bloody room?' Cat remonstrated. 'The podium girl, of course! Miss Coca-Cola!'

'*Monique*?' Ben exclaimed, placing his hand over his mouth, concealing whatever reaction was there.

'Whatever her name is,' Cat said, frowning with intent, 'and today, I see her crying her eyes out!'

'*Crying*?' Ben pressed from behind his hand.

'Yes!' Cat yelled. 'You're not going to do that to me!'

'Monique was *crying*?' Ben repeated. 'You heard her?'

'She was crying,' Cat growled.

'Did you *hear* her?' Ben persisted.

'I saw her!' Cat spat. 'Her eyes were red raw, for Christ's sake!' She stamped. 'She looked utterly miserable.'

Ben stared at Cat, took his hand from his mouth and regarded her.

'So would you be,' he said to Cat, 'if you had raging conjunctivitis.'

Cat stares at the Great Ophthalmologist, her eyes criss-crossing his face trying to absorb what she's just heard, make sense of the tangle, and figure out how she should respond. Turning away from him, which she does momentarily, seems like a good idea. But when she turns back he's still there, still silent, regarding her with a blend of reproach and amusement. The onus is on Cat and it's onerous. She's biting

191

her lip so hard that it's throbbing but she can't seem to release it. Slipping past him to take refuge in the lovely bathroom seems like another good idea so she does just that.

She's sitting on the edge of the tub regarding her feet, now she's sitting sideways on the toilet looking at her knees. Now she leans her back against the basin. She's now knocking her head gently against the window. She turns and glances in the mirror, imploring her reflection to tell her what to do.

Jesus, have I blown it now! Stupid stupid girl.

Say sorry.

As if that would suffice.

Laugh it off?

That would seem too trite.

Give him a blow job?

My jaw is too tense. And anyway, he's hardly likely to rise to the occasion for a girl who's thrown slanderous accusations at him, for a girl who's made an utter fool of herself.

Well, what *are* you going to do?

Tell me what to do!

No, Cat – you figure it out.

Oh Fen, where are you!

Over the sea and far away.

Reflection – help!

It's only you in the mirror. Your call, Cat McCabe.

Shit! Have I been in here ages? Say he's left?

Cat opens the bathroom door. Ben is sitting in the chair seemingly engrossed in Rose Tremain. He glances up and then returns his attention to the book. Cat pads across the room, walks around the bed and sits on the edge so that her knees almost touch Ben's. She tips her head to one side, silently imploring him to look up. He's reading. She clears her throat, hoping she might gain his attention. He's reading. Rose Tremain is bloody good. Cat sighs, hoping he'll take sympathy on her humiliation. Nope. She gazes over to the window. It's gloriously dusky now, the portion of sky visible streaked with amber, the room bathed so aesthetically in half-light that Monet really should have been there.

Incongruous though it might seem, Cat feels an enormous sense of tranquillity, the willing captive of some strange hermetically sealed moment placing her in a beautiful room on a sultry evening with a man quietly reading. A blink returns her to the situation in hand. A glance to Ben reveals that Rose Tremain's text is closed around his index finger and his attention is focused on Cat entirely.

Cat licks her lips fleetingly and speaks without preparation or agenda.

'I. Am. So. Embarrassed.'

Ben does not reply but something about his demeanour enables Cat to smile apologetically.

'What can you think?' she continues with a humble shrug superseded by a sorry slump. Ben tilts his head and closes the book, clasping his hands loosely, sitting back in the chair, relaxed.

'Please forgive me,' Cat says, now sitting very tall, her hands demurely in her lap, her eyes cast down.

'You're fucking gorgeous when you're angry,' Ben says, deadly serious and with no jest.

'I'm sorry,' Cat says, looking straight at him, 'I hope I didn't offend you.'

'On the contrary,' says Ben.

'And I really hope,' says Cat, very measuredly, eye-locked, 'that I haven't gone and ruined any prospects here.'

'You're also very sexy when you're meek,' Ben tells her.

Cat can't hear the compliment, her concern to appease Ben, to undo any wrongdoing, her sole focus.

'I didn't mean to insult you,' she says.

'I'm pretty flattered, actually,' Ben says, 'that you should have thought me such a gigolo and so in demand.'

'What can you think of me?' Cat laments, looking at her lap but immediately yearning for Ben's gaze.

'I think you're a feisty girl who won't tolerate any crap,' Ben says openly. 'Fuck, what a challenge!'

They regard each other in the fading light, the soft tones, the hush of the evening, enhancing their reciprocated allure.

Cat flops herself backwards on to the bed, her arms above her head, and scours the ceiling. She hears the Loom chair creak. Her heart is beating fast and goes into overdrive at the touch of Ben's fingers on her knees. Goosebumps tingle their way over her skin as she feels her dress being lifted up and then lowered back.

'Cat McCabe,' Ben marvels in a low voice, leaning over her, his hands either side of her torso, 'where are your knickers?'

'Obviously, they were in a twist!' Cat jests softly. Ben sits on the edge of the bed and Cat runs her hand lightly up and down his back. She pulls at his shirt, gently at first, then with an insistent tug. He lies next to her. They look up at the ceiling and then, with film-worthy timing, they turn and look at each other. The shared gaze, the mutual desire caught in a sealed second of fabulous intensity before they are at each other's mouths; kissing and tasting and biting and uncontrollable.

Ben flings Cat's dress up so that she is naked apart from one breast and her shoulders. He has a hand enmeshed in her hair. The other is everywhere and fast. Trickling over her legs, brushing her bush, sweeping over her stomach, up her waist, into her armpit, over her exposed breast where he stops awhile. She wants to taste every part of his mouth. His body feels so tantalizing behind his cotton shirt. Off. Off. She pulls at buttons, at the tails, she slips her hand underneath and finds his flesh. Warm, prickling under her touch, a strong body, a little hair to the chest, to the lower stomach. His skin is so soft, almost incongruously so for his defined musculature and masculinity. She straddles him, she has to get that shirt off. As she is unbuttoning, he runs a hand up her inner thigh, cups it over her sex and inserts his finger effortlessly, deep inside her. She's gasping, he's glazed. He's moving his finger and she's moving on it. His thumb is stroking her clitoris. She wants the shirt off his back. Get it off. She wants to come. Fuck the shirt. Her whole body wracks with the orgasm, her voice comes through her gasping. She's coming on his finger, his thumb, in her stomach, through her nipples. Her body crumples with the pleasure of it all. She lies beside him, her leg slung over his, her sex grazing his jeans. He brings his finger to his mouth and sucks it and then he takes it to her mouth and she sucks it too. That's me. That's you.

'I'd like to have sex with you. Now. Please. Now,' Cat says, easing his shirt away and gazing desirously at his torso. She unbuckles his belt, her eyes drawn to and delighted by the bulge in his jeans, her fingers tracing the shape of him, her sex anticipating the feel of him.

'I'd love to have sex with you,' Ben says, his hand up the back of her dress, softly feeling her buttocks and tracing the crack down and under to her damp mound.

'*Now*,' Cat implores, leaning over his face and licking his lips, 'I want to have sex with you *now*.'

'I don't have any condoms with me,' says Ben, stroking her face and tracing her lips.

'I don't have any condoms with *me*,' Cat bemoans. Then she smiles mischievously, eyes his insistent bulge and regards him with delight.

'There are plenty of other ways I can think of,' she says.

'And,' Ben reasons, unpopping his jeans, bucking his hips to wriggle free from boxer shorts too, 'there's tomorrow. Come to me when you've had Luca.'

'Metaphorically speaking,' Cat chides, walking her fingers tantalizingly up his shaft.

'Come to me then,' Ben murmurs, closing his eyes with the pleasure of Cat's hand encircling his cock; gasping as he feels her lips at the tip of him, can sense them opening, anticipating her mouth taking him deep.

I want you to come in my mouth, Ben.

I'm coming, Cat. Jesus. Fuck.

STAGE 7
Computaparc – Individual Time Trial. 54.5 kilometres

'*R*achel – help.'

Vasily Jawlensky entered the Zucca camper van.

'Oh dear,' his *soigneur* said from behind an architecturally intriguing tower of energy bars. 'Och Jesus – look at you!'

She looked at him. Vasily Jawlensky, her team's key rider on whose shoulders the hope of the yellow jersey was today firmly placed. And yet, unlike the brooding Fabian Ducasse, currently barking and snarling at everyone, Vasily's comportment was no different than if he was merely going out on a training ride. His tall body, on to which lycra had seemingly been sprayed, dominated the interior of the camper van. He regarded his *soigneur* steadily and shrugged at her almost apologetically. Rachel saw that his skinsuit was split from underarm to hip and was aware that his Time Trial start time was in half an hour. She helped peel her rider from the lycra and assisted him in slithering his way in to a pristine suit.

'I go back to the blocks now,' he said graciously, focusing so intently on her neck that Rachel found herself cupping her hand against it. 'With thanks to you, Rachel.'

'That's good,' his *soigneur* replied. 'How are you feeling?'

'Tight,' Vasily replied, 'tense – you know?'

'I can imagine,' Rachel said. She stood in the doorway of the van and watched Vasily place himself on his stationary bike. He clipped his feet in and started to pedal, soon leaning down to take the handlebars. Rachel winced. The skinsuit had torn again, this time around the shoulders.

Fucking supplier – I'll kill them.

Vasily calmly dismounted, feeling the ripped material, his skin. He looked at his *soigneur*.

'You have another, Rachel?' he asked.

'Sure,' Rachel replied, closing the door on the fans craving every last glimpse, any glimpse, of the great Russian. Again, the two of them freed Vasily's body from its colourful sheath and he stood naked and contemplative whilst Rachel delved around a bag for another.

'Have you grown?' she asked Vasily, eyeing him objectively, or as objectively as such a particularly fine specimen of masculinity could be viewed by a young woman.

'No,' Vasily said, 'I am as I always am. No change.'

'Bloody suppliers,' Rachel elaborated with a thunderous frown.

'Yes, *bloody* them,' said Vasily ingenuously, liking the semantic taste of the word but intending no insult. Rachel puffed clouds of talcum powder over Vasily's torso and patted his skin lightly. And then, momentarily, she wavered. She stroked him gently down his chest. Smoothing the talc. No, stroking his body. She turned him around. Again, she wavered. She looked at his back – no, gazed at his back – before applying more powder. Stroking gives better coverage than patting. Yeah, right, Rachel. She took the new lycra, assessing the material with much concentration, trying to pay no attention to the downy blond hairs furled about his forearms. She'd never noticed them before; she certainly wasn't going to start noticing them now.

How can I not have noticed them before? How many times must I have massaged this rider?

Was Vasily staring at her? She didn't think so. How could

he be, with his Time Trial looming? His eyes might be focused on her, but she acknowledged that his mind was already engrossed in the Computaparc course. She'd obviously quite lost hers. She helped Vasily dress again, checked the seams of the new skinsuit and asked him to bend, to stretch.

'Well,' she said, 'that'll last you the 54 and a half k *and* the short trip to the podium this evening.' She winked at him supportively, wished him good luck and told him to go and finish his tuning up.

'Thank you, Rachel,' Vasily replied, continuing to stare at her so intently that she wiped her hand across her chin to remove whatever it was that had so caught his attention.

'Go!' Rachel said, glancing at her watch and wanting Vasily to be warming up five minutes ago.

'Yes,' said the rider. And then Vasily Jawlensky kissed Rachel McEwen. Quite quickly but very intensely. Too swiftly for her to have pulled away; too adeptly for her to have wanted to. He encircled her waist, lowered his head and took his lips to hers, slipping his tongue into her mouth immediately on contact. She'd never had a kiss like it. His eyes were open and so were hers. Their tongues danced slowly. It lasted seconds yet it was luxurious and measured rather than urgent. Then Vasily went directly to his bike and continued to warm up in earnest. Rachel closed the camper-van door and sat down heavily on the bench. She placed her head in her hands and took deep breaths. She could smell talcum powder. She inhaled deeply.

Then she wiped her hands urgently on her jeans.

What the fuck just happened?

There had been no warning, no prior hints, no clues at all in all the time she'd known Vasily. Not from him. She knew so little about the person behind the champion cyclist. Not within herself; she'd rarely thought about the personality behind the body which raced bicycles.

Have I ever fancied Vasily? Have I ever thought he's fancied me? Hand on my heart, no. I'm his soigneur. He's my charge.

What just happened?

I have absolutely no idea.

How can that be?

I don't know. I hardly know Vasily. Few people do. He's such a closed book – one so many are desperate to read. Not me. I know his joints and muscles off by heart but I've never really stopped to contemplate the man they belong to.

Why did you stroke and not pat?

I don't know. But I don't think it was me, if you see – I don't think he meant to kiss Rachel. Maybe it was an instantaneous reaction to me stroking, not patting – a chemical, hormonal, non-cerebral, male response. Shit, maybe it was the talcum powder itself. Maybe there's a substance in it that's banned. But it wasn't me. It can't have been. I'm just his soigneur. *How can he know me as Rachel? He does not know Rachel at all.*

You should get moving. You have a million and one duties to attend to.

I need to sit a while.

'I know what I need,' Rachel said, standing, glancing around the interior of the van, 'I need a girlfriend – I need the insight of a woman. I need female company, complicity – a confidante.'

Contre la montre.

What a lovely phrase. It was Cat's chant that morning as she gathered together her wits and her work effects. She was running late, having not been able to leave her bed for all the reliving of the night before and the projected ponderings for the day ahead. Sex? Perhaps. More than likely. Hurry up! *Contre la montre.* Against the clock. Morning, Josh. Morning, Alex. Hurry up, Cat. Sorry. Sorry. *Allons!*

'You're perky,' Josh remarked, pleased that she was.

'I had,' Cat reasoned, 'a very good – night.'

'*Moi aussi*,' Alex said, 'like a fucking log. Out for the count.'

'I slept really well too,' Josh added, glancing in gratitude at Auberge Claudette before driving away.

'Me too,' Cat recapitulated.

I am going to sleep with Ben tonight and I'll be most wide awake.

'I'm interviewing Luca this afternoon,' Cat said. 'He's riding early so I'll disappear for an hour or so. Will you fill me in?'

'Sure,' Alex said, looking to the back seat where Cat was sitting and staring out of the window with an inordinately expansive smile on her face, 'as long as you share any juicy Luca-isms.'

'Where are you going to do him?' Josh asked, curtailing any insinuation from Alex by stamping on the brakes to allow the race commissaire's car priority.

'In his hotel room,' Cat replied. Alex tittered. The others didn't.

The only time Jules Le Grand was going to leave Fabian Ducasse's side was when the Système Vipère rider and overall contender for the *maillot jaune* was actually on his bike riding the course. The rider had all but sleep-walked to his *directeur*'s room at four in the morning to say one thing.

'The Time Trial is a test of truth.'

For all Fabian's outward arrogance and confidence, he needed the support of his *directeur* if he was to take yellow at the Time Trial that afternoon and define the ultimate outcome on the podium in Paris a fortnight later. Though Fabian had returned to bed and, amazingly, to a deep sleep, his *directeur* stayed awake for him. In silk pyjama bottoms, Jules had gazed out of the window witnessing night simper into dawn.

Fabian needs me to yell 'Allez allez allez!', to torment him, to demand that he ride harder for fuck's sake.

Jules showered and shaved and treated his underarms and cheeks to liberal applications of Gucci toiletries.

Fabian also needs me to listen attentively when he repeats his concerns and strategy for the course.

'Often he does so in silence but it is always audible to me,' Jules said out loud, wondering if 6 a.m. was too early to phone Système Vipère's eponymous sponsor. He would leave it half an hour. No doubt his favoured journalist on *L'Equipe* would be glad to take a call.

'Ultimately, it is the paternal support of the *directeur sportif* that the rider requires after a Time Trial,' Jules said down the line to the reporter, 'to lift his spent body from his bike, to be there for him whatever the outcome.'

'*Merci*,' said the journalist, hoping Jules Le Grand had not heard him stifle a yawn, could not envisage him as he was, crumpled, in bed and still half-asleep.

Jules was dressed in Gucci top to toe. He phoned the team sponsors.

'Whatever the outcome, today,' he told them, 'Ducasse will ride the Stage as if his life depends on it which, to him, it does. The team are pleased that you will visit today to watch the Stage. It will be good for Jesper Lomers to see you.' There was a pause. 'Yes, yes, he is on the verge of renewing his contract – of that I'm sure.'

He'd better be – or Anya will have me to answer to. Not that she's answered any of Jesper's calls, I am informed. At the moment, that is not good for my rider's morale. But I can turn it to the team's advantage, I'm sure of it. When the time is right.

Jules Le Grand plucked at grapes from the fruit bowl and sipped at Evian from the minibar. He phoned *L'Equipe* again, making a well-rehearsed soliloquy sound positively conversational; so eloquent that the journalist could quote him word for word.

'Today, Fabian Ducasse will not be merely going to work, doing his job, earning his salary. For Fabian, this Time Trial will determine his purpose on this mortal coil. He will challenge the demons within himself. He will emerge triumphant.'

Jules ended the call.

If not – then what? he contemplated quietly, bursting a

grape against the roof of his mouth. *What will it all mean? Who would Ducasse be? What would be the point?*

'He needs me,' Jules said, leaving his room at 7 a.m. to check on the *soigneurs*, the mechanics and the weather.

Cat McCabe saw Fabian and Jules on her way to the *village*. Full of the bounce and confidence that the headiness of new passion can instil, she approached the two men.

'*Bonjour*,' she said, turning back on herself so she could walk their way a while. 'How are you feeling? What is your optimum time? If you don't take yellow today, can the Tour still be yours?'

Fleetingly, Fabian looked at her darkly, frowning, turning to his *directeur* for support, to make her go away. Intrusion. Distraction. Pointless. Jules Le Grand glanced at Cat. He'd seen her around. English *journaliste*. Any other day, he would have granted her a suave smile, an audience with himself, with his riders. Today, though, at this time, he regarded her with undisguised contempt.

'Leave Fabian,' he commanded, his hissed order rooting her to the spot while the men walked away from her and ever onwards towards their fate.

Josh looked up from his laptop.

'Hullo, Rachel,' he said in amazement, 'what brings you here? Fugallo had a great ride. Are you here to watch Vasily?'

'Actually,' Rachel said, 'I was looking for Cat.'

'She's interviewing Luca,' Josh informed her. He glanced at his watch. So did Alex.

'She's been bloody hours,' Alex remarked, 'little minx.'

'Is she coming back here?' Rachel asked, eyeing the unmanned laptop next to Josh.

'She has her report to file,' Josh said, glancing at his watch and shaking his head. 'You bet she'll be back.'

'We're all going out tonight,' Alex said thoughtfully, distracted from his work by the sight of Rachel's bottom which he thought very nice indeed, 'why don't you come too?'

Rachel swiftly assessed all she had to do, then she nodded. 'Cool,' she said, 'that would be great. Will Cat be there?'

'Of course,' Josh said, 'she's one of us.'

'Vasily's about to start,' Alex said, twisting his chair to focus on the screens. 'Watch it here.'

'Oh God no, I can't,' Rachel smiled, shaking her head, 'I'm far too nervous for him. I'd better go, I'll see you all later. Tell Cat I stopped by – that I'll see her later too.'

No one responded and Rachel left a hushed *salle de presse*, suddenly loving all the journalists for being so focused on Vasily's ride.

Why did the sod kiss me? Why am I giving it so much thought? Do I want more? But where the fuck did it come from?

When Luca told Cat that Ben had offered his own hotel room for the interview, Cat had to stop herself from leaping into the air, hugging the rider and saying come on, let's get it done quickly then.

'I'm rooming,' Luca had shrugged. 'Didier might want to rest. Ben will come back in an hour because then I must rest. But hey! I did well, no?'

'You,' Cat had responded, walking alongside Luca down the corridor to the doctor's room, 'are a star. It was a great ride – I'd say this is going to be a really fabulous first Tour for you.'

'You're a babe, Cat McCabe,' Luca had said as they entered Ben's room. 'Hey! I'm a poet! Let me be your boyfriend,' he had continued, 'we can make beautiful babies. Or we can practise anyway.'

'Work first,' Ben had cautioned the rider whilst glancing at Cat, 'play later. No sex during the Tour.'

'Fuck you,' Luca had protested.

'Fuck you,' Ben had responded, staring at Cat. With a sly

smile he had left the room, informing them he would return in an hour. Luca took to Ben's bed. Cat set her dictaphone on the bedside table and coiled herself into the armchair.

'So, Luca,' she had said, 'let's talk about you.'

'Love and sex, Luca?' Cat asks, glancing at her watch and seeing that the hour is almost up.

'Sure,' Luca shrugs, 'both – sometimes separately, occasionally together. This is off the record, right?'

Cat nods, regards the dictaphone but does not switch it off.

'I'm a young guy,' the rider shrugs, 'and I'm horny. I do a job where you can be superhero to many women. They don't know you – but they think they do. It's flattering, you know? If they offer, I'll take it – but only if I can make it the next day. So, even if there was a chick yesterday with tits out and legs open, I would have refused because the Time Trial was today. Yes? But tonight – tonight is different.'

'So you're going on the prowl?' Cat jests.

'If I can stay awake,' Luca responds ruefully, 'cos you know something? Soon the only humping for me will be going up and down those fucking mountains.'

'Are you nervous?'

'That is not a question for me to answer.'

'Are you?' Cat asks tenderly, as a friend. Luca regards her. Cat thinks how young he suddenly seems, how his body so lithe and virile in front of her is also one that could be destroyed without notice; a body, a spirit, whose strength is supreme and yet continually on the brink.

'Are you scared, Luca?' Cat repeats.

Luca observes her again. She has come to the edge of the bed and laid a hand over his wrist.

He nods, knowing it won't come out on dictaphone. She strokes his forehead and smiles down on him. He nods again.

Darling boy. Please be careful.

'Time's up,' says Ben. 'Luca, how's your pulse?'

'It's good,' the rider replies, unfurling himself from the bed. 'I'll go rest and bring it down further.'

'Thanks, Luca,' Cat says, her hand on his shoulder.

'Cat-the-Babe-McCabe,' says Luca, standing up, suddenly clad in the colourful public persona everybody loves and expects, 'my pleasure.' He kisses her three times and then leaves.

'Was that good?' Ben asks, going to Cat directly and lifting her T-shirt off.

'Great,' Cat replies, unbuttoning his jeans.

'How long do you have?' Ben asks, nuzzling his way down from her neck to her right nipple. 'Because I have about seven inches.'

'I have to write my report,' Cat says huskily. She takes his cock in her mouth.

'Jesus, Cat,' Ben pants. They gaze glazed at each other. Cat unzips her shorts and lets them fall. Ben cups his hand between her legs and can feel the heat and moistness seep through her panties. He moves his fingers as if he is playing a trumpet and watches as Cat sways with desire. He slips a finger inside the elastic and finds her flesh, burrows in a little and teases her. Her heightened breathing, audible, urgent, turns him on. The sight of his cock, stiff and straining and impatient, turns her on.

'I want you now,' he murmurs.

'You can have me now,' she replies. They wriggle out of their clothing, intermittently gorging themselves on each other's mouths. Breathing is deep and desirous, interspersed with a little laughter. The bed is creaky in places. Cat loves the sound of Ben, that he sucks in his breath when she runs her hands over his torso, that he gasps when her fingertips skim his balls. Ben loves the sounds of Cat, the little inadvertent moans she gives when he tweaks her clitoris, he likes the sudden gasp he causes when he treats her nipples to a bite or a suck. She's a sight to behold as he looks up her body while his mouth is buried in her sex. Her figure is trim and pert. She tastes delicious. He could drink her for hours. She doesn't have hours.

'Don't stop,' she pleads, moving against his mouth. But he takes his face away and now he is hovering over her, his cock probing at her bush, her stomach, her thigh, teasingly.

'Later,' he informs her, dipping down to kiss her.

'Now!' Cat remonstrates, smelling her scent on his face.

'Such matters should not be rushed,' Ben reasons, closing his eyes and groaning as Cat grasps his cock and starts to masturbate him. He steadies her wrist to his favoured pace and then holds it tight, motionless.

'Stop,' he tells her. 'We both have jobs to do.'

'But I want you,' Cat pleads, opening her legs, 'I do. Now.'

Ben smiles down at her, all lovely and soft and supine beneath him. 'Look on this as a taster,' he says, propping himself up next to Cat and slipping his hand between her legs. 'I'm going to whisk you away tonight, I know of a place.' He has two fingers inside her and her eyes are closed with the exquisite pleasure of it all. 'It's private and beautiful and we're going to have sex there.'

Cat's breathing is fast, she is moving herself against his hand, finding his fingers inside her, his thumb pressing lightly at her clitoris. She is feeling his cock. They are staring hard at each other, dipping faces close to tongue and bite, pulling away to breathe and gasp. Ben takes his hand away when he feels Cat's sex start to quiver.

'Don't go – oh God, Ben!'

He sucks on his fingers as he watches and listens to her coming, her hand between her legs, her body bucking gently.

'Tonight,' he tells her, despite the post-orgasmic vision of her all languid and soft making him harder still. 'Go now. I'll find you.'

I can't wait for tonight, Ben decides once Cat has left. *Literally, I can't wait.* His erection has hardly subsided. He returns to the bed. Cat's intoxicating scent lingers on the pillow. Ben breathes deeply and wanks to an explosive, vociferous reward.

*

'What a day!' Josh exclaimed, distributing bottles of *Seize* in an intimate bar near the Auberge, refreshingly if anomalously devoid of Tour personnel.

'What a day!' Rachel echoed, taking a hearty swig, closing her eyes and leaning back in her chair.

'One fuck of a day!' Alex said, raising his bottle and drinking most of it down in one.

And it isn't over yet! Cat thought to herself whilst nodding in agreement with the others. They relived the Time Trials of the key players and asked Rachel how the Zucca boys had reacted. She was discreet and, when Vasily's ride came under analysis, gave away even less. Cat observed her friend and thought she seemed quiet. She didn't look tired, but preoccupied, distant – a little down, perhaps. Cat followed when Rachel went to the toilet.

'Hey, Rachel,' Cat said when she emerged from the cubicle to find Rachel staring at a streaming tap. Rachel regarded Cat, and then the water, and then the floor and then her friend again.

'Are you all right?' Cat prompted gently, busying herself by washing her hands and then drying them meticulously, not wanting to pressurize Rachel.

'No yes no yes – fuck knows!' Rachel declared almost miserably.

'Do you want to talk?' Cat asked. 'Anything I can help you with?'

'No yes – ditto ditto,' Rachel smiled forlornly, 'fuck knows.'

The women's toilet was almost as large as the bar, airy, clean and really quite conducive to female revelations. There was a bentwood chair and a deep window-sill. Rachel chose the former and Cat happily settled herself into the latter.

'Vasily,' Rachel said quietly.

'Well,' Cat said supportively, 'for what it's worth, I think he'll still do it. Fabian isn't as strong in the mountains – but he won't want to let go of the yellow jersey so he might well be spent by the last Time Trial.'

'No,' Rachel said, looking up at Cat, 'I mean, *Vasily*.'

'I know,' said Cat eagerly, missing the point that Rachel wasn't making very well. Cat slithered down off the window-sill and shuffled alongside Rachel on the chair. Rachel was about to speak when Cat's mobile phone intruded.

It's Ben!

'Hullo?' she said.

'Where are you?' Ben said. 'You can talk, you can't talk? Are you near the hotel?'

'Yes,' Cat responded, thinking she ought to dampen her elated grin.

'Are you more or less than a five-minute walk away?'

'Yes,' Cat said again.

'Yes, more?'

'No.'

'Ah! Less. Good. Meet me round the back of your hotel in five minutes.'

Ben hung up. Cat turned to Rachel. What had Rachel been saying? Something about Vasily. Poor sod who missed the *maillot jaune* by so little. He must have dumped the burden of it all on his *soigneur*, poor girl. Cat tipped her head and smiled at Rachel. She held up her mobile phone.

'I can't believe it,' she said, careful not to lie, 'I've been summoned – in context of this afternoon. I'm going to have to go.'

Rachel nodded, hiding her disappointment well. 'Sure,' she said to Cat, 'you have a job to do.'

And this is one of the perks, Cat did not say out loud.

She observed Rachel still looking somewhat discomfited. 'Rachel,' she said, 'can I shadow you tomorrow?'

Rachel looked at Cat. 'Sure,' she said, 'but there's no feed as it's a short Stage – how about the day after?'

'That would be great,' Cat enthused. 'I might pop by in the morning as the start isn't till one-ish.'

'Sure,' said Rachel. 'You'd better go,' she continued, suddenly wanting to be alone anyway. Cat went. Rachel remained in the toilet a few minutes more. She stared at her reflection.

Saved by the bell – if Cat hadn't had that call, I'd be deep into revelation by now.

'Fuck it,' she said softly, 'there's nothing to discuss really anyway. It probably didn't mean anything to Vasily – he's more than likely forgotten it already.'

And for you, Rachel? What did it mean? You've thought of little else.

'The clear light of tomorrow, after a night's sleep, will render whatever it was insignificant.'

But you're not speaking for yourself, that's just your conjecture for Vasily.

'It was just somewhat disconcerting, that's all.'

Rachel returned to the bar. Alex and Josh had replenished her *Seize* and were on to their fourth apiece, aided and abetted by a packet of Gauloises with a fair few missing.

'Are you all right?' Josh asked, leaving the chair that had been Rachel's and taking his place back on a stool.

'Got the shits?' Alex asked in his inimitable way.

'I'm fine,' Rachel said.

'Where's Cat?' Josh asked.

'Has *she* got the shits?' Alex asked.

'She got a call through,' Rachel shrugged, 'she went directly to work.'

'Oh,' said Alex.

'Oh,' said Josh. Both men wondered how the novice *journaliste* could possibly have usurped them in the scoops stakes. It was just somewhat disconcerting, that's all.

Ben took Cat to Arcachon, where the sand dunes were emphatically moonlit and all was gloriously private and, though a short car ride from Bordeaux, a million miles from the Tour de France, from the times and trials of journalism and medicine. Foreplay hardly figured. The last twenty-four hours had seemed to both Cat and Ben to have been a prolonged preparation for penetration.

209

The sand was cool and though Ben had thoughtfully brought a towel, they did not lie on it. They undressed themselves; standing naked and silent, Ben passed Cat a condom which she unwrapped and placed on him. They knelt, kissed and he entered her smoothly, easily. The feeling of being filled by a man whom she so desired, the sensation of a cock inside her after a barren few months, the sensitivity with which he kissed her eyelids, licked her neck, slipped his tongue into her mouth, the adeptness with which he moved his body into hers, made her come almost immediately. He let her orgasm subside. The feeling of a tight pussy of a girl he was mad for, the pleasure of hearing her gasp, the excitement of sensing her sex quiver and pulsate around him, the surprise of her tongue dipping in and out of his nostrils, his ears, made him come soon after.

The towel did come in useful. Ben and Cat skinny dipped, talking to each other with ease, embracing in the water. Ready for more sex. No more condoms though. No matter – there would be tomorrow. And there really would be tomorrow. This wasn't to be a one off. Neither of them knew what it was to be but they were aware that tomorrow they would be together, the day after too, and the notion thrilled them privately.

What happened today, Cat? Apart from your fair share of orgasms, a head full of daydreams and a heart newly nourished and beating hard for more? The Tour de France? The Time Trial? Who won? What's happening?

Read my report, I'm tired. I want to go to sleep. I can taste salt water on my skin. I can taste Ben still. Good night.

COPY FOR P. TAVERNER @ GUARDIAN SPORTS DESK FROM CATRIONA McCABE IN BORDEAUX

Against the setting of Computaparc, where a massive turnout of cycling aficionados rubbed shoulders with a huge crowd of somewhat nonplussed techno-geeks, the 54.5 km Time Trial of the Tour de France was run today and won in outstanding style by Fabian Ducasse of Système Vipère. Vasily Jawlensky, last year's winner of the yellow jersey and contender for overall victory this year, rode brilliantly but Fabian rode better. It took 1 hour 9 minutes and 38 seconds for the French heart-throb to claim the maillot jaune and a 1 minute 18 second lead over the Russian defender, who now lies second.

Though there is no certainty that Ducasse will ride every day in yellow from here to the podium in Paris, the golden fleece will assist his passage and he will not relinquish it without the fight which many anticipate will take place between him and Jawlensky in the looming mountain Stages.

Fabian set his pace and held it, averaging just under 51 kph. He chose a huge gear and stuck to it, enabling his bike to gulp as much tarmac with each turn of the pedals as possible. He maintained his prawn-like position all the way; folded aerodynamically, his head tucked lower than his shoulder blades, his knees close to the frame, shoulders steady. Technique, however, went only part of the way in securing his victory today, determination played much the key role.

A Time Trial is lonely to ride and heart-wrenching to watch. Tarmac is ever unfurling and the wind seems to relish buffeting a cyclist out there alone, with no shelter, no slipstreams, no stretch where he can ease the pressure. How was it for Megapac's Didier LeDucq, standing on his pedals to contend with the climb an evil 15 km from the finish, to have Ducasse power past him sitting deep and steady on the saddle? Time Trialling requires supreme strength, it needs calculation and brains and, ultimately, dogged determination to discredit suffering. Acknowledging pain does not win Time Trials. If your pulse is racing at 180 bpm and lactic acid is forming in your muscles but there are only a few kilometres to go – so what? Your soigneur, glucose and electrolytes can help later. Health does not matter to a rider midway through a Time Trial. A rider who can calmly dismount and walk himself to his soigneur *did not Time Trial*. Jules Le Grand, directeur sportif *of Système Vipère, literally carried Ducasse from his bike. Similarly, Rachel McEwen, Jawlensky's* soigneur, eased the rider away from his machine, her supportive embrace holding him up, holding him together, as she escorted him to the privacy of the team bus.

<ENDS>

STAGE 8
Sauternes–Pau. 162 kilometres

*B*en York awoke with an erection, as frequently he did, however this morning he knew it was not a physiological vagary of his reverie that caused it, but a lucid awareness of Cat's existence down the road now replacing the image of her which had inhabited his dreamtime. He fingered his cock, gave himself a few soothing tugs and grinned, closing his eyes.

She's quite something.

What are you going to do with her?

Something along the lines of what I did last night – but without the sand.

You have a sizeable grin on your face.

And a proportionately equivalent hard-on too.

You're feeling pleased with yourself then?

Pleased? Yes. Happy.

You like her?

I've never met anyone quite like her.

You like her.

Yes, I think I do. I like the way that she's a little naïve but feisty. She was so adorable all in a dither about Luca's unintended innuendo a few Stages ago. And when she was mad at me with the Monique misunderstanding — all gorgeous fury and indignation in a see-through dress. Yet last night she blew my mind as much as she blew my cock. For one who's so easy to wind up, she's very sure of herself sexually. It's surprising. I like that.

You like her.

I do.

Isn't that something of a first for you? Recently, you've slept with women because you've liked what's on offer more than you've considered whether you've liked their persons.

Touché. *But true. I've had sex with women because I can. With Cat, I wanted to. I want to.*

It was eight in the morning. Ben rose, showered, shaved, packed and then stood by the window of his hotel, its nondescript features providing an opportunity for his mind to wander approximately a kilometre away. He envisaged Cat sleeping soundly, her body supine, soft and at rest beneath the linen on the old iron bed in Auberge Claudette. He wanted to spy on her like that as much as he desired to be in the full throes of fucking her right now.

Is she awake yet?

'I wonder if Ms McCabe would care to join me for breakfast.'

Fabian Ducasse awoke very much the accomplished pro cyclist with his mind settled, focused and full of his *maillot jaune*. Fabian also awoke very much the healthy virile man, his cock stiff and proud. He thought of his girlfriend. Fleetingly. He zapped through the television in search of porn but found only cartoons, quiz shows and the Tour de France. He began to masturbate but his right hand was not enough of a turn on, not even when coated with the hotel's complimentary body lotion. And then he remembered one of the clerks at the desk. Fuck, remember her name. Shit, what was it. Ah! He remembered. He picked up the phone.

'This is Fabian Ducasse,' he barked with some irritation to

the male voice which had answered. 'Is Francine on duty?'

'*Oui*, Monsieur Ducasse,' the man informed him.

'Give her to me then,' Ducasse commanded.

'*Bonjour*?'

'Francine,' Fabian drawled, 'yesterday, you said if I needed anything, to speak to you.'

'*Bien sûr* – what can I do for you?'

'I need something in my room,' Fabian explained. 'You will come.'

'Directly,' said Francine, turning from her colleague to hide her flush and the surreptitious unbuttoning of her shirt by one notch.

Fabian assessed the room and looked at his watch. He would not be wanting her on the bed. Not least because, after he had done what he intended to do with her, he would sleep for another hour or so. He did not want her on the bed because he desired no intimacy. He had no need, no wish, for a woman to be curled up and languid under white cotton, not leaving. Fundamentally, he did not want her on the bed because it would add time and necessitate seduction; his time and his seduction skills were precious commodities Fabian was not about to waste.

There was a discreet knock at the door. Fabian padded across the room and let Francine in. He was a sight to behold; naked and with an erection so arrogantly defiant that it needed neither introduction nor justification. She was pretty with a lovely figure but Fabian hardly clocked the facts. All he knew was that she had previously offered her services which, he deduced, meant warm, welcoming pussy. That was enough. That was what he wanted. That was all he wanted. And if he knew women, or at least those who made overtures to him midway through a Stage Race, she would be pleased to be fucked by Fabian. So, everyone was going to be happy. Let's get on with it, *tout de suite*.

He backed her up against the closed door, unbuttoned her blouse and feasted his eyes on her impressive cleavage. He wasn't going to waste time unhooking and unfastening, he just yanked the bra cups down so that her breasts were squeezed out and on display. He reached up her short skirt and ripped down her panties. She wasn't very tall so it was good that she was wearing high heels; they could stay on. The skirt would have to go, though, as it prevented her spreading her legs wide enough. But the clasp and the zip – too complicated. With a desirous growl, Fabian ruched the skirt up until it was bunched around her waist like a deflated life ring. He took a step back and regarded what was on offer. Great tits. High heels. Shaved pussy. Best of all, utterly silent. Yeah!

Fabian placed the palms of his hands on each of her inner thighs and spread her legs easily. He took his hands to her breasts and moulded and fingered and grabbed at them, fixating on her nipples between his finger and thumb. Then he grasped her buttocks, bent his knees and bucked up hard, entering her with what he assumed was pleasurable force. Certainly, her gasp would have him believe that. He fucked her hard and came in about ten thrusts. No doubt she came too, *oui*? He grinned triumphant, proud at the glazed response he'd caused in her. He righted her skirt, buttoned her blouse albeit wrongly, handed her the panties and kissed her on both cheeks. It was the first and only time his lips had touched any part of her.

'*Merci*,' he murmured, '*merci bien.*'

'*Bonne chance*,' she said, leaving his room.

He did not watch her walk down the corridor trying to restore order to her blouse and her mind despite the trickle of semen dribbling down her leg. The power Fabian experienced fucking the clerk had flooded him with strength he could utilize on his ride that day. But the desired result which he had attained fucking her was nothing compared to the power that saturated him when he put the *maillot jaune* on his back.

'How do you feel, Didier?' Luca asked, sensing that LeDucq was awake and staring at the ceiling.

'Better,' Didier answered.

'Completely?' Luca probed.

'No,' Didier confided, 'but I haven't been sick for two days and my arse is – how do you say?'

'Bricks instead of mortar?' Luca ventured.

'I like that,' Didier laughed.

'Zucca make bricks and mortar,' Luca mused.

'And I shit on all of them,' Didier bantered.

'I need to have a wank,' Luca said, rising from the bed and disappearing courteously into the bathroom.

As Ben walked through the streets to Cat, he placed a hand against his stomach. He felt a little queer but diagnosis of the symptoms eluded him. He decided that hunger and lack of sleep were to blame, that breakfast with Cat and then perhaps a spell in her bed, or in her bed under her spell, might be curative measures to take. It was only when his stomach turned over, shot down to the soles of his feet and then rocketed up to the base of his throat when the auberge came into sight, that Ben deduced from what it was that he was suffering.

Butterflies. Fucking butterflies. When did I last have these? I've gone soft.

He was so disconcerted by the affliction that he very nearly bypassed the auberge. But not quite. Soon enough, he was knocking at Cat's door with tiger moths rampaging around his abdomen. Then Josh appeared down the hallway.

'Morning, Ben,' he said affably.

'Hey, Josh,' said Ben.

'Are you looking for Cat?' Josh asked.

'Yes, I am,' said Ben, 'actually, yes.'

'I think Rachel said something about she and Cat having breakfast together on account of today's afternoon *départ*,' Josh informed Ben. 'We had a great night last night – how come you didn't show?'

'Oh,' Ben said breezily, 'I had medical matters to attend to

– bodies, rest and motion – you know the kind of thing.'

'All in a day's work,' said Josh, nodding ingenuously. He regarded Ben. 'Why do you want Cat?'

Because she's gorgeous and sexy and I haven't wanted anyone so much for bloody years.

'She left her dictaphone in my room,' Ben said.

'What was it doing in your room?' Josh asked, now just a little intrigued.

'It was picking up the glinting gems which trickled like a golden waterfall from the ruby lips of one Luca Love Me Jones,' Ben said wryly.

Josh laughed and then held out his hand. 'Do you want me to give it to her?'

No. That's my privilege – I'll be giving it to her. And I'll be returning the dictaphone too.

'You're all right, Josh,' Ben said. 'I feel I should deliver it to her myself – it's safe in my hands, you might steal her scoops!'

Josh shrugged. 'Ben?' he called after the doctor who was about to descend the stairs. Ben turned and regarded him. Josh wavered and then waved the air dismissively. 'Nothing,' he said, returning to his room. Josh was going to say something, and he knew what it was he was going to say but the fact that he was unsure quite why he wanted to say it ultimately prevented its disclosure.

Josh always thinks before he speaks. Alex, however, does not. When Ben passed him on the stairs on his way out, Alex also asked his purpose in the auberge.

'I'm after Cat,' Ben explained.

'Who isn't!' Alex exclaimed with an excited growl.

Cat McCabe had awoken early and sat up in bed gazing at her surroundings, already missing the room she'd have to check out of later. She committed the wallpaper design to memory, soaking up the beauty of the light filtering through from the bathroom like a waft of fine muslin. She felt so at home here and suddenly she thought of her family. She called Fen but there was no reply. She tried Pip but finding only her sister's voice on the answering machine, albeit claiming to be Martha the Clown, she decided not to leave a message. Finally, she dialled Django.

'Who's there good God?'

Django only ever answered the phone like that when he was elbow-deep in some culinary venture. Forlornly, Cat cancelled the call. Less than a minute later, her phone rang.

'No recipe,' Django boomed, 'no matter how intricate the instruction – regardless of milk curdling, sauce clogging or egg whites misbehaving – no recipe takes precedence over any of my nieces.'

'Hullo, Django,' Cat said.

'What's up, pretty girl?' Django asked, slipping a wooden spoon, sticky with something resembling wallpaper paste, into the back pocket of his jeans.

Cat smiled small.

How can he tell?

'I did something last night,' she explained, with no shame, no embarrassment, but quietly.

'With whom?' Django asked, taking the spoon from his pocket and seeing whether it would stick to the glass pane in the kitchen door. It did.

'With the doctor,' Cat confided.

'How lovely,' Django enthused, because his other two nieces had provided enough details for him to deduce that the doctor was a very good idea indeed.

'I know,' Cat said, her voice faltering beyond her control, 'I know.'

'Why the tears?' Django asked while all around him the sauce separated, egg whites collapsed and bananas went brown.

'Because it means He's gone,' Cat said, 'I've made Him go.'

'Don't capitalize that scoundrel,' Django all but barked before softening his tone. 'I know, darling. But you've let go because you could. Well done you.'

'Haven't I gone and scuppered any future chance?' Cat asked, knowing the answer full well.

'Catriona,' Django said gravely, 'that man deserved neither your future nor your sparkle. That he dared to try and strip you of the one means most certainly that he was never entitled to the other.' Cat nodded. Django could sense it. 'It's good,' Django continued, 'believe me. Those who love you are so excited for your life – great things come to those who deserve them. Dr Who is one of them. Good for you.'

'Think so?' marvelled Cat on the verge of amazement.

'Know so,' Django declared.

Half an hour later, Cat all but skipped to the Zucca MV team hotel, forsaking forays into foyers in search of riders, for swift circumnavigation of the grounds to locate the Zucca team bus and *soigneur*. She found Rachel sitting on its steps, face up and eyes closed into the morning sun.

'Rachel,' Cat greeted.

Rachel opened her eyes and blinked, continuing to squint at Cat even when she could see her clearly. 'Hey,' Rachel said, 'you look very chirpy.'

Cat smiled. 'You wouldn't have a spare pair of Oakley sunnies I could borrow?'

Rachel disappeared into the bus and came out with a pair of sunglasses. 'They're Vasily's spares – I gift them to you for an hour!'

'Thanks,' said Cat, greatly honoured, putting the glasses on and seeing from her reflection in Rachel's that she looked quite good in them.

'So?' Rachel probed, suddenly realizing how relieved she was for the excuse not to talk herself.

Cat tipped her head to one side. 'It's funny, isn't it? The more you're surrounded by men, the more you crave and value female company.'

Rachel frowned and cast her eyes down, suddenly realizing she'd love the excuse to talk, to confide her antics for constructive analysis.

'Are *you* OK?' Cat asked, suddenly sensing Rachel's introspection. Rachel wiped her hands on her jeans and said she was fine and would Cat like to help mix the dextrose powder into the bidons? They performed their duty in affable silence until monotony made Cat's mind meander.

'Hey Rachel,' she said, alighting on a fine topic, 'pick up where you left off yesterday. You were talking about Vasily.'

Rachel was silent for a second too long.

'Vasily?' she replied in a way simply not noncommittal enough.

'In the bar,' Cat said in what she hoped was a tempting way, 'in the loos?'

'Vasily,' Rachel declared, 'nothing to say. Yesterday was the Time Trial. He wasn't himself.' Cat said nothing because Rachel needed to say nothing more. Cat knew that intonation, those kinds of sentences. She turned to Rachel, screwing on the lid of a drink bottle and giving it a good shake. 'Tell me,' she suggested, Rachel's lack of eye contact confirming Cat's hunch.

'It's nothing,' Rachel said, fiddling with things that needed no attention, 'it was nothing.'

'What was nothing?' asked Ben, suddenly at the foot of the bus.

'Ben!' Cat exclaimed with joy without checking.

'Hullo, Ben,' said Rachel, the briefest glance at Cat's illuminated face telling her all she needed to know without recourse to the glint in Cat's eyes which the Oakleys were hiding from view anyway.

'Cat,' said Ben quite formally, 'here's your dictaphone.'

'Thanks!' Cat said effusively.

'Do you women want breakfast?' Ben asked.

'We've had,' said Rachel, speaking for both, though Cat would have been quite content with a second sitting. Cat looked at Rachel. Slowly, she removed the loaned sunglasses and handed them to the *soigneur*. The girls conversed expertly by glances.

You've slept with Ben Bloody York, haven't you!
I know! What do you think?
Go for it.

'Wait up, Ben,' Cat called after him but only once she'd

been granted Rachel's nod. Ben stopped a few yards off, the morning sunlight catching his features so aesthetically that Cat had to catch her breath.

'Tell me,' Rachel said connivingly, 'why does he have your dictaphone?'

'I must have left it in his bedroom,' Cat said.

'Oh,' said Rachel, nodding sagely, 'couldn't he just have used his finger then, like a normal bloke?'

It took a while for Rachel's jest to filter through Cat. When it did, she roared with laughter, nudged her friend, all but leapt from the bus and approached Ben most jauntily. As they walked away, Cat turned. Rachel was standing in the doorway of the bus, cleaning the Oakley sunglasses she had lent Cat, on the rim of her T-shirt.

Shit! Cat faltered, looking over her shoulder at the bus, *Vasily! What were you going to say, Rachel?*

It can wait, Cat – don't worry about it – it can wait. It was nothing.

When Cat and Ben had disappeared from sight and the bidons were all done, Rachel cleaned the Oakleys once more.

'Vasily, Vasily,' she said under her breath, 'what am I meant to think, let alone do?'

A little later, Rachel did something she had never done. She went to her rider. Two of the team had come to her room for a leg rub, another had come for fresh socks but she hadn't seen Vasily. Vasily probably didn't need clothing or massage or to be disturbed, but still Rachel went to his room.

'Hey,' she said.

'Hullo, Rachel,' he replied.

'Can I come in?' Rachel asked.

'Please,' he said, holding the door and welcoming her. She was deflated that he left it ajar.

'Can I do anything for you?' she asked.

'It's a short Stage,' Vasily shrugged. 'I am fine, please do not worry.' Rachel was standing with her back to the window, Vasily was leaning leisurely against the wall, the bed was between them. Rachel noticed that Vasily had, for some reason, made it.

'OK,' said Rachel, hovering, wondering if he'd forgotten, remembered or merely dismissed the day before. 'About yesterday,' she started.

Vasily raised a hand. 'Please,' he said kindly, 'do not worry.'

Rachel regarded her feet.

I'm not worried. I just want to know if there might be more from whence it came.

'Don't worry,' she echoed, her fixed smile contradicting the darting of her eyes.

'Oh,' said Vasily dismissively, 'I won't. I forgot it already.' He wondered why Rachel had suddenly cast her gaze away. 'Rachel,' he said softly, advancing towards her, 'it was not meant to be. If I am OK with it, I expect you – my *soigneur* – to be so too.'

Rachel looked up at him, he was close and lovely and she wanted to touch his lips with her fingertips. She nodded, not able to wrest a forlorn edge from her gesture.

'You look sad,' Vasily said.

'I'm fine,' Rachel said a little too loudly.

'It won't last,' he continued.

'You're right,' Rachel confirmed.

'It won't last, I will have it again,' Vasily continued, his apparent contradiction distracting Rachel momentarily from the fact that he was fingering the buttons on her denim shirt.

'I don't think so,' Rachel said, quite crossly.

Who does he think I am? Some fucking groupie willing to dispense sex when he so demands?

'Rachel!' Vasily remonstrated.

'What?' Rachel objected.

'I say it won't last, I will have it again,' Vasily said, 'and you tell me *no*, that I *won't*?'

'You bloody won't,' said Rachel.

'I don't need bloody shit like this,' said Vasily.

'And nor,' Rachel declared, 'do I.'

She brushed past him and made to go. Vasily caught her arm. 'You think it's not possible?' he implored. Rachel looked at him coldly, her jaw locked with indignation and hurt. She snatched her arm away and stomped towards the door. 'It won't last,' Vasily declared. 'I will have it again.'

'Fuck off, Jawlensky,' Rachel hissed.

'Yesterday meant nothing. You will see,' Vasily proclaimed to her back, 'I will take the *maillot jaune* in the mountains.'

Rachel stopped stock still, closed her eyes and grimaced.

You stupid, idiot girl. He's a fucking cyclist. He was talking about a piece of bloody yellow lycra all along. Not you. Not kissing you.

Rachel turned.

And now he looks hurt and confused. And why wouldn't he be? His faithful soigneur *has just doubted his pedal prowess.*

Rachel went back to her rider and laid the palm of her hand gently at his cheek. 'Oh shit,' she whispered, 'I didn't realize. I thought you. I meant about.'

Vasily tipped his head to one side and regarded her. 'Please,' he said, 'you speak better for Vasily so he can understand.'

'Understand this,' said Rachel, standing on tiptoes and planting a small, apologetic but emphatic kiss on his mouth. Suddenly he was kissing her back, his tongue leaping around her mouth on a mission of its own.

'Rachel,' he murmured, wonderfully gravelly. He took her hand and placed it against his groin. She could feel him, rock hard. Rachel took his hand and placed it over her breast. Then she guided it under her shirt to her bare flesh, her nipple enticingly at the centre of his palm.

'What do you want?' she whispered, dabbing her tongue tip on the dimple in his chin. He encircled her with his arms, pressed his groin against her and moved his body gently.

'I want to stay out of trouble,' Vasily murmured into the

224

top of her head. 'I need to ride near the front today but not too hard. Tomorrow, the Pyrenees. Tomorrow, I am at war with Ducasse.'

Cat's job was not just easy to do that day, it was a true pleasure. On a glorious sunny afternoon refreshingly punctuated by a gentle breeze, the race headed out from Sauternes and through lines of the famous lime-green vines striping the land like corduroy. The route headed due south, down through Gascony to the Béarn region and its capital, Pau; gateway to the Pyrenees, harbinger of the first mountain trials of the Tour de France but also a lovely old university town crowned with a picture-perfect fourteenth-century château. Cat was excited to be there; not even a nondescript modern motorlodge could dampen her delight.

It was an easy Stage to report and she whacked out 500 words effortlessly. It was easy to work diligently when a certain euphoria tided you along, when the person responsible for that euphoria was willing you to finish your work because he was waiting for you. The route had been raced fast with an exciting photo-finish between three riders, a paragraph-worthy mass pile-up near Brocas-les-Forges, no change in the general classification nor the jersey wearers and no abandonments. Tomorrow, out of the original 189 starters, 180 would be heading towards their nemeses at altitude.

'*Finito!*' Cat exclaimed.

'Are you on a mission or something?' Alex probed.

'Yup, Rachel and I are having a drink before dinner,' Cat said, her eyes glinting, 'so I'd better shoot. I'll see you later, boys.'

Josh watched Cat all but skip out of the *salle de presse*. He thought her to be ridiculously excited over a pre-dinner drink with a girl she'd had breakfast with that morning.

'Rachel and Cat,' Alex guffawed, nudging a bemused Josh for good measure, 'kinky!'

'You're a prat, Fletcher,' said Josh. 'I'm going out for some air.'

And there was Rachel. And there was Ben.

'Hey, Josh,' Rachel called.

Josh approached them. 'Cat's just left,' he said to Rachel, knowing instantly why Rachel looked momentarily puzzled. 'You're meeting for a drink?' he said, as if reminding her kindly though he analysed her response. He glanced at Ben as if to say, my! aren't girls dippy.

'Oh yes,' Rachel said, tapping her temples, 'I'm losing my mind.' She returned Ben's shot glance in what she hoped was a legibly conspiratorial way.

'I think she's gone to phone her boyfriend first,' Josh heard himself say before he allowed himself to check his words and consider his point. He was looking steadily at Rachel but he could feel Ben regard him abruptly. 'Didn't Cat say something about him coming out for some of the mountain Stages?' Josh continued to Rachel.

'Um,' Rachel faltered as if pondering Josh's query rather than wracking her brains for any clue that Cat had given her of a boyfriend back home.

'Anyway,' Josh said lightly, 'that's where she's gone – her daily indulgence of long-distance sweet nothings.'

'That's nice,' Rachel said distractedly.

'I'd better shoot,' said Ben, turning and walking away.

'Me too,' said Rachel, doing the same.

'Yes,' said Josh, 'and me.' He returned slowly to the *salle de presse* hating himself but not kicking himself. What had he just done? Was he trying to protect Cat? From Ben? For her boyfriend back home? She so sparkled in the doctor's company. Was he trying to keep Cat chaste? And if so, for whom? The boyfriend? Or himself?

Cat was waiting for Ben in her room. He was later than she had anticipated and she was so highly charged with desire that when he knocked, she flung open the door and greeted him with a torrent of kisses. She didn't want him to use his mouth for an explanation, she didn't need an apology. Kissing was all she required to come from his lips.

Ben, who was thoroughly disconcerted by what he'd just learned from Josh, had intended to ask Cat for some information and honesty. But her mouth was so sweet and kissing her was so tantalizing and her hands were running all over his body and his cock was responding in fine style. So, Ben allowed Cat to lead and she took to her role with relish, stripping herself first and then Ben. She went on top and held her position there. She felt fantastic to Ben and, as he came, his hands on her firm buttocks, his tongue deep in her mouth, his body thrust high into hers, their eyes locked together, he thought how he never wanted to let her go. As he left, he considered how she wasn't even available for the taking.

STAGE 9
Pau–Luchon. 196.5 kilometres

*F*en opened the door to her Kentish Town flat to find Pip clutching the *Guardian* and two cappuccinos in polystyrene cups. Pip had phoned not half an hour before and Fen had told her that she was working from home because she was desperate for no distraction. The fact that Fen was embroiled in a relationship with a colleague, as well as dithering over another man in Derbyshire, was distraction incarnate. Pip, who did not have a conventional job, never mind the choice of one man let alone two, assessed that if her sister was not physically at her place of work, or getting physical with a male, it meant she was at play and available for confabulation. The fact that Fen was visibly flummoxed, surrounded by papers and fluorescent Post-its, was of no relevance to Pip. She bustled in, removed the plastic lids from the coffee and licked each one clean. Fen, exasperated, motioned to her papers and files.

'Very nice,' said Pip, handing her sister a coffee, turning straight to Cat's report on the procession down to Pau the previous day. 'She's very good, our baby sis,' Pip murmured as Cat's passion for the Tour filtered through the newsprint and infused the reader.

'I'm dying to know what's happening,' Fen said, now enjoying the cappuccino and grateful for her sister's intrusion.

'Me too,' Pip enthused. 'Both Cat and that nice Paul Sherwen chap from Channel 4 say that the race starts in earnest now, in the mountains, that the challenge for the yellow jersey will be at its most intense and consequential.'

Fen stared at Pip. 'All that – yes,' she said, 'and Fabian Ducasse is a spunk and a half, but I was referring to Cat – and the doc. Where do you think *they're* at?'

'Oh blimey, of course,' Pip said, sitting cross-legged at her sister's feet, 'brawny Ben.'

'Shall we phone her?' Fen suggested, already dialling. Pip grabbed the phone from her, scooping cappuccino froth from the side of the cup with her index finger while waiting for Cat to answer.

'Hullo?' said Cat, sounding like she was just around the corner, sounding like she had just woken up.

'Have you shagged him yet?' Pip all but squealed.

Though she really shouldn't have been startled by her sister's trademark bluntness, Cat found herself answering with an affirmative giggle. While she listened to her sisters shrieking with delight in the background, Cat considered that, though she had indeed shagged Ben, that they had quite categorically fucked each other's brains out, gorged on each other to satisfy a very base hunger, there had been an edge to it all. Right from the start. Sexual desire, yes, but something else, something more too. Merely confirming that she had shagged the man did both him and herself something of a disservice. It had been more than just sex, but what, exactly? Surely the sex could not have been so good without this enhancing extra layer of something or other? Physical attraction is one thing on but one level; to be mutually attracted to each other is something else and multi-faceted. And somewhat perplexing.

'He's lovely,' Cat said to Pip's 'Come on come on come on!'

'What was it like?' Fen asked excitedly. 'Was he good?'

'It was great,' Cat replied.

'Where did you do it?' Pip butted in. 'When? How many times?'

'I like him,' Cat reiterated, thinking, deluded, that she was being discreetly noncommittal, 'it was great.'

And then Cat changed the subject. 'The weather is absolutely appalling here today – it's cold and very wet. It's going to be torture for the boys. Promise you'll watch? Promise you'll pray for them? You're going to meet a host of new characters today – all those powerful sprinters so familiar last week will now be gone from sight. They've passed the baton to the *grimpeurs* – lithe, wiry, crazy, brave boys. Watch what the mountains do to them. Watch what they do to the mountains.'

'The fact that she changed the subject in a way she thought was so subtle—' Fen starts, replacing the handset, finishing the coffee and reordering her piles of papers.

'Means one of two things,' Pip completes.

'Either the sex was a bit disappointing and reality has let her daydream down,' Fen theorizes.

'Or,' Pip continues for her, 'Cat's gone and fallen for him.'

'In some ways,' says Fen, very slowly, 'I rather hope she hasn't.'

'I know,' says Pip, 'I do too. She'd be safer.'

'But I rather think it's the latter,' Fen clarifies, 'and I don't want her to be hurt.'

'I mean, he's probably a really lovely guy with honourable intentions,' Pip says, 'and has massive desire for Cat, which is great for her – but if she is falling for more than his ability to bring her to orgasm, she is somewhat vulnerable.'

'And I don't want her to hurt,' Fen states, 'she's had enough of that.'

Pip was staring at Fen's calendar from the Musée Rodin.

'The Eternal Idol, 1899,' Fen whispers rather hoarsely. 'Isn't that clit-quiveringly wonderful?'

'Huh? Oh yes!' Pip says, changing her focus to observe the photo of the sculpture. 'But I was thinking – fancy a weekend in the Alps?'

Fabian Ducasse has spent the least accumulative time in the saddle which is why he is wearing the yellow jersey. He's been racing for eight days and has covered over 1,570 kilometres in 41½ hours riding. He has over 2,000 kilometres to go, twelve further days in the saddle with two rest days during which he'll be on his bike, of course. Fabian Ducasse, twenty-nine years old, will climb five mammoth Pyrenean passes today. Tomorrow, another five. All in all, there are seven days in which mountains are to be tackled. By our boys. On their bicycles.

As Cat told her sisters, we have new characters to meet who have spent the last week wisely sheltering safe in the air bubble at the centre of the bunch, conserving their energy for the mountains. The pure sprinters have now had their apportionment of fame. Their current concerns are merely to survive the next week if they are going to make it to Paris at all. Last week, they surged and pumped hard at the front of the peloton in front of the world, now they'll gladly join the grupetto, the bus of riders that forms the back of the bunch, just keeping together, keeping going, living to ride another day, riding for a living though it nearly kills them. Jesper Lomers and Stefano Sassetta will continue to duel for the green jersey to prove who is the Tour's most consistent daily finisher; one who can cope with the mountains in the second week, as much as he shone at sprinting in the first. Jesper's wife Anya has not yet made an appearance. Jesper is doing battle with himself to keep his professional and personal lives separate. And he is at war with Stefano. A handful of points separate them.

We met the two major contenders for the polka dot King of the Mountains jersey before the race but we've hardly seen them since. *Donna* magazine's 'Sexiest Man on Two Wheels', Zucca MV's dashing Massimo Lipari; the face of a popular chocolate-hazelnut spread and a familiar fixture in the Italian music charts each summer when he releases synthetic Europop in honour of the Giro, his nation's Grand Tour. Massimo has been King of the Mountains for the last two years. However, the man that Système Vipère transferred at great expense to put a stop to Massimo's run is the Pocket Rocket – small but charismatic Carlos Jesu Velasquez. A Spaniard riding for a French team, he is taciturn, a family man. Lipari and Velasquez's style on bike and off are vastly different. Their ability this year is neck and neck. Their aim is the same. The polka dot jersey. A slip of white lycra, spotted red, well worth the pain of pelting up peaks for points.

'The hills are alive!' Luca warbled at breakfast, the rest of Megapac regarding him with a mixture of pity and contempt. 'Come on, guys,' he continued quietly. Ben looked at him unseen, sensing the rider's bravado was but a thin veneer laid unconvincingly over his truer anticipation, dread and fear.

'Eat,' Ben said, eyeing the plates of pasta. 'Your bodies are going to use a lot of energy keeping warm today.'

The team were well aware of the rain teeming down the windows. 'Climb every mountain,' sang Luca, rather forlornly. Hunter pointed his knife at him but said nothing.

'It's wet but all of you must drink as often as you can,' Ben said, 'and lots of Vaseline on your feet so wet socks won't rub.'

'It's too wet and cold for bikinis,' Luca rued, taking more pasta though he wasn't hungry in the slightest, 'such a shame. Maybe there'll be some wet T-shirts instead, hey guys!' Travis shot him a withering look that went unseen.

'Luca,' Ben said, rising from the table, 'take your negligible brain cells from out of your dick and stick them where they'll serve you best. Jesus, you can be a bloody headache sometimes.' Ben left the dining-room, refusing to acknowledge Luca's look of hurt. Returning to his room, Ben hated himself for foisting his own unrest upon his young rider. He stood still in the centre of the bedroom, then switched on the TV, turning the volume high on whatever channel came on. He didn't want silence; ironically, he wouldn't be able to hear himself think. With the TV droning away, he began to bundle his clothes into his case.

'Would I have felt differently about Cat had I not found out she has a bloke back home?' he asked himself, sniffing at a shirt and tucking it deep down into the case. 'Is it the fact that she is unavailable that makes me want her more?' Ben sat on the edge of the bed for a moment before moving to the chair and then to the window-sill against which he rested the small of his back. 'Is that what disconcerts me?' He pushed himself away to lie down on the unmade bed. 'Bloody women. It's proof – as if I needed it – that any involvement that goes beyond a mere physical exchange is hassle I don't need.'

Ben left the bed and went to the bathroom. He looked at himself. 'Who the fuck said I was involved anyway?' But the two images of Cat which solicited him in quick succession answered him. The first was watching her, unseen, engrossed in her work in the *salle de presse*; her foot tapping, her lips moving – parting into a smile at certain sentences, into a pout when vocabulary eluded her – her whole self focused, a little frown now and then, a twitch of her nose, the brace of her back, accepting a drink from Josh, a quick banter with Alex, a glanced smile at an Italian journalist. She was in a little sundress that day, white pumps and a white, tight T-shirt. Ben had left the *salle* and walked away with a grin to his groin. The other image accosting him was of Cat climaxing last night, her eyes never leaving his, just glazing over with the pleasure and gazing deep into him. He'd found it an incredibly intense moment. She had been straddling him, gyrating to her peak, moving around and down on to him; his hands had been on her thighs, at her waist, cupping her breasts, and then she stilled herself, gasping and staring at him and he felt her sex suck him deep inside her, her gaze drawing him into her. And then she all but crumpled down on to him with post-orgasmic exhaustion and he wrapped his arms around her, tenderly encircling her as her throbbing subsided. She had smelt wonderful. He could have feasted on the scent of her, the sight and sound of her and never have had his fill.

That any imagery, let alone two vivid and contrasting ones, were deeply ensconced in his soul and mind's eye, was a disconcerting fact in itself.

It isn't that I've consciously not allowed many women to take residence in my head, to say nothing of my heart – it's that none of them have really warranted the space. Bloody Cat is bloody everywhere.

Ben knocked his head gently against the mirror, knowing full well that the action would have done little to dislodge Cat from there, that when he turned away to drop his pants and have a piss, he needn't even close his eyes to summon an image of her. Uninvited? Perhaps. But even if he wished to banish her, he would be unable to.

'Hey, Rachel,' Cat said, walking past the *soigneur* on her way to meet Josh at the car.

'Morning – but not a good one,' said Rachel glowering at the sky and then appearing to scrutinize Massimo Lipari's legs before rubbing them with great consideration. Elsewhere, riders rubbed udder cream or Vaseline on to their nether regions to prevent chafing; the sight alarming neither girl.

'I think I'd better leave shadowing you till tomorrow,' Cat said.

'Wise,' said Rachel, 'that's fine by me. I'm going directly to the hotel anyway.' Massimo stood, walked a step and a half to his bike and then cycled slowly away, for a last coffee and another piss before the start. Cat began to walk away. Rachel called after her.

'Yesterday,' she began, 'I mean – I didn't know.'

'About Ben?' Cat said with a spirited smile.

'No,' said Rachel, regarding her straight, 'about the other one.'

Cat looked puzzled.

'Ben's a really nice guy,' Rachel continued, 'I've known him for a few years now.'

Cat grinned, reading this as Rachel's seal of approval which she was flattered to receive.

'So?' Rachel prompted.

Cat shrugged.

'This guy?' Rachel continued. 'Back home?'

'Who?' said Cat, genuinely confused.

'Josh was telling us you are deeply involved with a guy back home.'

Cat was rooted to the spot, her jaw had dropped and her eyes were flitting all over Rachel's face.

'*Us*?' Cat said in hushed horror, half-knowing what she'd hear. 'Who was the "us"?'

'Me,' Rachel said, 'and Ben.'

'Oh God,' Cat cried, turning away and then back again. 'Oh fuck. Jesus. I've got to go.' Rachel watched her jog away. She'd learnt no more. In fact, she felt she now knew Cat less. That upset her.

Alex and Josh told Cat she ought to drive the route to gain a true feel of the drag of the mountains and the plummet of the descents. Although she had wanted initially to confront Josh immediately, she was ultimately glad of the chance to restore her composure and concentrate on being a *journaliste* on the Tour de France.

Everything happens for a reason, she told herself in Django's words and tone as they reached the base of the fearsome Tourmalet. What the reason might be, she was as yet unsure. The Tourmalet not only provided welcome distraction, it absorbed her entirely. She was driving the 18½ kilometres to the 2,115 metre summit of the mighty mountain. There was nothing average about the gradient; 7.7 per cent was the mean and it was just that.

How are the boys going to get up this, with the Aubisque coming right before? And the d'Aspin and Peyresourde after? In this rain and mist? With thousands of fans clinging to the slopes like birds on a cliff and the tifosi – *the truly obsessed – thronging either side of the road as the summit nears; crowding in, yelling and running alongside, making it all so narrow, so claustrophobic, so treacherous. How can the riders descend as fast as they can, but safely? Far faster than a car can manage. Look at these bends, the drop. It's wet. I can hardly see. How are my boys going to cope?*

With wills of steel, legs of iron, the snap-quick eye reflexes of an eagle, hearts of a lion, and no nerves to mention.

The terrible grandeur of the mountains elicited fulminations from Alex so colourful and effusive that Cat wondered if he was suffering from Tourette's syndrome. Josh was capable of little more than whistles and tuts. They made it in one piece to Luchon knowing full well that some of the riders would not.

If Cat had found the drive itself a physical and mental trial, watching the riders do battle with themselves, with each other, with the awesome gradients up and down, was emotionally exhausting. She swallowed down a sob as she watched the excruciating but not unfamiliar sight of a rider weave semi-deliriously all over the road at a snail's pace half-way up the Tourmalet. Despite the impassioned pleas and helpful if illegal running shoves from fans, the rider finally stopped, quit his bike and the Tour, had his race number ceremoniously stripped from his back by an official before he was escorted to the ignominy of the broom wagon which transports deserters funereally along the route behind the race.

'How on earth can you put into words what we've just witnessed?' Cat marvels to Alex once the Stage has finished. 'I'm utterly exhausted, I'm speechless. I want to cry and go to sleep.'

'Fuck off and stop being so girlie,' Alex declares, envious

of Cat's entitlement and ability to express emotions mirroring his own but which bravado in the *salle de presse* dictates he should keep close to himself.

'I know,' Josh says sympathetically, giving her arm a squeeze, 'I know.'

You know nothing, Cat thinks miserably, suddenly wanting to be shot of her work so she can enlighten Rachel and appease Ben. In privacy.

Her phone rings and she goes to the back of the *salle* before answering it.

'Oh my God,' Fen all but wails.

'I can't believe it,' Pip whispers.

'Jesus, what's wrong?' Cat gasps. 'Is it Django?'

'Django?' Fen retorts, 'God no. He's fine. He's having to have a stiff brandy though – we've just phoned him.'

'*Today*, stupid,' Pip cries, 'how did they do that? Why were they made to do that?'

'Huh?' says Cat.

'The Tour de Bloody France,' Pip protests.

Cat grins.

My two sisters. In the fold. Part of the fraternity.

'That guy – the weeny Spanish climber,' Fen says, 'how did he do that on the final climb? It was like there was suddenly a motor on his bike. Was it my imagination or did he actively choose the steepest part to suddenly power away from the faltering?'

'Strategy,' Cat replies, 'undoubtedly – Velasquez always bides his time and then attacks. Imagine the effect it has on those he pulls away from.'

'And all for a spotty jersey,' says Pip contemplatively.

'And Jawlensky finished ahead of gorgeous Ducasse and diminished the Frenchman's lead to a minute,' Fen rues. 'Did I pronounce Vasily's surname correctly? With a "y" not a "j"?'

'Perfectly,' Cat confirms. 'What with Velasquez – that's a "th" not a "z" at the end of his name – in polka dot, and Lomers and Sassetta still at loggerheads for the green jersey, this Tour is being waged on a personal level between Système Vipère and Zucca MV.'

'But it was so cold, so misty and grim today,' Pip says plaintively.

'And that boy went careering off the side of the mountain,' Fen remarks.

'David Millar?' says Cat. 'He's fine – thanks to a bush. He lost his bike but managed not to lose too much time.'

'What do you think will happen tomorrow?' Pip asks.

Suddenly, Cat wonders. 'Today changed many things,' she says, 'tomorrow, I would say, even more so.'

'What do you mean?' Fen probes.

'Read my report – it's all in my concluding paragraph.'

'Er, Cat,' says Pip, her mind switching from lycra and bikes to flesh and beds, 'how's Ben?'

'Fuck,' Cat bemoans.

'What?' Fen says.

'It's complicated and horrible and I've created a sorry mess for myself.'

'Details, please,' Pip demands. Cat gives her sisters a nutshell version which more than suffices.

'Well, don't you dare back off from unravelling it,' Fen cautions.

'Humble pie can be quite nourishing,' Pip says encouragingly.

Django phoned almost as soon as Pip and Fen had gone.

'They're bloody lunatics!' was his opening statement.

'Who are?' Cat said, startled at the severity of his accusation.

'Your bloody bike boys,' Django brandished. 'Fancy wanting to ride a push bike up five fuckers of mountains. Bloody mad. Are they on drugs? I'm on double brandy after that.'

'Good question,' Cat said a little despondently.

'Why all the sex?' Django demanded.

'The sex?' Cat exclaimed, wondering if Django would move on to rock and roll next. 'Where?'

'On the mountains,' Django said ingenuously, 'that lovely Liggett commentator was telling us that certain riders bonk whores.'

'*What*?' Cat exclaimed aghast.

'Oh yes,' Django continued, 'on the mountains them-selves.'

Cat fell silent and then grinned. 'Are you talking *hors catégorie*?'

'That's the one!' Django confirmed. 'Would it have some-thing to do with those mountains being such a bitch to climb?'

Cat roared with laughter, much to the consternation of a posse of Portuguese journalists near by. '*Hors*,' she stressed, spelling it out, '*hors catégorie* means "beyond classification" – and yes, I suppose they are the bitch climbs.'

'And the bonking?' Django probed, most interested.

'When a rider bonks, it's like a marathon runner hitting the proverbial wall,' Cat explained.

'Have you bonked?' Django asked.

'I *am* knackered,' Cat conceded.

'Yes but have you *bonked*,' Django pressed, 'your doctor?'

Oh God. Ben. The boyfriend. The bullshit.

'Ben?' Cat used the house phone in the foyer of the Megapac team hotel.

'Not a good time,' Ben said, quite plausibly, though there was no one else in his bedroom and nothing urgent requiring his attention.

'Come to me later?' Cat said softly.

'Perhaps,' Ben said. 'Don't wait up for me, though.'

'Rachel?' said Cat, using the house phone in the foyer of the Zucca MV team hotel.

'Hullo,' Rachel replied.

'Can I come up?' Cat asked. 'I'm desperate for a chat.'

'Of course,' said Rachel, intrigued and feeling too that she was entitled to an explanation. She placed her portable grocery store at Cat's disposal. Gratefully, Cat filled a bowl with cereal and munched thoughtfully.

'It was bullshit,' she said at length, 'what Josh told you.'

'You didn't tell him you have a boyfriend?' Rachel probed.

'No!' Cat wailed. 'I mean, I did tell him I have a boyfriend.'

'Do you?' Rachel pressed, obviously suspicious.

'No,' Cat said a little sadly, but quite categorically, 'I don't. Not any more.'

'Since when?' Rachel enquired, wondering if Cat had chucked him that evening.

'Since a few months ago,' Cat defined quietly.

Rachel regarded Cat. 'Why did you tell Josh that you did,' she asked quite reasonably, 'if he no longer exists?'

'I regret telling Josh that I did,' Cat said, 'but I told him very early on because – well, because it felt like protection. I didn't know if he was trying to come on to me. I didn't know there'd be Ben.'

Rachel nodded slowly. 'Did Josh come on to you?'

Cat smiled and shook her head. 'He's a lovely married guy,' she said, 'but I didn't know until after I'd spun my yarn.'

'Well, you've created some tangle. You should put him straight. He Who No Longer Exists – as I think I'll call him – has a stature he obviously doesn't deserve.'

'I know,' Cat sighed, 'I know. There hasn't been the right time.'

'Och, bollocks,' said Rachel with fine Scots directness, 'there's never a wrong time – not when it concerns people of whom you are fond and who care about you.'

'I know,' Cat nodded, 'I know.'

'Have you cleared things with Ben?'

'Not yet,' Cat said, 'but not from want of trying.'

'Bloody boys,'. Rachel said, somewhat connivingly. 'Was he bloody? Your ex?'

'Yes,' Cat admitted, 'he was.' She would have been pleased to elaborate, to tell Rachel all about Him and all about Ben had there not been a rap at the door. Vasily entered wearing only a towel – a skimpy one – around his waist. Cat's eyes bulged and she flitted an impressed glance over to Rachel whose gaze was exclusively focused on the rider.

'Rachel,' Vasily said in his gloriously Slavic way, 'you said you had something for me.'

Cat bit her lip.

'Of course,' Rachel exclaimed, smacking her forehead, 'I suggested a bath.' She looked over to Cat. 'Epsom salts and vinegar – *soigneurs* of yore swore by them. If it soothes, it's good, I say.'

'I'd better go,' said Cat.

'Yeah,' Rachel said, sternly but kindly, 'you have work to do.'

'Great ride,' Cat beamed at Vasily, who was used to such praise but always accepted it graciously. 'You might do it tomorrow, hey? You need only put a minute into Fabian.'

'Shadow me tomorrow, Cat,' Rachel said. 'I'm doing the feed. You'll get a great view – you'll get my view – there may be an article in it.'

'Too right,' said Cat, adding a call to Andy at *Maillot* slightly higher on her mental list than transcribing Luca's interview.

Cat left the hotel, omitting to ponder on the Vasily–Rachel situation about which she was faintly curious. She was much more concerned with returning to her hotel room, for Ben to come to her. She didn't wonder whether or not Rachel would slip into the bath with Vasily. She did not consider how recuperative a bath of Epsom salts and vinegar might be. Nor did she ponder the effect of 5 hours, 49 minutes and 40 seconds at an average speed of 32 kph on Vasily's libido.

There is a rap at Cat's door. It has gone midnight but she knows the code of Ben's knocking. She does not put the light on. She answers the door and Ben pushes her back into the room.

'Ben,' she whispers, 'I need to—'

He clasps his hand over her mouth. It turns her on. He pushes her roughly on to the bed.

'But I want to—'

This time he hisses at her to shut up. His forcefulness is thrilling. She lies there and lets herself be taken. He places his arms under her waist and thrusts his cock into her with absolutely no preamble. He hasn't kissed her yet. Hasn't touched her at all really. Once he's inside her, humping her vigorously, he finds her mouth and tongues her voraciously. Her hands are enmeshed in his hair, their mouths are fused together, their limbs are intertwined, their bodies moving in frantic unison. He comes very quickly. She hasn't climaxed but the sex lacks nothing for her. Suddenly he's away from her. She can hear him fiddling with the condom.

'Cheers,' he says, into the dark.

He's left the bed.

'Ben?' she calls after him. 'There's something I—'

'Not now, Cat,' he says. He leaves the room. Cat is simultaneously exhilarated and yet unnerved.

'Ben,' she says quietly, though she knows he is gone, 'there's no one back home. You can have my undivided attention.'

And my affection, I rather think.

Say that out loud.

God no. Far too risky.

STAGE 10
Luchon–Plateau de Boudin. 170 kilometres

*I*f she was to shadow Rachel intently, it meant following in her footsteps from the moment she woke. As Cat left for the Zucca hotel, Josh and Alex were still fast asleep, Ben was tossing and turning. Though Cat was eager to talk to both Josh and Ben, she was also looking forward to the refreshing and welcome opportunity of a whole day in female company. She'd never seen so many men *en masse*. Though she was increasingly fond of those with whom she travelled, worked and ate, though she was admittedly smitten by him with whom she slept, if she was brutally honest she was starting to crave quality time with her own sex. Chatting with her sisters had highlighted this; as had the lengthy periods spent with Alex and Josh. The very presence of Rachel, that work commitments and the pressure of the race made extensive exchanges rare, underlined it. Josh and Alex were touchingly protective towards her – Josh to an extreme (he'd raid the press buffet for her even if she wasn't remotely hungry and had, on occasion, insisted on swapping hotel rooms on some pretext or other – towel quality, hanging space, number of mirrors), but Cat was starting to feel swamped by the unremitting prevalence of males. Even the timbre of their voices, whatever their language; the gait of their walk, whatever their footwear, could make her feel somewhat isolated.

Rachel drove Cat along the route, through the stunning Haute-Garonne and on to the Ariège region, with the luxury of a classical music channel rather than Radio Tour providing a rousing score to the scenery. The land was quite staggeringly verdant and lush, the villages gorgeous, all being blessed with unabated sunshine and no remnant of the cloud cover which had scourged the race the day before. The mountains looked woolly with their cloaks of vegetation and seemed to encircle the valleys in an amicable embrace. Whereas yesterday's foul weather had made the mountains all the more menacing, this morning, in 27 degrees, they seemed almost benign. For those experiencing them on anything other than a bicycle, that is.

When the girls had set up at the feed station some 95 kilometres along the route, they indulged in sunshine and time on a grassy bank, tanning their legs with eyes closed and ears tuned gratefully to the novelty of hush, the gift of shared solitude. The riders, however, had three mountains and a sprint point to contend with before they could fly past and snatch their lunch *musettes*. Yesterday, the peloton had been hammered by rain. Today, they would be drained by the heat. Tomorrow, their bodies would pay. The pace of climbing, at about a third of a rider's normal speed, provides only minimal draught. In this heat, Cat hoped they'd be taking it sensibly, for their own sakes primarily, but also to permit her and her friend the luxury of let-up.

'This is the life!' Rachel proclaimed as if she was on holiday, stroking the downy grass as if it were Caribbean sand.

'This is the life!' Cat echoed and meant it. With eyes closed, her sense of scent was highly attuned. France. Definitely not England. Specifically, midway between

Biarritz and Perpignan, close to Spain, far from Camden Town. Behind closed eyes, she replayed her coupling with Ben and projected imagery of future liaisons with him. She turned on her side, propped herself on an elbow and regarded Rachel. The *soigneur* looked at her, but was obviously seeing something quite else. Cat knew that look.

'Vasily,' Cat prompted, with what she hoped was a conspiratorial tone of camaraderie.

Rachel said nothing but nodded very slowly, rolled on to her back and remarked that the publicity caravan of floats and music preceding the race by an hour would soon be approaching.

I'll let it lie, Cat decided thoughtfully. *There's a time and a place – it isn't here but hopefully she might let me take her there sometime soon.* She lay on her back and her mind streamed off to the tangents that sky-gazing generates.

'We,' said Rachel breezily, before closing her eyes to forestall the tongue-loosening effects of the troposphere, 'oh. Nothing. I was. I was just.'

Cat knew very well what incomplete sentences were all about. She also knew that silence was not the best medium for revelation. The gaiety of the caravan, however, could well provide the perfect ambience. She awaited the raucous, garish publicity snake; daydreaming and sky-gazing until she could detect the distant toots of the approaching carnival.

'Tell me,' she prompted gently while the floats came upon them in a wave of colour, lousy music and grinning personnel scattering freebies like modern-day winnowers. Bolstered by a *panini*, Rachel spoke. Sustained by a ham roll, Cat listened attentively.

'We kissed,' Rachel began, with the hint of a grin she then saw wise to curtail. 'I don't know why,' she shrugged, 'but we kissed. Just before the Time Trial. I mean, *really* kissed.'

Cat's jaw dropped.

You and Vasily – wow! Hearts will be breaking amongst the female fans world-wide.

Cat regarded Rachel. 'Lucky you, I'd say. Just the once?'

Rachel shook her head. Then she shrugged. She did not look as ecstatic as Cat felt that someone kissed regularly by Vasily Jawlensky really ought.

'Well,' Rachel declared, standing, 'it was probably nothing. Anyway, they'll be along soon – come on, Shadow Girl, action stations.'

'You liked it?' Cat encouraged, following Rachel to the trunk of the car, thrilled to be given a Zucca MV jacket to wear to assist the riders looking for their lunch. 'Or you didn't? You want more – or you don't?' Cat observed a blush, barely perceptible but emphatically there, bloom across Rachel's cheek.

Isn't it funny what a man can do even to the most seemingly sussed and self-contained, self-content woman. Strong, sassy Rachel who keeps Zucca MV in order, shipshape, is here beside me churned up by a kiss.

'It's odd,' Rachel elaborated, handing Cat a clutch of *musettes* like a bunch of balloons upside-down, 'in all the time I've been involved in pro cycling, I've never even had to keep my professional and private lives separate – the one has never infringed on the other. I've not really been tempted. To be honest, apart from a wee dalliance last year with a journalist – a Dutch one, in case you're wondering – I haven't really had a private life at all and it's not something I've minded. I'm a *soigneur* – I'm at the beck and call of the team. I don't resent it.'

'And now there's a spanner in the works?' Cat broached.

'Yes,' Rachel agreed, 'I don't know how to deal with it. I can't really figure out what the fuck happened.'

'Did you see Vasily this morning?' Cat asked.

'I'm his *soigneur*,' Rachel said simply. 'Of course I saw him, I massaged him.'

'And?'

'I had a job to do, massaging my rider,' Rachel shrugged. 'He likes silence.'

'Well,' said Cat in a businesslike way, 'have you ascertained what *you* want?'

'I'm trying not to,' Rachel said, 'for fear of it not coinciding with what he may want. As I say, I'm at his beck and call.'

'You can pander to the needs of your riders,' Cat said emphatically, 'that's your job. But your own needs are paramount within the grander scheme of things.'

Rachel considered this. 'I don't know what I want. I was so damned tempted to get in to that salt and vinegar bath yesterday. But I didn't. Because he didn't ask.'

'And you would have?' Cat asked. 'If he had?'

Rachel shrugged.

'I can't think why Vasily wouldn't,' Cat said supportively. 'We just have to figure a way to verify his desire without disrupting his ride.'

'Maybe snogging helps his ride,' Rachel said wryly.

'Thank God it's you who's his *soigneur* – not your portly, bearded colleague!' Cat returned.

'Vasily is such a dark horse,' Rachel continued quietly, 'you rarely know how he feels let alone what he's thinking.' She regarded Cat and winked. 'But if he kisses like Casanova, even speculating on his bed skills sends me spinning.'

Cat laughed. And then she thought of Ben.

How can I miss him?

'But,' Rachel said with a touch of resignation, 'it's probably a terrible, crazy idea.'

'Say he doesn't think so?' Cat posed, it suddenly dawning on her that, if she actively missed Ben, it meant she herself had become embroiled. With a lurch, she was at once aware of the merits and dangers therein. 'What you need,' Cat continued, keen to concentrate on her friend's situation instead, 'is clarification – on how he feels, what he wants and where you stand.'

'You never know with Vasily,' Rachel mused, 'you just don't know what's in his head or if his heart races for anything other than cycling.'

'Providing a leg rub is one thing,' Cat said, 'sexual therapy is something quite else.'

'Well,' Rachel replied, 'it's certainly not on my job spec!'

Suddenly, the police outriders were visible in the distance. Rachel and Cat took their action stations. Megapac's Travis Stanton streamed towards them and swished past them in a blink.

'Ready?' Rachel yelled, not looking at Cat but at a small bunch pelting through the heat haze towards them. With her heart in her mouth, Cat held out her arm, proffering the *musettes* which were swiped away, whipped from her hand almost instantly. It stopped her heart and then sent it into overdrive. The hiss of wheels, the zip of colour, tension tangible, adrenalin a taste. Then they were away. Gone. Flashed past. And yet their impact lingered. Massimo Lipari. Gianni Fugallo. Speechless, grinning, transfixed, Cat had her gaze pulled after them until they were a blur and then out of sight. Suddenly, her attention was magnetized back to face the second rush, slightly larger, just coming in to view. The noise of the boys, shouting, whistling, swearing. The pace. The energy.

Luca! Fabian – oh my God – not with Vasily's group.

Gone and distant more quickly than they'd approached; heading for the Col de Port, not particularly high but a 1-in-20 climb lasting 12 kilometres. Onwards to the Plateau de Boudin, the final climb and altitude finish; *hors catégorie*, viciously steep at the outset and almost 1,800 metres high. Best known as a cross-country ski station. Claim it by bike? Racing? After 154 kilometres in which there were four other mountains and two hot-spot sprints? Why? A touch of insanity? Or the pursuit of glory? What?

I'm going to have to confront her.

Ben York assessed the gash on Hunter's elbow and decided three stitches would suffice.

But if I do, and she backs off, then I risk losing her altogether.

'Cutting off my nose to spite my face, I suppose,' Ben said out loud.

248

Why on earth do I even give a damn?

Hunter felt his nose. 'Huh?'

'Nothing,' said Ben, 'I was talking to myself. First sign of madness and all that.'

'Well, can you kinda like fix my arm before you flip out?' Hunter said, quite serious.

Ben smiled and drew thread through a needle.

If wanking can make you go blind, a lack of sex can make you go crazy.

'Tell me about Tayla,' Ben murmured whilst setting to work on Hunter's elbow.

'She's my girl,' Hunter sighed, suddenly missing his fiancée terribly, more so when he realized he hadn't given her a second thought let alone a first one over the past two days.

'How did you two meet?' Ben probed.

Hunter, presuming Ben was trying to distract him from the unpleasant sting of the stitching, reminisced gladly. 'I stole her from Richie Budd, just after the Motorola team disbanded, the season before I turned pro.'

'Did she come willingly?' Ben persisted, giving his head a quick shake to dislodge the sound of Cat coming willingly.

'Sure did,' Hunter nodded, 'in fact, she made a play for me. But we'd known each other for a while, living in the same town and all.'

Ben swabbed the wound, dressed it, and sent Hunter on his way. 'Well ridden,' Ben said, wondering who had truly initiated whatever it was that was going on between him and Cat.

Is it simply control that I crave and feel I've lost?

'I can smell the top ten!' Hunter sang, loping out of Ben's room.

Or, great sex aside, is it Cat herself that I crave and all the more so because she's not mine?

Luca came in.

'Yo, Doc!'

'What's up?' Ben asked.

'I've got the squits.'

Ben gave Luca a pill.

'The Babe was asking for you,' Luca said.

'Who?'

'McCabe!' Luca elaborated. 'The Babe. You know – the Babe McCabe. She hates when I call her that. She's so cute.'

Ben glanced at his watch. It was eight thirty.

I wish I'd never met her.

I want her right now.

This is no good.

This could be brilliant.

What a head fuck.

It is 8.30 and the *salle de presse* is chilly. Only a third of the press corps are left. Cat saw Josh briefly but decided Alex's presence was a good enough excuse not to talk. She hasn't seen Ben but she does want to talk to him. Cat has written less than a third of her piece. Taverner wants her copy by 11 p.m. at the very latest. She looks at her screen. She's written but one paragraph. Not very well. She's somewhat distracted and very tired. She only started work half an hour ago, having literally shadowed Rachel until she was off duty and about to take a shower. She stares at the screen but, instead of seeing the words she's written, she can suddenly read the pith of her current situation.

Shit. If Ben knows that I have a boyfriend but is still happy and at ease about sleeping with me, what exactly does that say about how he views me?

A Swiss man called Franz is frowning at her, now raising his hands. Cat looks away, realizing she had unwittingly fixed her expression of horror on him.

He must think me an utter tart. What does that tell me about Ben?

'I'm not!' she declares, to the bewilderment of two Belgian reporters sitting in front of her.

But it doesn't seem to bother him.

'Fuck,' Cat hisses, her head in her hands. The Belgians

presume she's struggling with how to report on the magic of Massimo Lipari's triumphant attack on the Plateau de Boudin.

Is that all it is for him? A convenient fuck? He can't respect me much.

'I want him to like me,' she whispers behind her hand clasped to her mouth, 'I want that to be the driving reason why we're sleeping together.'

I want him to know me. Obviously he doesn't.

'Do I want an embroilment with someone like that?' Cat asks her keyboard softly. A Spanish journalist nearby regards her but doesn't understand English.

I want Ben. But who's who here? I want him to want to sleep with me because he knows me and likes what he knows.

'But he doesn't know me at all, then,' she says ruefully.

'Who does not?' a French reporter called Pascal asks.

'No one,' Cat rushes, 'nothing.'

I'm obviously a no one to him, a bit of nothing.

'Time to back off, Cat,' she tells herself, going to one of the fridges for a can of Coke. 'I must look after myself – that's what Fen would say.' She returns to her seat. Her lower back nags after eleven days in ergonomically substandard chairs.

In fact, I'd better not tell Josh that the boyfriend doesn't exist. If I do, and then Ben finds out, I'll have made a fool of myself in his eyes as much as I've currently made a slut of myself.

Her phone rings. She looks at the number displayed. It is Ben. She bites her lip. Her thumb hovers over the answer button.

What should I say? Why is he calling? Because he wants sex? But I so want to sleep with him. Tonight. Again and again. But dignity – I need to leave here tonight, in a fortnight, to return home and to my future with my dignity intact.

She glances around the emptying *salle de presse*. Her phone continues to ring. An Italian journalist tuts at her. She switches her phone off. She removes her treasured pass and holds it to her cheek. Catriona McCabe. *Journaliste. Le Guardian.*

'This is the Tour de France,' she almost shouts, 'I'm here, I am!' Journalists of many nationalities stare at her, wondering if she's suffering from writer's block or too much Coke or not enough caffeine. A French reporter called Jacques, who's old and friendly, approaches and offers her a glass of the locally produced Fitou.

'*Merci,*' Cat says, downing almost the entire glass. Her body shivers as the alcohol slicks down to her empty stomach and the cold night breeze courses up her spine. She flexes her fingers, blinks hard, deletes most of her work and starts anew.

COPY FOR P. TAVERNER @ GUARDIAN SPORTS DESK FROM CATRIONA McCABE IN PLATEAU DE BOUDIN

Though on paper not as taxing as yesterday's Stage, with only one hors catégorie climb, the cyclists on the Tour de France left Luchon already disadvantaged – their limbs sore and stiff from the chill and damp of almost 6 hours' exposure to terrible weather yesterday. Today, the sun shone unabated with little breeze on the climbs, little warning of the drop to 12 degrees at the summits and the shock of severe cold which lashed the riders on the descents. Such extremes in temperature can play havoc with a rider but the tifosi, the maniac fans, were there in force, handing out sheets of newspaper indiscriminately. This was not for the peloton to catch up on world news, but to use as padding beneath their jerseys to protect against destructive windchill on the descents. On the Col de Portet D'Aspet, the race was neutralized as the riders paid their respects at the stone memorial to Fabio Casertelli, the 1992 Olympic champion who was killed, aged 22, after a horrendous crash there in the 1995 Tour.

Fabian Ducasse, the current yellow jersey, punctured at the base of the penultimate climb, the Col de Port. Three Système Vipère domestiques dropped back to assist. The

Viper boys had practically to ride a Time Trial up the mountain to minimize time loss. Using his domestiques' slipstreams until they were spent, Ducasse had ultimately to make much of the passage by himself. His main contender, Vasily Jawlensky, observed peloton etiquette and did not launch an attack until Ducasse's had rejoined the lead group. The Russian then motored away, flanked by his team's superclimber Massimo Lipari. With no Viper boys in Ducasse's group, if the yellow jersey wanted to catch Jawlensky he would have to do all the work. That's the law of the race and four other riders just sat on his wheel as Fabian pursued his Russian adversary.

On the Plateau de Boudin, Jawlensky's team-mate Massimo Lipari, defender of two consecutive King of the Mountains triumphs, launched his trademark attack. Riding out of the saddle, he found perfect rhythm and swallowed up the seconds, the gravelly tarmac, and soon enough two stunned riders who thought they were well clear. Ultimately, he had enough time to zip up his jersey and approach the summit finish, clapping, waving and blowing kisses to the fans and to the heavens. His rival, Carlos Jesu Velasquez, victor of yesterday's Stage, still wears polka dot but Lipari is only a few points behind. With three days of a flatter profile, the battle for the King of the Mountains in this year's Tour de France will resume in the Alps.

<ENDS>

Rubbing her eyes, Cat packs up from the table and goes to transmit her work down the line to London. She arrives at the hotel nearing 11.30.

Too late to talk to Josh.

She goes to her room and slumps into a chair.

Is it really too late to talk to Josh?

She goes and hovers outside his door, pressing her ear against it. There is no sound. She won't disturb him. It can wait. Tomorrow. Definitely.

Back in her room, curled on the bed, she dials Ben's mobile phone and stares at the number. Her phone beeps at her. *Call?* She leaves the phone on the bed and goes to the window. There's a draught. She's chilly. The phone beeps again. *Call?* Cat rummages around her rucksack and retrieves a sweatshirt. She hasn't yet worn it. It smells of the fabric conditioner she always uses, of being tumble-dried in her local launderette. She inhales, closing her eyes. She can smell home. Now there's a place! A beep from her phone brings her back to reality. *Call?* Cat goes to the bathroom and glances briefly at herself in the mirror.

That's me. I know who I am.

She returns to the bedroom and stares at her phone. It beeps again. *Call?*

No.

STAGE 11
Tarascon sur Ariège–Le Cap D'Arp. 221 kilometres

*L*uca Jones had a childhood fascination with prehistory that has never left him. He collected fossils, knew everything about dinosaurs and still loves the idea of cavemen and women. However, that morning, with one Stage left to take him away from the Pyrenees and to the Rest Day, he was not remotely distracted by the fact that Tarascon-sur-Ariège, with its famous local caves, was one of the great centres for its study. Nor had he given much thought to, let alone passed comment on, the fact that they'd be riding through the hottest part of France where bikinis would abound, that the area of coast to which the race was headed was popular with naturists. Luca was anomalously quiet. Yet his spirit was good. He felt very well. His legs were tingling to get going. It was scorching hot but the sun's rays seemed to be nourishing him deep to the marrow of his bones. He loved his job passionately on days like this.

There was a great turnout to see him and the remaining 177 riders on their way. As they rolled out and along the route, the crowds thinned but the strength of support did not diminish. On a quiet stretch of road, Luca saluted with heartfelt gratitude a corps of firemen standing to attention outside their fire station, the lights of the fire engines flashing, the hoses providing a refreshing arc of water. And then, despite an estimated further five hours in the saddle, in the heat, Jacky Durand, as was his wont, picked up the pace and the pack started to pelt along.

'Jesus, we've covered a fuck of a lot this first hour,' Luca yelled to Hunter who tweaked the computers on his bike and confirmed they'd been racing at an average speed of a fraction under 50 kilometres an hour.

'You're looking strong, Luca,' Hunter shouted, 'go have yourself some fun. Go flirt with the TV cameras and grab yourself some new fans.'

'Whatever you say, boss,' said Luca guilelessly, heading off through the pack as if the leaders were pulling his bike towards them.

'Great tailwind,' he said to Vasily Jawlensky who didn't quite hear him but smiled warmly anyway. Vasily was cycling with his faithful *domestique*, Gianni Fugallo. Luca and Gianni knew each other well.

'Stick with us,' Gianni said as they approached the fourth-category climb Cote de Mouthoumet.

'I'm not going anywhere,' Luca replied.

'You are,' said Vasily, 'you're coming with us.' The Russian suddenly powered away, flanked either side by Luca and Fugallo, his wheel taken by a Belgian rider called Tommy, an old friend of Vasily's from a previous team. The four-man break spoke little, they worked together to read the wind and build a good distance from the bunch. Cross-winds had splintered the peloton into small fractions and organization to bring back the breakaway was tardy. Luca swept to the head of his little group feeling utterly invincible, consequently he was somewhat disappointed when Fugallo came alongside to take the brunt at the front. The motorbike scoreman rode up, brandishing the blackboard which proclaimed they had a 2 minute 12 second lead. It meant Vasily was now the yellow jersey on the road. The peloton behind was in disarray despite the wrath of Fabian Ducasse, the frustration of Jules Le Grand barking orders to his Vipers through their earpieces.

65 kilometres from the finish, with the medieval town of Narbonne a few kilometres off, Vasily Jawlensky sat up, appearing to stream backwards as the other three, momentarily unaware, kept the pace high. When they looked over their shoulders, he waved them on. His hands were off the handlebars, he was sitting upright, pedalling leisurely, eating a power bar, enjoying a drink. They stared at him. Now he wasn't so much waving them on as shooing them away. Emphatically.

'What the fuck is he doing?' Luca asked incredulously. 'He's giving up the fucking yellow jersey.'

Fugallo, listening to his *directeur* through his earpiece, had tears in his eyes. 'Vasily is doing it for me. He knows the pack will chase hard – our *directeur* says that Système Vipère are now setting the pace very strong. Vasily knows that it is him they want. He knows that the bunch don't care about us as we pose no threat in the overall classification. Vasily is doing this for me – giving me a chance for a Stage victory.'

'He's a fucking hero,' Luca yelled and Tommy nodded vigorously.

'Let's not let him down,' Gianni said. 'You guys ready to work?'

'Sure,' said Luca, 'and I'll work for you – the Stage is yours in Vasily's honour. Let's hit it!'

Off they went, men with a mission, men riding on the legacy of a true champion.

'Vasily does not want to take *maillot jaune* just yet,' Fugallo reasoned, 'too much pressure. He is only 53 seconds off Ducasse. The *maillot* is his for the taking whenever he so chooses.'

'Let's ride!' Luca cried, heading off.

'The bunch will subconsciously slow down when they're retrieved him,' Tommy judged.

'Fuck, Luca, you're on a roll!' Fugallo marvelled. 'What are you on?'

Luca shot him a look. 'Passion,' he said. 'It's legal, it's effective, it's safe, there are no side effects and the results are true.'

20 kilometres later, Gianni blew. Not a tyre but his legs. Having finished minutes ahead of Luca and Tommy in the previous two mountain Stages, after a week of hard work for Stefano Sassetta, the price of selflessness was unfortunately paid for by the body. Luca dropped back immediately, urging Gianni to dig as deep as he could to find a second spurt.

'It's no good,' Gianni said magnaminously, 'poor Vasily. But it's no good. I'm hurting, I'm through. You guys go on. You take it. I don't want to hold you back. The bunch are two minutes away. You're wasting time on me. I'm spoiling it for you. Go, Luca. Tommy, go. Fuck off and go.'

Luca and Tommy were torn. They actively wanted Gianni to recover. They wanted to do justice to Vasily's altruism, to bring to fruition the great Russian's munificence.

'Go,' Gianni pleaded, 'please. Another time. Another Tour.'

Luca and Tommy both put a hand on Gianni's shoulders. And then they surged forwards again, without Gianni but on his wishes. However, at Beziers, with only 21 kilometres to go, Luca could sense Tommy was starting to flag.

'Come on,' he urged as the motorbike drew alongside and held up the blackboard which now said '1 minute 54'.

'Go,' Tommy commanded. 'I can't. You can.'

'Please,' Luca encouraged.

'Think of your team,' Tommy said. 'You're as strong as you were 50 k ago. Go for it. I've won a Stage in the Tour de France. I won't win one today and that's no reason for you not to.'

Luca looked at Tommy, bloodshot eyes, dried spittle at the corner of his mouth, his legs so tight they looked almost flayed.

'You sure?' Luca stressed.

'Fucking go!' Tommy yelled, his shoulders moving far too much.

All Luca had ever learnt from his trainers and managers, from listening to other riders, from watching miles of footage of pro cycling, surged through his blood and nourished his muscles. He went.

Don't look over your shoulder. Keep your head down. Don't even look ahead. You know the route profile off by heart because you studied it before you went to sleep.

Luca noted the red and white 10 kilometre banner.

Hug the side of the road, stay close to any fence or barrier, take any shelter from the wind, however minimal.

Luca could hear the crowds yelling for him. He picked out his name, time and again, from all the others painted in whitewash across the tarmac by the fans.

Jesus, I feel strong.

The motorbike pulled alongside. His lead was down to 1 minute 30.

I'm still 1 minute 30 ahead. I haven't slowed down, they've picked it up, the fuckers. Let's give the fans something other than a predictable sprint finish. Mama, this one's for you.

Luca thought alternately of his mother, and of nothing but maintaining his momentum. His legs were stiffening, his arms were tired but his spirit was not phased by his lead diminishing. With 3 kilometres to go, he had just over a minute on the bunch. There was a taste in his mouth. Ambition. Victory. There was no way he was going to let anyone wrest this perfect moment from him. He thought of the great Miguel Indurain, he remembered Lance Armstrong, he recalled Vasily powering up the Col de Port yesterday.

They knew where to find that little extra. I need to access it right now.

He started to chant the names of past Tour giants. Merckx. Hinault. Indurain.

'And Luca Fucking Jones!'

Merckx. Hinault. Indurain.

'I don't care to win the Tour de France five times. I just want to win today. On Stage 11. Tarascon-sur-Ariège to Le Cap D'Arp. 221 k.'

He passed under the final kilometre banner and the motorbike warned him 58 seconds. He ached across his shoulders. His throat was burning dry. He should have drunk more. There had been no time. His legs were hurting. His eyes were stinging. Mama.

And then just an atom of the combined gifts of Merckx, Hinault and Indurain seeped through into Luca's soul and sent a current of strength through his knackered limbs. His legs did not feel so abominably sore. His arms were not insurmountably tired. Come on! Luca, ride for your life, take the Stage. Not just for your Mama, sitting at home with various family members all cheering and sobbing and clutching their hearts. Do it for everyone who knows you and all those who will know you ever after. Show them triumph over adversity. Become the personification of glory.

The crowds were roaring and thumping anything they could, including each other. Luca could see the finish. He allowed himself the briefest glance over his shoulder; the bunch were metres away. In a flash, he knew he was nearer to the line than they were to him. Near enough, moreover, for him to think not only of his Mama but of the TV cameras, the press photographers and his world-wide audience. Accordingly, he zipped up his Megapac jersey, clapped high above his head, punched the air, waved a double-handed victory salute, blew kisses to everyone and God, and gave his bike a final hurl towards the hallowed line. He crossed it 9 seconds ahead of the chasing sprint. Ultimately, he crossed it sitting up, not pedalling, his arms loose at his sides, his eyes closed, tears streaming, his smile ecstatic. The taste of tears. The taste of success. It was exquisitely beautiful. The greatest moment of his life.

I have won today. I am the Tour de France.

All journalists have not merely a favourite rider but one

whom they feel they can appropriate as their own; whose career they always follow closely, whose triumphs they wax lyrical about, whose defeats they play down. It's favouritism, it's widespread and it's allowed. For Cat, though mighty Miguel Indurain was her hero, Luca Jones had long been her special boy.

Cat had watched the last 10 kilometres of the race standing very close to one of the press TV sets. She winced at the welt of sunburn across the back of his neck. She noticed that he'd taken off his gloves, was transfixed by his hands, pale pink in contrast to his bronzed arms. She could practically count all the separate muscle groups in his legs. When Luca had only 700 metres to go she started jumping up and down. As he crossed the line, she leapt high into the air and cheered and squealed.

'Luca!'

She kissed the person closest to her, which happened to be Josh, whispered, 'Luca's done it!' and ran with the pack from the gymnasium requisitioned by the *salle de presse*. Luca, of course, was swamped by a mass of men but she hugged Hunter, cycling to his *soigneur* hot, wet and ecstatic himself. Then she bounced on tiptoes at the edge of the swarm around Luca before skipping off merrily towards she didn't know where. Just skipping. High. Delighted. Skipping towards – ah! The team cars.

She slowed her pace to a reverential walk as she neared the Zucca MV bus. Rachel was wiping down Vasily's legs with a green flannel.

'Thank you,' Cat said, bowing her head at the rider. 'How is Gianni?' she asked Rachel.

'He's OK,' Rachel nodded, 'he's OK. Exhausted. But he can rest a little tomorrow.'

'Tell him he's an absolute star,' Cat said.

'Ms McCabe,' said Rachel, stepping away from Vasily and tipping Evian water on to the flannel, 'have you done your work?'

'Taverner says I can only have 400 words,' Cat rued.

'I meant,' said Rachel, 'your *work*. Ben? Josh? He Who No Longer Exists?'

'Almost,' Cat said, imploring her friend not to give her a hard time at such a joyous moment. Rachel raised her eyebrows. 'Imminently,' Cat promised. Rachel allowed her eyebrows back down. Cat walked away but within a few yards she was jigging triumphantly again. She practically collided with Fabian Ducasse talking with Jules Le Grand, but she gave them only a cursory '*Pardon*'; for her, Luca Jones might have been 42 minutes behind the yellow jersey in the overall classification but he was the true hero of the Tour de France that day.

Team cars were already whisking riders to their hotels, though the Megapac entourage was besieged by press men and TV crews. Cat changed direction and went to the podium instead, beaming and applauding extravagantly when Luca took to the dais to claim his fame, his trophy, his kisses from the Coca-Cola girls and adulation from the crowds.

Kiss him again, Cat implored them, whilst whistling hard through her thumb and little finger (a skill painstakingly learnt aged nine from Django and put to use only on the most special occasions).

Kiss him some more, he'll like that and he deserves it.

She left for the *salle de presse* while Fabian received his fifth yellow jersey of the Tour and his fifth Crédit Lyonnais toy lion and his fifth round of kisses from the sleek Crédit Lyonnais podium girls.

And then she saw Ben from behind and she felt her body swoon at the sight of him; his shoulders, the backs of his ears, his bottom, his walk. And she forgot about resolutely not phoning him last night, she forgot that she had decided he was not a very good idea, she forgot that she had work to do, she forgot that Rachel had told her she had work to do, she forgot Rachel, and Josh, and Him. She jogged to Ben, put her arms around his waist and spun herself around him as if he was a maypole. She threw her arms around his neck, kissed him clumsily and then proclaimed, 'He did it!

He did it!' to Ben's startled expression.

Only Ben's startled expression did not abate, in fact it transmuted into one of polite irritation which Cat misread immediately.

'He did it,' Cat said earnestly, should Ben have missed her point. 'Luca did it.'

Ben smiled and walked on, with Cat inviting herself to accompany him. She jabbered nineteen to the dozen, mainly analysing the race, until they reached the *salle de presse*.

'Can I see you later?' she asked, a twinkle in her eye reflecting the sparkle of her intent, merely a glint of the shine that enveloped her.

'I don't think so,' Ben said. Cat jerked. 'It's a bit –' Ben continued, his hands churning the air in front of him for want of words, 'it's just – well.' Cat's focus was on him entirely but the only response she could give was via the immediate disappearance of her sparkle which Ben could not see as he was studiously not looking at her. 'It's a bit too complicated, wouldn't you say?' he said, though Cat was too dazed to detect the patronizing edge to his voice.

'No!' she whispered, 'you don't understand – I need to talk to you.'

'Oh,' said Ben nonchalantly, 'actually I *do* understand. But it's cool. It's fine. Don't worry about it.'

'No,' Cat said, 'you *don't* understand.' Ben's reply was a raised eyebrow; his aloof expression rendering him at once so unobtainable, and yet attracting Cat to him all the more, hopelessly, helplessly.

'Listen,' he said, 'I have to shoot – we'll have a drink some time. No hard feelings.'

As he walked away from her, as she found her legs taking her to her occupation, both of them touched upon the irony of hard feelings. Feelings had of course been there, over and above the physical evidence that Cat had aroused Ben to a level no woman had for ages; that Cat herself had not been made love to for a long, long time by a man so hard for her.

She returned to her seat between Josh and Alex without a

word or a glance. Her mind was in a muddle. The Stage was being replayed on the televisions but it was Ben's words, echoing in her head, which provided the incongruous commentary.

What should I do? Find him? Phone him? Phone Fen? Run to Rachel? Write? Cry? Hit Josh? Thump Alex? In what order? Oh, for order, for some sense of control.

'Cat,' Josh said, placing his hand on her shoulder and making her flinch, 'can I borrow your Luca interview?'

'God yeah,' Alex enthused, 'and me?'

'I haven't transcribed it yet,' she said to Alex, unable even to look at Josh. 'Perhaps once I've done so,' she continued, staring at her screen.

With all that was buffeting around her mind, writing her article was the perfect way of taking time out from it all. Amazingly, the words flowed on the tide of emotion subsuming her whenever she replayed Luca's victory in her mind or caught snatches of it on the screen. She pleaded successfully with Taverner to let her have an extra 150 words purely for the purpose of purple prose and finished her work well before Josh and Alex. When she came back from transmitting her piece, she took her seat, glanced at Alex and then turned to Josh.

'Josh, I need to talk to you.'

He turned his cheek slightly towards her but kept his eyes on his screen and mumbled, 'Sure.'

'No,' Cat said, looking at him, 'I really want to talk to you.'

Josh stopped typing and looked at her ingenuously. Why shouldn't he? After all, what had he said? What, if anything, had he done wrong? There was not a malicious cell in his body, only affection for Cat.

'What's up?' he asked.

'In private,' Cat said quietly, regarding his fingers resting, mid-sentence, over the keys.

'Are you OK?' Josh asked. Cat shrugged and tried to raise an eyebrow in a Ben-like way, unaware that the result was more startled fawn than nonplussed doctor. 'Let me just finish up,' Josh continued, 'then we'll go for a quiet drink, yes?'

Cat sat quietly, happily watching the replays on the TV screens. What a tremendous day's racing. Luca Jones. Four hours, thirteen minutes and sixteen seconds. It should be written in full. He deserves glory for every fraction of each moment.

Here's Luca heading home with just under 5 kilometres to go. This is when the cameras focused on his hands. Here they are. Gloveless. Pink. One silver ring. Slender fingers. Cat found that she was standing up and knew she had just said, 'Oh my God!' out loud a number of times. She looked from Alex to Josh, both of whom were regarding her somewhat puzzled. 'Oh my God!' she said. 'I have to go.' And she went.

En route to her hotel, Cat makes a detour to the water's edge. In contrast to the fiery Atlantic Coast which provided the backdrop to her initial coupling with Ben, the Golfe du Lion is mellow and affable. The water is lapping lazily, as if it always does so, as if this is the preferred pace of the place, regardless of whether 175 men (two retired) hurtled into town at 60 kph that afternoon. She lays her hand lightly in the spume and feels the bubbles tingle and effervesce, senses them burst in a tickle when the water pulls back. It is dusk, the water is warm. If she was wearing a bra she'd undress and swim in her underwear. But she isn't, so she doesn't. She looks at her hand, all glistening, and dabs her tongue against her salty fingertips, sucking them at length and thoughtfully.

Hands. That was it. That's when I knew. Hands.

Hands, Cat?

It was seeing Luca's hands.

What did you see?

That's when I suddenly realized.

Realized what?

I'm going to say this out loud.

265

'I know Ben's hands off by heart. It's his hands that I can conjure. I can't recall the hands of Him – and is that surprising? After all, Rachel pointed out that He No Longer Exists. I can't remember what they look like. Not even if I scrunch my eyes tight shut and concentrate. And yet I can envisage Ben's hands effortlessly. It doesn't bother me at all that I no longer know what that other man's hands looked like. It's Ben's that I know. It's Ben that matters. I'm going to find him.'

How easy should this be for Cat? Should Ben be in his room, reading, relaxed, receptive? Might Cat come across him right now, strolling along the beach, nicely contemplative? Maybe he'll be having a quiet beer alone in a harbourside bar with a spare chair conveniently close? Perhaps he'll be coming to find Cat as she goes to locate him. And they'll see each other a way off. And, as they near, their smiles will spread. And they'll grasp hands, kiss and confide and feel elated and go straight to bed.

Actually, Cat doesn't even know at which hotel Megapac are staying and her booklet with that information is in the boot of the car parked at the *salle de presse*.

Should I just phone him? Or perhaps Rachel?

Cat dials Ben. His phone is switched off and she has to work hard at not attaching great significance to this. She dials Rachel who gives her details of the Megapac hotel but who is not given the chance to have a chat or suggest a drink. Cat goes as directly as she can to the Megapac hotel, though she makes two wrong turnings and almost collides with an irate woman on a scooter. The hotel foyer is thrumming with fans and press. She goes to the lifts, scans the information of the team rooms and goes to the fourth floor. It is eerily quiet and she can sense that the doors are closed on empty rooms. It's the *Repos*, the Rest Day, tomorrow, after all. Megapac have the perfect opportunity to celebrate their Stage victory in their first Tour de France.

'Where would they do that?' Cat asks Ben's shut door, at

which she continues to knock gently. 'Where are you all?' Cat goes to the car park in the hope that a *soigneur* or mechanic might be finishing duties. Why would they be? It's the Rest Day tomorrow, the one opportunity for things to be put on hold for a night.

'Well, I'll just have to lie in wait,' Cat says to the silent, lumbering team buses. And she does. For over an hour. Thinking what to say. Planning how to say it. Becoming word perfect, perfecting intonation, facial expressions, gestures. Soon enough changing her mind and her soliloquy. Now fretting that she'll fluff her new lines and ruin the depth and sincerity of it all.

She walks around to the front of the hotel and promenades to and fro, delivering her soliloquy quietly. There's Ben. Over there. On the other side of the street. He's with a group of people, Cat. Men and women.

He's with Luca. Luca looks slightly pissed.

So does Ben. Who are the women?

No idea. They looked pissed too.

They're with the American journalists.

Yes.

They also look somewhat drunk. They've bypassed the hotel and gone into that bar.

Yes.

Is that where you're going?

Yes.

When Cat walked into the bar, which was smoky and packed, she was instantly relieved to see that in the far corner the women, whoever they were, were draped over the journalists. The swarm of people was as dense as at the finish-line media scrum but Cat squeezed and prodded and weaved her way forwards.

'The Babe!' Luca sang as she tripped and stumbled on her final approach to their party, steadying herself with a stranger and the edge of a table.

'Luca!' Cat beamed, trying to look composed, wondering

why she couldn't feel Ben's gaze upon her, sensing icy stares from the women that the journalists were now wearing like football scarves.

'You came to see me!' Luca proclaimed.

'Congratulations,' Cat breathed, wondering if she was going to cry and whether it would be for Luca or herself, 'I'm so proud of you.'

'Ah!' said Luca, nudging Ben. 'The Cabe McBabe came to see me.'

'Actually,' Cat heard herself all but interrupt, 'I came to see Ben.'

'She came to see you!' Luca laughed.

'Can it wait till tomorrow?' Ben asked. 'We're taking time out here to celebrate.'

'No,' said Cat, not blaming him for his reserve though it hurt, trying to remind herself that he was still under the illusion that she was a two-timing fraud.

'Have a drink, McBabe,' Luca said ingenuously with a small hiccup, 'sit on my lap.'

'Your legs are far too precious to have my bum on them,' Cat said jovially, before regretting such an uncouth comment. 'Ben?' she implored. He glanced at his watch and asked the group to excuse him. The noise level was very high and Cat could barely stay her ground for all the jostling.

'Outside?' she asked, making her way with pencil-sharpenered elbows through the mass.

'Cat,' said Ben, once outside but before she had the chance to suggest they walk to the seafront, 'I haven't really got time – I told you, don't worry about it.'

'We could go to the beach,' Cat blustered.

'Huh? I'm midway through a party,' Ben said.

'I know, I know – I just.' She looked at him and put her hands on her hips, mirroring his stance. 'You *don't* know,' she said emphatically.

'Yes,' said Ben, scratching the back of his head and glancing over his shoulder to the direction of the bar, 'I do.'

'No,' Cat remonstrated with a light stamp of her foot, 'it's your *hands*.'

'Pardon?'

'You see, it's your hands that I *know*,' she shrugged, sitting in a deflated hunch on a low wall, 'I know your hands, Ben.'

'That's because they're the most recent pair to have been all over you,' said Ben. 'Listen hon, I have to go.'

He walked away.

He's walking away, Cat. Bloody go after him. Forget your speech and just talk honestly with him.

'Ben!'

He raises a hand but does not turn around or even slow down, as if to say, 'Please – another time, Cat.'

Cat jogs after him and uses him as a maypole again. He tries to walk on but she gives him a forceful shove and he stops and regards her, irritated.

'Ben,' she says, knowing neither what to say next nor where to look. Her eyes are drawn to his. He's regarding her sternly, as if he's allocated her a final two minutes before he's bloody going back to the bar. 'Ben,' Cat says, feeling a smile spill across her lips in advance of the liberating truth, 'there is nobody back home for me.'

Ben says nothing.

Say something, Ben – alleviate her ordeal.

No. I think I ought just to listen.

'There *was* someone,' Cat says quietly, 'a very significant other – but that was some months ago.'

'Really,' says Ben but not as a question.

'Honestly,' Cat implores.

'Why lie?' Ben asks after a moment's contemplation. Cat shrugs. 'Don't shrug, speak.'

'Because it felt safe – at the start – before you,' Cat elaborates. 'I'm in a minority out here,' she continues, 'I'm surrounded by blokes – I had no idea and no intention of falling, I mean fancying anyone.'

269

Say something, Ben.

Like what?

'I told Josh,' Cat continues in earnest, 'very early on, before I knew him, let alone you.'

'Why haven't you told him that it was a lie?'

'Because we're on the Tour de France and it's a race. Every day is a fucking race. To pack and check out. To get to the *village*, to scrounge quotes, to glean gossip. To rush to the *salle de presse*. To write the report. File it. Eat at some point. Sneak time with you. Sleep.'

God, she's almost as gorgeous all in a dither as she was when she was livid with me over Monique.

Well, tell her.

No. This is to savour.

You're a bastard.

No. But a very quiet, private part of me has been, dare I say it, just a tiny bit – oh God, oh all right – hurt. No, no, not hurt, just disconcerted. Yes, that's it. So I'll let the balm of her honesty soothe me a while. I'm entitled.

'So,' says Cat with a shrug, 'that's kind of my story in brief. I'd be happy to elaborate. Suffice it to say, I am quite categorically single. I am desperately sorry for the misunderstanding. I rarely lie. And I'm hoping, very much, that we can pick up from where we left off. And run with it.'

She's exhausted. Ben can see that.

'And,' Cat concludes, taking his right hand and scrutinizing it though she knows it off by heart, 'I know your hands, you see. And I can't remember those of this other bloke – it's weird but liberating because it doesn't bother me. I no longer care. I know yours and I *do* care.'

Ben is stalled. He finds himself taking her hand flat between both of his. Against what he presumes to be his better judgement, but helpless to do anything about it, he finds he has kissed her knuckles, turning her wrist to kiss the palm of her hand, licking it suddenly.

'You're salty.'

Stating the obvious.

Cat nods and says, 'So is the sea,' which is a daft thing to say but neither of them reflect upon it.

Ben shakes his head and savours the bewilderment criss-crossing Cat's face before he alleviates it with his smile. He pulls her against him and finds her mouth.

I've never met anyone quite like you. You thrill me and unnerve me and I don't know what I'm meant to do about any of it.

Tell her, Ben.

It's probably not a good idea. None of this. But I can't let common sense allow it to go.

'I have to go,' Ben says. 'Come in with me. Come and join us.'

Cat shakes her head. Her job is done and she desperately needs to rest. And have a bath. And find Josh and confess.

'Come with me,' Ben repeats but again Cat shakes her head. Ben does not even bother to check who is around, who is staggering out of the bar or forcing their way in, or who is on the other side of the street, or in earshot, or who might see. He cups Cat's face in his hand and kisses her, lightly at first and then deeply, his tongue dancing in delight at the taste of her which he has foregone for almost forty-eight hours. 'Tomorrow's the *Repos*,' he says, eyes alight. 'What are your plans?'

'I need to transcribe Luca's interview,' Cat says, her eyes still closed, her head tilted upwards presenting lips eager to be kissed again. Ben licks her mouth with the tip of his tongue, swiftly, gently, from corner to corner. Cat is utterly light-headed between her legs.

'And then?' he asks.

'And then, Ben,' says Cat, looking at him and laying a hand against his chest, another against the bulge in his trousers, 'I'm all yours.'

'What was that about?' Luca asked Ben. 'Where's the Babe?'

'She's gone,' Ben shrugged, taking a hearty drink.

'She OK?' Luca asked.

'Hands,' said Ben with a slow nod, displaying his for emphasis.

Luca, pissed on two bottles of *Seize* and hyper after too many bottles of Coke, nodded earnestly. 'All that typing,' he justified, looking at his own hands, 'quite a tough job, I would think.'

REPOS

*C*at couldn't believe she was singing 'Oh, I do like to be beside the seaside', but she was. She had started to hum it whilst cleaning her teeth and now, sweeping back the hotel curtains and looking out over the navy-blue water, she was singing it with gusto. She needed to call Taverner at the *Guardian* and Andy at *Maillot*, she had her Luca interview to transcribe and she planned to have everything wrapped up before lunch-time to warrant the rest of the day alone in Ben's company.

'First, I must find Josh. I'm not only going to tell him about He Who No Longer Exists but also about He Who Most Definitely Does. I owe it to Josh, he's my pal and he cares about me.'

She went along to Josh's room and knocked on the door. Josh grinned at her. 'You like it, don't you?' he brandished.

'Yes?' she answered. 'Do I? What?'

'Cat McCabe,' he smiled and then broke into song most operatically, '*beside the seaside, beside the sea*!'

'Oh shit,' Cat declared, hiding her face behind her hands.

'The walls are paper thin,' Josh said, casting a glance towards Alex's room on the other side of his and shaking his head.

'Was Alex singing too, then?' Cat asked artlessly. Josh snorted but the explanation came soon enough in the form of a buxom woman opening Alex's door, stepping out in to the corridor, rearranging her clothing, murmuring, '*Ciao!*' back into the room and then nodding most courteously to Josh and Cat as she passed.

'Fletcher!' Josh cried once he'd closed his jaw, while Cat stood stock still and flabbergasted. 'Bloody show yourself.'

Alex appeared, with a John Wayne swagger and a Benny Hill grin. 'I'm shagged!' he declared. Then he steadied his head with both hands and moaned, 'I'm also still pissed, I think.'

'What's her name?' Cat whispered.

'Oh,' Alex fumbled, waving the air dismissively, 'Mary, Margaret, Molly – something like that,' though he knew full well that her name was Maria Angelo because it had taken him most of the previous evening, his entire repertoire of chat-up lines, an exorbitant amount of Pernod and the false promise of Laurent Jalabert's autograph to lure her back to his room. 'Come on, I desperately need caffeine. And food. I need to replenish. I'm knackered. Shagged. Fucking hell.'

'I'm going to the *salle de presse*,' said Cat, looking imploring at Josh who was looking reprovingly at Alex.

'See you there,' Josh said, glancing at Cat. 'I'd better chaperone this jerk all the way.'

'Oh,' faltered Cat, 'OK.'

'Are you going to transcribe your Luca tape?' Josh asked.

'Yes,' Cat said pensively. She tried to communicate via loaded glances but, whereas Rachel would have read her perfectly, Josh just thought he had shaving cream on his cheek or toothpaste on his lips or sleep dust in his eyes. 'If you have a mo',' Cat said to Josh, realizing Alex was too distracted and hungover to eavesdrop, 'I wanted to talk – remember?'

'Oh sure, yes of course,' said Josh. 'Later? After breakfast?'

Cat nodded, hoping that a slightly worried twitch of her

eyebrows would signify that she wanted to talk in private too.

'But Luca won the bloody fucking Stage yesterday,' Cat fulminated in fine *salle de presse* style down the phone to Andy at *Maillot*, 'and I've got an exclusive.' Andy pointed out that she had interviewed Luca *before* he was a Tour de France Stage winner. 'How about a fun little piece on how the riders spend the *Repos*?' Cat suggested, undeterred.

'Who've you got?'

'Um – not a problem.'

'Sure, but *who*?'

'It's no problem – honestly. Who do you want?'

'Cat,' Andy cautioned.

'Any news on my job?' she continued, thinking her idea for a Rest Day vignette very good and wondering to whom else she could pitch it.

'Not as yet,' said Andy.

Frustrated but not discouraged, Cat plugged an earpiece into her dictaphone and set Luca's interview running. Alex and Josh arrived when she was half-way through it. Ben rang her at much the same time as the boys beeped their laptops into life.

'Hurry up,' was how he greeted her, 'I'm horny.'

It gave her the impetus to decline a coffee break, to concentrate hard on Luca's gems and hardly touch the pause or rewind buttons.

'The only humping for me will be going up and down those fucking mountains.'

Darling Luca.

'Are you nervous?' Cat murmured out loud, in sync with her final question to the rider.

'That is not a question for me to answer,' she replied, alongside Luca in her ear. And then she remembered asking him if he was scared and he'd nodded and it wouldn't have come out on tape and she'd never impart his answer anyway. Finished. Done. She set her dictaphone to rewind,

saved her work, flexed her over-exerted fingers, raised her eyebrow at Alex who looked ghastly but self-satisfied and raised her eyebrow at Josh, hoping he'd read it as a request for a moment's privacy.

'Finished?' he asked.

'Yup,' said Cat, her eyebrow still at work. Her phone rang. It was Ben.

'Get your gorgeous ass over here, McCabe. I have wheels, wine and wanton wishes. Come *on*!'

My slate is clear – it's Fate! thought Cat, gathering her things enthusiastically.

'Did you want to nip out?' Josh asked, seeing that Alex was staring gormlessly into the middle distance. 'For a quick chat?'

'Oh,' said Cat, suddenly flummoxed, 'later – would that be OK? I mean, I wouldn't want to prolong your work – it *is* the *Repos.*'

'Sure,' said Josh, 'can I borrow your Luca tape?'

'Sure,' said Cat, handing over her dictaphone, a swarm of butterflies making her all but float out of the *salle de presse* with huge anticipation, much lust, a sizeable smile and a veritable gleam in her eyes.

If the *salle de presse* was like the university library at the end of term, airy, fresh-smelling, laid back and less than half full; the town of Le Cap D'Arp was like a cycling holiday camp. Cat was passed by Tour de France riders in little posses twiddling through town on their way out for a few hours to keep their legs turning. On the beach, Cat noted those who'd trained early and who were now sunbathing in a futile bid to neutralize the demarcation of their bronzed legs, necks and arms from their lily-white T-shirt chests and pale feet and hands. Elsewhere, others were with their families, being treated like royalty by the local cafés and those not in view were obviously indulging in time and space with their wives and girlfriends. Or being massaged. Or playing computer games. Or sleeping. Vasily Jawlensky had become the Pied Piper of cycling; when he left his hotel with Fugallo to ride, scores of kids, teenagers, amateurs and fans pedalled alongside, behind, some even taking their chance in front; everyone smiling. A little way out of town, Vasily glanced at Gianni and the two of them streamed onwards, giving the impression that their followers had come to a complete standstill though they all continued to pedal their hearts out.

Directeurs sportifs sat in the bars, mobile phones at the ready. Journalists not at work took the opportunity to launder their backlog of smalls. Mechanics played volleyball on the beach; *soigneurs* shopped locally for bananas and Vaseline and honey and fabric conditioner for sensitive skin. Cat passed Jules Le Grand, two mobile phones on his brasserie table, a clutch of fans and journalists hovering near by. He tipped his head to one side and proffered his hand which she took and shook whilst he stood and kissed her on both cheeks before taking his seat, answering one phone, having to switch the other to his messaging service. Where was Rachel, Cat wondered? Was Vasily back? Would he and Rachel sneak any time together? She'd phone later. Anything and everything could wait till later. For now, her undivided attention was for Ben.

Initially, she felt a little shy when she saw him, half-wondering whether she should repeat and reaffirm all she told him the night before. Tenderly, he put his hand around the back of her neck and kissed her softly on the lips.

'*Allons*?' she smiled.

'Not quite,' he replied. 'I have to have you – and now. I won't be able to think straight let alone drive straight and my trousers won't hang straight, otherwise.' He led her to his room and made love to her urgently, panting her name as he came, his orgasm precipitated by hearing her call him God and Ben as she climaxed. She felt fantastic to him; tight and hot and extremely wet. It was flattering, immensely arousing, and he was rock hard for her in return. They lay, Ben on his back, Cat on her stomach, Ben grinning at the ceiling, Cat smiling into the pillows, before he gave her buttocks a rap of friendly slaps. 'Come on, McCabe, we're going for a little excursion.'

He drove down the coast towards Perpignan where they ate *moules* and *frites*, drank cold, innocuous lager and strolled amongst the boats licking ice-cream from cornets. He now knew all about Fen and Pip, the layout of Cat's flat, Django's dress sense and culinary proclivities and the quite overwhelming fact that Cat's mother had run off with a cowboy from Denver when her daughters were very young.

'I'm not a million miles from Denver,' Ben said, as they sat on the harbour wall, swinging their legs, 'you could try and locate her when you come to visit.' Cat smiled a little bashfully and glanced at Ben. 'You will come and visit me,' he stated. She nodded confirmation and then grinned inanely whilst the boats bobbed and Ben stroked her bare knee.

Cat learnt about Ben's background, about his somewhat burdonsome mother, about his father with whom he didn't really connect, about Amelia of whom Ben said he rarely thought. Ben didn't learn much about He Who No Longer Exists because Cat said there wasn't much to say.

After all, he no longer exists, does he? Certainly he no longer warrants personal pronoun capitalization.

'Ben,' said Cat contemplatively as they drove back midafternoon. She looked at his cheek and placed the back of her hand softly against it.

'Yep?' he replied, his eyes leaving the road momentarily, alighting on Cat's for a second yet scorching her to the core instantly.

'Who did you think I *was*?'

He glanced at her again; she was gazing out of the window. 'I mean, when you thought I had a bloke already. You must have thought me something of a slapper, right?'

Ben did not reply.

'A sure shag,' Cat pressed, 'pussy that puts out – right?'

'Wrong,' said Ben thoughtfully, doing much mirrorchecking. Cat looked at him but he did not take his eyes from the road. 'I *was* disappointed,' he said, a few kilometres later, '– not in you so much, but in the situation. However, believing you had a boyfriend actually didn't make me want you any less. It didn't make me want you any more either – because I was at my pinnacle of desire anyway.' He glanced at himself in the rear-view mirror, called himself a soft bastard but was unable to do anything about his grin.

'I don't have a boyfriend,' said Cat, firmly but quietly, seeing from the wing mirror that the blush she felt within had manifested itself in virulent scarlet across her cheeks.

'No,' Ben said, 'you only have me. And I don't have a girl-friend.'

'No,' said Cat, 'just me. And this is the Tour de France.'

'The Tour de France,' said Ben, 'and it's over half-way through.'

Something quite ghastly is going to befall Cat on a day hitherto as close to perfection as she's ever known. She feels simultaneously peaceful and utterly exhilarated, as only being on the brink of falling headlong in love with someone can instil. Perhaps she shouldn't fall in love with Ben, not if she's sensible and considers that the Tour is over half-way through and her beau lives in Boulder. But how can you decide not to fall in love with someone? Especially if you've already been treated to a glimpse of the potential that such a state could provide. It would be pointless. It would be impossible.

However, Cat's euphoric state is going to be shattered, her world is going to go haywire and her confidence is going to collapse. Worst of all, she will soon doubt her standing as a respected member of the Tour de France family. I have no idea how she'll cope or how she'll recover or why this has to happen to her. She deserves an easy ride, after all, doesn't she?

It's a beautiful day. She wants to go for a swim in the sea later. With Ben. Have a long, boozy supper, with Ben, perhaps with Rachel and the others too. Sleep with Ben tonight and wake up in the same bed as him tomorrow. She could even stroll through the *village départ* hand in hand with him. First, though, she has to go to the *salle de presse*. She is ready and eager to confess to Josh, to hug him and thank him and apologize for the fact that she spun him a yarn she should have unknotted days ago. So she's going to the *salle de presse*, a spring in her step, a head-turning smile on her lips and in her eyes, energy and well-being instilled in her every move. I'm sorry. Poor Cat.

Alex and Josh were at home and happy in the *salle de presse* on the *Repos*. They had no pressing urge to swim or stroll. To pack up at tea-time, as they intended to do, was treat enough. They liked it that the pace was down a gear, that the *salle* was populated today only by the diehard cycling enthusiasts who masquerade as journalists.

'Would you mind finishing the last part of the tape?' Josh, who types at a fraction of Cat's speed, asked Alex. 'I hate transcribing. It means we need only do it the once between us.'

'Sure,' said Alex, yawning, 'sounds about all I'm capable of today. Fuck, I'm shagged.'

'I'll go and get caffeine,' Josh informed. Alex fiddled with the earpiece before deciding to dispense with it. He set the tape running, turned up the volume, and transcribed from where Josh had left off. When Josh returned with coffee, Alex paused the tape and drank the liquid as if it were nectar.

'Good old Luca,' Alex laughed, 'he says the only humping he'll be doing is going up and down the mountains – "*the fucking mountains*"!'

'God,' said Josh, rewinding the machine, 'did Cat just ask him if he was nervous?'

They listened. 'Yeah,' Alex confirmed, 'but he didn't bloody reply. We'll have to ask her if he gesticulated positively or negatively or whether he kept a poker face. Fuck, she just asked him if he's scared.'

'No reply. I think that's probably about it,' Josh surmised, flicking down the volume.

'I'll just check,' said Alex, turning the sound up again.

How long do you have? a male voice but not Luca's seeps out of the dictaphone, *Because I have about seven inches.*

I have to write my report, a female voice, too British and unmistakable to be anyone other than Catriona McCabe, *journaliste, le Guardian*, is heard to reply.

All heads in the *salle de presse* turn to Alex and Josh and Cat's dictaphone; delighted, flabbergasted, hungry for more. Thank God only a third of the press men are working.

I want you now, the man is murmuring amidst much rustling.

You can have me now, the English girl replies whilst bedsprings creak.

There is the sound of deep, desirous breathing and some laughter and some moaning and some bed bouncing. Penetration or not – and the recording doesn't divulge – it is indisputable what has been recorded; it is obviously an aural sex show and the press men are transfixed.

'Come on,' Josh tells Alex, 'switch the fucker off.' But neither of them silence the machine because both of them know they are listening to Cat and Ben.

Don't stop, the girl pleads.

'Whoa whoa whoa,' says Alex, grabbing the dictaphone but not touching the volume, let alone switching the thing off.

Now! the girl is remonstrating when the man tells her *'Later'*. She is panting and gasping and audibly on the verge of orgasm.

Cat came into the *salle de presse* just as she was about to come on tape. And when she came in, all eyes were on her in the here and now whilst all ears were still trained to her in the then and there. There was silence amongst the press corps. But not from the dictaphone.

'But I want you – I do – now!'

Cat was rooted to the spot.

'Look on this as a taster – I'm going to whisk you away tonight, I know of a place. It's private and beautiful and we're going to have sex there.'

Cat remembered distinctly how, at that point, Ben had had his fingers inside her. And even if she'd forgotten, the sound of her rhythmic, lust-urgent breathing would have reminded her.

Isn't technology marvellous! How sensitive dictaphones are! See, it can pick up and project the unmistakable rasps and clicks of two people kissing and it can preserve crystal clear and loud the sound of Cat imploring, *'Don't go – oh God, Ben!'* It is a shame that the *salle de presse* isn't quite so sensitive to allow a private situation to remain so. But can you blame them? Have you ever heard anything like it? Luca Jones. Sex. Gossip. On the Tour de France. Compulsive listening. I dare anyone to switch it off.

What did Cat do? What could she do? What do you think she did? What would you do?

She gave a strangled yelp. She turned on her heels. She ran. Fast. Just to get the fuck away from there. And fast. It probably wasn't the most logical thing to do, nor the most constructive because it would of course make her return – and she would *have* to return, it was her *job* – all the more difficult. But she acted on impulse, reacted to the sheer horror of it all, and all her senses barring common sense had told her to bolt.

Was the dictaphone then switched off? What? And miss Ben having his private wank? The tape must run to the end. After all, say Luca came back with a fantastic quote? Fast forward? No, no – wouldn't want to run down the batteries.

I could fly home from Toulouse.
But you'd have to inform Taverner at the *Guardian*.
And he'd want to know why.

And then, of course, so will *Maillot.*

And yarn-spinning obviously lands me in more trouble than the truth.

Plus, if you left under a cloud, you'd have no control over the way this whole débâcle will be recounted.

Jesus. Before you can say maillot jaune, *legend will have me live on video shagging the entire Megapac team.*

How long have you been sitting there? It's drawing to dusk. Isn't the sand damp and your bottom wet?

I didn't go to the hotel for fear of being followed. I found this secluded chink away from the main beach. There are rock pools. The sand is dry.

There *is* a funny side, Cat, you *do* know that? But you alone can orchestrate the way this afternoon is preserved for posterity.

I know. It would only take Rachel or my sisters to point it out, but I'm actually too humiliated to contact anyone. Even Ben.

Instead, Cat opted out of the present tense and sat a while longer, by herself. She analysed how the clouds simpered up to the moon and over it, having their edges singed brown like the circumference on a cup of espresso coffee. Then she made the clouds appear to stand still so that she imagined the stars to be making a reverential pilgrimage towards the moon. Then she saw the night clouds as a slow, silent procession; like a line of melancholy people moving quietly, secretly away. Finally, she scoured the sky for the constellations she knew and she mused a while on how, at different times and in different places, she'd seen Cassiopeia as a W, an M and a 3. Finally, she admitted that such meanderings were just pointless displacement activities and that facts had to be faced and that faces had to be braved.

So she switches on her mobile phone. There are six messages. Rachel wants to know if she'd like to have tea and a window shop. Ben says hasn't she finished her work yet, he thought she was just going to the *salle de presse* to retrieve her stuff. Josh says Cat, where are you, please call, he's worried. Alex says you're cool, McCabe, don't worry about it, your street cred has just rocketed. Ben tells her he's just spoken to Josh, asks her to call, call now. Josh implores her to call, please Cat, just call.

It is because Cat can feel their affection and detect no ridicule that she decides she won't be flying home from Toulouse. She knows she will be able to enter the *salle de presse* tomorrow, even if she won't quite be able to hold her head high. Who to phone? Who else.

'Josh?'

'Cat,' Josh sighs, relieved, delighted, 'where the fuck are you?'

'Oh,' Cat says, a wavering voice coming through more clearly than her breezy tone, 'just sitting. Having a think.'

'Do you want company?' Josh asks.

'Can we just chat on the phone?' Cat replies, dipping her fingertips into a rock pool.

'Sure,' Josh says.

'Josh, I'm *so* sorry,' Cat says, hugging her knees and wishing she was hugging him.

'You don't need to be,' Josh assures her.

'No, I *do*,' Cat confirms, her voice breaking, 'I lied to you and I don't feel good about that and I should have set records straight ages ago.'

'About the non-existent boyfriend?'

'Yes,' Cat gasps, 'how do you know about him?'

Josh wasn't about to tell her that he was in Rachel's room, eating cereal, with the Zucca MV *soigneur* and the Megapac doctor trying to hear both sides of the conversation. 'I didn't know you then,' Cat was continuing, 'when I, um, *fibbed*.'

'Fibbed!' Josh laughs. 'It was a fucking whopper!'

'I know,' Cat concedes, trying to lean back against a rock but finding it singularly uncomfortable, 'I know. But I did it for many reasons, many of them daft but mainly for my own security.'

'I understand,' says Josh honestly because, after lengthy

conversations with both Ben and Rachel, he does.

'I adore you, Josh,' Cat says from the heart, clutching hers for unseen emphasis, 'I truly value our friendship and I hope I haven't hurt you.'

Josh smiles. He's glad Ben and Rachel didn't hear that. He wants to keep it for himself. He's touched.

'So,' Cat says, 'I'm not an immoral slapper.'

'Good God no!' Josh replies with great affection. 'You're just a sex-crazed compulsive liar.'

To be teased in such a way but with such affection at such a time is a true tonic for Cat and she is further soothed by Josh imploring her to come to the Zucca MV hotel to raid Rachel's veritable grocery store.

'Have you been with Rachel, then,' Cat asks, 'this whole time?'

'Yes,' says Josh, 'and Ben's here too.'

Cat poked her head around Rachel's door with her eyes trained firmly on the carpet. She noted Rachel was wearing pretty sandals, Ben was in his lovely Docksiders and Josh was in trainers. Very slowly, she let her gaze travel upwards over three pairs of legs of varying degrees of hirsuteness. Rachel was sitting in a chair, Ben and Josh were on the edge of her bed. Gradually, Cat lifted her head and finally her eyes alighted on the three faces. Rachel was shaking hers slowly, with a wry smile etched across her lips. Josh had tilted his, broadcasting a supportive smile as loudly as he could. Ben was simply looking at her.

God, you're gorgeous, Cat.

'Hullo,' Cat said to all asunder, bashfully.

'Do you want some food?' Rachel asked, rising and slipping her hand around Cat's waist, giving her a squeeze.

'Yes, please,' said Cat, shuffling further into the room.

'Fuck it, Cat, you mad girl,' Josh said, coming over and enveloping her in a bear hug. He kissed her cheek with a sonorous 'mmwah!' and then helped himself to a banana which he munched thoughtfully.

When Cat had consumed two bowls of cereal and a yoghurt, Ben yawned, stretched and rose. 'Come on, you,' he said, going to her and running his fingers through her hair. Cat knew she blushed at the sudden public display of his affection, but up she stood obediently, beamed gratitude at Rachel and said, 'Come, Josh, let's go.'

Josh, Ben and Cat strolled leisurely back to their hotel. Every now and then, Cat glanced gratefully at the moon, checked on Cassiopeia's whereabouts and observed that the queue of clouds had dispersed. It was going to be a fine day tomorrow.

The journalists' hotel was small and the foyer served as an impromptu bar. Alex was there with the buxom woman, ensconced in sagging seats and surrounded by several empty bottles of *Seize*.

'Cat McCabe!' he bellowed, unravelling his gangly limbs, extricating himself from the capacious chair and the drape of the woman. He loped over to her, picked her up off the floor, swung her around and then deposited her somewhat cack-handedly. 'Cat McCabe,' he said again, with a veritable twinkle in his eye, 'you little vixen you.' Then he turned to Ben. 'You're a wanker of a bastard,' he praised the doctor, 'you're loathed and envied by the entire *salle de presse* right now.' Ben thanked him courteously for the compliment, Cat kissed Alex goodnight and raised her eyebrow quite saucily in reference to Mary or Margaret or Molly.

'Maria,' Alex whispered. Cat winked and they left Alex to his questionable yet obviously relatively effective seduction.

'Sweet dreams,' Cat said to Josh, laying her hand on his arm before hugging him tightly.

'You too,' Josh grinned. 'Night, Ben.'

'Goodnight,' said Ben.

Cat had the most horrendous headache, slicing right across her brow and searing into the centre of her skull. Ben said that, ironically, the best cure for a headache was sex. Cat was happy to believe him and needed no spoonful of sugar to facilitate such medicine. He was a doctor. She trusted him.

STAGE 12
Frontignan La Peyrade–Daumier. 196 kilometres

*B*ack in London, Pip, who'd hardly slept, phoned Django at 5.30 a.m.

'Can you lend me some money?' she said.

'Jesus Christ – are you in trouble? Are you in jail?' Django cried, throwing back the bedcovers, ready to dress in a second and pelt down to London at a moment's notice even if his eyes were still firmly shut.

'God, I'm fine,' Pip laughed, 'only I'm a bit broke this month. So can you?'

'Can I what?' Django asked, rubbing his eyes and his head and trying to massage his memory into recalling what his niece had phoned for.

'Lend me some money,' Pip repeated.

'Money?' said Django. 'What for? Are you in trouble?'

'God, no,' said Pip, 'I want to go to France to visit my sister.'

'You want to go to France to visit your sister,' Django repeated attempting, at this ungodly hour, to recall which niece was not in England and why.

'Yes,' said Pip, 'Cat.'

'Well, why didn't you say?' Django exclaimed. 'Of course

you can have some money – if I have some.'

'You have lots,' Pip prompted, 'somewhere.'

'Of course I do,' Django said, as if thanking his niece for reminding him, 'I'll send some down.'

Pip phoned Fen immediately. 'I have some money,' she said.

'That's nice,' said Fen blearily. 'Fuck, it's twenty to *six*.'

'I have some money,' Pip repeated, 'so let's go to France this weekend.'

'Can't afford it,' said Fen, pulling the duvet up to her chin and keeping her eyes closed.

'Bollocks!' remonstrated Pip. 'One of your boyfriends is loaded.'

'But the other one is broke,' Fen said softly.

'Yes, but which one have you chosen? Who is it to be?'

'I still don't know,' Fen wailed.

'Yes, yes. But will you come to France?'

'Sure,' said Fen.

Luca lay in bed with an inordinately large grin on his face, his eyes wide open and sparkling, fixated with a particularly uninspiring run of cornice.

'Come on come on come on!' he chanted. Didier awoke.

'Fuck it, man,' Didier remonstrated, 'it's 6.30!'

'I want to start!' Luca declared. 'I want to get going.'

'Go to sleep,' Didier mumbled, pulling a pillow over his head.

'I can't!' Luca declared. 'I haven't slept a wink.'

'Not amphetamines again,' Didier exclaimed, hurling the pillow away and fixing an accusing stare on his room-mate.

'Don't be fucking stupid,' Luca said, quite offended, 'I'm as clean as they come. I want to win another Stage, goddamn it. Those feelings of euphoria, of adulation, of strength – they're far more addictive, and much more effective too. I'm raring to go.'

'Well,' Didier reasoned, 'you're not going to win a Stage on no sleep, for fuck's sake.' He turned his back on Luca, mumbled, 'Sweet dreams' and then went off to have some of his own – mainly about glory in the mountains and winning a Stage himself.

Cat moaned when Ben woke her, not least because the awakening was rude in the extreme. She cupped her hands around Ben's head and lifted his face from her pussy.

'I don't want to wake up,' she lamented. Ben crawled up her body and she kissed him, tasting her own salty-sweetness on his mouth. 'I'm dreading today,' she confided. 'How on earth am I going to manage the *salle de presse*?'

Ben lay on his back and looked at her sideways. 'Are you embarrassed?'

'Embarrassed?' Cat exclaimed, propping herself up on her side. 'I've never been so humiliated in all my life.'

'Yes, but are you *embarrassed*?' Ben pressed. Cat frowned. 'About whatever it is that's going on here – between us.' Ben was regarding her steadily.

'God, no,' Cat said quietly, gazing at him and punctuating her statement with an emphatic kiss to his shoulder.

'Well then,' said Ben, 'you just lie back, close your eyes and figure out who is in the wrong, who has the dignity, who should be embarrassed, while I satiate myself on your gorgeous pussy.'

Rachel didn't have any time with Vasily on the Rest Day. After his ride, he'd had deep massage from another *soigneur*, followed by a little ultrasound on an old knee injury. This morning, when she delivered clean gear to the team, she had a few minutes alone with him. She was hoping for quality time. When she gave him his lycra, she kissed his cheek; seductively close to the corner of his mouth, she hoped. She noted how, initially, he looked utterly startled until she saw the cogs of his memory start to turn. When he then kissed her back, on the lips with a tantalizing flick of his tongue, it was enough to put paid to the unease she had fleetingly experienced.

With the Tour over half-way through, Cat had long absolved many in the press corps for their diabolical taste in footwear, their deplorable typing skills and their excessive addiction to nicotine because, for the most part, they were a nice bunch with such passion for cycle sport that Cat could even turn a blind eye (if still-attuned nose) to their diminishing concerns for personal hygiene. There were individuals, however, who were simply not likeable; for smelling just too bad, for not loving cycling enough and for general antisocial behaviour that went far beyond footwear fancy and nicotine predilection.

A small man called Jan Airie was perhaps the most odious of all. He never went to the *village*, never ventured near the finish, let alone the scrum, never took his chance amongst the team vehicles or hotels; yet he always crept around scrounging quotes from the other journalists, wheedling his way up and down the banks of laptops, invariably clearing his chest or picking his ears. Sometimes, Cat sensed him scavenging from her screen over her shoulder; or rather *scented* him, for he was prone to belch with the force and regularity of a Tourette's sufferer, his feet were spectacularly vile and oral hygiene was obviously of no concern. He made her jump. He made her skin crawl. She knew it would have been too much to hope that he hadn't been in the *salle* the day before.

I'm too full of adrenalin to be able to digest even a spoonful of humble pie, Cat bemoaned to herself as Josh parked the car near the *salle de presse* in Daumier.

'I'm starving,' yawned Alex, stretching expansively and clonking Josh on the ear as he did so. 'You're very quiet,' he remarked to Cat who did not reply. Josh glanced at her from the rear-view mirror but she looked away before she could receive his supportive wink. Taking a few deep breaths, with eyes cast down though the serene and elegant town of Daumier well deserved her attention, Cat traipsed behind the boys to the *salle de presse*.

'Wait up,' she said to Alex and Josh, 'can you two flank me?'

'Oughtn't you be wearing sackcloth,' Alex teased, 'not that floaty little sundress – a bag over your head at the very least?'

'But it's hot,' Cat remonstrated.

'And the press gang'll be even hotter,' Alex remarked, eyeing her up and down.

'I can't go!' Cat declared, coming to a standstill.

'Come on,' said Josh, linking arms with her. They escorted her in, which was a good job really as she was too busy scrutinizing the ground just millimetres in front of each foot fall to take notice of where she ought to be headed and obstacles to avoid.

Shit. Has everyone gone quiet? Or is my heartbeat just drowning out every other sound? I daren't look up.

The boys sat her down between them and Cat started typing immediately; furiously and with her head close to the keyboard and masked by the screen.

COPY FOR P. TAVERNER @ GUARDIAN SPORTS DESK FROM CATRIONA McCABE IN DAUMIER

The memory of yesterday's Repos *faded fast* (God, I wish it would – I'm going to have to relive it again when next I speak to my sisters) *as the Tour de France headed for Provence. The deep massage and physiotherapy the riders would have had yesterday was in retrospect not so much to soothe their limbs from the exertion of 11 days of racing, as to prepare and cajole their bodies for a further 9 days.* (Jesus – what's that? Oh my God, people are clapping.)

Though a slow round of applause intruded on Cat's concentration, she decided to give everyone the benefit of the doubt that maybe, just maybe, they were merely applauding a breakaway or hot-spot sprint. She was desperate to watch the race, the *Repos* had been very nice, thank you, but Cat had withdrawal symptoms for cycling. However, she didn't dare raise her head though her neck was aching and her shoulders stiff. Josh sweetly whispered a running commentary and Alex supportively denounced the clap-happy posse as a bunch of tossers. Neither could do much about warning Cat that Jan Airie was leering behind her because he had slunk up unannounced, as was his wont.

'Catriona!' he breathed pungently and invasively close to her ear, forcing her to retreat even further into the questionable space offered by her laptop. 'I do believe you interviewed young Luca Jones – I'd love to hear your tape – I'm sure it is very interesting.' Then, though his humour stank and his laughter reeked, he wheezed himself silly at what he perceived to be his great wit. Cat wanted to throw up or hit him, but as the former would mess up her keyboard and the latter would entail face-to-face propinquity, she sat stock still. Airie, proud of himself, skulked off, taking a seat directly in front of Alex and taking a good look at the computer screens of his immediate neighbours. He helped himself to a cigarette from one and stole a swig of Coke from the other.

'Vile!' hissed Josh under his breath.

'Loathsome,' Cat agreed.

'Total wanker,' Alex contributed.

The three of them pulled themselves up primly and settled down to their work, sensibly ignoring Airie exclaiming, 'Don't stop! Don't stop!' in falsetto under the pretext of urging some Banesto rider's bid for freedom.

With the high mountain Stages approaching, the main contenders for the yellow jersey will keep their energy expenditure to a minimum. With the Alps looming, the non-specialist riders can relish the chance to make a break and glean some glory before the Alps blow them away. Système Vipère, the team behind the yellow jersey of Fabian Ducasse, need to stay near the head of the bunch, to monitor the pace and control which riders they will tolerate in a breakaway. (Thank God for that, Jan Airie seems to have his imbecilic tendencies under check. Where was I? Oh yes, mountains and breakaways.)

But then Jan Airie started to sigh. And then he added a moan or two. Soon he was delivering a clangorous caricature of the female orgasm, soliciting the attention of the whole of the *salle de presse*. Tittering developed into chortling which was soon full-blown laughter.

Cat is starting to feel angry. She feels something else too. Ben's lips. They touch down first on the back of her neck and then along the stretch of her shoulder. The laughter subsides but Airie's faked orgasm, which he is delivering with eyes shut, does not.

'It sounds like you're sick,' Ben tells him very loudly.

'He is sick,' Alex confirms.

'I think he needs help,' Josh adds.

That shut him up! Cat marvels. *Kiss me again, Ben.*

Ben kisses her again and runs her hair through his hands, scooping it into a pony-tail, tugging it so her face tips back for him to kiss her forehead. Then he chats easily to Josh and Alex, massaging Cat's shoulders all the while and fixing Jan Airie with a steely stare. And then, job done, he goes; telling Airie, very loudly, that if drugs don't help a sanatorium might; telling Cat, very loudly, that he'll see her later.

Darling boy, Cat thinks of Ben, as she gazes at the TV screens, noting that Hunter Dean is in a six-man break. Another darling boy.

The riders are racing in 36 degrees, with the sly winds of the region, the mistral and the tramontane, lurking in the wings as if deciding whether or not to have some sport and wreak havoc with the pack. (Ben York, Ben York – you've declared yourself my boyfriend; only how can you be if this is the Tour de France and in ten days' time you'll be in Colorado and I'll be in Camden?)

*

'That's not my primary concern at this precise moment,' Cat says to herself, eyes glued to the TVs, her concern and affection for the riders manifesting itself as a furrow to her brow and a swell in her heart. 'Can my heart beat so hard in two places at once?' she wonders quietly. Obviously it can.

'It's fucking hot,' Luca says to Travis, 'and the wind's picked up – it's north-westerly and it's a bitch.'

'I'd say it's around 50 kph,' Travis confirms. 'It's cool that Hunter's in the break.'

'Yeah,' Luca agrees, 'my legs feel great – I might go for a little gallop.'

'Whatever,' Travis says, 'I'm happy hanging out with this lot.'

Just after the feed, Luca Jones jumped gear and tore away. Though he accomplished a minute's lead on the bunch at one point, he made little headway on the 3-minute lead of the six-man break. 10 km later, aware of the TV helicopter hovering close behind him heralding the imminence of the bunch, Luca sat up and returned to the fold with dignity and his infamous grin.

'Creeps!' Travis hisses to Luca, referring to four young riders from four different teams taking turns to ride headfirst into the wind at the arrowhead front of the bunch.

'I'd say they're shrewd,' Luca counters.

It was a day for young riders acting alone to take turns at the head of the peloton, hauling the Zucca and Viper boys along, to garner favour in the hope that it might be returned in the mountains. 22 km from the finish, the riders faced the second-category climb of the Col de Murs.

'It's a fucker of a descent,' Travis warns Luca as they approach the mountain.

'Too right,' Luca agrees, 'you can't see where the hell you're going.'

'Careful!' Travis calls to Luca who's gone ahead again.

'The publicity caravan leave slicks of rubber and diesel and crap – it can be pretty dangerous.'

With the mountains of the region being densely tree-clad, descents are fast and dangerous as it is difficult for the riders to judge the lay of the land, the severity of the hairpins, which way the mountain slips away around the corners. Travis Stanton was flung from his bike having hit a skid of diesel half-way down.

'Nice road rash!' Luca teases Travis once the road has levelled out into a wide lush valley of breathtaking beauty. Travis glances at his grazed, glistening forearm, his scraped, red raw knee. He pours water over his wounds and shrugs the sting off. 'Where's the break?' he asks Luca who doesn't know.

'Where's the break?' Luca asks David Millar.

'Still three minutes plus,' the Cofidis rider replies. 'You've got Hunter there, right?'

'Yup,' says Luca with pride, 'he's our main man and if I continue to send him my Stage-winning vibes, he's gonna do it. Yo, Hunter!'

'You're a jerk, Luca,' Millar laughs, riding ahead.

The breakaway streamed into the elegant town of Daumier where huge crowds had been chanting and singing all afternoon. The tight corners and barriers of a civic finish, plus the sudden change from unabated sunshine to tree-dappled light, enforcing the riders to steady their pace. With no true sprinter amongst them, psychology was going to decide the victor of the Stage. Though Hunter Dean hung back to judge when to go and who to take, all six riders stormed the last few metres abreast and fellow countryman Marty Jemison (US Postal) took the Stage by a rim, 2 minutes 32 seconds ahead of the main field. Fabian Ducasse takes his sixth yellow jersey but Vasily Jawlensky plays psychological warfare, still a mere 53 seconds off Ducasse's lead. The peloton head for Grenoble tomorrow. Tonight they rest under the imposing presence of the Giant of Provence; the mighty, fearsome Mount Ventoux where Tom Simpson, English rider and yellow jersey wearer, lost his life in 1967.

<ENDS>

Pip and Fen watched the Tour coverage on Channel 4 television with their hearts in their mouths, their passports in their laps, their bags packed and a cab ordered. As soon as the programme finished, they charged to Waterloo, took the Eurostar to Paris, changed stations and boarded a train headed for Grenoble.

'Should we have phoned Cat, do you think?' Pip asked.

'I wonder,' mused Fen. 'No, there's nothing like a surprise.'

'How will we find her?' Pip asked.

Fen shrugged. 'We'll track her down,' she said, wondering for the first time how on earth they would, 'she said she's one of only a dozen women there, after all. How difficult could it be?'

'Where are we going to stay?' Pip asked.

'We'll find somewhere,' Fen assured her. 'How difficult can that be in the land of *gîtes*?'

'And *pommes frites* – I'm starving,' said Pip.

'Did you know,' said Fen, looking up from her Channel 4 guide to the Tour de France, 'the first ever yellow jersey was actually given in Grenoble?'

Pip shook her head and looked fascinated. 'Oh yes,' Fen continued earnestly, 'in 1919. I don't even know why it's yellow.'

'It is yellow,' Pip discoursed, pulling her eyes away from her copy of *Procycling*, 'because the race was sponsored by *L'Auto*, a newspaper whose pages were yellow.'

'How interesting,' said Fen, flipping through *Cycle Sport*, 'and Eddy Merckx collected ninety-six yellow jerseys in his career.'

'Listen to this,' Pip said, consulting *Maillot*, 'scandal and skulduggery! In the second ever Tour, the *maillot jaune*,

Maurice Garin, was disqualified when it transpired he'd done one of the Stages by train!'

'I think that was the Tour when the other top three riders were eliminated for having set up barricades and scattering nails on the roads!' Fen contributed. She looked out of the window. Whilst hurtling through such peaceful countryside, it was hard to believe the huge, hermetic world of the Tour de France was just hours away. What was it going to be like? 'I'm sure we'll find Cat,' Fen said, 'and Fabian Ducasse.'

'Of course we will, I hope we will,' said Pip, referring first to her sister and second to the French rider. It was dawning on them that they hadn't made the journey so much to spend time with their sister, but to see the boys on bikes in the flesh, to experience the Tour de France first hand.

STAGE 13
Valadon–Grenoble. 186.5 kilometres

COPY FOR P. TAVERNER @ GUARDIAN SPORTS DESK
FROM CATRIONA McCABE IN DAUMIER

Against the shimmer of lavender fields and the stab of cyprus trees, amidst the rustic stone buildings tiled in terracotta, under the gaze of the inky mountains of the Vaucluse, the Tour de France found itself in the midst of a Cézanne painting. However, in 40 degree heat, with only a simpering south-westerly hardly easing the humidity, the peloton's interest in art history was negligible as they laboured towards the Alps and to the promise of cooler climes, if torturous climbs.

Today was a medium mountain Stage, hard but tolerable, with the race traversing the Vercors Alps south to north. The final climb, 50 km from the finish, was the second-category Col de Rousset; the pink flesh of the mountain from where the hairpin bends were gouged contrasting with the dense indigo shrubbery crowning it. Though the gradient is not severe, it is a long slog panning out at the summit to a taxing plateau continually undulating for almost 60 km. A seven-man breakaway stayed clear of the field by 10 minutes, but posed no threat to the leaders. As the ugly outskirts of Grenoble gave way to the elegant boulevards of the city centre, the small group played cat and mouse to the delight of the phenomenal crowds. No one wanted to start the sprint but nor would they tolerate a lone bid for glory. Ultimately, David Millar sneaked away at great speed to take the Stage in 4 hours 31 minutes and 40 seconds, leaving the other six to sprint to a photofinish for second place. Massimo Lipari, Zucca MV's pin-up climber and last year's King of the Mountains, scooped more points today to bring him within a hair's breadth of the polka dot jersey currently with Système Vipère's Carlos Jesu Velasquez, the diminutive but charismatic Spaniard. Similarly, though the green jersey is with fellow Viper Boy Jesper Lomers, Zucca MV's Stefano 'Thunder Thighs' Sassetta could well claim it by Paris. Fabian, still in the maillot jaune, *completes the jersey trilogy for Système Vipère but Vasily's designs on the hallowed* maillot *are both realistic and imminent. This year, the three jerseys are not merely the ultimate accolades of the Tour de France, but the trophies of a duel being fought exclusively between Système Vipère and Zucca MV.*

<ENDS>

'And I really don't know who I'd most like to win,' Cat smiled, returning to her chair having transmitted her report to London.

'It's for you,' Josh said, handing Cat his mobile phone, 'it's Taverner – he says he can't get through on yours.' Cat checked her phone and saw there was no signal. She took Josh's and immediately pleaded, 'I know you said 350 words but I'm only 26 over!'

'I let you have "dark duke Sassetta" last week,' Taverner said, 'but I'm drawing the line at Stefano "Thunder Thighs" Sassetta.'

'Why?' Cat probed. 'He'd bloody revel in it.'

'And,' Taverner continued, 'will you *stop* calling the guys by their Christian names? Are you shagging them or something? Luca this, Fabian that, Vasily the other.'

'But they're individuals,' Cat tried to justify, 'not anonymous pedal turners.'

'And finally,' Taverner persisted, 'enough of the arty-farty bullshit waffle. Cézanne's one thing, but "pink flesh of a mountain"?'

'I just get carried away,' Cat tried to justify.

'Change it, please,' Taverner ordered, hanging up.

'I *like* pink flesh,' Cat said somewhat petulantly and inadvertently loudly. A number of press men glanced round at her and enjoyed a little snigger. Though Cat revised her article and spelt names out in full, she defiantly left the Thunder Thighs exactly where she felt they should be.

Fen and Pip sat in a daze at a café.

'We have nowhere to stay, we can't reach Cat and we caught just a glimpse, just a flash, of cycling.'

'And only by standing on our tiptoes, standing on other people's toes and elbowing complete strangers,' Pip interjected.

Fen twitched her mouth, frowned and looked at her sister. 'We get to see more on Channel 4,' she said extremely quietly.

'How are we going to get from Grenoble to L'Alpe D'Huez tomorrow?' Pip asked. 'I doubt whether we can hop on a bus or cadge a lift.'

Fen shrugged and contemplated her kir. 'If we do make it there, where are we going to stay? Under the stars?'

'Where are we going to stay *tonight*, more to the point,' Pip pointed out.

'Come on,' said Fen, 'let's find Cat. Let's go back to the *salle de presse*.'

'But we hovered for ages,' Pip bemoaned, 'with no luck in any language.'

'Come on,' Fen said, boosted a little by the sight of a team car with its roof-load of bikes.

On their way, they passed Ben York but it meant nothing, of course, to any of them. Though Ben is head-turningly handsome, Pip was too engrossed in a map and Fen's head was already cramped with two men jostling for attention. Ben glanced at the women but his priority was half an hour with Cat before he dispensed electrolytes and glucose.

The *salle de presse* in Grenoble was housed in the Palais des Sports, built for the Winter Olympics. Every entrance was guarded by officials refusing to understand English or establish eye contact with anyone not wearing a pass. Which was a shame as both Fen and Pip were excellent in the art of doleful eyelash-batting. It was most unfortunate therefore, that the first journalist they accosted happened to be Jan Airie.

'Ex you sum wah,' Pip enunciated in plummy English, hoping that the journalist might be American and his heart might soften at her accent alone.

'Huh?' Jan said, puffing halitosis liberally.

'Cat McCabe?' Fen suggested, rather nasally.

'Catriona?' Pip added. '*Journaliste, le Guardian*?'

The man sniggered. 'Whore!' He waddled away, laughing to himself.

'What a charming chap,' Pip muttered. They took it in turns to approach other journalists leaving the *salle* but their English, their poor French and their pigeon Italian met with apologetic shrugs.

'Everyone looks shattered,' Fen remarked, 'bags under the eyes, crumpled clothes.'

'Some look like they need a good scrub,' Pip added, 'and a haircut, and a cutthroat shave. There – that bloke looks friendly – your go, Fen. Try him.'

'*Monsieur*?' Fen asked Josh.

'*Oui*?' Josh replied, thinking she looked familiar but, seeing no pass, not dwelling on it.

'Cat McCabe?' Fen asked.

'*Journaliste, le Guardian*?' Pip interjected.

'What about her?' Josh said.

'Oh good, you're English, we're looking for her,' Pip replied.

'Who are you?' Josh asked.

'Who are *you*?' Pip retorted, wondering why everyone was so accusatory.

Josh looked down at his pass and twisted it the right way round. 'I'm Josh Piper, as it goes,' he said, 'and let me guess – you're her bloody sisters, aren't you?'

'We are her bloody sisters!' Fen exclaimed delighted.

'I can't believe you're Josh,' Pip cried, leaping into the air and having to exercise enormous restraint not to do a line of cartwheels, 'I can't believe it!'

'Why?' Josh exclaimed. 'How did she describe me?'

'No,' Fen laughed, 'she means that we found you – we asked one vile man who referred to Cat as a whore and then – bingo! – here you are.'

'That'll be Jan Airie,' Josh said, 'fuck him.'

'My sister's not a whore,' Pip said defensively.

'Of course she isn't,' said Josh.

'Do you know Ben, then?' Pip probed. 'Ouch!' she said as Fen dug her in the ribs.

'Of course I know Ben, then,' Josh said, contemplating Fen's caution.

'She doesn't have a boyfriend, you know,' Fen explained, just in case Josh still thought she did.

'I know,' said Josh, 'though she has Ben – mind you, what you'd call him, given that she's landed him whilst on the Tour de France, I don't know.'

'Where *is* Cat?' Pip asked, as if suddenly remembering their mission to the *salle de presse* in Grenoble.

'She's finished for the day,' Josh said, 'so has Alex. I'm the last of the lot. Jesus! Where are you staying? Does Cat know? Bloody hell! When did you arrive? When are you leaving? What are you even doing here, for fuck's sake?'

'We've come to watch the Tour de France,' Fen said as if Josh was dense.

'We don't have anywhere to stay,' Pip said, as if it really wasn't a problem.

So where is Cat?

She's with Luca.

Where?

Round the back of his team hotel, sitting under a tree in the still-considerable heat of late afternoon.

What's she doing? What's the purpose? Does she have that dictaphone with her again?

They're having a chat.

'Luca,' says Cat, who feels they've analysed the Stage for long enough, 'I have something to tell you.'

'Sure, Babe,' he says. He regards her. Though she looks uncomfortable, this is strongly contradicted by the veritable glow enveloping her. Her mouth might twitch but her eyes sparkle. She shrugs and smiles simultaneously.

'Ben,' she says, 'and me.'

Luca considers this and then he nudges her. 'If I was a doctor instead of a cyclist – would you love me instead?'

'Don't you dare even muse upon being anything other than a cyclist,' she chastizes him, nudging him back. 'The world would be a poorer, duller place.'

'I knew of course, I knew all along,' says Luca, holding Cat's hand in his and tapping at his thigh gently, 'back in Delaunay Le Beau, all those years ago, before the Tour had even started.'

'At the medical?' Cat reminisced. 'That's when I first saw both of you. Sitting together on a bench.'

'Yup,' Luca says, now tapping his handful of hand on Cat's thigh, 'that's when my main man Ben went skippy.'

'What's skippy?' Cat laughs.

'It's a word, no?' Luca says earnestly. 'I say it to mean that's when Ben – well – *went*.' Cat's eyebrows twitched. 'OK, in sensible English, I tell you that's when Ben got the horn.' They both laugh heartily.

'Did he tell you?' Cat probes.

'Ben York?' Luca exclaims. 'Bastard didn't have to. You know why?'

Cat shakes her head.

'Usually, if I joke about women – you know my style – *yeah, she's a fit chicky*, or maybe I say *yo! tasty honey-babe*,' Luca says, all excited, suddenly finding a hearty gossip most reviving, 'well, that boy Ben would normally join in, pass comment – you know?' Cat nods. 'Whenever I talked about you,' Luca says, raising a finger to emphasize significance, 'if I talked about *Gatto*, or the Babe, you know what?'

Cat realizes she has to say, 'No – what?' for Luca to continue.

'I'll tell you,' Luca says, 'Ben doesn't say a fucking thing. So then I knew. I had fun.'

Luca releases her hand from his, Cat stands and pulls Luca to his feet.

'I have to go,' Cat says.

'*Gatto!*' he calls after her. Cat turns. 'I can still call you the Babe McCabe, right?'

'I don't think I could answer to anything else,' Cat assures him.

Cat returned to her hotel which, though clean and bright, smelt of mothballs and the type of disinfectant used liberally in schools when someone's thrown up. A note had been slipped under her door from Josh, informing her that they were in a bar around the corner. Her chat with Luca, talking in the open about Ben, had infused her with extreme happiness, the likes of which she had not felt for some too long time. She floated off to find the bar and, from a way off, saw that joining Alex and Josh were Ben and two women she thought she knew. From a distance, out of context, far from home, on the Tour de Bloody France, there was no way she was going to recognize them instantly as her sisters. As she neared, she squinted, then she grinned, then squinted again and tried to grin at the same time but it was not possible.

'Fen?' she shrieked. 'Pip? Josh! Ben! Alex!'

'Cat!' Pip squeaked.

'Pip!' Cat declared. 'Josh? Alex! Ben? Fen!'

'Cat!' Fen cried.

'Fen!' Cat responded. 'Pip!'

The sisters stood and bounced and hugged and repeated each other's names *ad nauseam* until Alex said for fuck's sake, settle down and have a drink.

'You look shattered,' Pip told her sister, 'you need a haircut and your clothes are all crumpled.'

'If I'd known you were coming, I'd have asked you to bring knickers and hair conditioner,' Cat assured her.

'You look thin too,' Fen said sternly.

'I've put on about half a stone,' Alex bemoaned.

'Fuck that. Do you know what I'm thinking?' Josh said, looking at Alex. 'I am thinking that it's been a long time since Bordeaux.' Alex regarded him and then punched the air, hissing, 'Yes!' under his breath.

'What would you kill for?' Josh asked Cat, shaking his head when she said she'd kill for a ride in the Système Vipère team car.

'Try closing your eyes,' Alex said, noting how his command was obeyed by all three sisters, 'now recall how much frigging baguette, stinky cheese and *jambon* you've had or spurned day after day.' He was amused how Pip and Fen could nod and frown so sincerely alongside Cat. 'Now tell me what you'd kill for.'

'Big Mac,' Cat whispered, eyes still closed, 'large fries,' she continued though an excess of saliva made her voice a little odd, 'and a vanilla milk shake.'

'Now and only now,' said Josh, squeezing her shoulder, 'are you a true press man of the Tour de France. Congratulations.'

And so, over supper at MacDonalds, while Alex, Josh, Cat and Ben indulged in their fantasy meals in appreciative silence, Fen and Pip told Cat all about their journey, their arrival, their day and what on earth and where on earth would their night take them.

'They could have your room,' Ben said, removing a glob of

Special Sauce from Cat's chin. Everyone nodded, especially Alex, who, resuscitated by the splendour of such a meal, suddenly had designs on both sisters and enormous self-belief that he could have the one, the other, or both, whenever he so chose.

'Tomorrow,' Alex said, 'we're staying in an apartment at the ski station – so you two can crash with us there.'

'Please,' Pip said, thinking Alex quite handsome actually, 'where's best to watch the race? We hardly saw a thing today.'

'L'Alpe D'Huez,' Cat said, 'but there will be at least a quarter of a million people on the mountain – many of whom have been there for days, literally.'

'Oh,' said Fen, dejected.

'Oh,' said Pip, disappointed.

'I could drive you there at the crack of dawn,' Cat said, immensely touched that her sisters had come to find her, but moved to the extreme that they had come to see the Tour de France.

'Ben?' says Cat, as they lie on their backs, post orgasm, with their heart rates thundering, their bodies gratifyingly sweaty and their erogenous zones well satiated.

'Yes, Cat?' Ben says woozily.

'I think I'd like to go back to my hotel, if that's OK?'

Ben rolls over, takes Cat's hands above her head and regards her in the half-light. Everything about her is glossy; her eyes, her hair, her skin. She smells fantastic, she had tasted wonderful. 'Is that OK?' Cat says again.

'Of course it is,' Ben whispers.

''Sme,' says Cat, knocking at her hotel room door. The sisters snuggle against each other, as often they have, in a rather small double bed. They stroke faces and hold hands and natter well into the night, as often they have. They settle into a very short sleep before waking at an ungodly hour to make the pilgrimage to cycling's mecca, L'Alpe D'Huez.

STAGE 14
Grenoble–L'Alpe D'Huez. 189 kilometres

'**J**esus, how are they going to get up this?' Pip gasped as Cat turned off the flat road and L'Alpe D'Huez soared skywards immediately.

'Twenty-*one* hairpin bends?' Fen asked Cat, hoping there'd been some mistake and the peloton would actually have only half that number to contend with.

'Yup,' said Cat, driving around the third, 'a 14 k climb.'

'And they'll have ridden three other big 'uns first?' Pip said, holding on tight as the car swept around another bend.

'Yes,' Fen answered, holding on to her stomach, 'including the Galibier – is that right, Cat?'

'Yup,' said Cat, gripping the steering-wheel and swinging the car around another bend, then up, always up, interminably up, 'the Galibier is over 18 k and at 2,646 metres, even higher than L'Alpe D'Huez.'

People were sleeping on the slopes of the mountains, their sleeping bags emerging from the shadows like huge slumbering slugs. Elsewhere, opulent campervans protected their inhabitants from view and dew. Already, people were milling about, ghostly grey in the pre-dawn light, some holding cups of steaming liquid, others draped in the flags of their nation, carrying tins of whitewash, some carrying tins of beer. Cat pulled over three-quarters of the way up the mountain. 'It'll be a slog for you to walk the rest after the Stage – but you can spare a thought for the boys who've biked it,' she said.

'Look!' Pip marvelled at a posse painting riders' names across the tarmac. 'Whenever I see the graffitied roads on the TV coverage, I worry that some riders might have been overlooked. Let's befriend someone with paint, Fen.'

'Will you do one for me?' Cat asked, suddenly wishing that, just then, she could have the freedom of a fan rather than the restrictions of a *journaliste*.

'Sure,' said Pip, 'who?'

'Luca, of course,' said Cat.

'Give us some names to paint,' Fen implored.

'Xavier Caillebotte,' Cat said, 'or Didier LeDucq.'

'Ones we can spell,' laughed Fen.

'I'm going to do Ducasse,' Pip proclaimed.

'Are you now!' Cat teased.

'Who's the yummy Yankee?' Fen asked. 'The dark one?'

'The postman,' Pip clarified.

'George Hincapie,' Cat said, 'US Postal.'

'Him,' said Fen, 'I'll do him.'

'Lucky George,' said Pip.

'Do Marty too,' Cat said, 'and Tyler.'

'Better make a list,' said Fen, anxious now to be on foot, on the great mountain, painting names and waiting for their holders to pedal past.

'What time are they due?' Pip asked Cat.

'About five-ish,' Cat said.

'It's six-ish now,' Pip remarked, not at all concerned that eleven hours separated her and the cyclists.

'He looks friendly,' Fen nudges Pip, 'ask him.'

'*Monsieur? Parlez-vous anglais?*' Pip asks the man.

'Yes,' the man says, 'you speak Dutch?'

'Um,' says Pip, 'not terribly well.'

'OK,' the man laughs, 'we stick with English.'

'Could we have some of your paint?' Pip asks assertively.

'Sure,' says the Dutchman thinking that eleven hours in the company of these two would be most welcome.

```
        L
L   U   C   A
    C
    A
```

Pip paints for Cat.

VASSILY

Pip paints for herself.

'One "s", stupid!' Fen says, midway through **F A B I** and trying to remember if it's **E N** or **A N**.

'Must remember Didier,' Pip says, 'let's do his name really huge.'

DIDIER

'I haven't had so much fun in ages,' Fen says, flicking Pip surreptitiously when her back is turned. 'Mind you, I'm a bit bloody cold.'

'Maybe Mr Rembrandt will have something warm for us,' Pip says prior to collapsing into giggles with her sister before they compose themselves and return to their whitewash duties.

```
    T
    Y
        L
            E
            R
```

MARTY! MARTY! MARTY!

GO GEORGE

'Look,' says Fen, 'someone's painted Lance Armstrong's name!'

'But he's not riding this year,' Pip remarks of the rider who had won the Tour spectacularly having beaten cancer.

'Nope,' Fen says, 'his wife's just had another baby.'

'I'm going to do another Vasily,' says Pip, 'just with the one "s".'

'OK,' Fen enthuses, 'I'll do Svorada – he's a spunk.'

'And then we'll return the paint and ingratiate ourselves to Mr Van Gogh,' Pip says very earnestly.

'Absolutely,' Fen says, finding room for an exclamation mark after **ALLEZ MILLAR**. 'I'm cold, thirsty and hungry already.'

By 11.15 a.m., when the race rolled out of Grenoble, Pip and Fen had painted the names of most of the peloton and made many friends on L'Alpe D'Huez. Consequently, coffee, beer, junk food, transistor radios and expertise had been laid generously at the English girls' disposal. Mr Van Gogh was called Marc and Pip whispered to Fen that, in daylight, he appeared to be looking more and more like Johnny Depp. Fen decided her sister probably should not have had a beer for breakfast so she told her to pee behind a boulder, which Pip dutifully did.

'Remarkably like Johnny Depp,' she said to Fen on her return. 'I'm covered in whitewash.'

'What makes a great climber?' Fen asked Marc, while Pip gave him a fleeting flutter of her eyelashes.

'Basically, a strong will and a high strength-to-weight ratio,' Marc explained, 'though, being light and nimble, they often lose time to the heavier riders when descending.'

'Have you ever been to England?' Pip asked Marc.

'What makes a good descender then?' Fen interrupted his reply.

'Confidence,' Marc said, 'supreme nerve.'

'Your English is so good,' Pip flattered, beer for breakfast increasing her confidence, 'you must visit London.'

A cheery Belgian called Fritz offered paprika-flavoured potato chips around. 'Eye reflexes have to be really sharp and honed,' he told Fen. 'That's OK for the first descents but later, when the riders are tired – ppffp!' He motioned with his hand a rider careering off the road.

'Also, the change in rhythm,' a Danish girl called Jette interjected. 'It's very pronounced for the riders to go from the big gears and flat roads to small gears and long climbs – they have to spin rather than churn.'

Fen nodded earnestly.

Pip gazed at Marc.

'Nerves,' Marc said, gazing at the gradient of the mountain road unfurling in front of them, 'the belief you can go a step beyond your limit.'

Pip whistled slowly.

'Massimo Lipari could well take the Stage,' said Jette, 'and claim the King of the Mountains jersey.'

'Today,' said Marc, thoroughly enjoying the way that Pip hung on his every word and occasionally his arm too, 'Jawlensky will challenge Ducasse for the *maillot jaune*.'

Cat did not see her sisters as she drove Alex and Josh to the *salle de presse* but, from the look and sound of the clamouring crowd, she was convinced they'd be having a party and she needn't worry about them. In fact, she did not have time to spare them much thought. Bad weather was forecast. Dramatic action was prophesied. Jersey-switching was predicted. Frantic rewriting of copy was a foregone conclusion. She had driven the route because, as with the Pyrenees, she needed to experience just a snatch of the haul of the mountains the peloton were going to confront. It had been an arduous drive, well over 100 kilometres longer than the *itinéraire direct* and L'Alpe D'Huez seemed even more severe than it had in the early hours.

The coverage on the *salle de presse* TV screens, however, was not good. Driving rain spattered the camera lenses and, combined with the altitude, the transmission was distorted.

It was raining in squalls. Wind sucked and blew as if the heavens were hyperventilating. It was cold. Worse, much worse, than the first day in the Pyrenees. But what the journalists were denied in terms of clear pictures, they gained in terms of drama via snatches of grainy footage of riders battling the elements on the Col du Telegraphe. They were drenched. The descent was going to take them straight to the gruesome north face of the Galibier.

The conditions were appalling. A miserable 12 degrees in the valleys dropped to a little above 3 degrees at the summits. Earlier, drizzle on the *hors catégorie* Col de La Croix de Fer had deepened to driving rain on the Col du Telegraphe. Massimo Lipari had been first over both peaks and if he could win the Stage, Velasquez's polka dot jersey would be his. Ensconced as they were in the warmth and brightness of the Palais des Sports et Congrès near the finish line, the journalists shuddered for the bunch. But no amount of encouraging vibes and heartfelt hopes could reach the riders, out there, in the Alps, contending with the terrible conditions, the terrifying gradients, and their own personal demons taunting them with fatigue, cramp, cold, breakdown.

'*The Galibier towered above on the race, glowering down on the men who had the audacity to scale its heights by bike*,' wrote Cat. '*For a mountain whose bleak wastes are inhospitable even in sunshine, in the rain today it was grim and desperately dangerous too.*'

She was paragraphs into her article though the race was a long way from the finish. Though she was going to exceed her word limit, she needed to recount the awesome magnitude of the day, to do justice to the men who were out there; just let Taverner dare edit!

Luca and Didier were in a small group with the green jersey of Jesper Lomers, way ahead of the toiling gruppetto, but an insurmountable distance behind a breakaway containing Lipari, Velasquez, Ducasse and Jawlensky.

'Welcome to hell,' Didier said to Luca when the descent of the Telegraphe had at once become the climb of the Galibier.

'This isn't rain,' Luca remarked, 'it's fucking sleet.'

'We need our rain capes,' Didier said.

'Can't we just keep going?' Luca suggested, not wanting to slow down, let alone stop, wanting only to be done with the Galibier.

'We'll freeze, we'll never make it,' Didier insisted.

'I can hardly see,' said Luca, 'and I'm bursting for a piss.'

'Just piss yourself,' said Didier, 'it'll keep you warm.'

'God, this is horrible,' said Luca, not at all comforted by the hot trickle that seeped its way around his shorts. His group tried to work together to combat the headwind, the flurries of sleet but ultimately it was each man for himself. Luca's legs felt appallingly heavy, his eyes stung, his feet were numb and his fingers felt welded with ice to the handlebars. He was dropping back but knew that if Didier was to survive the Galibier, he must be allowed to do it at his preferred pace and rhythm. Luca was on his own and he was hurting badly across his forehead and the back of his neck. His arms ached supremely, the fronts of his thighs and inside his knees were scorched with pain and felt on the verge of malfunction. His breathing, laboured and painful, filled his ears.

'Help me,' he whimpered, 'oh God!'

A fan ran beside, chanting encouragement and pushing Luca for a few yards. His team car drew alongside and his *directeur* yelled hard and heartlessly at Luca to fucking keep going. Somehow, Luca clambered and straggled his way to the Galibier's summit; thirty-five minutes behind Carlos Jesu Velasquez and Massimo Lipari, thirty minutes behind the group with Fabian and Vasily, eighteen minutes behind Didier's group and fifty-eight minutes in front of the gruppetto. Luca's limbs froze on the descent and so did the blood in his veins. It was absolutely terrifying. He was dangerously stiff. Visibility was but a few metres. He felt he had little control over his bike or brakes, with fingers frozen, mind numbing and spirit dying.

I don't want to be here. What the fuck am I doing? I don't know how the fuck I am going to carry on. I want to be in Italy. I don't want to be on a bike. Sunshine. Mama.

On L'Alpe D'Huez, Massimo Lipari stood on his pedals and danced away from Carlos Jesu Velasquez, commandeering the invisible motor that should be the advantage of the polka dot jersey wearer. The Spaniard could do nothing but ride his best and he could do nothing about the fact that, today, Massimo Lipari was simply riding better. It was going to be a legendary Stage finish. Système Vipère's Velasquez had won at altitude in the Pyrenees, now Zucca MV's Lipari was set to do the same in the Alps. The *salle de presse* and their editors back home were ecstatic about the copy such a day was generating.

On L'Alpe D'Huez, Fabian Ducasse bonked. In the *salle de presse*, fingers went apoplectic over keyboards, but not Cat's. Though she had been grinning transfixed by Massimo's great bid for victory, her jaw dropped in awe as she watched Vasily Jawlensky pull away and power up the mountain, sitting calm in his saddle, his shoulders, his eyes, his resolve, rock steady. Incredibly, Vasily hugged the inside of each hairpin, riding the shorter but steeper route as if it were the easier option, the most direct route to the yellow jersey after all. Cat's mouth remained agape in disbelief to see Fabian unable to counter Vasily's attack.

On L'Alpe D'Huez both the polka dot and yellow jerseys changed backs, yet excitement amongst the press for the new victors was countered with compassion for the vanquished. It was gut-wrenching to watch Fabian flounder, to watch the yellow jersey himself slip away from his group, the jersey slip from him. No one helped him. Their pace had not changed. His had. Will power is one thing, grim determination is another, but limbs shot away with pain and muscles ravaged by lactic acid is something else entirely. Fabian simply could not turn the pedals with the force and effect that the other riders could. His eyes were swollen, his mouth was agape, his upper body could not pull and his lower body could not propel. Whatever was going through his mind, no matter how deep he dug within his soul, his body was emphatically on strike and he was utterly at its mercy.

On L'Alpe D'Huez Luca Jones dismounted. Now Cat gasped alarmed, having watched in silent horror her rider weaving and wavering before quitting his bike.

'Get back,' she murmured, 'don't stop. Don't stop, Luca. *Please.*' She closed her eyes, willing him to continue. Opening them, she saw the Megapac team car alongside Luca.

'Make him get back,' she implored, stirring the journalists around her but having no effect on Luca, 'don't let him stop. Tell him he can do it. Please.'

'Let me stop,' Luca sobs.

'No! I will not have you fail. Get back and move. You are paid to do a job,' the *directeur*, merely doing his, barks.

'I can't,' Luca pleads.

'You ride for Megapac,' the *directeur* shouts, 'you are not sick, you are lazy – ride on.'

'*Please*,' Luca pleads.

'Last week you were the personification of success, today you are the epitome of failure.'

Luca remounts and slowly, painfully, painfully slowly, pedals onwards. He makes it up and around two further hairpin bends before dismounting again, this time sitting down on the tarmac, his fingers fixed as if still gripping the handlebars. His team car draws alongside. He looks at his *directeur* through his bloodshot eyes sunken deep into his skull. He is too cold, too desolate, to speak.

'Luca, you will finish this Stage, you will not let L'Alpe D'Huez do this to you. How dare you even think of doing this to the team!'

'My hands,' Luca wails, 'so cold.'

'Piss on them,' his *directeur* commands. 'I forbid you to give up. You will not leave the Tour today.'

*

On L'Alpe D'Huez, Fen and Pip, drenched but warmed by Fritz's schnapps, watched aghast as Luca Jones all but collapsed off his bike and sat shivering and hunched on the tarmac. They watched dumbfounded as he stood, stooped, rolled down his shorts a little and pissed. They watched stunned as he attempted to direct the flow over his hands. They watched in awe as he remounted. He was pushed along, from fan to fan, until his legs could take him forwards and his bike crept upwards and away. Pip chastized herself. She had been on the verge of moaning to Fen that she was wet, that it wasn't much fun, that Channel 4 and a cup of tea were far preferable. But, having watched Luca, her triteness and selfishness appalled her. She needed to make amends. She summoned her spirit, found her voice and, with Marc and Fen and all her other new friends, cheered and urged each and every rider who passed her on their passage.

On L'Alpe D'Huez, four riders abandoned the Tour de France, bringing the number of riders retiring on Stage 14 to twelve. Luca Jones was not one of them. It took Massimo Lipari a phenomenal 36 minutes 51 seconds to climb the mountain, win the Stage and claim the polka dot jersey, a true King of the Mountains. It took Luca just under an hour to limp to the line. Ben was waiting in the team bus. When Luca crawled up the steps, Ben thought how his face was like that of a wizened old man, but how his fragility, his comportment, was that of a child. Luca looked to Ben and, just then, all the doctor felt he could do for the rider was to open his arms, into which the young rider collapsed. He sobbed, his body shaking in spasms of cold and fatigue.

On L'Alpe D'Huez, in the *salle de presse*, wearing Josh's fleece and with Alex's sweatshirt over her knees, Cat wondered how on earth to finish her article. She was thrilled for Massimo to be wearing the polka dot jersey after an epic Stage won in 5 hours 43 minutes and 45 seconds, she was ecstatic that Vasily was now the *maillot jaune* of the Tour de France, having come home with a hissing, livid Carlos Jesu Velasquez two minutes later. However, her heart bled for

Carlos and of course for Fabian, now lying second and nearly four minutes behind Vasily; she felt for the whole of Système Vipère who had relinquished their two prized jerseys on this horrible day. But it was Luca Jones, though, who captured her sympathy and haunted her. With no defining jersey on his back apart from his sodden Megapac strip, he was, in general, just another rider from the peloton who had suffered beyond comprehension today. To Cat, though, he was a champion. Luca had given every ounce of his physical and emotional capacity to finish the Stage for his team, for his *directeur*, for cycle sport, for the fans and lastly, for himself. For Cat, even those ten riders who abandoned, even the two riders coming home well over the time limit only to be sent home, were victors commanding her respect, her compassion and commensurate columns in her report.

Today, I am not writing sport reportage, my piece is not a commentary on the day's Stage. It is my deeply personal response, as honest and emotional as a private diary entry.

'Hey, Cat,' Rachel's voice crackled through bad reception on the mobile phone.

'Rachel,' Cat said, 'what a godforsaken day.'

'I know,' Rachel agreed.

'I mean, well done Zucca – but the *conditions*, Jesus! How are the boys?'

'Too exhausted,' Rachel said, 'absolutely shattered and shot through to the marrow.'

'You sound low, Rachel,' Cat detected, 'it must really take it out of you, too.'

'It does,' the *soigneur* confided. 'Today Zucca have the yellow and polka dot jerseys – but the team are supremely exhausted, their bodies brutally battered. I have to pick up the pieces and it's knackering.'

'Would you like some company?' Cat asked, seeing it was eight o'clock and wondering when Taverner was going to lambast her for exceeding her word limit by 100 per cent.

'Please,' said Rachel, 'come by the hotel.'

'Shit,' said Cat, once she'd hung up, 'my sisters.'

Cat's sisters had trudged up L'Alpe D'Huez, very wet and a little drunk. They'd walked the finishing straight, thinking how, amidst the debris and lingering vibe, it was as if a circus had come to town and then gone again. The rain had settled into an eye-squinting mist and it justified more schnapps and a good sit-down somewhere warm.

'I can't believe Cat's pissing off to see some physio friend,' Pip said petulantly, a hearty glug of liqueur dissolving a mouthful of cake. She was also piqued that Marc had not invited them to thaw out in his campervan, that Fritz had not enquired where they were staying, that Jette had merely said *ciao*, see you on the Col de la Madeleine tomorrow.

'*Soigneur*,' Fen corrected, 'Rachel. Zucca MV. Cat's at work, remember.'

Pip nodded reluctantly, concentrated on her cake and then brightened up. 'When are we meeting Josh and Alex?'

'In half an hour,' Fen said, 'at the apartment. Another drink?'

'Let's raise a glass to Vasily and Massimo – *le maillot jaune* and *le maillot à pois*,' Pip declared, knocking her drink back in one.

'And here's to Fabian and Carlos,' said Fen, doing the same.

'We'd better have another,' said Pip sincerely, 'we must toast those who bowed out.'

'And Luca,' said Fen.

'I wonder if he's had a shower,' said Pip, the sorry sight of the rider urinating over his hands indelibly printed on her memory.

'Can we talk about anything but cycling?' Rachel asks Cat, welcoming her in to her room.

'Of course,' says Cat. 'You look ghastly.' The *soigneur* has dark circles around her eyes, her hair hangs lank and there is a visible slump to her characteristic energy and poise.

'I should toast the team,' Rachel remarks, as if it were a requirement of her job, 'taking two jerseys from Système Vipère in such fine style.' She stifles a yawn and lies back on her bed. 'Well done, Vasily and Massimo. Well done team for just making it today.'

'I'll nip down to the bar and bring a couple of drinks up,' Cat offers sweetly. 'Beer?'

'Make it whisky,' says Rachel, 'and if it isn't Scotch, bugger it, I'll have vodka instead.'

To Rachel's delight, Cat brings her a large tot of Glenfiddich.

'When were you last home?' Cat enquires.

Rachel scrunches her eyes. 'Far too long ago – I miss it and yet when I return it doesn't really feel like home. I soon miss the camaraderie, the familiarity of life with the peloton. Anyway,' she says, taking a hearty glug, her eyes watering at the severity of the liquor, 'enough about work. Let's talk about boys.' Though her eyes are slightly bloodshot, a sly twinkle courses its way through. 'Let's get He Who No Longer Exists out of the way first.'

Am I ready for this? Cat wonders.

Yes, you are.

Rachel was so proud of Cat's level-headed analysis of her failed love that she delved into a bedside cabinet and retrieved an immense block of Cadbury's chocolate as a reward.

'Bliss,' said Cat, filling her mouth and closing her eyes.

'The One Who Is No More,' Rachel toasted, 'well done.'

'Any developments with Vasily?' Cat asked.

'The *maillot jaune* is the development,' Rachel defined quietly. 'Until the race is over, I would think the only thing he'll desire next to his skin is yellow lycra.'

'Are you frustrated?' Cat asked. 'Hurt?'

Rachel considered this. 'Frustrated?' she mused. 'No. Hurt? No. Confused – very.'

'Why?'

'I adore Vasily,' Rachel defined, 'but you know something? I don't think I feel any true chemistry – I think I've been searching for it because when a man like Vasily wants to kiss you, you sit up and take notice.'

'Because he's such an enigma?' Cat clarified.

'Exactly,' Rachel nodded, 'no one knows of any woman Vasily has had. And yet it seemed he wanted me. That fact in itself was enough to turn me on. It was so flattering – I kept thinking, wow! What is it that I have that's seeped through his armour?' Rachel paused, cleared her throat and continued in a whisper, 'I don't actually fancy Vasily Jawlensky.'

'That's tantamount to blasphemy!' Cat cajoled.

Rachel shrugged. 'It's a fact.' She munched on some chocolate. 'I adore him, he's a bloody good kisser, but I don't burn for him. You won't believe this – it's taken me a couple of days myself – actually I quite fancy someone else.'

'Who?' Cat exclaimed, intrigued. 'You slapper!'

Rachel poked Cat. 'André.' She bit her lip.

'André?' Cat contemplated, not knowing anyone of that name in the peloton, let alone Zucca MV.

'André Ferrette,' Rachel said, beckoning Cat close for disclosure, 'is the Système Vipère mechanic.'

'Fucking hell!' Cat declared, about to take a lump of chocolate. 'A *Viper* boy? For a *Zucca* girl? We're talking Montagues and Capulets here.'

Rachel winced. 'Don't I know it – our respective *directeurs* are not going to be best pleased. I bet you we'll have accusations of sabotage and espionage thrown our way before long.'

'So what's happened?' Cat implored, curling up on the bed as Rachel had. 'I can't think when you've had time to form a new union, let alone theorize so lucidly on Vasily.'

'Aye, that's what's weird,' Rachel stated. 'I haven't even come close to kissing André, yet my lust for him is, um, fairly pronounced and something of a distraction!'

'I rather think you hadn't been kissed for way too long,' Cat mused, 'and perhaps you believed you fancied Vasily on account of all the oscular activity.'

'In English, do you mean I was desperate for a snog?'

'Something like that,' Cat laughed.

Gianni Fugallo knocked and entered, eyed the chocolate longingly, eyed the two women supine on the bed hopefully, but made do with a banana and a copy of *Marie Claire*.

'Now let's talk about Ben,' Rachel said, her revelation having quite exhausted her. 'I've heard quite enough about your Other One and anyway He Is No More.'

'Yup,' Cat smiled, 'he's firmly in the past.'

See, no capital 'h'.

While Cat continued to gorge on chocolate and girlie gossip, her sisters, her colleagues and Ben ate liver, tongue and various indefinable parts of cow and pig at a hearty, rustic mountain-top restaurant. It was joyous and noisy, with yelling coming from the kitchen and animated chatter from the diners who were mainly *presse* apart from a hirsute group of men Pip decided were goat-herders, a comment which Alex reacted to with excessive chortling. Red wine flowed, as did the conversation. Especially, Josh noted, between Pip and Alex. Fen also noticed, but her attention was given to Ben.

'Where do you live, Ben?' Fen asked.

'Boulder,' said Ben.

'In the New Forest?' Fen exclaimed, heartened. 'Near Lymington?'

'Er, Colorado,' said Ben, almost apologetically.

What'll happen to my sister when the Tour de France finishes? What is she to you, Ben? A French fling? Might you have another lined up for the Vuelta? Was there someone during the Giro?

'I've invited Cat to visit,' Ben was saying. 'She told me about your mother running off with a cowboy from Denver – we thought we might track her down.'

'What, on Cat's paltry freelance pay?' Fen derided, unnerved that Ben was so *au fait* with her family history.

When has Cat ever wanted to track our mother down?

Fen wondered why she wanted to dislike Ben; especially as, having now spent time with him, she could not dispute that his seemly exterior complemented a strong, likeable character.

Nourished and rejuvenated by the wholesome food, lubricated by the wine, Ben regarded Fen quizzically.

I know I don't have her seal of approval and the bizarre thing is, it matters to me and I rather want it.

'I don't mind saying I was gutted when I thought Cat was involved with someone back home,' he said frankly, continuing while Fen was still wondering what sort of reply a statement like that necessitated. 'But I felt,' Ben paused, 'I felt not just relieved but pretty damn delighted when she told me he was just an ex from months ago.'

Just An Ex? Fen thought to herself. *Why hasn't she told Ben much? Why has she played down the impact it all had on her? Her past is defining her present and will shape her future. Why, and what, does she not want Ben to know? She's either protecting herself – or she is not being herself at all.*

'More wine, Fen?' Ben asked, raising an eyebrow at Josh with a glance in the direction of Alex and Pip who were sporting matching flushed cheeks and looking particularly cosy.

'Thanks,' said Fen, who sipped and smiled politely and tried unsuccessfully to catch her sister's eye. 'Ben,' she started, her conscience warning her to bite her tongue but the wine letting it loose, 'I love my sister. She's extremely precious,' Fen persisted, with more than a hint of warning to her voice.

'Fen,' said Ben, tilting his head and regarding her.

'I love Cat very very much,' Fen interrupted again.

'I know you do,' he said, nodding again.

And I do too. But I'm not going to say it out loud. Not

because I know I'm drunk, but because I'm certainly not going to tell you unless I've told Cat herself.

'To Cat,' he said instead, raising glasses that he'd refilled once more.

'To Pip and Alex,' Josh murmured, suddenly missing his wife desperately.

As Cat walks down from the Zucca MV hotel, she contemplates how she hasn't seen Ben at all today. They haven't even spoken. Not since yesterday.

And I've missed him. Shit.

The notion simultaneously warms Cat and worries her.

She approaches the apartment block at the same time but from the opposite direction to her sisters, her colleagues and Ben, whose status she has great difficulty in defining.

'They're pissed!' she observes, wondering whether Pip is linking arms with Alex purely for stability and, indeed, whether it is for her own stability or his. Cat's eyes are locked on to Ben's. She's delighted to see him.

I have missed him, I really have.

Fen observes how Cat sparkles at the doctor. She regards how her sister practically sings, 'Hullo!' to the rest of them before she beams at Ben, focuses on him exclusively and they kiss. The affection between the two of them is pronounced. It simultaneously warms Fen and worries her.

*M*ost courteously, Alex and Josh had taken the room with bunk beds so that the sisters could have the room with the small double and tiny single bed. Pip told her sisters she ought to take the single bed as she feared she was developing a cold. Josh was well aware that Alex presumed him to be asleep when his colleague crept from the room and when he returned in the early hours. Fen and Cat did not hear Pip leave their room but they heard her return. Facing each other in the double bed, they opened their eyes, raised eyebrows, bit back grins and pretended to be fast asleep.

Cat's mobile phone woke them for real an hour later, at seven in the morning.

'Cat?'

'Rachel?'

'Are you busy?'

'Er, no.'

'Are you asleep?'

'Er, no.'

'I need some help – can you come? Bring your sisters. It's women's work and I need all hands on deck.'

Rachel welcomed them into the Zucca MV team bus. Cat observed her sisters' open mouths and wide eyes and realized with a certain warmth how initially she too had been staggered at glimpsing such a different, special, self-contained world; but how now all of this had become the norm to her, a plausible, preferable way of life.

It's my world too, now. Part of my life. I'm happy here. I feel I belong.

'Now,' said Rachel, most officiously, 'down to business.' From a carrier bag, she laid out a selection of porn magazines.

'Shit,' Pip gasped, 'where did you find those?'

'Are they banned?' Fen whispered ingenuously. 'Did you have to confiscate them? Have you to surrender them to Jean Marie LeBlanc?'

Rachel and Cat laughed, though Cat, aware that porn mags were not a banned substance, was not yet sure of their purpose.

'The boys had a really tough day yesterday,' Rachel said, flipping through a magazine leisurely, 'and today the forecast is very hot.'

'And today they have five mountains to climb,' Cat added, peering over Rachel's shoulder at female limbs in a quite startling configuration.

'So,' said Rachel, 'I thought, to hell with tin foil – I'll wrap their race food in something far more appetizing. We need a production line. Fen, would you mind going through this pile, Pip you have that.'

'What do you want?' Fen asked, deadly serious. 'Big tits?'

'Split beavers?' asked Pip soberly.

'Perfect,' said Rachel, 'only try to find bodies where, if there is a face, it's a pretty one. Bugger the readers' wives and fuck the ones with so much silicone that their nipples spread out like a rash. Just go for the bimbos – I really want to treat the boys.'

*

In the front seat of the Système Vipère team car, Fabian Ducasse is pugnaciously silent and aggressively focused. Jules Le Grand is driving him down L'Alpe D'Huez, down the very mountain which the day before Fabian had ascended in his own funeral cortège. He stares straight ahead, not looking at the road, the gradient, the debris from yesterday. His eyes, today the colour of graphite and as seemingly insensate as the rock of the fearsome Alp itself, give nothing away. Fabian's aquiline features are as sharp as the boulders. A scar scores through his soul in much the same way as the road slices into the mountain. Behind closed lips, his teeth are clenched. However, the external manifestation of his inner turmoil is one of brooding steady focus; he resolutely refuses to allow any hint of emotional turbulence to be visible. It's strategy. The media must not know. Nor must any rider in the peloton. Nor, he thinks somewhat deludedly, must his *directeur*.

But it is Jules's job to be in tune with his riders; though he has read Fabian's condition in a glance, he knows that diplomacy is crucial if the great rider is to race well today. Personally, Jules detests seeing his team leader back in regular Système Vipère colours; Fabian looks wrong some-how, like he's in mufti after eight days wearing the yellow jersey. Though his primary concern is for Fabian's physical and mental recovery, Jules is also thinking of the Système Vipère sponsors, intending to phone them, reassure them, flatter them, once the Stage is under way. Jules has hardly spoken to Fabian because he knows there is little the rider wants to hear. When Fabian finished the Stage yesterday, Jules had grasped his shoulders, shaken him until eye contact was established and said, '*Bien, Fabian, bien.*' Jules curses the fact that the only way to today's start is down the very route that decimated his rider the day before, stripping him of his *maillot jaune*. Jules is painfully aware of the irony that L'Alpe D'Huez, in glorious sunshine, looks positively *Sound of Music* this morning.

'Can he reclaim the *maillot jaune*?' was a question posed

to Jules by fans, by TV, by phone and in the press conference yesterday.

'Tomorrow is another high mountain Stage,' Jules had replied nonchalantly, 'and there is of course another Time Trial to go.'

He had not said this to Fabian. There was nothing that could be said to Fabian that Fabian wouldn't have told himself already, time and again.

Fen and Pip caught a ride to the Col de la Madeleine with another Zucca MV *soigneur*, a quietly spoken man with whom they conversed sparingly in pidgin Anglo-Franco-Italian. He felt it his greater duty to consolidate his passengers' burgeoning passion for the sport by driving them along the race route than to go direct to the hotel to unpack for the riders. From Vizille, the summer seat of many a French president, through the Chatreuse Massif, they journeyed on a road laid down by Napoleon, unaware that the day was to bring a French revolution in the form of Fabian Ducasse's comeback. Pip and Fen were seduced by pretty chalets in sleepy mountain villages where, in July, the Christmas lights were still up because the ski season alone defined such places' existence.

Sunflowers, lavender and cow parsley provided a gentle aesthetic antidote to the rock faces on which firs clung precariously. Local women, laying claim to their favourite spectating spots, sat under parasols, compounding Fen and Pip's feeling that they were driving through an Impressionist painting. Until, that is, the *tifosi* began to gather in force and *en masse*, their sodden clothes from yesterday drying on mountain safety barriers, shrubs, even the tarmac itself. The sisters grinned proudly while the fans cheered, waved and rang huge cow bells as the Zucca MV car passed by.

'Madeleine,' said the *soigneur* with hushed reverence, stopping the car near the summit of the great mountain. 'Please,' he said, hand on heart, as if it were his grave responsibility, 'I wish you to have a very good day.'

'*Mille grazie*,' said Fen.

'*Trille zille grazie*,' said Pip.

'*Prego*,' said the *soigneur* with a humble but flattered shrug and smile, '*prego*.'

'Everyone is so lovely,' Fen remarked to Pip as a vast Spanish family made room at the roadside for them, and an elderly German woman whose face was painted like her national flag offered them cold sausages.

'It's like a huge family,' Pip agreed, thanking three young Spanish boys for sharing their orange juice. 'I can't believe you're making me go home tonight.'

'I *have* to go to work tomorrow,' Fen bemoaned, wanting to stay in the Alps, stay on for the Time Trial, for Paris, rather than head home to trying times and impossible choices.

'And Ben is going to drive us to the station in Grenoble,' said Pip. 'He's lovely, isn't he?'

'It's only about 70 k from Gilbertville,' Fen retorted, wondering how on earth she had the space in her mind to be confused about Ben when she was dithering over two men of her own. 'Wouldn't you rather Alex drove us?' Fen crossed her arms and raised her eyebrow at her sister who almost choked on her orange juice before brandishing a very wicked smile.

'Naughty Philippa,' Pip chastized herself with great pride.

'And?' Fen pressed.

'Who would have thought the Tour de France was sex and drugs and rock and roll?' Pip marvelled as a nearby Danish contingent danced terribly to terrible Europop and a Dutch posse enjoyed cake whose main ingredient was obviously far more mood-enhancing than just flour, butter, eggs and sugar.

In the Gilbertville *salle de presse*, a large marquee by the Arly river, Cat sat on a rickety plastic chair as if it were a veritable throne.

Taverner didn't cut a bloody word! she marvelled to

herself and anyone else who chanced upon the *Guardian*, spread before her. *If this doesn't swing the favour of the* Maillot *office, what the fuck will?*

'Andy? This is Cat McCabe in Gilbertville.'

'Hullo, Cat McCabe in Gilbertville,' said Andy from offices in Pentonville.

'Have you seen the *Guardian*?' Cat said, trying hard not to squeak with excitement, nor sound deflated when Andy said he hadn't. 'Well, I gave Taverner twice as much as he'd asked for and he hasn't cut a word.'

'And *Maillot* would want to employ a girl who doesn't do as she's told?' came the response, the tongue in cheek not being audible via mobile phone. Cat hung up and speed-read yesterday's article to keep despondency at bay. 'I need a break,' she said quietly, 'I deserve the chance.'

Fabian Ducasse wanted a break too, but the peloton were still bruised from the previous Stage, their bodies bewildered by the sudden heat, so they rode together in an unspoken ceasefire. Fabian's team-mate Carlos Jesu Velasquez, the dethroned King of the Mountains, had conquered the first three narrow twisting mountain passes to bring him within spitting distance of the polka dot jersey Massimo Lipari had taken from him yesterday. No one went for broke on the penultimate climb, the Grand Cucheron, so there were no great time gaps as the riders raced in the still, dry, high heat along 40 kilometres of flat roads towards the Col de la Madeleine.

There, Fen was tanning nicely and Pip's nose was starting to burn a little until she caught a souvenir baseball cap flung from the publicity caravan. The vibe of the approaching race could be felt from way off and the McCabe sisters were soon standing in anticipation with the excited hordes, ten people to every metre along the climb of the Madeleine. A whisper surged through the crowds that Fabian had launched a surprise attack in the lower reaches. Those further up could not witness it but ears were glued to radios and, in the *salle de presse*, eyes were stuck to the TV screens. What Cat saw she deemed to be nothing short of genius and she intended to tell her *Guardian* readers just that.

> *Fabian Ducasse read astutely not only the requirements of the 19.5 km climb of the Madeleine, but also the state of his rivals' minds and bodies. As the 7.6 per cent ascent commenced, he appeared tired – continually dropping off the back of his small lead group and then labouring hard to claw his way back. Ultimately, he was calling their bluff. Suddenly he steamed from the back and headed off at speed, plucking Velasquez with him. Sitting deep and resolute in the saddle, his shoulders steady, his gear arrogantly huge, his body appeared to snub the gradient of the climb. His Spanish team-mate and* grimpeur *extraordinaire, stood on his pedals and danced alongside the Système Vipère leader. Zucca MV's Jawlensky launched a counter-attack immediately, assisted by the heroic Gianni Fugallo – arguably the* super domestique *of the Tour. However, having offered Vasily his slipstream in the Pyrenees and the Alps, having worked tirelessly to bring Stefano Sassetta to the sprint finishes of the first week, today Fugallo only managed to haul his team leader two thirds of the way up the Madeleine before dropping back. It was enough, however, to keep the Russian strategically close to his Système Vipère adversaries and Fugallo's efforts were instrumental in ensuring that the* maillot jaune *stays with Zucca MV tonight.*

While Fen and Pip were too high up to see the *super domestique* at work, they would later see what Cat could not: how ravaged a state Fugallo was in. The pictures beamed in to the *salle de presse* focused on the race lead, not the *domestique* struggling with the mountain in a body struggling to cope. Fen and Pip yelled and leapt as Fabian and Carlos, and soon enough Vasily, passed by.

'I can't believe I've been so self-centred with my Evian,' Pip said in horror, watching the fans pour water over the riders as they passed. 'You can have one last sip, Fen,' she said.

'Look at all these people,' Fen marvelled, taking two sips less than she actually required, 'they're like an ever-converging corridor, stepping aside but a wheel away from the approaching riders.'

'If you were a dog,' Pip reasoned, scanning downhill for the cyclists, 'you'd have to wag your tail up and down, it's so narrow. Here they come!'

'Two and a half minutes off the lead,' said Fen, checking her watch and focusing on four specks of lycra approaching. 'Look! Someone's bolted off.'

'Lipari! Lipari!' sang neighbouring Italians who'd been most generous with their Amaretti biscuits and their Amaretto, and they burst into the Zucca MV climber's Giro pop tune.

'Will he catch them?' Fen wondered. 'Fabian and Carlos and Vasily?'

'He's Massimo,' one Italian said to her, raising his hands as if her question bordered on blasphemy, 'of course he catch them – he eat them!'

'Indians,' says Hunter to Luca in a group of twelve, 24 minutes behind the leaders.

'What?' says Luca, who feels surprisingly strong but is riding carefully.

'Indians,' Hunter repeats, nodding ahead. Luca follows his gaze and his heart drops.

'Oh fuck,' he gasps, 'no way, man, no fuckin' way.'

He'd thought the summit couldn't possibly be much further off. But, as he looks ahead, he spies lines of fans in the distance, snaking up and around the mountain, a zig-zag of spectators demarcating horribly clearly the severity and length of the route to the summit.

'You can do it,' Hunter says, 'we can both make it.'

'*We* can,' says Luca, 'but I'm not sure about poor Fugallo. Shit, did you see the state he was in?'

Still none of the McCabes knew how Gianni Fugallo was suffering. When Luca's bunch neared Pip and Fen, Pip glanced at her sister, beamed a smile of inordinate proportions, grabbed the bottle of Evian and ran along the tarmac splashing the water over as many riders as she could. Cat saw her sister on the press TV, thought *that's my girl* and wondered if any of the riders were as drenched as Pip appeared to be. But, with the three leaders beginning the descent, the cameras focused on the head of the race and Cat did not see Gianni Fugallo limp his way up the Madeleine, almost thirty minutes behind.

Fen and Pip, of course, did. It was the most repulsive yet poignant, heart-rending yet stomach-churning sight.

'What's that?' Fen gasped in horror though she knew the answer, eyes hopelessly transfixed by the cyclist's legs.

'It's shit,' Pip whispered, staring in horror at what appeared to be trickles of slurry coursing their way down.

'It's fucking dysentery,' Fen exclaimed, with revulsion but more with sublime respect that someone suffering so much, so publicly, was doggedly climbing a mountain by bike and obviously had every intention of finishing the Stage.

It *was* fucking dysentery. When Fugallo made it to the finish, 1 hour 20 minutes behind the leaders but defiantly just ahead of the gruppetto, Rachel had been radioed by the team car on the route. She ushered the exhausted rider into the team bus, all blinds drawn, and peeled away his stenching shorts. Tenderly, she washed the rider down by hand, going through three flannels and bottles of water. Then she helped him into a tracksuit and escorted him to a team car where the other *soigneur* whisked him away.

The only time anyone heard Gianni Fugallo protest, let alone complain, not only on this specific Tour de France but in his professional cycling career as a whole, was later that night when the Zucca MV *directeur sportif* instructed Gianni Fugallo, on doctor's orders, to retire from the race.

*

The demands of team laundry saw Rachel cancelling her drink with André, the Système Vipère mechanic. It was not just Gianni's shit-sodden shorts she had to contend with. When Massimo handed in his washing, she could detect a smell familiar yet undefinable. As she sorted through the clothing, she recoiled and all but retched when she came across his shorts. They were covered in a thick, greyish brown, viscid mess. She ran to his room, seriously concerned for his health.

'Massimo, Jesus!' she said, bewildered that he should look so well and indeed relaxed; a vision in Prada with sunglasses atop his head and goatee immaculately trimmed.

'What is it, Rachel?' the King of the Mountains, but only just, asked her.

'Are you ill?' Rachel asked. 'Your shorts!'

'I am very well, I am King!' Massimo laughed, putting on his sunglasses and approaching her. 'And my shorts – it is banana.'

'Ba*nana*?' Rachel exclaimed.

'It is big ladies' story, yes?' said Massimo.

'Old wives' tale,' Rachel corrected. 'What is?'

'That banana is good for bumps,' Massimo said ingenuously.

'There is no medical proof that bananas have any function in the treatment of piles, Massimo,' she said, her relief manifesting itself in fury, 'not by ingestion and certainly not by slipping a peeled, ripe one between your arse.'

'So tomorrow maybe I try raw liver?' Massimo asked ingenuously. 'Steak, perhaps?'

'No, you fucking won't,' said Rachel, leaving only to return moments later with conventional ointment for haemorrhoids.

Cat decided she had to write a profile on Gianni Fugallo. Whether *Maillot* or *Procycling* or *Cycle Sport* would want it was beside the point, she felt compelled to do it as her tribute to the rider himself. If it meant she was unable to accompany her sisters and Ben to Grenoble, then so be it.

I'm working, remember. This is not a holiday but my livelihood. My presence here is as an accredited journaliste. *If my work is to gain credit, it must be done. I have to think laterally. I have to think ahead. I am a woman in a man's world and must work twice as hard for half the recognition.*

She nipped outside the *salle de presse* to hug her sisters farewell and treat herself to a snatched moment's intimacy with Ben.

'I'm sorry,' she said whilst embracing Pip. 'Are you pissed, Pip?'

'Amaretto,' Pip hiccupped apologetically.

'At least you'll sleep well,' said Cat.

'Gianni pooped his pants,' said Pip, on the verge of tears.

'Rumour has it he'll abandon,' said Fen.

'Rumour confirmed,' said Cat.

'Poor Gianni,' said the McCabe sisters.

'He'll be fine,' the doctor soothed.

'Couldn't you stay?' Cat said, suddenly sad.

'Some of us have conventional jobs in the real world,' Fen said, drawing her sister close and whispering, '*Take care, Cat, take care.*'

'I will,' Cat said firmly, 'I'm fine.' She glanced at Ben and smiled at Fen. 'I'm more than fine.'

Yet Fen regarded her with an expression that would haunt Cat during the evening.

Was it concern? Fear? Doubt? Does she not believe that I'm fine? Does she think I'm not?

Fen was ultimately pleased that Cat chose to stay and work conscientiously and she was relieved that Pip was drowsy from drink and fell asleep in the back of the Megapac car. She had Ben to herself for 70 kilometres, which was what she'd wanted and yet suddenly she could think of nothing to say.

'Back to the real world,' said Ben, providing Fen with a perfect opening.

'Exactly,' Fen said. She looked out of the window and felt enormously tired; she thought of the cyclists and another mountain Stage to come.

'Ben,' she said, glancing at herself in the wing mirror.

'Fen,' he said, detecting the portent in her voice and glancing in the rear-view mirror to assess how deeply asleep Pip was.

'You said it,' said Fen.

'Said what?' said Ben.

'About the real world,' Fen said, 'being far from the Tour de France, Planet Tour – the bubble.'

'For you,' said Ben, 'but for me, it is my world and,' he said, taking his eyes from the road to regard her because he'd just grasped her point, 'it welcomes your sister in to its fold.'

'If she can get a job,' Fen countered.

'She's bloody talented,' Ben retaliated.

'She's not having much luck,' Fen remarked. She could feel Ben observing her but she cast her gaze away. 'I find nothing in you to dislike or disapprove,' she said tartly, 'but I don't want my sister to be hurt.'

They drove on in silence.

'I wouldn't want to hurt your sister,' said Ben.

They drove on in silence.

'Someone did,' said Fen.

'I gather,' said Ben.

Fen shook her head at the pain of remembering the intensity of her sister's pain. 'I'll never let that happen to her again.'

'Nor, I would have thought, would she,' said Ben.

'But next week she'll be in England,' said Fen, wishing that they weren't approaching Grenoble, wishing she could stay and keep Cat close, 'and all this will be some distant Gallic dream.'

'And I'll be in Colorado,' said Ben, amazed that Grenoble had crept up on them so quickly.

'Exactly,' said Fen.

'Exactly, indeed,' said Ben.

'I wish you weren't nice,' Fen rued, 'I wish you and my sister had never met.'

'Charming,' said Ben with equanimity.

'Ben,' Fen sighed, 'I am warning you – I really am.'

'Fen,' said Ben gravely, regarding her, 'thank you. You don't have to.'

'I won't have her hurt,' Fen whispered, not wanting to look at Ben, taking her wrist away from his proffered hand, 'but that's inescapable.'

Ben was driving very slowly.

And me. I will too. Hurt. Miss her. Like I've never experienced.

Tell Fen. Just say it out loud.

No. Not until I've told Cat.

Ben is back at his hotel by eleven o'clock. Cat is asleep in his bed. He slips between the sheets quietly and spends a few minutes observing her; moonlight sifting into the room through ill-fitting curtains and whispering silver highlights over her body. Gently, he hovers his hand over her bare shoulder and then lets it rest lightly on her skin. She makes a small noise in her throat and it makes him smile. He strokes her arm with his fingertips and brings his body close to hers. He breathes deeply into the top of her head.

I know that smell. It's not shampoo. It's Cat McCabe. She says she knows my hands. Well, I know her scent off by heart.

STAGE 16

Gilbertville–Aix-les-Bains. 149 kilometres

*T*he Tour de France lasts for six more days. In that time, loose ends need to be tied and those currently knotted need to be unravelled. The race is now about loss and gain. Both on the bike. And off. The riders of the peloton have each now lost an average four pounds in muscle which their bodies have resorted to pillaging for energy. Luca lost his nerve but found it again. Fabian has lost his yellow jersey but has designs on gaining it back. Vasily wears the yellow jersey and has no intention of losing it. Jesper Lomers wonders whether his marriage is lost. He leads Stefano Sassetta by just a few points. However, though Jesper defended his jersey ruthlessly in the mountains, Stefano rode strategically. Consequently, the Rotterdam Rocket Viper Boy is tastily clad in green lycra, but Dark Duke Thunder Thighs has ridden without the pressure of defending a jersey and has thus conserved crucial energy. Vasily Jawlensky leads the race with a 2 minute 33 second lead over Fabian Ducasse. Of the 161 riders remaining, the Lantern Rouge of the Tour de France is the twenty-year-old Portuguese rider, José Ribero. He is 3 hours 5 minutes and 18 seconds behind the *maillot jaune*.

When Jules Le Grand dressed this morning, he dressed for business. He chose a lightweight navy suit, a silk shirt in sky blue and fine leather loafers which he wore sockless. Though he would be driving the team car along the route and his clothing would become creased and crumpled, he has enough suits in pristine condition to last until Paris. During the first two weeks of the Tour, Jules's presence in the *village* each morning had a public relations function for Système Vipère; he had made himself readily available and consistently charming to journalists, officials and VIPs alike. This final week, Jules will go to the *village* as *directeur sportif* to the world's number-one professional road racing team. He has no interest in journalists, officials and VIPs; in fact, he is all but blind to their presence, even contemptuous of their overtures. His sole mission, the *raison d'être* for his presence, is to seduce riders, to lure them into his fold. Other *directeur sportifs* will see him at work, stalking, talking, schmoozing, perusing. Short of keeping their entire teams tethered, they will be unable to prevent Le Grand's inveiglement. They might avert their riders defecting providing they outdo Jules in the wage packets and flattery stakes. Jules is well aware that other *directeurs* will approach his Viper Boys, but he is confident that his team will remain loyal; apart from one *domestique* whose contract he has not renewed, and Jesper Lomers whose contract still needs signing.

Luca Jones visited the barber's stall in the *village* for a haircut. Pleased with the result and buoyed by the glances from many a *bella signorina* (and *signora* too), he went to the Maison du Café stand for a cup of sweet coffee.

'Allow me,' said Jules Le Grand, suddenly at Luca's side, fanning three sachets of sugar, adding the contents to the rider's plastic cup without relinquishing eye contact or saying anything else. 'I know what you like,' Jules continued once he was stirring the cup which Luca held, 'coffee with three sugars – right?'

'Yes,' said Luca, off his guard and self-kickingly dumb-struck.

'Come,' said Jules, walking well ahead, knowing, without turning, that the young rider would follow. They walked past the giant omelette stand, past the Coeur de Lion cheese extravaganza, to a small, open marquee to one side where there was a table with two chairs free towards the back, the others having been taken by local dignitaries and VIPs. Jules held back a chair for Luca and sat down himself once the rider was seated.

'Yesterday,' Jules started, 'I witnessed something extraordinary. Something which once again filled my heart with passion for this great sport of cycling.'

Luca nodded earnestly. 'Fabian,' the rider interjected, 'is an awesome rider. To suffer so much, to lose the *maillot jaune* and then to come back the very next day and win the Stage – incredible.'

'I am not talking of Fabian Ducasse,' Jules said surprisingly derisively, 'I am talking of a young rider on his first Tour de France who suffered to the depths of his being on the heights of L'Alpe D'Huez.'

'Oh,' said Luca, thinking he should sip his coffee and make use of the caffeine, but wondering when he might need to speak again.

'I am referring,' Jules continued, 'to a rider who shows more than promise. Indeed, this rider has the promise of sheer brilliance. He recovered supremely yesterday – his morale was high and his legs were strong. He rode sensibly and scaled the General Classification by eight positions.' Luca nodded and thought he really ought to drink the coffee if he was to manage to pee and then absorb two more doses of caffeine.

'Please,' said Jules, 'drink – I know what you need, what you like. Coffee with three sugars.'

Luca drank; a little faster than he'd like, but with Jules now silent and staring intently at him, relaxing over coffee was not a possibility.

'This rider of whom I speak,' said Jules rather theatrically, looking to the middle distance as if seeing a vision of his subject there, 'has enormous talent. But it must be nurtured, it must be nourished, loved. It must be developed and honed. True potential must never be wasted.' He paused till he knew he had Luca's gaze. 'Sometimes true talent can remain untapped.' He paused again. 'Travesty!' he spat. Luca nodded earnestly, now needing to pee rather urgently. 'This rider I speak of,' said Jules, 'is you, Luca Jones. You are a good *rouleur* but you could well be fantastic. You have the makings of a true champion. Système Vipère would be honoured to have you as a team member.'

Luca Jones almost pissed his shorts and his coffee very nearly fountained out of his mouth. But he crossed his legs and swallowed hard so he could murmur, 'Fucking hell!' instead. Jules was standing. 'Think about it, Luca,' he said. 'I would of course say "name your price" but once I tell you of what I have in mind – the salary, the apartment, the bikes, the Système Vipère super micro hi-fi – I don't think you will need to negotiate.' He laid his hand on Luca's shoulder, bent to his ear and spoke a figure that was roughly double Luca's Megapac wage. And then Jules was gone. And Luca sat immobile, murmuring, 'Fucking hell!' desperate to phone Mama, to find Ben, to piss, to absorb caffeine, to run around the *village* yelling. 'I have the makings of a true champion! I have enormous talent as long as it's nourished and nurtured!' Of course he did none of these. He sat alone, utterly speechless apart from 'Fucking hell!' whispered to himself at regular intervals.

There's a Viper Boy, Luca remarked to himself as he was leaving the *village*. *I could be riding with Jesper Fucking Lomers.*

'*Ciao*, Jesper!' he greeted, making a detour, presuming, for some reason, that the whole team must have colluded on the potential acquisition of Luca Jones.

'Luca,' Jesper acknowledged, a little baffled at the magnitude of the young rider's smile but pleased to respond to this likeable newcomer to the peloton. Briefly, Jesper watched Luca go on his way, before making his own way to Maison du Café. He took his coffee and went to sit with a posse of Dutch riders from various teams who liked to gather at one of the marquees each morning to sit in affable silence or chat quietly and usually, for some reason, in English. Today, Jesper chose silence but his was more reflective than sociable and the others sensed this and steered tactfully away from intrusion. Jesper looked around the *village*.

This is my world. It is all I have ever dreamed of, wanted, worked to have.

Metres away, he watched as a young woman was approached and embraced by a man.

Or is my world with my wife? Where is that world? Who am I within it? Where is Anya?

Suddenly, Jesper longed for a woman, for feminine tenderness and attention.

Just what is it that defines me? What is it that makes me feel whole? My bike? My woman?

He reflected on the irony that, as second in command in Système Vipère, he had privileges not afforded to the lesser riders. His own room. The company of his woman if he really required it.

And yet the domestiques *sneak in pussy to their shared rooms and my wife has not made one appearance.*

En route to the *village* for a quick cup of coffee, Ben was concerned to spy Didier LeDucq engrossed in furtive conversation behind a generator. Didier was in bad company. Jan van Loth wa a Flemish rider with a flagrant lack of respect for clean riding and a notorious ability to keep a step ahead of the dope controls.

Van Loth saw Ben before Didier and stealthed away in an instant. When Didier saw his doctor, he smiled and raised his hand in an atypical display of affection and hastily employed innocence. As Didier approached, Ben racked his conscience for how best to handle the situation. His job was to oversee the riders' health and well being, his duty was to maintain their confidence and trust.

It is an exceptionally delicate balance and I'm holding fragile scales in hands which are unsteady.

But the only way for the triumph of evil is for good men to do nothing.

'*Bonjour*, Ben,' said Didier, all smiles, standing tall, the picture of innocence and a curse upon anyone who would dare think anything else of him.

'Hullo, Didier,' said Ben breezily instead, 'lovely morning for it.'

Ask him what the fuck he thinks he's doing. What is he thinking of taking. And when.

'A lovely morning,' said Didier, still smiling easily, 'indeed. I saw Luca being talked to by Jules Le Grand.' He raised an eyebrow, a gesture which Ben returned.

And I saw you talking to Jan van Loth.

'Didier,' Ben said, 'there are just five days of racing left now.'

The rider shrugged and nodded and retied his pony-tail.

'My elbow's sore,' he told his doctor.

'I can fix most things, Didier,' Ben said, manipulating the rider's elbow, 'it is my job. Your health is in my hands.'

'*Merci*,' said Didier.

He watched the rider lope away and kicked himself for feeling so impotent. And then he caught sight of Rachel and knew at once how he could help Didier. She was leaning against a tree and, visible from some distance, was the sparkle she was bestowing on a man. Ben was amazed. Zucca MV and Système Vipère were all but entwined. It was so public. So scandalous. Key figures in the support staff of two rival teams flirting in full view. Should he leave them to it? She was his friend after all. He stopped and looked around him. No sign of Cat. Nor of Luca – what was it that Didier had said? Where is Didier? It was scandal overload on the morning of Stage 16 of the Tour de France and Ben felt enormously tired.

Oh, for the life of a regular doctor. With a surgery in a suburb. And a receptionist. And a legion of elderly people with gout and hypochondria. Perhaps a Well Woman clinic every Tuesday. Prostate awareness once a fortnight. Flu jabs. And a desk. With a photo of my wife and two kids. And my spaniel. I could have a Saab parked outside in a reserved space.

'Hey, Ben,' said Rachel, bringing him back to the balmy present of picturesque Gilbertville, to the sounds, the scents, the sense of excitement of the Tour de France. Ben closed his eyes and took a deep breath, acknowledging how, though fleeting, his daydream was not just deluded but utterly suffocating and essentially undesirable. There was only one place he wanted to be, and only one way he could possibly practise medicine.

'Have you met André Ferrette?' Rachel continued, eager that Ben should. The men shook hands.

'I need your help,' Ben said, prophesying that Rachel might well need his when the respective *directeurs* discovered that their staff were mingling.

'Sure,' said Rachel, sensing instantly that he required her capacity as friend.

'I'll see you later,' André said, taking her hand. Rachel beamed and Ben noticed how she now radiated femininity and allure, having kept such qualities invisible until she saw fit to unleash them on the man of her choice. So very Rachel. Strong. Sussed. Independent. Nobody's fool. Her own boss.

'What's up, Yorkie?' she said, reverting to the demeanour and look of Ben's friend, the Zucca MV *soigneur*.

'It's Didier,' said Ben gravely, 'and Jan van Loth.'

'You need Vasily,' Rachel said astutely, 'he rates Didier. I'll see what I can do.'

Ben felt easier but was still apprehensive. Though Rachel understood the urgency and gravity, he longed for Cat. His job was highly stressful. He wanted to talk through, to unwind, to offload, to be soothed. But it was 11 a.m. and, dependent on developments in the Stage, Cat would not be off duty until the evening.

'What's the time?' Cat asks Josh.

'Almost nine,' he replies. 'Are you through?'

'Yup.'

What happened in the Tour today, Cat?

It was utterly bizarre. Vasily lost a whole bloody minute. He didn't so much lose it but threw it away. No one knows why – there was no press conference. It must be strategy – but certainly not as we know it. Fabian and Carlos streamed off at the foot of the middle climb and Vasily just sat in a chasing group not actively pursuing at all.

So he is only 1 minute 33 ahead of Fabian?

Yes. And Carlos Jesu Velasquez took the polka dot jersey today with a truly ruthless ride. Poor darling Massimo suffered a double puncture on the first Col and fell off pretty badly on the descent. Though it violated race etiquette, Carlos took full advantage and zipped away. Massimo really floundered after that – he was incapable of mind over matter and there were no domestiques to raise morale and physically lead him back. Zucca were catastrophically lax today.

So his dream of a King of the Mountains hat trick has vanished?

I know. And I can't get hold of Rachel to find out how he is. Her phone's switched off. And I know her well enough to know there must be a reason for that. And I'm hoping the reason is that, for once, she's prioritizing herself. If Rachel's phone is not on, it's a blatant Do Not Disturb sign. And I'm happy to respect that. As long as she gives me a full report in glorious Technicolor tomorrow.

'What's the time?' Rachel asks André whilst she folds and refolds the batch of laundry just retrieved from the dryer in the Zucca MV team truck.

'Nearly nine,' he replies, checking his watch fastidiously. 'Your team had a very bad day.'

'My job is not to judge, not even to comment,' Rachel responds, 'but you're right. Your boys must be pleased – Fabian taking a minute from Vasily and Carlos taking the polka dot jersey from our Massimo. Poor Mass, he'll probably shave his goatee off. Or dye it.' She leans out of the truck and pulls the door shut, locking it from the inside. 'I really should be tucked up in bed,' she muses, taking an empty bidon to her lips and sucking thoughtfully.

'Early massage for the boys, early night for Rachel?' André laughs, hoping she won't take him literally.

'That's what I told them,' Rachel says a little guiltily, wondering whether a white lie warrants comeuppance. André glances around the truck. It's pretty much identical to the Viper's. He turns the taps on and off at the sink and Rachel fiddles with a scrunched-up piece of cling film.

Just bloody kiss me, you bastard!

André, however, is expressing polite but excessive interest in the quality of the melamine fittings.

'Your English is very good,' Rachel says as huskily as she can. André responds to the flattery not with a lunge for her breasts, as she rather hopes, but with a chronological account of his schooling.

Oh fuck it, Rachel thinks to herself, *I'll bloody kiss you then*.

André is saying something about something or other when Rachel flicks off the light in the truck and, knowing the layout of her second home off by heart, finds the mechanic, holds his face and presents her lips to his.

There's something about the situation, the furtiveness of it all; the scent of the almonds from the frangipane, the hum of the washing machine, the smell of chain grease, the confinements of the truck interior, the build up of a few days of glances, of emboldened flirting, that touchdown between these two pairs of lips inflames. Suddenly, clothing is being torn away, André's textbook English is replaced by throaty Gallic exclamations and Rachel's tough talking transmutes into soft gasps and moans.

Massimo Lipari couldn't sleep – what was the point when his dreams had already been dashed? Whenever he closed his eyes, the nightmare of reality accosted him. His body was sore, he had bad road rash down his entire left side. His head hurt, scorched by the incessant what ifs, if onlys, why didn'ts and I should haves tormenting him. He had a room to himself and though he had craved the solitude in which he could weep unchecked, now he did not trust or particularly like his own company. He was more appalled that he had bonked than he was outraged that Carlos attacked when he was down.

Humming his Giro pop song brought no solace, a funeral dirge seemed more appropriate, but he opted for the sad song of love and loss his grandmother had crooned to him under the olive trees when he was a child. He had so wanted to be King of the Mountains; the title suited him as much as the jersey. He made a solemn procession to the bathroom, took a razor and shaved off his goatee beard. He almost wept. And then he saw how the skin around his chin was ever so slightly, but certainly recognizably paler. He yelled in frustration. He needed fresh air. He eased up a window and gulped deeply. He gazed at the team truck, envisaging the bike that failed him hanging from its hook. Let it hang!

Fifteen minutes later, Rachel answered her door in her towel, so insistent was the rapping and banging and hollering outside her room.

'What you think you do?' Massimo spat, pushing past her, his eyes searching every nook of the room.

'I'm about to have a bath!' Rachel remonstrated, noting that she ought to change the dressing on his knee first.

'You bad bitch,' Massimo growled, 'what you do? You poison me?'

'Mass!' Rachel exclaimed, flummoxed and truly taken aback.

'Or you are stupid and maybe he put something in my

drink, no?' he shouted. 'He make me bonk.'

'Who?' Rachel pleaded, thinking she ought to work also on Massimo's shoulder to prevent it stiffening.

'Maybe he turn you away from me,' Massimo declared, 'make you not look after me so well?'

'Who?' Rachel implored, prophesying that Massimo would either hit her or burst into tears.

Massimo did the latter. Rachel secured her towel and sat on her bed beside him, laying an arm across the rider's quivering shoulders.

'Poor Mass,' she said, 'what a terrible day for you.'

'Bad bitch,' he sobbed.

'What have I done?' Rachel asked, trying not to be offended.

'I see you in the truck – with the Viper mechanic. You are stupid! He is dangerous!'

Rachel, who was utterly at ease with her level of intelligence and with the authenticity of André's virtues, was nonetheless agitated by Massimo bombarding into her personal life.

'I go tell our *directeur*!' Massimo cautioned. 'Then I go tell *L'Equipe*.'

Though Rachel would have quite liked a profile in France's famous sports paper, she knew that it would not be her sex life which warranted any such exposure. She accepted that Massimo's concerns were legitimate, for the good of the team, but still Rachel was exasperated.

'I'm entitled to some privacy, Massimo,' she said.

'Why you do it?' Massimo demanded. 'You spy? Who you poison next? Vasily? He ride like shit today.'

'For Christ's sake,' Rachel said emphatically, 'I was just having a shag.'

Massimo regarded her blankly. 'You?' he gasped, utterly staggered, as if considering for the first time that Rachel McEwen had a libido, let alone an active sex life. 'You? *Rachel*?'

'Me, Rachel,' she said with steel in her voice.

'You had a fuck in the truck?' Massimo exclaimed, wide-eyed and gobsmacked.

'Not that it's any of your business,' Rachel replied. It irritated her to see that Massimo's primary concern and immediate relief was more that she was not a spy or drink spiker, than he was pleased for her to have found someone she liked.

'Good,' he said, 'I apologize. You great *soigneur* and lovely lady. Why you not choose a guy from some other team?'

'For fuck's sake,' said Rachel, now thinking it all so tedious, 'as if I chose the team before the man. Give me a break.'

'You are very hard biscuit,' Massimo said earnestly.

'A tough cookie,' Rachel deduced.

Massimo rubbed his newly shaved chin. 'I fail, Rachel, I am no good,' he rued, his voice cracking.

Rachel was relieved to have the focus taken away from herself. 'You didn't fail,' she told the rider.

'I lose my jersey. I lose my dream,' he sobbed. 'I lose my beard. Now I live a nightmare.' Rachel put a supportive arm around his shoulder because there was no way she could massage his ego just then.

'Oh,' he wept, 'I cannot return home. I must exile myself. How could I do this! To the team? To the sport? To my family? To the people of Italy!'

Rachel let the rider sob and rant, accepting it to be a fundamental requirement of her job. She listened attentively and said soothing things that he was incapable of hearing and which would have had little effect anyway. She would have liked to let her mind wander back to André, to how he made her body feel, to relish the excitement and anticipation she felt. But all that panoply would have to wait. She had a job to do. She changed Massimo's dressings, did a little work on his shoulder, and made him hot milky malty cocoa to take to bed.

STAGE 17
Aix-les-Bains–Neuchâtel. 218.5 kilometres

*W*hat on earth are you doing, Ben? It's just gone two in the morning and you're creeping along the hotel corridor, listening hard at the doors of your riders. You're opening the door to Luca and Didier's room – why are you doing that? See, they're both sleeping soundly. You can hear them breathing. So go. But you're hovering and listening attentively – why?

I had to check something.

What?

That if Didier wasn't dangling himself from a door frame, he was sleeping soundly.

You're talking about EPO, aren't you?

Yup, erythropoietin.

The recent drug of choice for cyclists?

Er, the tennis and athletics associations might do well to ferret around their sports too.

Doesn't EPO simulate the advantages of altitude training on the body?

It's a hormone produced naturally by the kidneys. Administered, it boosts the red blood cell count and increases the amount of oxygen that can be carried in the blood; as the bloodstream can transport more oxygen around the system, endurance is enhanced and aerobic capacity is increased.

It sounds wonderful.

Undoubtedly – when used by the medical profession to treat people with kidney failure, anaemia and alleviate the side-effects of some AIDS treatments.

How fantastic.

It can also turn the blood to jam. A few years ago, there was a spate of riders dying mysteriously in their sleep. Cyclists' superfit hearts can pump at around 190 bpm and then rest as low as 30 bpm. That's when EPO can become lethal. The slower the heartbeat, the thicker the blood, the quicker it begins to clot and the heart begins to stall. That's why I wanted to check if Didier was hanging off a door, stretching out to thin his blood. That's why I needed to listen to his breathing pattern in his sleep.

And he was OK, so why not go back to bed?

True, Didier is sleeping soundly but maybe he's taken a good dose of aspirin. The danger of taking anticoagulants to thin the blood is the risk of haemorrhaging should Didier crash.

Do you think Didier is on something?

I don't know. I really don't. The thing with EPO is that it must be taken up to a week in advance and then every couple of days. He wasn't well, if you remember, towards the end of the first week of the Tour.

But where would he get it?

Shady characters and clandestine deals aren't restricted to grim alleyways and crack cocaine.

We're talking about a banned substance, not a class A illegal drug. Doesn't pro cycling have one of the longest lists of banned substances in professional sport?

Yes. However, riders can spout the disclaimer 'I've never tested positive' – that's different from saying they've never used dope.

But isn't this the sport with the most dope controls and the lowest number of positive tests?

Some riders will always seek ways to stay a step ahead of detection. Ever heard of Michel Pollentier? In the 1978 Tour, after he had taken the yellow jersey on L'Alpe D'Huez, he failed the dope test by attempting to pass off someone else's urine concealed in a rubber tube hidden in his shorts.

That's actually quite funny.

Yeah, right – did you hear the one about the cyclist who went to dope control and was told, 'You've tested negative and congratulations, you're also pregnant'?

Oh, very droll.

EPO, however, is for the most part undetectable – it is virtually impossible to tell the difference between a rider who has a naturally high haematocrit level because he trains at altitude and a rider whose levels are high because he's pumped with EPO.

Can't a limit be set?

The UCI, cycling's governing body, have set one. But somewhat arbitrarily. If a rider's red blood cell count is over 50 per cent, he is forced to take two weeks rest until his level is lower.

That's a start.

Hardly. Say Didier's natural haematocrit level is 42, and say Luca's is naturally 48 – Didier can legally dope himself to Luca's level, to within a hair's breadth of the limit, suffer no penalties and reap the benefits of an artificially stimulated performance from a prohibited substance.

That's cheating.

Correct.

So when does doping begin exactly?

Precisely.

And where does medical care end?

Exactly. Just before the infamous 1998 Tour – where brilliant riding was utterly overshadowed by the drugs scandal cum witch-hunt despite not one rider testing positive – well, another team approached me. The directeur made it very clear that I was to maximize the riders' performances under stringent medical control.

What did that mean between the lines?

It meant that doping was part of team policy expressly to prevent the riders obtaining drugs for themselves and threatening their health in doing so.

You didn't take the job, then.

God, no. I'm a conventional gentleman doctor and I'm also a romantic when it comes to sport – I like to admire supreme muscle tone without suspicion as to its provenance, to marvel at consummate athletic triumph without wondering if it's synthetically enhanced.

Haven't drugs always been synonymous with cycling?

In the 1930s, it was tiny doses of strychnine, soon enough and for a long time, amphetamines. Now EPO, human growth hormone. There's PFC – a chemical relative of fucking Teflon. Oh, and the charming Belgian Pot.

Belgian Pot – surely a laid-back stoned cyclist is a contradiction in terms?

I'm not talking marijuana but a delightful combination of up to ten drugs – amphetamines, cocaine, heroin, analgesics, nasal or bronchial dilators, corticoids, morphine. Very pleasant.

Tell me that Belgian Pot isn't rife?

It isn't. But it's there. Think of the pressures on a rider – not just the physical duress of three weeks, two mountain ranges and 4,000 k sandwiched between the equally taxing Giro D'Italia and the Vuelta Español. Consider the pressures of riding for a team sponsor on a short contract. Ride better, ride faster, reap glory. The pursuit of success can be just as addictive as substances.

But their health – are the riders stupid?

Not stupid. But consider, on the one hand, how many come from small, rural, simple backgrounds. They join a team. They ride for all they're worth, their bodies are ravaged, their spirits are exhausted. The directeur, the doctor, the soigneur say, 'Take this, it's recuperative, it will help, it will do you good.' Why wouldn't they? These are the rider's mentors, their father figures. They trust them and they depend on them.

And on the other hand?

Some riders proclaim themselves victims duped into dope but these are the same shrewd guys who ruthlessly negotiate huge contracts.

And you, Ben?

'Trust me, I'm a doctor' can be the most dangerous words in pro cycling and that frustrates and depresses me. Personally, I believe my duty as a doctor is ethical as much as medical. My obligation to my vocation, my employer and my riders is to ensure that my charges suffer as little and recover as quickly as possible. I study each man intensively and I administer a range of substances – nutritional, hormonal, anabolic – to maintain optimal balance. My scientific background enables me to do this – what the fuck and why the fuck would a rider know anything about how much beta-hydroxy beta-methyl butyrate and how often?

And Didier?

I can't sleep, that's why I'm in the corridor. Feeling impotent. Feeling pretty enraged. I can't have drugs on my team. I will not tolerate such a flagrant abuse of the team ethos, of all the work I do to maintain my riders' health. I fear Didier's stupidity and selfishness – if he dares, if he even dares, he could put all our jobs, our credibility, the very future of the team, on the line – to say nothing of his health.

And Vasily?

Vasily has a checkered past. He is now a crusader. I'm hoping his experience and the respect he now has universally, will enlighten Didier.

> Why comes temptation but for man to meet
> And master and make crouch beneath his foot
> And so be pedestalled in triumph?

But I don't know how Robert Browning translates into Russian or French.

Through breathtaking scenery, incredible overhangs of rock, tunnels burrowing through the mountains, stunning bridges old and new, the peloton of the Tour de France headed for its brief sojourn in Switzerland. Luca and Didier had woken in contemplative self-engrossed moods, having gone to sleep much the same the night before. Neither were aware that their doctor had eavesdropped on their slumber. Now they were cycling quietly side by side in a throng of yakking Spanish riders; through the beautiful town of Seyssel, elegantly atop a picturesque river, through the lovely flower-festooned old village of Billiat where Sassetta took the hot-spot sprint while aged men waved slowly and widely. The Tour de France — every year, since these septuagenarians were boys; defining their calendar, compounding their patriotism, affirming their past and confirming the futures of their grandsons. There would always be the Tour de France. A birthright. A heritage. An heirloom. Wave and smile and then a leisurely reminisce over Pernod about Louison Bobet, Jacques Anquetil, Thèvenet, Hinault, Fignon. Look forward to next year. *Vive le Tour.*

After 126 kilometres, a sprint, a fourth-, a third- and a second-category climb, Didier and Luca snatched their *musettes* as they flew past the feed station.

'I'm so tired,' Luca said, 'I'm not even hungry.'

'Me too,' Didier agreed. 'Mind you, I've been fantasizing about a day-long MacDonalds binge when the Tour is over.'

'I'm going to have oysters and champagne,' said Luca, brightening up. It was the first thing either had said all day.

'On Jules Le Grand's expense account, no doubt,' Didier tested.

Luca regarded him and shrugged. 'What would you do?'

'What you mean is, what do I think *you* should do,' Didier responded astutely.

'What *should* I do?' Luca asked quietly.

'Are you tempted?'

'Fuck, man! Système Vipère!' Luca exclaimed, as if resting his case.

'Loads of money, cool hi-fi, great bikes, cool team strip, the greatest team in the world,' Didier defined nonchalantly while Luca cycled a few metres ahead. 'So why,' Didier asked, catching up, 'are you asking me what to do? Why aren't you telling me that you're already signed up, that the cap fits, that you're a Viper Boy in the making? Why do you even need to ask?'

Luca sighed but decided instead to wonder why the spectators were waving ski poles. Didier let him sigh again before fixing him with a searching stare.

'It's blown my mind,' Luca said honestly. 'There has to be a catch.'

'Did you see Le Grand this morning at the *village*?' asked Didier, having waited for Jesper Lomers to overtake and be out of earshot.

'Yeah,' Luca replied, 'talking to Magnus Backstedt.'

'I saw him in a corner with Bo Hamburger,' Didier remarked.

Luca pedalled on ahead to reflect and, instinctively, Didier held back. Luca wondered whether those riders had also been told that it would be a travesty not to nurture talent, that they too had the makings of true champions and that Système Vipère would be honoured to have them? Two women bouncing ebulliently in bikini tops provided timely distraction and Luca cycled on, living for the moment, riding the day's Stage, his body knackered, his soul exhausted. Eventually, he sat up and looked back to see Didier, his team-mate, room-mate and friend, riding along-side the yellow jersey. Neither Vasily nor Didier spoke but Luca could sense some deep communication between the two. Like yesterday. Intrigued, he dropped his pace and returned to the bunch at the same time as Vasily, Fabian and a clutch of final-week glory-seekers sped off the front.

'Fuck! You're going to Zucca MV, aren't you?' Luca asked Didier accusatorially. Didier looked confused. 'You and your new best friend Vasily,' Luca probed. 'He's been sent to lure you, hasn't he?' Didier looked resolutely ahead, picking up the pace to pursue the breakaway. Luca matched his speed. 'We can't be on rival teams,' he bemoaned, 'and anyway, I can't believe he's picked you and not me after I rode with him that day I won the Stage.'

Didier glanced at Luca. 'I'm not going to Zucca, I'm staying with Megapac.'

'But Vasily *asked* – right? He's been wooing you,' Luca probed, 'all that shoulder-rubbing yesterday. When I came by, he flicked me – stopped talking and his stare said it all, said for me to fuck off.'

'It was a sensitive subject,' Didier said.

'He was trying to poach *you*,' Luca said sulkily, 'and I really thought he rated *me*.'

'Listen to you!' Didier snapped. 'You've got transfer fever bad – it's affecting your ride. It's affecting me. I'm completely knackered but I'm away. *Adieu.*'

Cat contemplated Didier's ride. For a quiet rider, a bulwark for Megapac, a stalwart of the peloton, LeDucq was suddenly making a huge splash, pelting after the breakaway, dropping anyone attempting to take his wheel.

'Blimey,' Josh marvelled out loud, 'what's he on?'

'Nothing, I hope,' said Cat.

Vasily is pleased to see Didier coming up to his group but instead of slowing the pace to welcome him, he accelerates forward causing Fabian to motor after him and the hangers-on to grip hard to hang on. It doesn't offend Didier. He understands the Russian's motive and Didier is motivated to reach them and ride on. There are 50 kilometres to go, Didier's head is down and he is cycling strongly, attaining great rhythm and maintaining utter focus. Conversation is sparse amongst the group but it is clangorous in Didier's head. Over and again, he hears Vasily's confrontation of yesterday.

'You cannot make a thoroughbred from a donkey,' had been the yellow jersey's opening line. Didier remembers how he had not known how to respond, that he could not fathom what Vasily meant, nor why the Russian had let a break containing his main adversary go so he could hang back and talk equestrianism. 'You are no donkey,' Vasily had continued, 'nor are you a thoroughbred. But you are a fantastic workhorse. I have respected you for many seasons.' Didier had nodded his gratitude, still baffled and even more so when Vasily had played his next card. 'I don't want to lose respect for you – it would pain me.'

Didier LeDucq checks the computers on his bike and his pulse monitor. He's racing well, strong enough to take a turn at the front, well enough to allow his mind to wander back and reflect on what had been said the day before.

'When I used to do amphetamines, my eyes were like piss holes in the snow,' Vasily had launched, 'my skin was terrible – I was covered in spots. I was more aggressive off the bike than on and I could rarely sleep. Unless I had valium.'

'Speed is shit,' Didier had said, hoping it was what Vasily wanted to hear.

'EPO is worse,' Vasily said. 'When I first took it, my kidneys felt like balloons full of water bashing the base of my back. My vision went queer, my joints hurt, I'd get nose bleeds. The migraines – terrible.' Vasily had stared hard at Didier who felt that to nod energetically was the best reply. 'But,' Vasily continued, 'soon enough it was like waking in a new land. I wanted to train hard, I could ride with reduced suffering and I recovered quickly. What a drug!' Again he had confronted Didier with his hypnotic stare.

'Yeah!' Didier had responded; simultaneously utterly crushed that his greatest hero was giving the notorious drug an apparent seal of approval, and yet knowing he wanted this drug badly himself.

'Yeah, what a drug,' Vasily had all but spat at him. 'I beat dope control – what a sportsman.' He fixed a penetrating stare on Didier who believed he ought to nod his head in an impressed way. 'What a clever, lucky guy I am – I beat dope control, won through cheating and the only price I'll pay is probably to die prematurely.' Didier's face dropped and

Vasily continued in a more genial tone. 'The iron level in my blood was so high – and for such an extended period. If I'm lucky I might avoid kidney failure. If I'm truly blessed, I might not suffer liver failure either. If God is on my side, I just might not contract cancer.' Vasily looked at Didier. He had taken a hand from the handlebars to lay it on the Frenchman's wrist. 'But you never know,' he had said in conclusion, 'and will it have been worth it? You decide.'

Gutted and speechless, Didier had ridden on in silence. Vasily had ridden alongside, also silent. At the end of the Stage he cycled alongside Didier towards the team vehicles. 'You know, LeDucq,' he said, 'I often wonder about the guy who won the Giro three years ago – and all his other victories that season.'

'But it was you,' Didier responded, 'three years ago – it was you who took the Giro, the Tour and all those other triumphs.'

'No,' Vasily said stonily, 'it was not me. There was no victory. The triumph was not true. There was no sense of achievement. It was all bullshit. I cheated – I cheated everyone.' Though the Megapac vehicles were close by, Didier automatically stopped, unclipped a foot and rested his bike and stared at Vasily transfixed, imploring him to continue. 'More than being ashamed for cheating my fellow riders and the race commissaires is the disgust I feel for having cheated myself. How pathetic!' Vasily had spat, shaking his head at himself in abhorrence. 'I regret it deeply. What did I achieve? Where's the pleasure? I recall that period with shame and no pride. I will not recount it to my grandchildren.'

Didier was looking hard at the ground. 'LeDucq,' Vasily said, taking his hand to the back of Didier's neck to embrace the rider, 'Didier.' Didier had raised his eyes to meet Vasily's. 'Now I can sleep at night – without valium – knowing that my victories are genuine, my losses fair. I ride *à l'eau*. I am clean. My dignity is intact, as is my responsibility as a professional sportsman. However, my liver,' he said with no hint of self-pity, 'is not so good. The price I will pay will be far more expensive than the winnings I earned when I was charged on crap.'

He had then given Didier a friendly slap between the shoulder blades before riding off slowly towards the Zucca vehicles.

So here is Didier today, riding alongside his hero, mentor and saviour. Didier had asked Ben for glucose and vitamins and anything else the doctor suggested. He had asked his *soigneur* to work on his knees, had asked the mechanic to check the measurements on his bike. Today, he knows he is tired but the strength of his spirit and resolve is manifesting itself in a fantastic ride. Vasily is making everyone ride hard. However, the Russian's pressure is not intended as a gauntlet to Fabian but as a challenge to Didier. Didier has accepted the challenge; he is riding on the rivet, he is suffering, but the pain is steeped in reality and he is glad of the self-knowledge it is establishing.

'What a great Stage,' Cat said to Alex, 'true classic racing.'

'Hurry and finish your piece,' Alex remarked. 'I want to have a shower and then go somewhere for raclette.'

'I want Toblerone,' Cat countered, her fingers skittering over the keyboard.

'I'm happy to settle for the Swiss bank account,' Josh piped up from the row in front.

'I want Heidi,' said Alex.

Cat recalled the concluding action of the day's racing and grinned at the vivid memory of it and preserved it for posterity in the concluding paragraph of her report.

In the final kilometres, with the other four riders lagging behind, Jawlensky surged ahead with Ducasse and LeDucq sticking resolutely to his wheel. The pace was fast, the bike handling consummate and the road dancing breathtaking. The three riders exercised enormous skill and focus to match, counteract and produce strategic manoeuvres. The Stage was won in 4 hours 52 minutes and 26 seconds. Fabian crossed the line just ahead of Didier. The yellow jersey placed third. No change to the overall classification. Sassetta came four points closer to claiming the green jersey. Pick of the peloton today was undoubtedly Didier LeDucq, a normally quiet, unassuming rider who today displayed a beautiful and complementary mix of superb riding and utter passion for his sport.

<ENDS>

'Well done,' Vasily says casually to Didier though it is obvious he has had to make quite a detour to come by the Megapac vehicles, 'you rode better than me and the result is fair.'

'I am happy,' Didier replies, 'because I am exhausted.'

'It's a good feeling,' says Vasily, 'something you can recall to your grandsons.'

'Indeed,' says Didier, not too tired to smile.

Ben and Rachel have seen their riders in close proximity but have not heard the exchange. Rachel catches Ben's eye. Ben nods.

That's Didier saved, for the time being. But though I'm relieved, I must be constantly vigilant. Drugs are just too damn tempting. When you're a Tour de France rider, pain alleviation is seductive in any form; legal, banned or even life-threatening.

Ben glances back at Rachel. André is slipping a hand around her waist, planting a fleeting kiss on her neck. It makes Ben yearn for Cat. Ben catches Rachel's eye but she looks right through him. She feels high, on fire, too preoccupied to acknowledge Ben, to observe that Jules Le Grand has thunder etched across his brow.

STAGE 18
La Chaux de Fonds–Lautrec. 242 kilometres

'Where is Rachel?' Stefano Sassetta bellowed in the corridor at an ungodly hour, having found no reply and no entry to his *soigneur*'s room. His outburst woke many of his Zucca team-mates, but as it was an occurrence with which they were familiar, pillows were placed over heads and dreams for the most part were uninterrupted. Stefano stormed back to his room, looked out of the window to the car park and noted that the team trucks were dark and obviously unoccupied. He phoned Rachel's mobile phone. To his fury, it was switched off. He left a livid, gabbled message about her round-the-clock duty to him and the importance of his thighs, before rubbing them himself sulkily and then falling asleep.

There you are, Rachel, scurrying back to your hotel under cover of darkness. It's almost five in the morning, need we ask where you've been?

To heaven and back. I can't wait to tell Cat. Mind you, only Cat – I think I'd die if anyone else found out.

Found out what exactly?

That I've been indulging with André to such an extent I fear I must be walking like John Wayne.

Would that swagger be caused by your spirit, then?

That and the fact that my legs have been akimbo for the best part of, well, all night.

Why do you dread others finding out?

Because it took me long enough to land this job and then twice as long, working twice as hard, to earn respect within my field, within this world. I've always been exceptionally discreet and steered well away from any attention whatsoever, adverse or otherwise.

If you're respected and liked, with a squeaky-clean record, might people not be thrilled for you to have found romance?

Romance? Who said anything about slush? I'm talking unadulterated passion here. Like Cat. Mind you, everyone can see that she and Ben are a fine pair, in love and all.

Maybe everyone would think of you and André as a fine pair and, in time, perhaps, in love and all.

And the hatchet between Système Vipère and Zucca MV would be buried? Hardly. One or both of us would get the sack, more like. I'm going to leave a message for Cat right now. Oh, I have message waiting. Stefano. Whoa! Abuse! Bloody men. Stefano and his bloody thighs. I'll have an hour's kip and then I'll wake him with a rub so vigorous he'll weep for mercy.

'I have a surprise for you,' Ben murmured, tickling Cat to awaken her. Cat regarded him with mock supplication and spread her legs obediently, a winsome expression on her slumber-soft face. Ben smiled at her, shook his head, was about to tell her instead that he loved her but, glancing at the clock, decided against it for the time being. 'No,' he said, whispering his fingers up her inner thigh, 'not that kind of surprise – but I like the way you're thinking.'

'What, then?' Cat asked sleepily, a little disappointed.

You could tell her you love her now, Ben.

Not enough time. Not the right moment.

'You'll see,' was all Ben would say, leaving the bed though Cat tried valiantly to grapple him to stay.

Jesper Lomers woke alone and lonely. Jules Le Grand had talked to him at length the previous evening about contracts and the future. Jesper knew that, in terms of his career, staying with Système Vipère was the only option. But he couldn't fathom whether his career should be his life or whether his marriage should be his career and if, therefore, Anya were to be his partner, whether they could build a strong enough business of their marriage.

How could he be most happy, he wondered, as he went to the bathroom. Surely one's happiness is ultimately one's own responsibility, he pondered as he smothered his legs in shaving foam and began to shave. He remembered how Anya used to love shaving his legs for him, taking her task most seriously, turning him on intensely. Shaving foam fights. Sex on the bathroom floor. Laughter. Togetherness. When was the last time? The last time that she had shaved his legs? The last time he had felt her, fondled her thighs? When did they last laugh together? When were they last together and actually experiencing togetherness? He nicked himself with the razor but did not curse, merely put his finger against the blood and then licked it pensively.

Could he be happy *not* riding for Système Vipère, he wondered, using a new disposable razor for his other leg. Could he be happy not cycling at all? He knew the answers to these questions. But oughtn't life to be about sacrifice? Wouldn't that make him a better person? Would he thus experience more of a sense of achievement there, than in keeping the green jersey for a second year running? He patted his legs dry and phoned Anya at his home, then on her mobile. No reply. He did not leave a message.

The *village* at La Chaux de Fonds was extremely crowded. The caged area in the centre of town delineating those with passes from those without was anathema to the memory of architect Le Corbusier whose birthplace this was. Accredited people mooched about within the confines, avoiding eye contact or establishing it quite brazenly with the clamouring members of the public who circumnavigated the enclosure and craved the rectangle of laminated plastic that would permit entry. Children outside clutching autograph books whose pages were bare, stared imploringly at the children of guests who milled about, bedecked with freebies and collecting autographs from any rider they saw. Cat contemplated how many of those outside would probably be far more appreciative of a pass than those who had them. She herself felt humbled, privileged; but also proud and just a little smug.

Look at me. I'm part of this club, this family. And I know you wish you were too. But I appreciate my very good fortune. I will nod at riders for you. Aren't I lucky?

'Cat,' said Ben, presenting two men to her, 'this is Mitch Mulready, General Manager of Team US Megapac.' Cat beamed at Mitch, a portly man in his fifties, with mirrored sunglasses and a toothsome smile.

'It's a pleasure to meet you, Mr Mulready,' she gushed, her hand swallowed between both of his in a lengthy handshake.

'And this,' said Ben, touching her elbow, knowing instinctively when to curtail what would otherwise be a stream of sycophantic cyclespeak from Cat, 'this is Jeremy Whittle.'

'Hullo,' said the man, extending his hand for the shaking.

'Hullo,' Cat responded, though her hand was practically numb from Mitch's grasp, 'weren't you English?'

'I still am!' Jeremy laughed.

'I mean – you were big in cycling correspondence in the UK?'

'That's right,' Jeremy confirmed.

'He's now big in cycling correspondence in the US,' Mitch interjected, slapping Jeremy firmly between the shoulder blades.

'Jez now heads up the cycling division of Sportsworld,' Ben furthered, referring to America's premier sports publishing house.

'*Cycle, Pedal Power, Road Race, Mountain Bike, Jersey,*' Jeremy listed affectionately, as if naming his pets.

'How fantastic,' breathed Cat, excited to learn of two new titles and hoping they'd be available in England.

'I've enjoyed your reports for the *Guardian*, I used to work with Taverner,' Jeremy said. 'I might well have some work for you – Ben said Luca gave you an exclusive?'

'Yes,' said Cat forlornly, remembering *Maillot*'s lack of enthusiasm, 'but that was *before* he won his Stage, you see.'

'He's a rider to be reckoned with,' Jeremy said soberly. 'Perhaps you could let me have a read?'

Cat grinned from ear to ear, humbly accepted Jeremy's business card and gave him one of hers.

'Fancy a ride in the team car?' Mitch asked her, as if it was an invitation no more enticing than a cup of coffee from Maison du Café. It was as if the ground beneath her feet began to undulate, as if a shaft of sunlight shot through her from a break in the clouds to radiate out from every pore.

'An answer would be good,' Ben suggested, adoring her gobsmacked face and wanting to cup her cheeks in his hands and kiss her right there, in front of his employer. Cat nodded eagerly, eyes asparkle, and shook Mitch's hand anew in vigorous gratitude before skipping off to find Alex or Josh, or anyone for that matter, to inform them that she had her own transport today, thank you very much.

The team cars moved off in a hierarchy according to the general classification of riders and Cat had to sit on her hands to stop herself from waving at all the people waving and cheering. Short of riding on a tandem within the peloton, this was as close as she could be to the inner sanctum of the Tour de France.

'So Cat,' boomed Mitch, from the back seat, 'what kind of job is this for a girl?'

'A dream job. Megapac are my favourite team,' Cat gushed, wincing at her clumsy effusiveness which Mitch luckily deemed artless and rather touching.

'Sure is pretty round here,' Mitch remarked, and Cat

momentarily changed her focus from the profile of the route to feast her eyes upon stunning verdant scenery as they journeyed through Switzerland and back into France.

'You think we'll have a bunch sprint finish?' Mitch asked her.

'Perhaps, unless a break goes clear,' Cat said, 'but once we're into vineyard territory, the lie of the land is pretty rolling and the bunch will be able to move over the little hills much faster than a small break who'd have to be pretty strong to hold them off.'

'I fancy a good glass of Burgundy tonight,' mused Mitch, giving his stomach a veritable drum roll of patting, 'it's why I chose this part of the race to come over for.'

Cat was too engrossed in Radio Tour to ask which Burgundy – Côte de Beaune or Côte de Nuits – Mitch was intending to enjoy with his *boeuf bourgignon*. 'Thirteen riders have gone clear,' she said, 'at the 17 k mark – including Hunter and Luca.'

'Yee hah!' Mitch sang, making Cat jump. 'Way to go, boys!'

'Jesper and Stefano are there too,' Cat said.

'Lomers and Sassetta?' Mitch clarified. 'I just love this battle of the bands – Viper boys versus Zucca guys.'

'Luca, 58 seconds,' the Megapac *directeur sportif*, driving, spoke to Luca through the two-way radio. 'Thirteen riders, 58 second lead. No counter-attack as yet.'

The channel crackled and Luca's response filled the car. ''Kay,' was all he said.

Cat was moved. Somewhere out there, 58 seconds ahead of the bunch, out of sight for the moment, Luca and the breakaway were working hard.

'We have to follow the break,' the *directeur* announced, nipping his car out of the convoy, tooting and revving past the others, heckling and joking with the other *directeurs*. Cat held her breath as they sped through towards the break.

'This is great!' Mitch exclaimed, as if it were a display put on for his benefit. 'Fucking awesome.'

Momentarily, the car was deeply ensconced within the

peloton itself and Cat felt a rush of excitement and emotion. There was too much to see and absorb. It was a blur of colour within a capsule of pure energy. She wanted the *directeur* to slow down, the riders as well, so she could take stock thoroughly, preserve it all and commit it to memory. Every detail, every rider, every expression of effort, pain, exhaustion, focus. Then they were behind her and she was being driven onwards towards the breakaway. For a few seconds, she gazed backwards until the peloton had become a single bolt of colour before disappearing from sight. Her eyes were scouring ahead for the thirteen breakaway riders.

There they are!

Here they are! Tiny amidst the cars, the motorbikes, yet seemingly unaware of our presence. Move over, Viper and Zucca team cars, can't we come through?

'Seven minutes, Luca,' the *directeur* said into the walkie-talkie. '6 k distance.'

''Kay,' the breathless answer crackled back.

'You OK?' the *directeur* asked him.

'Yeah,' came the reply after a fuzzy delay.

'Hunter too?'

'Yeah,' Luca said.

'Will they do it, Cat?' Mitch asked, not testing her but actively seeking her opinion as the *directeur* was obviously utterly absorbed with the driving.

Before she could reply, 'Megapac, please' came through over the radio, 'US Megapac.'

The carload fell silent. The *directeur*, swerving the car in between the others, headed towards the thirteen riders themselves. Cat was speechless with anticipation and delight.

See the boys, tiny on their bikes from afar? Look, now we're here; so strong and powerful. Their effort is so tangible. See the focus on their faces.

She gazed too at the neat bottoms clad in aesthetically panelled black lycra, the beautiful legs ever working; bronzed and glistening, the musculature long, lithe and delineated, calf muscles tapering like inverted teardrops, tendons taut, sculpted thighs exuding power, shoulders broad, tanned arms with wonderful definition. Breathtaking. Cat was holding hers.

'Open your window, Cat,' the *directeur* commanded her, 'Luca needs something.'

Wow, just listen! We're absolutely in the pack now. It's incredible. The noise – men breathing, wheels whishing, someone spitting, another shouting. Tension is a taste, a smell, I can reach out and touch it. My senses are utterly seduced. What does he want me to do? I can hardly think straight. I want to touch.

'Luca wants to hand his jacket in,' the *directeur* told her, 'take it from him. Pass him a power bar. Pass him two – one for Hunter as well.'

Luca! Luca? It's me, it's Cat. Gatto. The Babe McCabe. Hey!

See? He doesn't clock me at all. I take his jacket. I pass him the food. I have touched his hand but I am invisible. And I am not offended. This is Luca Jones, doing his job. The focus, the commitment, the mastery. Jesus.

The break was not caught though the peloton were hot on their heels, swallowing up the intervening minutes and kilometres. Cat, in the Megapac team car, followed the boys to within 500 metres of the finish where the vehicles were directed off.

Ultimately she was glad not to have seen the finish live. She would not have been accountable for her behaviour in the *salle de presse* had she done so.

'Fen! It's on, come *on*!' Pip yelled, opening two packets of crisps in preparation. 'Salt and Vinegar or Beef and Mustard?'

'S.A.V.,' whispered Fen, taking a seat on her settee next to her sister and passing her a bottle of *Seize* – a daily tradition since their return from France. They watched in informed silence and phoned Django during the adverts.

'That's Cat boyfriend's young rider,' Pip informed her uncle of Luca.

'So is Hunter,' Fen added.

'Hunter is her boyfriend too?' Django asked, a little disconcerted, wondering whether yet another of his nieces was hopelessly bigamous.

'No!' Pip laughed.

'Same team,' Fen explained.

'Well,' said Django, clearing his voice and taking a glug of gin and tonic, 'you can't blame me for asking – she may have taken a leaf out of your book, Fenella.'

Fenella bit her lip.

'Fen still can't make her mind up, Django,' Pip informed him.

'Can't she palm one off on to you?' Django reasoned very earnestly. 'Am I going to meet this boyfriend doctor of Cat's?'

'Not unless you jet out to Colorado,' Fen said glumly.

'Quick! It's on again!' Pip exclaimed, ordering her uncle to phone them when the programme finished.

The Stage was fast and furious and in the 350 metre finishing straight, the unthinkable, the terrible, the desperately unfair happened.

'Oh, fuck,' Fen gasped.

'Luca's down.'

'So's Jesper.'

'Sassetta's won the Stage.'

'That means he's taken the green jersey.'

'Jesper's up.'

'Luca isn't.'

'Oh, Jesus.'

Luca regained consciousness in the ambulance and was in absolute agony.

'You've broken your collar bone. You have concussion,' someone was telling him.

'I'm fine,' said Luca valiantly, 'I need to get back on my bike.'

'You need to get X-ray,' the paramedic told him.

'But my bike!' Luca cried. He tried to sit up but searing pain prevented him. This could not be happening. He had to finish the Stage. There were less than 100 metres to go. He knew just how he was going to ride them. 'Let me out!' he yelled, the paramedic's shrug of pity serving only to aggravate Luca's emotional pain and physical frustration. 'I have to finish the Stage – you don't understand.'

'Sure I understand,' said the paramedic with typical Gallic defensiveness that his judgement should be so questioned, 'you need to finish the Stage or you are out of the Tour de France.'

'Exactly,' Luca said croakily, 'so fucking let me out – please.'

'You are out of the Tour de France,' the paramedic said excruciatingly slowly, a matter of fact, a subject closed, a dream denied, before giving Luca a shot of sedative.

The information filtered through on Radio Tour before Cat had left the team car which then turned on a sixpence and roared off, under police escort, to the hospital. Ben was already there. He walked briskly to converse with the *directeur*, hardly acknowledging Cat's presence, indeed turning his back on her as the Megapac personnel discussed the situation.

'The press are starting to turn up,' Mitch said and hospital staff ushered them through corridors to a small ante room. The doctor came in, took Ben to one side and spoke in medical terms that transcended language barriers.

'His collar bone will need pinning,' Ben explained, 'they want to do it tonight. I say we give them the go ahead – he'll be ready for Spain and the Vuelta next month.'

'Can we see him?' Cat pleaded.

'They need to operate now,' Ben said, tension tangible in his voice, signing forms with the *directeur*.

'But he's all on his own,' Cat said, her voice trailing off when the *directeur* regarded her with a certain exasperation.

'You may see him for a moment,' the hospital doctor decreed, putting out a hand to prevent Cat from advancing with Ben and Mitch.

'No *presse*,' the doctor said.

'But I'm Gatto,' Cat protested. Her distress was of no interest to the Megapac doctor, *directeur* and chairman who were led through to see Luca.

Ben appeared a few minutes later and put his hand to the back of Cat's neck. 'Luca's devastated, he needs to rest. You can see him tomorrow.'

Ben rubbed the back of his own neck hard. There was a greyness to his skin. He looked exhausted. Cat did not protest though she felt excluded, a little hurt and still desperate to see Luca, to comfort and commiserate. It was a little disconcerting to have Ben as a doctor foremost, rather than her beau. To see him work, suffer, his attention directed elsewhere than on her. Her status was vague.

I feel both flimsy and in the way. I'm not part of the Megapac team. I'm not here to represent the press. My thoughts are for Luca Jones – yet on the face of it, I'm not entitled to feel the same concern as Megapac – and my distress is disproportionate for a member of the press corps.

'Pardon me, Cat,' Mitch said, still wearing his mirror sunglasses but not the wide smile. 'Ben, we need you to give us his condition in normal folk's language, we have a press conference to prepare.'

'Sure,' said Ben.

'You OK to make your own way back to the *salle de presse*?' the *directeur* asked Cat. She nodded. Ben and Mitch were too deep in conversation to notice her go.

Feeling a little forsaken for herself, and devastated for Luca, Cat returned to the *salle de presse*, today a voluminous tarpaulin on the edge of a serene lake with a McDonalds obviously sent from heaven to be in such close proximity. Not that she was hungry. Neither Josh nor Alex were around. Not that she wanted company. Zucca MV, Système Vipère and US Megapac press conferences were happening one after the other. Not that she was interested.

Cat contemplated her workload.

I have to write 700 words on today's Stage but I want to devote them entirely to one Luca Jones, noble soldier, brave boy, who fought valiantly for almost three weeks and is currently under the surgeon's knife.

Cat, write like that and Taverner will come out to France to sack you in public.

Fuck off. Luca deserves an epitaph.

He's not dead, he's just broken a collar bone – he'll be fine. He'll be racing again. He'll probably hoover up a Stage or two in the Vuelta.

His heart will be broken. He should have finished. He deserved Paris. It's what he wanted. I'm going to phone Taverner.

And?

He said I have to write about Sassetta taking the green jersey after a stray and empty can of Coke interfered with the wheels of the sprinting riders, bringing down Luca and Jesper and two others. He says I have to write about the race being in Charolais country; he wants a little vignette about the great fluffy creamy bovines. And the local Burgundy. He wants me to wax lyrical about the colourful tiled tessellations on the roofs in Beaune. He can piss off.

So?

I'm going to phone Andy at Maillot.

And?

He said he's already asked Josh to pen a piece because I wasn't answering my mobile phone. That's because I was at the hospital, I said. As presse, he asked. I wasn't there as presse, I was there as Luca's friend. But did I get to speak to

*him, he asked. He was about to have a fucking operation,
I retorted. No go, said Andy. Fuck him.*

So?

*I'm going to phone Jeremy Whittle, who I met this
morning.*

And?

*He said to call him Jez. He wants a profile of Luca Jones's
Tour de France for next month's* Pedal Power *magazine.
Two thousand words. I'm going to rattle off my race report
for Taverner and then get cracking for Whittle. It's odd. I
should be thrilled, I should be brimming with ambition. I
don't even know how much he'll pay me. However, my main
drive, my only motivation, is to honour the valorous Luca
Jones. I'm going to write my heart out for that boy, just as he
rode his heart out for all of us.*

REPOS
Transfer by road and rail. Lautrec–Disneyland-Paris

*P*ain woke Luca, but more than that which affected his shoulder was the deep wrenching hurt in his heart coupled with a searing headache. He wanted his Mama. He wanted his bike. He would gladly die young, gruesomely even, if he could only be given the gift of reliving the day before, of doing yesterday again. The pain in his heart was caused by his desperate desire for Paris, to finish the Tour de France. In the top fifty. With a Stage win under his belt.

His headache was caused by fear that perhaps he'd blown his career; that Jules Le Grand would no longer want him for Système Vipère. He was a broken machine, one in need of repair, one that might perform somewhat crankily until all the moving parts were well oiled and functioning well once more. What perplexed him most was that, riding along with Hunter yesterday, he'd all but decided to stay with Megapac. This morning, the possibility that he had blown his chance to be a Viper Boy was devastating. Lying now in his hospital bed, he craved Le Grand's advances, he needed the affirmation that, no matter how battered and broken his body, he was still a rider with great potential to be nurtured, a champion in the making.

But could he do it without those who had brought him this far? Could he ride without Hunter? Could he cope with a multi-day Stage Race without Didier as a room-mate? Could he function physically and mentally without his friend, his mentor, his physician Ben? Sleep soothed him for an hour but when the knock on the door awoke him, the pain in his head and in his heart had not abated, and that around his collar bone had intensified.

'Hey soldier,' said Ben, taking a seat next to Luca's bedside, 'did you sleep?'

Having mostly seen Luca in colourful lycra, out in the fresh air, riding in the sun, it was bizarre to see him now in a hospital gown, stationary in bed in a small little room. His golden curls were in disarray, his cherub-soft cheeks were invaded by bristles, the sparkle from his eyes had gone. His lips looked dry, but most worryingly, his voice was silent. Without the bike, his health, his vitality, this might not have been Luca at all, just someone who looked vaguely like him.

'Are you hurting?' Ben asked. Luca gazed at him, experienced enormous pain on trying to shrug and let a fat, solitary tear seep out of his eye to slither forlornly down his nose and evanesce over his lips in reply. Just as at L'Alpe D'Huez, Ben knew instinctively what medical attention he needed to dispense. He knew there was nothing he could administer to take away Luca's pain, nothing he could say to make him feel remotely better, nothing he could do to expedite healing, the only option (and flimsy tonic though it was) was to sit beside his charge and just be there. He looked at Luca attentively when Luca regarded him. He puckered his brow in unison with Luca. He gazed out of the window when his rider decided to do so, and he sighed the same sigh. And felt the same pain.

When Cat turned up at the hospital an hour later just after breakfast, she found Luca's door closed with the blind pulled down and entry barred. Cat of course respected this and perched herself on the window-sill, sniffing thoughtfully into the clutch of cornflowers she'd bought for him and wondering whether she'd written too much or said not enough in her card. Nurses bustled about in staunchly starched aprons and extraordinary wimples. Cat felt utterly flimsy, not merely in her insubstantial and rather creased sundress, but in her lack of ability to do anything constructive for Luca. Of course she'd tell him of her profile of him for *Pedal Power* but, just then, it seemed that the purpose of the piece was more for her own greater glory than it was a testimonial for Luca.

I've never been in hospital, she mused, remembering the numerous occasions she'd visited Pip when some acrobatic endeavour had ended in tears and a plaster cast.

Perhaps I have never needed looking after.

That people care about you is you being looked after.

I'm fine. Right as rain.

But you weren't.

Well, I am now. Don't dwell.

And here's Ben, walking up the corridor, handsomely dishevelled in the face having not shaved, attractively crumpled in attire, wearing yesterday's khakis and soft polo shirt.

'Hey you,' he says to Cat, going to the window-sill and kissing her bare knees.

'Hullo,' Cat says to him, placing her hand on his cheek and letting herself become lost in his eyes.

'Seen the patient?' Ben asks, glancing at his watch and noting that it's half an hour since he left Luca in search of breakfast in lieu of last night's supper.

'No,' says Cat, nodding towards the door, 'there's someone in with him.'

'A nurse?' Ben asks.

'A male voice,' Cat defines, 'been in there for ages.'

'Probably the surgeon,' Ben reasons, looking out of the window and feeling enormously tired and still hungry.

*

Luca's door opened. No surgeon came out. No doctor either, nor a male nurse. The man who emerged from Luca's bedside, who nodded most courteously at Ben and brandished a suave smile at Cat, was Jules Le Grand. In a cream silk suit, he swished away along the corridor not registering the dropped jaws and bulging eyes of the *journaliste* and doctor.

'How nice that Jules Le Grand came to see how Luca's doing,' Cat said feebly, persuading neither herself nor Ben in the process. They entered Luca's room and Ben swiped away his gobsmacked, brooding silence.

'Honestly, fuckwit,' he laughed jovially, 'I leave your bedside for a piss-awful cup of coffee and I return to find you in cahoots with slithery King Viper!'

Luca said nothing but stared at Ben very measuredly. Cat couldn't bear the loaded silence so she broke it.

'Hullo, Luca,' she said, all but tiptoeing to his bedside, 'how are you? I brought you flowers and a silly card. I couldn't sleep on your behalf and now I have a stiff neck in sympathy.'

'The Babe,' said Luca, a smile briefly lighting otherwise pain-dulled eyes, 'you're the Babe.'

Cat proffered the flowers for Luca to sniff and then she tore open the envelope and presented the front of the card for his perusal before unfolding it and holding it for him to read. It was the only card in the room.

'And Le Grand brought you his best wishes too?' Ben all but demanded.

'No,' said Luca soberly, 'he made me an offer I'd be a madman to refuse.'

Ben went over to the window and hated himself for hating Luca for loving Jules Le Grand and his ostentatious offer to join his fucking brilliant pro cycling team. Cat took a seat by Luca and fixed him with an expression of enthusiasm and support.

'Will you take it?' she asked. 'The offer, the opportunity?'

'*Gatto*,' Luca wailed, 'I love Megapac, my heart is there

377

because my friends are there and my friends there are as close as family.'

'It must be a desperately difficult decision,' Cat deduced, glancing at Ben's resolutely turned back, trying to implore him to offer advice, support, to join the conversation at the very least.

'It's terrible, Catriona McCabe, believe me,' Luca implored, 'terrible.'

Ben turned and looked down on his rider and his girl but he said nothing.

Luca regarded him. 'I should go,' he told his doctor, 'I really should. But I am afraid. Can I ever be as happy for another team as I have been with Megapac?'

Still Ben didn't speak.

'Will I regret it more if I leave or if I stay?'

Ben's facial expression remained unchanged.

'Can I trust Jules Le Grand? Does he truly rate me highly enough to ride alongside Fabian Ducasse, Jesper Lomers and Carlos Jesu Velasquez?'

Ben had not moved a muscle.

'Fuck, it gives me a headache,' Luca moaned, finding temporary relief in Cat stroking his brow tenderly. 'What would *you* do?' he asked her.

'I want you to be happy and to be the best rider it is possible for you ever to be,' she said honestly.

'But what would you *do*?' he pleaded. 'If you were me?'

Cat bit her lip and glared at Ben to help her, to help Luca.

'What would you do, Ben,' Luca asked, 'if you were me?'

Still Ben stood defiantly silent, as still and stony as a statue.

'What would you have me do, Ben?' Luca rephrased.

Cat saw Ben swallow and then she detected a just perceptible softening of his brow.

'I want you to be happy,' Ben said, finding his voice and discovering it to be rather weak, 'I want you to realize your true, possibly remarkable, potential as a professional road race cyclist.'

'So what *should* I do?' Luca whispered.

'I think you should grasp the opportunity and join Système Vipère, ride and train with the best in the business,' Ben whispered back.

The entourage of the Tour de France had their second Repos to transfer up to Paris, to Euro Disney, in preparation for the next day's penultimate Stage of this year's Tour de France, the final Time Trial. A TGV train was laid on for all the teams and any accredited personnel to use. Though Cat would have loved the experience, though she would have loved to have heard the announcement that the *maillot jaune* was currently driving the train, though she would have loved to listen to Vasily Jawlensky's incomparably husky, guttural voice announcing over the PA, 'Hullo, ladies and gentlemen, this is Vasily Jawlensky; I am driving you to Paris at 200 kph and I think I shall turn the corner – now!'; though all of this would have added greatly to Cat's experience of the Tour de France, provided her with yet another glorious memory, she forsook the event to journey alone with Ben.

Alex and Josh were travelling in their car, squabbling about the best route to take, who would drive which section and when and where they would stop for refreshments. They were both astutely aware that, had Cat been in the car, she'd have chided, 'Boys! Shut up and behave or you'll be sent to your rooms without supper.' As they drove along, they could both practically hear her wax poetic about some feature in the landscape or other. As their journey continued, they acknowledged privately that everything was more fun when Cat was there enlivening the proceedings quite unwittingly. This year's Tour had been the richer for her presence; consequently, it had passed far more quickly and had also been much more memorable. They'd miss her when they returned home. They hoped she'd be travelling with them next year.

'Twat!' Josh hissed. 'You missed the sodding junction.'

'Bollocks!' Alex retorted. 'I know this area – it's a short cut.'

'Short cut, my arse,' said Josh, with no malice.

'Oh, fuck off,' said Alex affectionately.

Rachel and André are not travelling together but they are communicating the whole route long. Rachel behind the wheel of the vast Zucca MV truck and André driving the enormous Système Vipère lorry. They are chatting most affably via indicators and hazard lights. They are taking it in turns to overtake so that they can draw alongside and grin idiotically and stare longingly and voice their desires by looks alone, saying things with their eyes that they'll fulfil in person later. Rachel couldn't even speak to Cat on the mobile phone. Not because to do so would be dangerous if not illegal, but because she claimed she was talking to André. Which she was. Not dangerous. Not illegal. Lovely.

And Ben York and Cat McCabe are travelling north together. They haven't said much. Ben is somewhat shellshocked by Luca's news and Cat is just plain exhausted. And if they were to speak, and the conversation was not focused on what it is that exists between the two of them, it would be instead only idle chatter. And a glaring effort not to broach sensitive issues that really ought to be confronted. I could suggest to them that they throw caution to the wind, bite the bullet and launch right in, but they wouldn't listen. I could yell at them to confide how they feel, but they wouldn't hear me. All I can do is eavesdrop. And wince that Cat has said 'glorious landscape' for the third time in an hour.

They fill the car with fuel, sit a while and have coffee that is absurdly good for a motorway service station. Ben mentions the weather. Cat hopes it will stay dry for tomorrow's Time Trial. Every time she looks at him, she has to glance away, for she surges with desire and finds herself wanting to grin inanely. To her, he is most handsome and his seemly exterior speaks volumes of the personality she has grown to know and adore. Love, Cat?

Ssh. Don't spoil the moment.

Why on earth would love spoil a thing?

Stop it. I just want to absorb everything of the present.

Ben buys a packet of Petite Beurre biscuits for the journey and suggests to Cat that they motor on. Cat, who has let the straps of her sundress hang down and who is turning her face to the sun, nods. She appears merely to be soaking up warmth, developing a nice colour to her cheeks and shoulders. Actually, her mind is in overdrive with thoughts bombarding her and sentences, some complete, some unstructured, all unspoken, racketing around. She wants to stay firmly in the here and now. If she opens her eyes, she will have to follow Ben to the car and they will restart their journey and the minutes and the kilometres will be swallowed up, taking her closer and closer to going home.

Why can't the Tour de France last for ever?

What a daft thing to say, Catriona McCabe. You're the *journaliste*, you know the pressures on body and mind of a Stage Race three weeks long as it is.

'Um,' says Ben, displaying a vulnerability in voice and choosing vocabulary that surprises Cat. He is fidgeting; tapping the steering-wheel, checking his blind spot an inordinate number of times though he has not yet switched on the engine. Cat, bizarrely, feels suddenly empowered and calm. She takes her hand to his wrist and strokes him.

'What?' she asks quietly. Her voice, so soothing, so familiar, relaxes Ben and he turns to her.

'I have something for you,' he says, twisting and leaning to the back seat, the sight of his torso delineated beneath fabric making Cat swoon and reach for him. He is rummaging in his jacket pocket and presents her with something concealed in a wad of crumpled tissue paper. As soon as she has it in her hands, he starts the engine and drives off somewhat aggressively.

Cat unwraps. It is a watch. An extremely plain, second-hand watch with bold roman numerals and hands telling the wrong time. The strap is pale tan and very supple, very worn. Cat, who has only ever had plastic Swatches, thinks it quite the most gorgeous timepiece she has ever seen and she stares at him, staggered.

'Beautiful,' she whispers and it is audible to Ben above the din of the engine. He glances in the rear-view mirror, in the side mirror, cranes his sight well ahead, looks to one side. Just not at Cat. And nods nonchalantly.

'It's from La Chaux de Fonds – the centre of the watch-making industry. Sorry it's not a Rolex,' he muttered, the whole business of pampering a loved one being rather strange to him. 'I saw it and thought it very you.'

'It's *so* me,' Cat declares in a whisper, the business of being pampered by a loved one being rather new to her too. She snatches off her blue plastic watch and sets the new one on her wrist. 'I love it.'

'You need to wind it up and set it to the right time,' Ben states the obvious ingenuously whilst doing lots of mirror-checking again. Cat does just that. The symbolism begins to dawn on her just as soon as Ben finds his mouth opening and words spilling out unchecked, uncensored.

'I'll be counting the hours, Cat,' he says, 'counting them. Wishing them away. Till I can have you again. Promise me you'll have work for the Vuelta?'

Cat can't answer because she's staring hard out of the window, at the landscape fleeing backwards, at the knowledge of the Alps, the Golfe du Lion, at everywhere she's been over the past three weeks, now so far behind but still on this very lump of land. She glances at her watch and has the crazy notion of turning the hands themselves backwards. Nobody before has spoken so beautifully, so emotively to her. He Who No Longer Exists would chastize her for being late, holler, 'Can't you tell the bloody time?' or else curse her for being petty should she ever dare to be upset that he hadn't come home at all.

Now here is a man who wishes away the hours that will

keep us apart. And has given me a watch so I can count down the minutes till we're together. Oh fuck, am I going to be able not to cry?

'I wish I'd bloody never met you,' Cat says in an extremely strangled voice.

'I wish I'd never met you too,' Ben agrees quietly.

'Cat McCabe,' Ben says, pulling over to the hard shoulder and switching off the engine, 'I am in love with you.'

Blimey, Ben!

It was easy to say. Now I'm exhausted. If my adrenal glands weren't in overdrive, I'd gladly fall asleep.

'I really do,' Ben emphasizes, most wide awake.

Cat can't speak, she can only nod. But the depth of her gaze and the sincerity of a tear which trickles cautiously down her face, speaks volumes to Ben.

They don't say much, just talk in clichés that don't seem hackneyed in the least. They agree that where there's a will there's a way, they reason that absence can only make their hearts beat stronger, they define that everything happens for a reason, they say that what will be will be, they theorize that one isn't given a dream without also being given the power to realize it. They grin and kiss and Cat sobs and Ben tastes her tears and reveals a few of his own, for the first time ever, to another person. This Cat McCabe, *journaliste*, whom he met less than a month ago, whom surely he has known all his life, whom he cannot condone spending time without, whom he craves and desires and loves and feels all his emotions reciprocated.

And then the police move them on. And they continue their journey towards Paris and two days concluding the Tour de France.

STAGE 19

Disneyland Paris, Individual Time Trial: 63 kilometres

'*A*lex, we *can't*,' Josh whispered, giggling behind his hand like a schoolboy.

'We bloody can,' said Alex, quite the playground bully.

'Poor Cat,' Josh laughed, 'she'll *die*.'

'She'll die if she doesn't,' Alex chortled at his Catch 22.

'It isn't fair,' Josh repeated with a certain glee, 'we really *can't*!'

'Can't what?' said Ben, suddenly appearing from Cat's room outside which Alex and Josh had been hovering furtively, sniggering, for the best part of ten minutes.

'We can't expect Cat to wear this,' said Josh, holding up a Minnie Mouse outfit, 'she'll die.'

Ben regarded the outfit and the two costumiers with an expression of horror which lasted but five seconds before transforming itself into one of wicked delight.

'You absolutely can,' Ben said, holding open the door to Cat's room and ushering in her two colleagues.

Cat was dressed extremely nicely in navy shorts and a navy and cream top. She was packing her bags and checking that her phone had recharged when she turned to see her two colleagues and Ben standing silently abreast. Alex was in the middle, holding a polka dot frilly dress by the shoulders; to either side of him, Ben and Josh each held an edge of the skirt. All were regarding her most gravely.

'Oh no,' she said, shaking her head vehemently, 'no no. Not in a million. No way. Absolutely not.'

The three men nodded very solemnly.

'Oh, but *yes*,' Ben said.

'Yes way,' said Josh.

'Abso-fucking-*lutely*,' said Alex.

When Cat attempted to back herself into a corner, the three men and the dress advanced on her.

'You're wearing it, Catriona McCabe,' Ben ordered.

'I am not, Benjamin York,' Cat wailed.

'You are,' said Josh.

'Full stop,' said Alex.

'I think it's ridiculous,' Cat fumed, 'this pathetic Americanization of the Tour de France. This is a serious sporting event and I think it profane that it should be held at a fun factory.'

'Oh, get off your high horse and in to your Minnie Mouse costume,' Ben retorted.

'It's all way too commercialized,' Cat bemoaned, 'it's all about profit at the expense of national character. All this Coca-Cola and Disney and Nike swooshes all over the place.'

'Cat,' said Josh in a gentle voice so patronizing that Cat gaped at him in horror, 'lest we forget that the very reason for the birth of the Tour de France in 1903 was for purely commercial ends.'

'To promote the newspaper *L'Auto*,' Alex reminded her sternly.

'The colour of whose pages became the colour of the leader's jersey,' Ben added for good measure.

'Why *me*?' Cat wailed, wondering quietly if the dress would fit and what on earth it would look like and when exactly was the last time she had dressed up. 'How come you lot get off scot-free?'

In solemn response, the dress was laid carefully on the

bed and all three men suddenly stood before her brandishing new ears. Alex became Dumbo, Josh became the Lion King and Ben, predictably, became Mickey Mouse.

'Change,' Ben, looking at his watch, commanded Cat.

'Quickly,' said Alex, proffering her the dress.

'We're running late,' said Josh, checking his reflection in the mirror.

Suffice it to say, Cat looked ravishing in her polka dot dress with its frou-frou skirt. She felt rather good too and it infused her step with a jaunty spring. She even wore mouse ears. And a smile. And used a length of red cord from her rucksack as laces in her white plimsolls. She gave the boys a twirl. Right there in the foyer of the motel, and was awarded a round of applause and many a wolf whistle.

Every rider in Système Vipère, the only team left in the Tour de France with all nine riders, wore some gimmicky accoutrement or other. Even Fabian Ducasse, ever brooding and aloof, went to sign on wearing a Pinocchio nose, though its comic potential, whilst delighting the crowds, left his sultry demeanour unaltered. The diminutive Carlos Jesu Velasquez, though resplendent in his polka dot jersey, was somewhat swamped by his Goofy baseball cap and whilst the *domestiques* came as six of the seven dwarves, Jesper Lomers opted merely for Mickey Mouse ears, quite sober in comparison. There was absolutely no way that Jules Le Grand was going to spoil the line or the cloth of his Armani suit with even a badge and his hair was far too perfectly coiffed to permit the presence of plastic ears or a baseball cap. He had made one huge concession to the atmosphere of the day, though nobody would realize. He was wearing socks with his suit. Emblazoned with Pocahontas. Not that anyone knew. It did, however, enliven his comportment and lighten his mien. And when he saw Anya Lomers, walking around the *village* looking thoroughly out of place so late on in the race, he greeted her warmly and gave her a pair of Mickey Mouse ears.

We have not met Anya yet; all we know is that she has caused Jules a headache and Jesper a heartache. She's handsome; tall and milk-blonde and we'd like to dislike her. But she looks lost, displaced; dressed so tidily in shirt and skirt and shoes all cream. Moreover, she feels lost. She has always felt out of place, here on Planet Tour, but she has never craved anything different. Her marriage has been as tough for her as it has for Jesper. The man she loves undoubtedly loves her but their requirements and commitments differ fundamentally. She wants children and a return to Holland. She is lonely and feels barren in her current situation, in France, with a husband she sees so sporadically. Jesper knows that he defines himself primarily by his ability to race a bike. He has to live in France. He races for the greatest team in the world. Anya is a woman turning thirty in a no-win situation. And she's wearing stupid Mickey Mouse ears when she's feeling deeply emotional on a morning she knows is to be hugely significant.

Stefano Sassetta had no need for fancy dress. Colourful enough in his regular Zucca MV gear, he was positively dazzling strutting around in his *maillot vert* with a self-satisfied smirk on his lips, thighs glistening with embrocation. The carry of his head, the brace of his shoulders, the draw of his chest, the meticulous arrangement of the bulges in his shorts, all proclaimed overflowing pride in his triumph. The ensemble delighted the crowds, amused the journalists and was an absolute treat for the photographers. The pictures taken of Stefano that day would soon adorn the walls of most Italian homes; from teenage cycling fans, to rampant women of all ages, to the entire gay population.

Sassetta wanted to be a living legend, and had carefully and successfully honed his image for posterity. The very look of him both excused and justified his sometimes questionable behaviour. In the *village* that morning, he ensured that he swaggered past Jesper Lomers at opportune times when the sun broke through the clouds and caught his jersey at its most resplendently verdant. Such a highly visible and antagonistic gesture brought him fame and notoriety and it was irrelevant that in fact he looked far more ridiculous than Jesper did in Mickey Mouse ears.

Jesper, however, hardly clocked Stefano's presence; the unexpected sight of his wife had him transfixed. The Dutch riders with whom he had been sitting and chatting quite affably forgave him his sudden silence and abrupt departure.

'Hullo, Jesper,' said Anya after they had stood very close and stared silently for a few moments.

'Great ears,' said Jesper, giving her Mickey Mouse head-piece a gentle flick.

'Yours too,' Anya said politely before scrutinizing some fascinating aspect of her footwear.

'I'm sorry that you don't see me in the *maillot vert*,' said Jesper, gravely apologetic.

'I am sorry for you that you have it no longer,' Anya said honestly.

'Ach,' Jesper shrugged with equanimity, 'I had it last year – but I believe I will win it for the Vipers next year.'

How the words hung, loaded and huge, as if physically there, on vast placards suspended from the clouds, emphatically and unavoidably legible. Jesus, the relief. Suddenly Jesper knew unequivocally where he would be on this day next year, even what he'd be wearing. It was as if he'd been granted some divine flash of the future and to abuse it, to do anything other than travel towards it, would be a sacrilegious travesty. And suddenly Anya knew exactly where her husband of today would be this time next year. And there was nothing she was going to do about it because there was nothing she actually wanted to do about it. She had no idea where she'd be in 365 days hence, but she knew that she would not be here, in a *village* of the Tour de France.

And so Jesper Lomers stands silent and still and solitary in the centre of the *village* while around him, journalists and guests and officials and a host of Disney characters mill about in high spirits. He watches Anya, his soon-to-be-ex-wife, walk away, her Mickey Mouse ears still in place, as are his. It is the penultimate day of this year's Tour de France. He has lost the *maillot vert* and he has lost his marriage. And yet, he has his health, his sanity and the priceless aptitude of knowing exactly what he wants to do with his life. What he lacks in happiness at this stage, he gains in a sense of peace.

Fabian Ducasse feels calm in that his thoughts are collected. He is not at peace though. His body is surging with anticipatory determination, adrenalin is pumping through his system. He is 1 minute 33 seconds from Vasily Jawlensky's yellow jersey. Both he and his rival are very strong Time Trialists; Fabian will ride with the extra spurt that ruthless desire and extreme ambition can instil, Vasily has the extra strength exuded by his golden fleece. Fabian Ducasse is capable of wiping minutes off other riders on today's Time Trial course. Vasily Jawlensky is capable of not losing a second.

Cat, Josh and Alex drove the course in a convoy of four press cars following the team car, hollering, '*Allez! Allez! Allez!*' at the Cofidis rider David Millar. The young Brit stormed the course and took the lead which he was still holding with only two men left to ride. Unfortunately, the men in question were Fabian Ducasse and Vasily Jawlensky; dressed for action in their skinsuits, equipped for battle on their aero-dynamic machines, prepared to plunder every ounce of their physical and emotional reserves.

Minnie Mouse McCabe was an exception to the rule amongst the press corps, today slogging out the words in an overheated room in a Disneyland hotel. With her hair washed regularly and skin bathed daily over the past three weeks, she looked nearly as fresh today as when the Tour started. The majority of hacks, however, had now resigned themselves to items of clothing which, whilst far from clean, at least were not amongst those fermenting at the bottoms of suitcases. The accumulation of three weeks of strong salami and *Seize* virtually on tap could be seen in expanded girths and heard in copious belching. Nicotine had stained fingers and teeth. Chins looked grimy – most razor blades having been well blunted since around Stage 16. Though noticeably weary over the past few Stages, today the *salle de presse* sat riveted by the action of the Time Trial relayed to them on the screens.

They watched Ducasse fly through the first checkpoint, swiping 34 seconds off David Millar's time there. At the second checkpoint Fabian's time was 42 seconds faster than Millar. He swept past Massimo Lipari who had started three minutes before him before storming through the final time-check now 1 minute and 11 seconds clear of David Millar. Hunter Dean, who started two men before Fabian, was staggered to find himself being overtaken by Ducasse. Système Vipère's great rider sprinted for the line. He'd completed the course in a phenomenal 1 hour, 15 minutes and 54 seconds and looked fresh and strong enough to ride the entire 63 kilometres again.

Vasily Jawlensky zipped through the first time-check a second faster than Ducasse. His fluid rhythm, comfortable position, his potent and fresh legs could have seen him swallow seconds with every kilometre. Only he punctured just before the second time-check. It was horrendous bad luck and, though the wheel change had been executed with military efficiency, he forfeited twenty-one seconds to Fabian. Nothing could have foretold nor prevented the unbelievable misfortune of a second puncture 6 kilometres later. This time, the wheel change, though fast, was not smooth and though Vasily willed the bike to perform, something jammed and he skidded to the ground. He flung thousands of dollars' worth of hi-tech machine on to the grass verge and had no option but to resort to a regular road bike for the last 28 kilometres. By the final time-check and with 15 kilometres still to go, he was 59 seconds slower than Ducasse. Though he rode for all he was worth, forcing his body to fold to the ultimate aerodynamic pose, to rebuff the drag of the headwind, to slight the technical demands of the small towns *en route*, Vasily crossed the line 1 minute and 2 seconds behind Fabian Ducasse.

The *salle de presse* roared, some in triumph for Fabian, others in sympathy for Vasily, all in reaction to superb bike riding. Cat looked contemplatively at her screen before answering an expected call from her sisters.

'If tomorrow goes smoothly,' she told them, 'Vasily Jawlensky will win this year's Tour de France. If a mishap befalls him – punctures, a crash – Fabian might just take the *maillot jaune*. You can never discount the danger of the unexpected.'

'Who do you think will win?' Fen asked.

'Who do you *want* to win?' Pip rushed before Cat had answered.

'The thing is,' Cat mused thoughtfully, 'I'd be happy for either rider to win and will mourn for the man who comes second. I'm going to cry tomorrow regardless. Probably throughout the day.'

Pip and Fen had already made a note to have a box of tissues at the ready, alongside the bottle of champagne already chilling in Fen's fridge.

'I can't believe tomorrow is tomorrow,' Cat wailed out loud in the *salle de presse*, 'that it will conclude my Tour de France. That the day after tomorrow, I'll be back in England.'

'You didn't say 'home'.

I can't really.

Are you deluding yourself?

I've never felt so at home as I have here, within this moving world, over these past three weeks. I'm exhausted. But look what's happened to me, see how I've changed, grown.

Good for you, Cat. Well done.

'Fabian is thirty-one seconds behind you,' said Rachel, peeling the skinsuit off Vasily Jawlensky, 'he will not be able to make up thirty-two seconds tomorrow. You are the *maillot jaune* and I'm so proud of you.' Vasily looked at his *soigneur*, and saw straight to the softness she liked to believe her wiry exterior hid from view. Rachel McEwen was one of the most important people in his life. He could not conceive of riding the Tour de France, any race in fact, without her.

Rachel handed her naked rider a pair of tracksuit bottoms and fresh socks. As he took them, their hands brushed and instantaneously their eyes were locked. Vasily made to kiss her and for a suspended moment, Rachel felt her lips yield. But she turned her head consciously and Vasily's mouth touched down on her cheek. His lips parted and confusion swept across his face. Rachel tried to smile kindly. A swift soft sadness clouded his eyes momentarily. He tipped his head to one side. Rachel shook her head, making the gesture meek and small. Vasily physically pulled his body taller by an inch or two.

'Thank you, Rachel,' he said huskily, 'for all that you do for me.'

'Hey,' said Rachel softly but lightly, 'I'm only doing my job.'

She watched her rider leave. It was the closest she had come to seeing true emotion in the man. Not that she knew it, it was the closest anyone had come.

Strong. Solitary. Enigmatic.

'Makes me sad,' Rachel said quietly to herself, 'for him and for the women he will never allow himself.'

Fabian's efforts pleased him on an objective level – it was the best Time Trial he had ever ridden – but frustrated him supremely on an emotional level.

It is still not enough to win the Tour de France.

He couldn't believe it. Reality dawned and he awoke to it as if trapped in a terrible dream.

Last year I said next year. This year I must now say next year. Next year. Le Tour de France. Le maillot jaune. Fabian Ducasse.

'André!' he called down to the mechanic in the hotel car park. André looked up and smiled. Fabian saw that Jules Le Grand was walking towards a team car. 'When you go to fuck the Zucca *soigneur*, sabotage their bikes, hey?'

Jules Le Grand jerked his head. He knew the sabotage part was a joke. But to confirm his suspicions that his mechanic was indeed involved with the *soigneur* of his rival team he found to be no laughing matter.

When André made love tenderly with Rachel later and for a leisurely, mutually gratifying hour and a half, he murmured her name as he came. At much the same time but for a fraction of the duration, Fabian was fucking some fan he had found loitering in the foyer when he went there expressly to prowl. He said nothing when he came. There wasn't anything to say. He hadn't asked her name. Actually, he had. But he hadn't listened to what she had said.

STAGE 20
Disneyland–Paris. 149.5 kilometres

We're getting there, all of us who've experienced this Tour de France on whichever level. We're almost in Paris, the finish line is 149.5 kilometres away. We just have to leave Euro Disney, travel up to Barcy, turn left, drop down, turn right and keep going due west until the outskirts of the exquisite city are upon us. Then we'll head for the hallowed cobbles of the Champs-Elysées, the most beautiful avenue in the world, where the Tour de France has had its grande finale since 1975.

Enter the circuit at the Avenue du Général Lemonnier, race alongside the Tuileries gardens, dash over the Place de la Concorde, whoosh up the Champs-Elysées to the Place Charles de Gaulle, curve round, pelt down the Champs-Elysées, back through the Place de la Concorde, along the Quai des Tuileries before turning to race the 6.5 kilometre lap another nine times. Having already covered 86.5 kilometres. Having previously raced 3,696.8 kilometres.

Cat almost couldn't bear to go to the last *village*, having had a lump in her throat since breakfasting with Josh and Alex that morning. A huge Mickey Mouse hot air balloon smiled inanely over the proceedings and Cat wandered about the *village* trying to absorb absolutely everything for posterity, to concentrate on the infuriating jingles in a bid to lighten the profound emotion enveloping her. She saw the pretty girls at the Coca-Cola marquee crying and hugging all the lithe bronzed Italian *domestiques* who had visited each morning over the past three weeks. She noted how the population of the *village* had swelled with the arrival of wives, girlfriends and families and she regarded them enviously but also with a certain satisfaction.

I've had the boys for three whole weeks. I've experienced it with them. From Vuillard to Le Cap D'Arp, from Valadon to Aix-les-Bains. I've shared their Tour in real time and at first hand.

Having said, 'Enjoy', as she had done recently to riders whom she now knew, and happy for them that finally today they could indeed do so, Cat drove the 30 kilometre *itinéraire direct* with a quiet Josh and a subdued Alex. Paris. *L'arrivée.* A staggering and rather unnerving contrast suddenly completing her three weeks with the peloton. She was used to the Tour de France being the largest entity, the centre of attention, in the places it had visited, enveloping the towns, the landscape and being welcomed and treated like some mammoth VIP. In Paris, it was swallowed up. Even the parking for the *presse* cars was today a far cry from the leafy enclosures near to the finishes, or spacious lots near the *salles de presse*. Today, in Paris, it was a free-for-all in the grim underground car park at the gargantuan Hôtel Concorde Lafayette. In the vast hotel where most of the entourage of the Tour de France, the teams, the officials, the *presse*, would be staying, the *salle de presse* was in a claustrophobic conference room.

There weren't enough cables. There was no complimentary buffet. No welcome. No pampering. Even the signs for the *salle* itself were comparably small against those for the boutiques and restaurants and those directing important businessmen to some convention or other.

Checking in to her room just to dump her bags, Cat noted the minibar, the satellite TV, the toiletries in the bathroom but she craved her beautiful little bedroom at the Auberge Claudette in Bordeaux. She even found herself reminiscing wistfully about featureless motels and insalubrious two-star establishments.

'I'm going to the Champs-Elysées,' Cat told Alex and Josh in the *salle*, bringing them Orangina and chocolate at enormous cost from her minibar.

'You won't see a bloody thing,' Josh warned her, but wondering where she'd set up her laptop anyway.

'You'd be better off staying here,' Alex advised, 'finish the work quick and then party.'

'I'm in *Paris*,' Cat explained, somewhat aghast, 'on the last day of the Tour de France. I can't possibly not walk the streets.' She ignored Alex's predictably raised eyebrow. 'I just want to experience the atmosphere,' she justified. 'If a socket comes free, can you plug me in?'

The atmosphere out on the streets bewildered her and she felt as lost and as small as when she'd first arrived in France. Though it was bringing her full circle, it depressed her. The fact that it was cloudy made yesterday, with all the sunshine, seem very distant. Remember the torrential rain from Pau to Luchon? The sleet on the Galibier? The phenomenal heat from Nantes to Pradier? Remember skinny-dipping in the Atlantic? Sitting and star-gazing at Le Cap D'Arp? When was all of that? This year? Surely not. A dream away. Was it real? Did it actually happen? Was I really there? Can I take it home? Can I come again?

Who are all these people milling about? Where have they been these past three weeks? Where were they when the boys were struggling up lonely Pyrenean passes? Or on monotonous stretches of landscape without even farmers on tractors to wave them on? How many here know what it's like at the Plateau de Boudin? How many stood for hours cheering for the Time Trial at Computaparc?

Why so harsh, Cat?

There are an estimated one million spectators in Paris today.

You should be pleased, they're all here in support of your precious sport.

Look at the throngs! See, the Arc de Triomphe is positively swamped by what look like, to all intents and purposes, football fans. They're rowdy. Urban. Unfamiliar.

How wonderful for the riders to return valiant and battle-sore to such clangorous support.

But most of this lot will only have seen the riders hitherto on television, mostly aerially.

Rather like you, hitherto. So, how lucky they are, then, to be treated to an afternoon with the lycra swarm in the flesh, close enough to smell and touch even.

I'm just feeling out of sorts. I don't want to go home tomorrow.

We know.

I don't see anyone I recognize. It's almost impossible for me to move around. My pass seems redundant. There's no family to belong to here. Just a huge city to contend with. I phoned Ben but we conceded we'd never find each other. I can't wait for tonight, to see him. And yet I'm dreading tonight because it's our last and will bring me within hours of having to say goodbye.

'It's not that I'm not good at goodbyes,' Cat said aloud, tripping over cables as she tried to avoid the crowds by choosing a taxing short cut through the battalion of radio and TV vans, 'it's just I'm not sure what I am saying goodbye to.'

'Cat.'

Cat McCabe stands rooted to the spot.

'Hullo, Cat.'

Her jaw drops and in her mind's eye, the past three weeks shrink rapidly into a tiny ball which is bouncing away, out of sight. Away. And fast. Catch it!

'How's things?'

A man stands before her. Tall. Broad. Relatively good-looking. Objectively speaking. If he's your type. Or Cat's type. It is He Who No Longer Exists. But he obviously does exist as he is here, in the flesh, standing in front of Cat, in Paris.

'Hullo,' he says again.

Still Cat is speechless. And there is no Josh, no Alex, no Rachel, no Ben, no one remotely near to sense her distress and come to her rescue.

'What are you doing here?' she gasps at last, hating her voice, hating the moment, wishing she'd stayed in the *salle de presse*, wishing she'd never come to the Tour de France, wishing He Who Is Standing In Front Of Her, wasn't.

'I was the one who kindled your interest in cycling, remember,' he says lightly. 'I came to watch the race. The grand finale. I came to find you.'

'Me?' Cat says, wondering if he's really here or whether this is some bizarre apparition, and if he really is here, does that mean perhaps the last three weeks never really existed? Was she really a part of the Tour de France?

'Can we talk?' he is saying.

'About?' Cat asks, her eyes flitting around, still seeing no point of reference, no known saviour (and, at a time like this, even Jan Airie would do) anywhere in the vicinity. She is cursing herself that, without her entourage, she suddenly feels so small and timid. Exactly as she was just under a month ago.

'Well,' he says, his voice known so well but making her chill as so often it did, 'I'm glad I came across you.'

Cat's eyes are trained on a large screen relaying pictures of the peloton live.

There's Stefano and Carlos and Vasily, the maillot vert, *the* maillot à pois, *the* maillot jaune, *riding amicably side by side just ahead of the bunch, chatting to the Tour's director Jean Marie LeBlanc who's handing them a glass of champagne from the window of his red Fiat. See them each*

*have a celebratory if abstemious sip. In the 1960s, when the
Tour passed through towns, the riders would leap from their
bikes and rampage through bars, grabbing people's drinks
regardless of what they were, food from plates, anything that
could be eaten or imbibed. It was an honour to have a Tour
cyclist snatch your refreshments. The bar owners would
then send the bills to the Tour organizers. Shit, but I'm going
off on dreamy tangents to escape from the situation in hand.
That He is here. Fuck, I've capitalized him. I'd rather watch
the big screen though.*

'Cat?'

'Um?'

'I was on for a Hollywood-style reunion. I'm out here after
all – hoping my gesture speaks a thousand words.'

'What?'

*No! Don't step towards me. Don't look at me longingly,
lovingly. Don't let me go back. Don't make me. Don't be the
person who says 'See! It was all a dream'.*

'Let's give it another go.'

'No!'

The vehemence of Cat's response staggers both of them.

'Are you shagging someone else, then?' he asks, pulling
himself upright and fixing her with the familiar look that can
instantly make her shudder and shrink and her blood chill.

'I have to work,' she pleads.

*I have to run! Go forwards to what I now know and believe
in. Not tiptoe backwards.*

'Where are you staying?'

I can't believe I've just told him. Walk away.

'And you're working there too?'

I can't believe I've just nodded. Run.

'I'll come by later. We'll talk. Try to sort things out. OK?'

And he's going. And Cat is swaying on the spot, unable to
keep tears at bay. She lets them fall but fixes her gaze on the
large screen as if watching the beautiful sport of cycling is
the sole provenance of her emotion.

*

'Jesus!' Alex exclaimed when Cat returned to the *salle de presse*. 'You told us you'd be emotional but you didn't warn us what it would do to your face.'

Josh tipped his head and regarded her. 'There aren't even any cyclists on the Champs-Elysées yet,' he reasoned, instinctively sensing that Cat was in some kind of torment. 'See, they're arriving just now. Cool! Chris Boardman is off the front.' Cat stared at the screen, lips aquiver, whilst her two colleagues observed her and winced at their impotence to do absolutely anything about her tangible distress. Josh knew that if he put out the supportive hand he so wanted to, Cat would possibly fall to pieces.

'Have you seen that thing down the corridor?' he asked instead, manipulatively ambiguous, voice easy. She shook her head a little more slowly than her body was shaking.

'You must see it, come on, I'll take you there.'

Obediently, Cat followed Josh. Tactfully, Alex stayed put and stared witheringly at any of the press men daring to stare.

Josh walked ahead of her before stopping just after the corridor turned a corner. He gave thanks for the fact that no one was around. He faced her, his head tipped gently to one side. His eyes implored her to trust him. And how she did. Josh Piper. Her colleague. Her friend. This time tomorrow he'd be on the opposite side of London to her.

'Josh,' she croaked.

'There there,' Josh soothed, having chosen those precise words with utmost care, 'what's up?'

'What am I going to do,' she whispered, 'without you, without all of this?'

'You'll have it again in Spain,' Josh encouraged, 'at the Vuelta.'

'But I haven't heard from *Maillot*,' Cat said, knowing that she was straying away from confiding the true reason for her distress. She sniffed and snorted, gave a little cough and dabbed her tongue against the mix of tears and snot forming a viscous moustache. Josh tucked her hair behind her ear, a touching gesture which made her feel safe. 'It's not *Maillot*,' she said very slowly, 'it's Him.'

'Who?' Josh asked, because why ever would he consider that Cat's ex-boyfriend, from whom she'd come to the Tour hoping to recuperate, from whom she truly thought she had moved on, was currently in Paris and intruding into the depths of her being, jeopardizing the confidence and security she had recently found.

'Who No Longer Exists,' Cat said quietly, 'Him.'

Josh faltered, this was not what he was expecting and he felt rather ill-equipped to help. 'Jesus,' he said, 'what does *he* want?'

'Me,' Cat shrugged.

All Josh really knew about the man was that he had hurt Cat very deeply. 'How do *you* feel?' he asked measuredly.

'Bewildered,' Cat defined.

Josh regarded her. Much as he liked Ben, he knew what he had to ask next. 'Do you want him?'

After a loaded pause, Cat shoot her head slowly. 'No,' she said, 'but he's here and he's an obstruction.'

Josh frowned.

'He's a horrible symbol of very unhappy times, and a harbinger of back home,' she continued. 'Though the last few months were terrible – communication was impossible – and the final throes were quite vicious, I had *five years* with him and did love him very much.' She looked out of the window. Paris. A little overcast. They'll be on the Champs-Elysées now.

'Still?' Josh asked.

'Once,' Cat replied. She was speaking clearly if softly. 'Eventually, the reason for us to be together, all the elements that once were so loved, were simply no longer known. I was wrong for him. He was increasingly mean to me. I was clinging to all that had been and, in an ideal world, all that we'd hoped for. He wanted out. I was so low I was convinced an unhappy life with him was preferable to all the uncertainties I'd face in a life on my own.'

'Your self-esteem was decimated,' Josh said.

Cat snorted. Then she was still. Finally she nodded. 'When someone scolds you enough, you end up believing it.'

'And yet you're confused now you've seen him again?'

Cat shrugged. 'He's come to find me. There were good times.'

'Do you love him still?'

'I love still the idea of it all.'

'Ben?' Josh asked, a tiny thought zipping into his mind that poor Ben might have been but rebound fodder.

'I am in love with Ben,' Cat declared. 'For me, he symbolizes everything that my future should be about. Through him, I got my bounce back.' She sighed. 'It's just my past isn't merely haunting me today, it has thrust itself across the path of my journey forward.'

Her eyes darted and she reached for Josh's shirt, giving it an absent-minded tug. 'My strength feels sapped,' she said, 'my mind is in a knot.'

'Don't let him do this to you,' Josh said fairly sternly, pressing for a lift which he didn't want, 'you owe it to yourself. And us.'

Cat nodded for Josh while her brow twitched for herself. 'Ben?' she whispered. 'Ought I to pull back now?'

'Pull *back*?' Josh said, amazed. 'From Ben? Why would you want to do that?'

'I have to meet him tonight,' Cat said, oily tears smudging her eyes.

'Ben?'

'No. Him.'

A lift arrived, its doors sweeping open, and Josh and Cat automatically entered.

'*Not* pulling back carries great risks,' Cat explained whilst Josh selected the fifteenth floor for some unknown but uncontested reason. 'If I don't pull out,' Cat said softly but lucidly, 'I lay myself bare to even the possibility of future hurt. That, for me, is reason enough.'

'Cat McCabe,' said Josh, leaning against the wall of the lift, 'you are way too strong to be so appallingly feeble. Don't pull out. I don't want you to. It would be very, very wrong. Ben is a lovely guy and he adores you. You would jeopardize so much if you don't go for it.' He watched her concentrating on the buttons of the floors, could sense that she was fighting tears. 'What exactly would you achieve?' Josh posed. Cat gave him no answer so he gave her the only one possible. 'Big bloody deal,' he said, 'that on your deathbed, aged ninety-seven or whatever, you could concede that you made it through the rest of your life never having been hurt again.' He gave her a gentle punch on the shoulder. 'You have too much to give – and with your generosity, your great propensity for friendship and love, it's inevitable that you draw people to you and that you'll receive back what you provide.'

The lift arrived at the requested floor. Josh and Cat stood stationary, regarding the corridor on view. The doors closed by themselves, as if misuse was an occupational hazard. Cat sucked her bottom lip thoughtfully and then pressed for the floor from which they'd come. She looked at Josh a little bashfully.

'I know,' she whispered, 'I wouldn't feel vulnerable if I wasn't involved. The fact that I'm involved, unequivocally, is alternately exhilarating and absolutely terrifying. Ben will be so far away. Missing him is going to hurt.'

'Well,' Josh said measuredly, 'I can't see your dilemma. Someone in love with you but far away. Someone who was mean to you but is near by.'

'*Near by*?' Cat whispered. 'He's in fucking *Paris*.' Alarm criss-crossed her face. 'Today. He wants me this evening.'

'Fuck him,' said Josh, ushering her out of the lift lest they should find themselves next stop in the bowels of the hotel via the lift with a mind of its own. 'You're coming out with us,' Josh ordered, 'it's our last night too. Do you think we're happy about having to let you go? About the end of a phenomenal three weeks? Another memorable Tour de France?'

'I have to feel good about my past if I'm to greet the future,' Cat said, 'maybe I need closure.'

'You sound like Oprah fucking Winfrey,' Josh said.

'Of course I'd rather he wasn't here,' Cat said, just before they arrived at the *salle de presse*, 'but he is and I'm having to deal with it. There must be a reason. I don't know what. I'm terrified about seeing him tonight. But I have to. Will I be OK?'

'If you're not, there's a posse of us who will gladly deck the bastard,' Josh said. His triteness, blended with affection, making Cat smile at last. 'Now, *journaliste* McCabe, you have your final report to write. Here – blow.' Josh held out a handkerchief and dutifully, Cat blew her nose sonorously into it. Unflinchingly, Josh tucked it, sodden, back into his pocket. He had loads of washing to take home tomorrow as it was. And anyway, it's one friend's duty to wipe away the tears of another.

Rachel McEwen was at the team vehicles in the Place de la Concorde, using half her brain to double-check she had plenty of everything whilst using the other half to make lists of items to audit, order and pack in the coming weeks of racing. She was aware that someone stood near by, watching her, but she was used to this and presumed it to be a fan hopeful of a free baseball cap or bidon. When her name was breathed huskily, with the 'R' rolled around leisurely at the back of the throat, the 'l' licked from tongue to teeth, she knew instinctively to whom the voice belonged.

'Monsieur Le Grand,' she said courteously, '*ça va?*'

'*Bien*. Jules – please,' he replied, swiping away the sides of his jacket as he slipped his hands into his trouser pockets. 'I have something for you, Rachel,' he said with great mystery, savouring her name on his tongue as if it was an oyster. From one pocket, he brought out a small package and gave it to Rachel, coming close within her personal space and changing the air around her from heavy with embrocation to scented with an inordinate amount of Gucci aftershave.

'For me?' Rachel asked, wondering what and why.

'Open,' he commanded, his eyes fixed on the package, 'please.'

His gift, rather predictably, was Chanel Eau de Parfum. An ostentatiously large bottle. 'Call it a bribe,' he shrugged, 'but I want you to come and work for me, for Système Vipère. I make you this offer because I respect you as a *soigneur*. I give you this gift because I respect you as a woman.'

Och, what a load of tosh, Rachel thought to herself whilst smiling sweetly out loud, *wait till I tell Cat*.

'Jules,' she said, 'I don't know what to say.'

'Shh,' he said on the verge of seductively placing his index finger against Rachel's lips, which parted flabbergasted whilst her eyes danced in disbelief. 'Just consider it.'

With that he was gone. But he'd been gone from the Système Vipère vehicles long enough for the Zucca *directeur* and chief mechanic to have paid a visit to André Ferrette. They did not flatter him with expensive scent or guttural overtones. They merely reasoned that, as he and their *soigneur* were now an item, wouldn't it be great for everyone concerned if he came over to work for Zucca MV?

The last laps of the Champs-Elysées. The last minutes of the race. The closing metres of the Tour de France. The peloton stream around the circuit wowing the crowds. The pace is fast and during the laps opportunists regularly pelt off the front, driving the crowds wild in the process. Though the likelihood of a Stage win by such riders, from so far out, is minuscule, the attention they attract curries great favour with their sponsors too, most of them ensconced in VIP enclosures.

With three laps to go, Hunter Dean from US Megapac pumps away from the bunch not just to taste glory and do his sponsor proud, but to savour precisely where he is and where he has been and just what he has achieved to be here, on heaven's cobbled paving of the Champs-Elysées, ahead of the peloton of the Tour de France. Three weeks ago, the crowds at Delaunay Le Beau had sent him on his way; a superfit rider with a golden tan, hope in his legs and a goal in his soul. The crowds in Paris welcome him home; a rider unfathomably fit, his face thinner, his limbs more sinewy, lighter by a fair few kilos, intensely bronzed if slightly grimy from the city streets. The hope in his legs and the goal in his soul have been tested to the limit but the self-belief that continues to pump through his system with every beat of his heart is what ultimately has brought him here. As he cycles in front of the bunch, he wants to cry. He can't wait to be on his knees, kissing the cobbles; an image he has called upon frequently over the past three weeks when his body threatened to give up and his mind said no way, no more, I can't. You can, Hunter, you did.

If L'Alpe D'Huez is mecca for the *grimpeurs*, the climbers, then the Champs-Elysées is the equivalent for the sprinters. Consequently, Carlos Jesu Velasquez rides along safe in the centre of the bunch, hissing and clicking in the polka dot jersey. Massimo Lipari rides nearby, bolstered by the fact that he is as much a hero for being vanquished as he would be were he wearing polka dots. There will be many people waiting for him at home, there will be a party in the local bar where the world will be put to rights and the Tour de France rerun to the outcome they would have preferred. And there will be plenty of *signorine* to soothe him, who will be desperate to stroke his ego and caress his brave body. A woman at the start this morning had touched his shaved chin and made wonderful innuendos about bare cheeks.

Into the penultimate lap, the sprinters' teams start to organize themselves. Stefano Sassetta seeks out Jesper Lomers and cycles silently alongside him. The riders regard each other. Jesper nods. Stefano nods too. Then Jesper's congenial smile is countered by Stefano's huge and affable grin. The Dutchman congratulates the Italian *maillot vert*.

'Next year I have to fight hard, hey? To keep it?' Stefano says reverentially, whistling and shaking his head at the prophesied effort of it all again.

'He wins it who deserves it,' Jesper replies with equanimity.

Stefano nods and places his hand between Jesper's shoulder blades. 'I may have the green jersey,' he says, 'but if you are crowned the most beautiful thighs of the peloton again, I will fucking kill you!'

Jesper laughs. He loves all this. The camaraderie. This family. This burgeoning sense of euphoria and relief that has been earned tenfold from the effort of the last three weeks. 'Let's race,' he says, allowing his lead-out men to guide him through the bunch.

Vasily Jawlensky and Fabian Ducasse ride side by side in truce and mutual respect. Vasily is about to win the Tour de France by a paltry 31 seconds. He ensures Fabian rides a wheel ahead, that he rides a pedal turn behind. Fabian accepts the gesture with good grace. They don't fight for the final line, they cross it together, a photofinish of the two greatest professional road-race cyclists in the world. Their *soigneurs* are soon upon them, skipping wet flannels up and down their bodies, but the two men just want to hug each other silently right there in the centre of the media scrum; regardless of how this impedes their *soigneurs'* jobs, blind to the barrage of photographers, deaf to the *presse* firing questions in various languages. Vasily Jawlensky has won the Tour de France, having cycled 3,761.8 kilometres in twenty days, in 91 hours 27 minutes and 44 seconds. Fabian Ducasse took a second over half a minute longer. The Lantern Rouge of the Tour cycled for an extra 3 hours 2 minutes and 39 seconds.

Did Cat cry when Stuart O'Grady took the final Stage win just ahead of Stefano Sassetta and Robbie McEwen? Did she cry when Vasily and Stefano and Carlos Jesu took to the podium? Did she cry when the riders cycled in their teams a final lap of honour? Did she cry when the TV monitors in the *salle de presse* were dismantled for the last time? Did she cry when she was handed the final sheets of race results? Did she cry when she placed the last full stop at the end of her final report for the *Guardian*? What do you think?

She's dried her eyes, washed her face and donned sunglasses for the sake of anyone who might catch a fright when catching sight of her. She goes to the foyer to check on Ben's room number. She doesn't need to. He's there and, joy of joy, so is Luca.

'The Babe!' Luca proclaims, looking far odder for his jeans, trainers and denim shirt than he does for having his arm in a sling.

'Come to the Megapac dinner,' Ben suggests, 'Mitch would love you to be there.'

'I can't,' Cat white lies, 'I ought to convene with my own team, the press gang.'

'Later, then,' says Ben.

'Of course,' Cat replies, feeling how Ben makes her bubble, remembering how the other man made her flat. It seemed extraordinary, therefore, that she was to forsake the one in favour of the other tonight.

'You dance with me later, *Gatto*?' Luca asks.

'Of course,' Cat assures him.

It's 10 p.m. Josh and Alex can't find her. She isn't in her room and her mobile phone is switched off. Ben says, I thought she was with you. The boys say, we thought she'd be with you. No, haven't seen her. No, don't know where she is. Leave a note under her door. She's probably gone for a stroll. Gone to be self-indulgently metaphysical amidst the debris on the Champs-Elysées which is all that remains of the Tour de France. Yes, that sounds like Cat McCabe.

Only she isn't on the Champs-Elysées. She's nowhere near anywhere the cyclists' wheels have been. I don't know where she is. I can guess. But she's permitting no access. No laminated pass can provide entry. No eavesdropping allowed. She wants no interference. She doesn't need me. She needs privacy. We can give her that. She's entitled. We trust her. We know she's strong enough.

'Where the fuck have you been?' Alex, pretty pissed, demands jovially when Cat turns up an hour later, at the infamous James Joyce pub just a stone's throw from the Concorde Lafayette hotel. She gives Alex a friendly whack. She stands still. Takes stock of where she is. Takes a deep breath.

'I need a drink,' she says.

Alex goes to the bar and Cat turns to Josh. 'It was tough,' she says, 'I left before pudding. It's good to be back.' Josh nods, Alex returns and while he rambles on, Cat looks around her. Phil Liggett and Paul Sherwen are supping pints. She sees Rachel and André sitting on bar stools, heads close, his hand on her knee, her hand over his, Rachel talking animatedly, André listening attentively. They suit each other. In some ways, they hold a mirror to Cat; being thrilled for her friend is being happy for herself too.

My God, it's Greg LeMond. Alex has great pleasure in introducing Cat to the legendary American three-times Tour winner, still the same fresh-faced bright blue-eyed boy whom she has revered for years. The decibel level is as high as people's spirits, the Guinness is as rich as the experiences being recounted. Laughter flows with the conversation, warmth envelops the proceedings. Luca and Ben turn up soon after and Cat whiles away the night until the early hours; the morning of the day when she will leave France, leave all of this, all of them, to return home.

She and Ben go to bed at 4 a.m., rather drunk and absolutely exhausted. They don't have sex. They can't keep their eyes open. They're too tired. Like everyone else who, in whatever capacity, has done this year's Tour de France.

DAY 27. MONDAY

Cat McCabe

Here she is. On the ferry. Was it only three and a half weeks ago that she clung to the railings, dreading the white cliffs of Dover disappearing from view and the great unknown unfolding before her? She is scorning the direction of travel to gaze wistfully at France, longing the land mass to remain in view. Oh, to time-travel backwards. That it all could be starting again.

Alex and Josh, where are they?

They're down in the bar, of course.

And Rachel?

She'll be on the road, driving the truck, everything shipshape and in order.

And Ben?

He's just phoned.

But where is he?

At the airport, accompanying Luca to the specialist in Colorado.

And the other riders?

Some will take a few days' respite from competition to train, of course. Others go headlong in to a round of Criterium races where, as heroes of the Tour de France, they're paid a sizeable start fee. August is a month full of Classics, of World Cup rounds. And then, of course, the grand tour of Spain, the Vuelta, in just under five weeks' time.

Will you be covering it?

I hope so.

For whom?

Well, Andy at Maillot *has suggested a strategy meeting. Tomorrow, in fact, though I really can't afford to hold my breath for the Features Editorship. My credit card bill is enormous. However, Jeremy Whittle has come up trumps and wants me to report the Vuelta for* Sportsworld's *website. That'll just about cover my expenses. Hopefully by then I might have a couple of freelance commissions. But you know, to be affiliated to the world of the peloton is riches enough for me.*

Who's meeting you at Victoria station?

I haven't told anyone what time I'll be home. I think it's important I make my return journey by myself.

I think it's important that you walk to the bow of the ferry, to bravely await the sight of the white cliffs of Dover.

Ben York

Ben sits in the departure lounge at Charles de Gaulle airport. Luca is milling about, delighted when anyone approaches him for an autograph or to commiserate on his bad fortune.

I had to say goodbye to Cat this morning.

You did?

It wasn't easy. It's been a phenomenally all-encompassing month.

Did you tell her how you love her?

Hearing it out loud, and hearing it back – I found it intensely emotional.

'Ben, look at this – fucking fabulous, hey?'

Luca has bought a lighter in the shape of the Eiffel Tower which plays the 'Marseillaise' when activated.

'But you don't smoke,' Ben laughs.

'But *look*,' he stresses, brandishing his acquisition, 'listen!' Luca sits alongside his doctor, frustrated that, though he is no longer in pain, he is still trussed up and out of action. He regards Ben. 'So,' he says. Ben looks at him. Shrugs and nods.

'It was some Tour, Jonesy,' says Ben, 'huge.'

'The Babe McCabe,' Luca muses, striking his lighter on and off, never for long enough to move beyond the opening bars of the French National Anthem. Ben nods. 'You're good together,' Luca says whilst nodding and humming thoughtfully. Ben looks away. 'You see her some more?' Luca asks. 'I hope so. You two should – you know? It would be a waste not being together.'

'Yup,' Ben says, looking around the departure hall, looking intently at the seam of his trousers, at Luca's hands fiddling with the lighter. 'She's quite something and she lives the other side of the Atlantic Ocean to me. But she's what I want.'

'And I always gets what I wants,' says Luca in distorted American. He regards Ben. 'Can it work? With your schedules? Your time zones?'

Ben falls silent. 'I hope so,' he says earnestly, 'I really do.'

'This month will shoot by,' Luca says encouragingly, 'before you know it – bam! The Vuelta. Give her a call,' he suggests, offering his mobile phone for the purpose.

'I just have,' says Ben, longing to hear her voice again, torturing himself with the vivid memory of the now unattainable reality of what going to sleep and then waking up alongside Cat is like.

Josh Piper, Catriona McCabe and Alex Fletcher
Josh spies Cat standing by the railings at the bow of the ferry. He can just about make out a glimpse of Britain.

'Hullo,' he says, drawing alongside, eyes tight shut against the buffeting wind.

412

'Hullo,' Cat says, turning her back on the sea to open her eyes and face the deck.

'Shall we drive *avant* or *arrière* today?' Josh asks.

'Well, I need to hang around the *village*,' Cat muses, 'I want to speak to Stuart O'Grady and Jay Sweet.'

'We'll go *arrière* then,' Josh decrees.

'OK,' Cat says brightly. 'I wonder what the *presse* buffet will provide us with today.'

'If it's crap,' Josh reasons, 'we can abuse my expense account and go for a blow-out dinner when we've finished our reports. A few bottles of *Seize* beforehand.'

'OK,' says Cat.

'What are you doing on the 7th?' Josh asks.

'Isn't that the San Sebastian Classic?' Cat responds.

'Well, I was thinking more along the lines of dinner at mine – meet my wife.'

'And reminisce?' Cat asks.

'Absolutely,' Josh confirms.

'It's a date,' Cat says.

They share the affable silence that is true testimony of good friendship. After a while, Cat turns to Josh. 'Yesterday,' she says quietly, 'was bizarre.'

'You'd never have known from the quality of your report,' says Josh, a rolled-up copy of the *Guardian* in his back pocket, 'your piece was great.'

'My final paragraph,' Cat elucidates, 'my last full stop – rather than bringing matters to a close, it flung the doors of my life hereafter wide open.'

'You have *so* much ahead of you,' Josh stresses.

'I know that now – unequivocally. But the realization would not have transpired so soon had he not turned up. I was finally able to conclude that chapter of my life, put the last full stop in place. Now I have a clean, fresh page. It's a little daunting but quite exciting too.'

'Did he want you back?' Josh probes.

'What if he did?' Cat replies. 'I don't know where my future will take me but I now know very clearly what I don't want. As I packed my rucksack one final time last night, I actually did some unpacking too. Things I don't need for my journey, things that were weighing me down.'

'That was then and this is now,' Josh defines. 'You know, Cat,' he continues, thinking himself very Oprah fucking Winfrey, 'we're often at our strongest when we decide to take risks — because we're ready and confident to tackle whatever the outcome will be.'

'You know something, Josh?' Cat responds. 'I feel blessed with that strength now.'

'I feel seasick,' moans Alex, joining them. 'Great hairstyle, Cat. Fuck me! We're almost home.'

'About ten minutes from docking,' Josh estimates, scouring the horizon and the land mass like an old sea dog. 'What are you doing on the 7th, Alex?'

'It's the San Sebastian Classic, isn't it?' Alex says.

'Or dinner round mine,' says Josh.

'Cool,' says Alex. 'Are you going to be there, Cat?'

'Most certainly,' says Cat.

'Cool,' says Alex.

Cat links arms with her colleagues and they prepare to disembark back on to English soil.

OCTOBER
Paris. The launch of next year's Tour de France

*C*at took the Eurostar from Waterloo to Paris the day before the launch and was booked to come back the day after it. Josh and Alex were travelling the next morning, making it a day trip. Though a train journey with them would have been fun and would have passed swiftly, Cat was thankful that she was alone even if the minutes seemed insufferably long. Ben was to meet her at Gard du Nord. She hadn't seen him since the Vuelta finished twenty-two days ago, a period of time the same length as a Tour de France and the trial of it just as arduous. And now she was on a train rumbling under the Channel towards three days and two nights with her beau. Paris couldn't come quick enough.

Though Cat and Ben, to each other, their friends and family, constantly rue the fact that they live thousands of miles apart, their relationship has blossomed and, with it, the fortunes of their respective telecommunications companies and postal services. Ben managed a stopover at Heathrow airport a week after the Tour de France ended and then they had twenty-five days together in Spain. With the *salle de presse* of the Vuelta being a quarter of the size of the

Tour de France, the pressures were much less too and Cat and Ben were able to indulge in each other's company. Luca had loved his profile written by Cat for *Pedal Power*. More to the point, so had Jeremy Whittle who had praised her, paid her handsomely and commissioned a daily website from her during the Vuelta. She still doesn't know if she will be Features Editor at *Maillot* but she should find out at the launch tomorrow.

During the Vuelta, Luca won two consecutive Stages and ensured he rubbed his collar bone theatrically, accidentally on purpose, when giving interviews at the finishes and for the benefit of his fans watching coverage on TV. He had become a hugely popular and well-known figure in the peloton. Press and fans and riders alike were interested that, next season, he was to be a Viper Boy. Fabian Ducasse won the Vuelta and, the week before last, the World Championship Time Trial too. Vasily Jawlensky came second. Last week, Lance Armstrong won the World Championship Road Race. Vasily Jawlensky came second. But the season will end with the great Russian's name still foremost on everybody's lips and it is his image which remains imprinted on everyone's memory of the season: the reigning *maillot jaune* of the Tour de France.

So how are you, Cat?

I'm fine. I'm happy. I'm broke. My train ticket is an early birthday present from Fen and Pip. Django has just paid off my phone bill. I'm twenty minutes from the Gard du Nord and the arms of Ben York. I feel like an excited, lovestruck teenager. It's a wonderful sensation and it doesn't dissipate in the slightest the deeper I get to know him.

So we're talking love, then?

Good God, yes.

The train trundles in to Gard du Nord and, with her stomach aflutter, her adrenal gland in overdrive and her heart evidently beating twenty to the dozen at the base of her throat, Cat disembarks and weaves her way up the platform. And there he is. She's never seen him in a thick jumper and she's struck by how very lovely he looks. All he can see is the girl he loves beaming at him. She's had a haircut, he notices, and she looks gorgeous. She looks robustly feminine with her healthy glow and assertive stride. He can't wait to kiss her, to whisk her away to the bohemian but rather luxurious hotel he has found for her on the rue de Buci in the heart of the Latin Quarter. He's about to say hullo, to take her bag, to tell her that they'll take a taxi but he can't squeeze out even a word because she has plugged his mouth with kisses. Never let you go. Missed you very, very much. Want you so badly.

In the Parisian rush hour, they gaze out of the cab windows at the city, whilst entwining their fingers together. Polite conversation is a necessity to curb their overwhelming desire to strip each other naked and ravish each other immediately.

'How's Luca?' Cat enquires. 'Did he send me his love?'

'Shit,' Ben gasps, 'I almost forgot, these are for you.' He cups her head in his hand and kisses each cheek in turn, twice over. 'They're from Luca for *Gatto* McCabe. Did I tell you he now sports a goatee beard and a pony-tail?'

'Does it suit him?'

'Judging by the amount of fan mail he receives, yes it does. How's Rachel?' Ben asks. 'What's her news?'

'She and André kipped at mine for a night last week,' Cat tells him. 'I phoned Jeremy Whittle last week, pitching an idea for a feature on Rachel – it's an excuse really, to have an expenses-paid weekend with her!'

'And?'

'Jez likes the idea.'

'She's still with André, then?'

'Oh, very much so. They went to their *directeurs* and told them that unless they accepted their relationship and allowed them to keep their respective jobs at Zucca MV and Système Vipère, they'd both leave and work for the Deutsche Telekom team instead.'

'That's some ultimatum,' Ben laughs, 'good for them. I'm

glad they're going strong, I like them both individually and they make a great couple.' Automatically, he squeezes Cat's hand and she knots her fingers frenetically to his. 'How about Fen,' Ben asks, 'has she made a decision? Is she now a one-man woman, so to speak?'

'She's fine,' Cat smiles, 'and yes, she made the decision – kept everyone guessing right till the very end.'

'And Pip?' Ben enquires.

'Pip's life is suddenly rather glamorous,' Cat tells him. 'In fact, she's been flown out to some tiny, luxury Caribbean island. But it's a long story and see – we've just crossed the river.'

'And Django, whom I've yet to meet?'

'Django, who's desperate to meet you, is fine. You'll meet at New Year. We all had a fabulous weekend up in Derbyshire. You're going to love it. Are we there yet? Soon?'

'Here's rue de Buci. And Josh and Alex?' Ben asks. 'What's their news?'

'Can we talk about them later?' Cat requests, already heading towards reception.

Both Cat and Ben had survived the previous few days on a frequent, semi-sustaining diet of envisaging lengthy fore-play and meaningful looks and long, leisurely lovemaking. However, because both had subsisted the last three weeks on memories of their past couplings and prophecies of those future; because they had frequently gone to bed alone craving each other and masturbating in honour of each other, now in Paris, in their hotel room, they all but tore their clothing off and fell to the bed, kissing wildly, their eyes closed with the exquisite pleasure of it all. Running hands just the once up and over one another's bodies was enough to have Ben as hard as he'd ever be and Cat as juiced and expectant likewise.

'Stop, stop, stop,' Ben gasped trying to still Cat's hips from gyrating him to premature orgasm. He flipped her over, pulling her on top and she sat astride him; only he had to close his eyes because the very sight of her could make him come against his wishes. They didn't stay in one position for very long because they were desperate to re-explore each other from every angle imagined and imaginable.

Lying on their sides with Ben taking her from behind, it was suddenly Cat imploring Ben to stop, stop, stop. They lay motionless, Ben feeling the vivid pulsations of Cat's sex sucking his cock deep into her, immensely turned on by hearing her gasp, her voice breaking through. He rolled her on to her stomach and lay himself on top of her, bucking up inside her deep and strong. He took his hands underneath her, burrowing his fingers between the lips of her sex to rub and twitch her clitoris. Cat was climaxing again and soon enough Ben was coming with her. He'd been on the point of orgasm since first entering her and it welled from the pit of his stomach before shifting down to the centre of his balls, zooming up his cock and firing out into the musky, hot welcoming darkness of deep inside Cat. It was a taste in his mouth, a scent in his nose. It was explosive. He could have passed out. Instead, they went out for a light supper and light conversation, drank much red wine and returned to their room to make love leisurely as they'd long envisaged.

'I do so love you,' Ben murmured to her, having locked eyes with her the whole session through.

'And I do you,' Cat responded.

'I love it that sex between us can be either romantic lovemaking, all sensitive and sensual, or else we fuck each other's brains out,' Ben defines. 'It's good to feel so comfortable with someone.'

'I love it that, whether making love or shagging each other senseless, post orgasm we frequently talk about some fine point of cycle sport,' Cat muses.

Paris dawned bright, cloudless and absolutely freezing cold. Ben and Cat strolled through the courtyards of the Louvre, through the Tuileries gardens to the Place de la Concorde before catching a cab up to Porte Maillot, to the Palais des Congrès de Paris for the launch of next year's

Tour de France. The foyer was packed. For Cat, it was like a family reunion and she wove her way through the throng, hugging and kissing and beaming at everyone; greeting people whom she had known previously by face alone but as if they were established close friends. The expansive grin that she wore, her face full of light and colour, contrasted with her sober black poloneck, black skirt of demure length, opaque black tights and black pumps. 'I'm working!' she had protested to a lengthy wolf whistle and a theatrical salute from Ben when she had dressed that morning. 'I'm a *journaliste*, remember.'

Is it seemly that a member of the press corps, one who hopes for recognition and respect, should then scurry around collecting posters and goodie bags and swiping the branded anti-macassars from the seats?

But everyone does. See! Look at Josh, he's asking Vasily Jawlensky for his autograph. And Alex has taken three copies of one poster. Those who follow this fabulous sport do so because they are passionate about pro cycling. We are fans foremost, the luckiest, most blessed of all supporters of the sport, for we are paid to indulge our love for it.

'Ms McCabe, hullo.'

It was Jeremy Whittle from *Sportsworld*.

'Hullo,' she replied, shaking his hand warmly, 'you know Ben, don't you?'

'Of course,' Jeremy replied, giving the doctor a congenial slap.

'How are you, Jez?' Ben said.

'I'm fine – but I want to talk business with Cat before the presentation starts.'

'I've spoken to Rachel McEwen about a profile,' Cat enthuses, 'and can I do one on Biarritz – many young riders are choosing it as their base? And I thought, how about a physiological cross comparison of Vasily and Fabian – their resting heartbeats, height, weight, VO2 max?'

'They sound great,' Jez said, 'and as Assistant Editor of *Pedal Power*, you can write whatever you like, really.'

'Please could I do Paris–Nice for you?' Cat continued, Jez's statement way too enormous to even hear, let alone contemplate.

'As Assistant Editor of *Pedal Power*, you would be expected to attend,' Jez tried again. It is a squeeze around her waist from Ben that jolts Cat into listening, absorbing and at once trying to fathom just what Mr Whittle means.

'Pardon?' Cat tries. 'Assistant Editor? Of *Pedal Power*? Who?'

'You,' Jez laughs, 'you'd be brilliant. It would mean moving to the States, of course.'

'Me?' Cat mouthed.

Jez nodded. 'We'll talk about salaries and the job spec after the presentation.' He placed his hand on her shoulder. 'Close your mouth, Cat,' he said affectionately before walking away.

'Morning, Cat,' said Andy Sutcliffe from *Maillot*. All Cat could do was nod and try to command her brain to close her mouth. 'Thanks for your e-mail,' Andy was continuing, 'I'd love to have you and I can provide you with a few perks too. The Features Editorship is yours, Cat. Shall we discuss it after the presentation?' Away he went.

Bloody hell, Cat. Two job offers within five minutes. The opportunity to move to the same country as Ben. By the chasm of your dropped jaw, I'd say you are positively gobsmacked. What are your immediate instincts? What do you think you'll do? We know what Ben would say. But what about Fen and Pip and Django? So much food for thought you'll get indigestion. But you have this time in Paris to muse. And whatever decision you make, the army of people who love you so, will furnish you with their support and best wishes.

I can't think about any of this now. I must go – the presentation is about to start.

Guess who has a large lump in her throat when footage of the recent Tour de France is beamed on huge screens?

The unveiling of the route for next year's Tour de France reveals a clockwise *grande boucle* with a sortie into Italy. Alps first, then Pyrenees. A whopping 3,850 kilometres. Twenty-one teams of nine riders will be invited to compete for the *maillot à pois*, the *maillot vert* and of course the golden fleece itself, the *maillot jaune*. Of the peloton, there will only be three or four serious contenders for overall victory and yet 189 riders will race their hearts out. Mont Ventoux. A Time Trial at Futuroscope. A Stage finish in Bordeaux. Cat has whispered to Josh that they simply must stay at Auberge Claudette, that she will book ahead next week.

Jules Le Grand, top to toe in Armani, sockless even in October, still tanned even in October, is in the audience with some of his riders and dignitaries from Système Vipère's sponsors. He glances across to the Zucca MV *directeur*. His gaze is returned. Steadily. The gauntlet is thrown down. Fabian Ducasse is already planning how and when he will launch his offensive to claim the yellow jersey for himself, for the glory of Système Vipère, for the pride of his country whose great race this is.

Having now seen the route, Ben York is devising and revising training schedules with the Megapac *directeur*. Megapac won't be a wildcard team next year. They have had a fabulous season and will be one of the sixteen teams automatically entitled to race. Rachel McEwen has requested that the route be faxed to her at the Zucca MV headquarters as soon as possible. Ever keen and conscientious, she wants to start making lists already.

It might just as well be July right now for Cat McCabe. She is already there, in her mind's eye, travelling through some of the most stunning parts of France following a bunch of brave boys on bikes. She is under no illusions that it won't be at times exhausting, stressful; often physically uncomfortable what with the heat, freak cold and an infernal selection of two-star motels. Her diet will be lousy. But if she stays off the brie and baguette from now till next July, she might just tolerate it on a daily basis for three weeks.

Cat McCabe can hardly wait. So many of her good friends will be there. Rachel to gossip with, Alex to be teased by, Josh always looking out for her. Maybe Fen and Pip will visit again, they might even bring Django this time. And of course Ben will be there, snatching time with her whenever possible, sharing beds that are often rickety, or too small or, once in a while, as at Auberge Claudette, near perfect. There is even the chance to retrace their trip to the dunes at Arcachon. Where it all began between the two of them. When Cat changed her life for the better. *Vive le Tour.*

ACKNOWLEDGEMENTS

*B*ack in 1991, whilst zapping through TV channels, I came across a bunch of boys on bikes. I had no idea what they were doing exactly, nor why they would want to scale a mountain in blistering heat by bicycle. However, it was the most hypnotic, compelling sight to me and soon enough I was obsessed. To be allowed to indulge my passion by basing a novel around the greatest sporting event in the world, I owe deep gratitude to my wonderful editor and friend, Lynne Drew, and my incredible agent and friend Jonathan Lloyd.

To the *Société du Tour de France*, for welcoming me into the fold and affording me so many privileges, I am truly honoured and immensely grateful. Personnel at the time included Agnes Pierret, Pascal Thomas, John Lelangue, Sonia Barjou-Rousseau and a special mention for Sophie del Rizzo. Teun van Vliet, thanks for the ride – I think I left my stomach somewhere on the descent of the Madeleine.

I'm indebted to the riders who were so helpful and generous with their advice, memoirs and anecdotes. Enormous thanks to Chris Boardman, to David Millar, to Graham Jones. Also, to Stuart O'Grady, Magnus Backstedt, Jay Sweet and all the riders who let me witter on at the *villages*. At the US Postal team in general, many thanks to riders past and present: Viatcheslav Ekimov, JC Robin, George Hincapie, Tyler Hamilton and to Jonathan Vaughters for letting me sit in on his massage. I'm grateful to Johnny Weltz for memorable and informative rides in the team car, to mechanic Geoff Brown and PR Louise Donald. Also, to Jill Jemison for dispelling myths and for that restorative ice cream at the water's edge in Aix-les-Bains. Much gratitude and love to Emma O'Reilly for incredible generosity with her frangipane and her time, both on and off duty – always a great *craic*.

In the *salle de presse*, my thanks to all the journalists who were so friendly and helpful; in particular Sam Abt, Andy Hood, Leon Bignell, Michael Enggaard, Susanne Horsdal, Stephen Farrand, Alasdair Fotheringham, Graham Watson and Rob Lampard. Also Phil Liggett and Paul Sherwen at Channel 4 and Simon Brotherton, Joanne Corrigan and Graham Jones (again) at Radio 5 Live. Also Christi and Phil Anderson, Shelley Verses and Greg LeMond.

Huge thanks to Sally Boardman, Peter Woodworth and all at Beyond Level 4. Much gratitude to all at Sports for Television and everyone involved with the Prutour, especially Alan Rushton, Rita Bellanca, John Herety, Tim Harris, Joscelin Ryan, Gerry Dawson and Clare Salmon. Thanks to numerous McQuaids, specifically Pat at the UCI, Kieren for driving me Stage 1 of the 1998 Tour and Ann for back issues and enthusiasm. Thanks, too, to Harry Gibbings and Simon Lillistone.

At *Cycle Sport and Cycling Weekly*, many thanks to Luke Evans, Keith Bingham, Phil O'Connor et al.

At *Procycling*, and *Tour Live* to William Fotheringham for increasing my understanding of the sport and keeping me constantly entertained; to Jeremy Whittle for his support and enthusiasm, for checking my facts and figures and for being such a good friend both in the *salle de presse* and out; to Andy Sutcliffe, for sending me that clutch of magazines back in 1996, for letting me ferret through his address book when I was ready to start my research and for the permanent loan (!) of books, back issues, videos and other stuff – my deepest thanks to you all.

This book is dedicated to the memories of Tom Simpson (1937–1967) and Fabio Casartelli (1970–1995), both of whom lost their lives during the Tour de France. Having battled cancer, Lance Armstrong won the Tour de France in 1999 and, for me, he personifies the essence of this great sport, this spectacular race. Triumph over adversity. Man against mountain. Whatever that mountain might be.

The Lance Armstrong Foundation, PO Box 27483 Austin, Texas 75755, USA

Look out for Freya North's fabulous new novel

FEN

Men . . . You wait ages and then two come along at once

Fen McCabe, 28, has only ever been in love with one man. To her sister's despair he's a nineteenth-century sculptor called Julius Fetherstone, whose rather erotic sculptures Fen adores.

But starting a new job leads her to meet not only young, handsome magazine editor Matt Holden, but also brooding landscape gardener James Caulfield, twenty years her senior. Though she fights it, Fen finds herself falling for both of them. Does she really have to choose?

From urban adventures in London to rural bliss in deepest Derbyshire, Fen develops her own north-south divide as sex, sculpture and severe indecision collide.

'Fen is a delicious creation . . . sparkling in every sense'
Daily Express

'The much-loved author returns with another delightful novel about the trials and tribulations of an irrepressible heroine . . . Funny, heart-warming and full of charm'
Hello!

'North's charming romp mixes art, sex and outrageous coincidences' ***Cosmopolitan***

Find a tantalizing extract from Fen overleaf . . .

FEN

Freya North

'Blimey mate,' said the cloakroom attendant at the Tate gallery when James handed him the rucksack containing the Fetherstones, 'what you got in there? Bleeding crown jewels?'

'You never know,' said James who then wished he hadn't because the attendant promptly opened his bag for a suspicious look inside.

The attendant smirked and raised his eyebrows at Adam and Eve clasped in ecstasy. 'Is that art, then?' he asked James.

'God no,' said James, 'pornography.'

Matt and Otter both knew why Fen had refused sandwiches with them. They knew exactly what her prior arrangement was. And, though they knew that she obviously wanted to keep her lunch-time lecture secret, they couldn't resist going.

'We'll keep out of sight,' Otter reasoned.

'We'll be silently supporting her,' Matt justified.

'We'll be fleshing out the audience,' Otter continued.

'We'll sit at the back and sneak out before the lights come up,' Matt concluded.

Only Fen's lecture was of course conducted not in an auditorium but in the sculpture hall, so Matt and Otter found pillars to hide behind.

'My God,' Otter exclaimed. Matt though, was speechless.

There was Fen, sitting on the lap of a large stone man whilst a stone woman pressed her back against his, her head thrown back, one arm extended down with her had firm over her pubis, the other arm stretching above, her fingers enmeshed in the male's hair. Fen sat very still, having positioned herself so that the male form seemed to be nuzzling her neck, his right hand masked from view by her body but apparently cupping his cock. Or wielding it. Or touching Fen's bottom. Or delving right in. The sight was quite something. Quite the saucy threesome. Matt's jaw dropped. Otter giggled involuntarily. James felt his trip to London was already proving well worthwhile though had yet to visit Calthrop's. Judith St John arrived late. She coughed when Fen was about to speak. Fen swiftly told herself that perhaps Judith simply had the beginnings of a cold. Judith St John had no interest in Julius Fetherstone, whom she considered a second-rate Rodin. But she was interested to hear just what this Fen McCabe had to say. Bloody double distinction from the Courthald Institute. She herself might only have one distinction but she'd graduated five years prior to Fen McCabe. Hardly second-rate. Standards had been much higher then. And the true distinction was that she was deputy director of Trust Art. And look at Matt Holden, all mesmerised. Oh for God's sake.

'Julius Fetherstone,' Fen started, assessing that Judith's cough had subsided and that the audience of around twenty was well above the age of consent, before stretching her arm above her, stroking the male's cheek before placing her hand over that of the female, 'was obsessed with sex.'

Fen slid from the lap of the sculpture and, with her hand on the male's hand which, it transpired, was indeed lolling over his cock, she ran her fingertips up his arm while she continued. 'Fetherstone seemed to delight in capturing in stone, or bronze, and in a frozen moment, all the heat, the moisture, the movement and, most of all, the internal sensation of the sex act.' She brushed the cheek of the man with the back of her hand and then rested her head gently on his shoulder, draping her arm down over his chest. The women in the audience wanted to be where Fen was, wanting to touch and clasp and grapple with the awesome sculpture. Many of the men in the audience, however, just wanted to touch Fen. Apart from Otter who was transfixed by the male sculpture. And by a rather athletic-looking tourist a few yards away.

'This work is called *Hunger*,' Fen said, standing back from it though it meant her all but pressing herself against two young women listening. She gazed at the stone and then faced her audience. She made eye contact with all of them, with Otter and Matt and James and Judith. But she did not glance away, or give a blink of discomfort or recognition. Fen McCabe, art historian, was rather different from Fen McCabe, archivist. Or was this merely the spell of Fetherstone's works? 'It's called *Hunger*,' she repeated, standing much closer to her audience than to the sculpture, 'but the couple themselves seem quite sated, don't you think?' The audience bar James was staring at the sculpture. 'Don't you think?' It was a question. James wanted to answer but could not establish eye contact and didn't really want to raise his hand. Anyway, the lecturer was staring directly, almost at point-blank range, at the two young women near to her. 'Don't you think?'

'Definitely,' one whispered. The other could only nod. They were both flushed. Not from humiliation or embarrassment. But from the effect the mass of copulatory stone had on them.

'Fetherstone worked on the theme of sexual abandon from 1889. His great treatise – titled *Abandon* – now exists in four supreme bronzes. Though the whereabouts of the marble *Abandon* – staggering even in the few photos we have of it – remains a mystery. Just look at them,' Fen implored, turning back to the sculpture, 'just look at them.' She gave her audience a tantalizing few seconds of silence. 'Now, this portrait bust of Jacques Lemond,' she said, moving to a plinth nearby, 'is not just conventional in conception, it was staid and boring even for the time in which it was executed.' Fen McCabe had cast the spell and then broken it. The audience had to follow her dutifully to another work, a rather uninspiring, if well executed, head and shoulders. But Fen was manipulating her audience. Her talk ended ten minutes later, having utilized a cross-reference with Maillol and a look at the two oil sketches by Fetherstone (which James was most pleased to deduce were inferior to his in execution and subject matter). She'd answered the obligatory questions (having anticpated, by the look of her audience, what they were to be) and then she'd left the gallery. Briskly. Perhaps to have a sandwich or something. Buy an *Evening Standard*. *Cosmo*, maybe. She knew well what would be going on in the sculpture hall. Most of the audience would remain. She'd observed their reaction to her lecture, to *Hunger*, to sculpture, on several occasions. They'd potter about half glancing at other works. Some would linger at Rodin's *The Kiss*. But all would gravitate back to *Hunger*, however long it took. To circumnavigate. For a deeper look. To feed their hunger.

POLLY

Polly Fenton loves her job teaching English in London, and she's mad about Max Fyfield. But she's leaving both behind to embark on a year-long teacher's exchange to Vermont. Swapping Marmite for Hershey bars and cornflakes for Cheerios is one thing. Trading lives with her American counterpart Jen is quite another.

But the minute Polly's feet touch down Stateside, she's swept off them altogether. She's dazzled by the brave new world; her letters become shorter, then less frequent. When she meets Chip Jonson, school athletic trainer, home thoughts from abroad cease altogether.

Meanwhile in London, her boyfriend, his brother, her best friend and her replacement are forming quite the cosy foursome. If, by the end of the first term, a certain amount of bed-hopping seems inevitable, who is it to be?

Spanning three terms and two countries, this is a sparky and sassy story of New England and Old England; fidelity and flirtation, receiving one's comeuppance – and making amends.

CHLOË

When Chloë Cadwallader's beloved godmother Jocelyn dies, she leaves Chloë a letter instructing her to give up her job (*lousy*) and her boyfriend (*awful*) to travel the four countries of the United Kingdom during the four seasons of the year.

Heavens. How can Chloë deny a godmother's last wish?

Off she goes, with a tremor of doubt and a letter marked Wales, to a farm deep in the Black Mountains where she finds an assortment of animals and the best looking man she's ever laid eyes on.

And as the seasons unfold, so too does Chloë's journey. From Abergavenny to St Ives, from the Giant's Causeway to the shores of Loch Lomond, join her as she discovers love, lust, and life – and a man for each season.

AVAILABLE TO ORDER IN ARROW

☐ Polly	Freya North	£6.99
☐ Sally	Freya North	£6.99
☐ Chloë	Freya North	£6.99

ALL ARROW BOOKS ARE AVAILABLE THROUGH MAIL ORDER OR FROM YOUR LOCAL BOOKSHOP.

PAYMENTS MAY BE MADE USING ACCESS, VISA, MASTERCARD, DINERS CLUB, SWITCH AND AMEX, OR CHEQUE, EUROCHEQUE AND POSTAL ORDER (STERLING ONLY).

☐☐☐☐☐☐☐☐☐☐☐☐☐☐☐☐

EXPIRY DATE .... SWITCH ISSUE NO. ☐☐

SIGNATURE ....

PLEASE ALLOW £2.50 FOR POST AND PACKING for the first book and £1.00 per book thereafter.

ORDER TOTAL: £................................. (INCLUDING P&P)

ALL ORDERS TO:

ARROW BOOKS, BOOKS BY POST, TBS LIMITED, THE BOOK SERVICE, COLCHESTER ROAD, FRATING GREEN, COLCHESTER, ESSEX, CO7 7 DW, UK.

TELEPHONE: (01206) 256 000
FAX: (01206) 255 914

NAME ....

ADDRESS...

....

Please allow 28 days for delivery. Please tick box if you do not wish to receive any additional information. ☐

Prices and availability subject to change without notice.